ELLIS ISLAND

ELLIS ISLAND

A Novel by

Fred Mustard Stewart

WILLIAM MORROW AND COMPANY, INC.
New York / 1983

Library of Congress Cataloging in Publication Data

Stewart, Fred Mustard, 1932–
    Ellis Island.

    I. Title.
PS3569.T464E4   1983   813'.54   82-14301
ISBN 0-688-01622-7

Printed in the United States of America

First Edition

1 2 3 4 5 6 7 8 9 10

BOOK DESIGN BY FRANK JAMES CANGELOSI

Author's Note

For her excellent suggestions I wish to thank my editor, Pat Golbitz. For his enthusiasm I wish to thank my agent, Owen Laster. For guiding me through Ellis Island I wish to thank Jonathan Russo. And thanks to Gabe Katzka and Pat Johnston.

For her unflagging support and enthusiasm, her wonderful ideas and her faith in the project, I not only thank my wife, Joan, but dedicate this book to her with love.

F.M.S.

Introduction

For millions of poor Europeans the dream was America, and the door to the dream was Ellis Island.

It is still there: twenty-seven acres of rock in Upper New York Bay, not far from the Statue of Liberty, southwest of the bottom of Manhattan. Originally called Gibbet Island when a pirate was hanged there in 1769, it later was renamed after its then owner, Samuel Ellis. Around 1800 the new nation turned it into a fort; the federal government took it over, and for most of the nineteenth century it was known as Fort Gibson. After the Civil War it became an ammunition dump. But in 1892 the deluge of immigrants pouring into America forced its conversion into an immigration station. The original wooden buildings burned in 1897 and a new complex of brick buildings was opened in 1900. It was through the main building, called simply enough the Reception Center, that the grandparents of perhaps a third of present-day Americans passed during the peak years before the First World War. Processing as many as five thousand immigrants a day, the government doctors and inspectors treated the would-be Americans with considerable humanity. Nevertheless, the prospect of passing through the Immigration Center—and the possibility of rejection—struck such terror in the hearts of immigrants that it was known to many as the Island of Tears.

Today, it is a wreck and a relic. Closed by the government in 1954 and put up for sale, it was left unguarded for ten years, during which time vandals rowed over from the mainland to steal the hardware, the copper flashing from the roof—whatever was not nailed down. Years of leaking roofs crumbled the old plaster; now, parts of the building are unsafe. But one can still wander through the Great Hall and many of its adjacent rooms. Here amidst the debris stands an old upright piano. There, an ancient Singer sewing machine that might once have been used by some peasant woman to mend the torn shirt of her son as they waited to be processed. In another corner stands an antique electric fan that stirred the air on some hot early-twenties summer afternoon.

It's all quiet now, except for the cawing seagulls swooping over the water and an occasional mournful ship's horn. If one approaches it from Manhattan, the red brick and stone Reception Center looms up through the mist of the bay looking rather eerie and sad, like an old house that time has passed by. But if you listen with your imagination, you can hear the babble of Greek, Yiddish, Italian, Norwegian, Russian. You can hear a baby crying, a mother soothing, two Italian peasants whispering nervously to each other, an Immigration Service inspector trying to communicate through a harassed interpreter with a frightened Turk. You can hear the young Sam Goldwyn, the young Felix Frankfurter. You can hear the voices of millions of people who radically changed and enriched America.

Most of them are ghosts now, but they must be proud ghosts. Ellis Island is America's haunted house.

ELLIS ISLAND

PART I
The Exodus

Chapter 1

Thirty horses galloped out of the woods and headed across a snowy field toward the tiny village of Gorodna. It was a few minutes before ten on the morning of April 7, 1907. The flat fields of the Ukraine were still in the grip of a hard winter, and the breath of the horses and the Cossacks who rode them steamed in the crisp air. The Cossacks, part of a regiment based in nearby Kiev, wore long-skirted scarlet greatcoats that reached to their boots, big black fur caps, and crossed cartridge belts over their chests. Each man carried a gleaming saber and a 1903 Springfield rifle, purchased for the regiment two years earlier by the Imperial War Ministry, which had been impressed by reports of the efficiency of the American-made gun. However, each rifle ended in an extremely lethal, extremely Russian four-edged bayonet. The Cossacks galloped in silence toward Gorodna. They looked as fierce as their reputation, and their reputation was enough to strike terror in the hearts of most of Europe.

Gorodna was a village of less than ninety. It consisted of an unpaved street lined with log huts. It was part of the Jewish Pale of Settlement, a geographical area in which Jews were forced to live, covering parts of Poland, Lithuania and the Ukraine, and set aside in 1791 by Catherine the Great. Every person in Gorodna was Jewish, part of the millions of Yiddish-speaking Ashkenazi Jews who had, over the centuries, fled into eastern Europe from the murderous anti-Semitism of the Germans.

The Cossacks had been ordered that morning to kill every Jew in Gorodna and put the village to the torch.

Lydia Rupinski was the first Gorodnan to spot the Cossacks. She was a twenty-four-year-old mother of two whose husband was a woodcutter. She was returning from Saul Panev's general store with a bag of onions, accompanied by her four-year-old son, Lev, when she saw the Cossacks crossing the field toward the town.

"Cossacks!" she screamed, grabbing Lev's hand and running toward her hut. It was then that the Cossacks started their infamous yell, a wild, bloodcurdling roar of lethal rage that filled the air with thunder. Others heard it. Saul Panev in his store heard it, as did his three customers. Natasha Mandel, doing her laundry, heard it.

Jacob Rubenstein, accompanying his father, Ilya, heard it and stopped playing the small, push-pedal organ in the one-room log synagogue.

Ilya Rubenstein, a giant of a man with a huge black beard, was the cantor of Gorodna's synagogue. A cultivated man who had once toured Europe with an opera company, Ilya had come home to Gorodna and persuaded the Orthodox rabbi—with much arguing—to permit the addition of a suspect Reform organ to the synagogue. Now his rich baritone stopped as he listened to the Cossack yell.

"Pogrom!" he said to Jacob.

In Russia, in 1907, the word had the same deadly impact that "Gestapo" would have thirty years later in Germany.

"The Torahs!"

Ilya ran to the rear of the room as Jacob stood up from the organ. Now the sounds of shots could be heard outside the synagogue, and screams mingled with the Cossack yell. Jacob froze with uncertainty and fear. He knew what a pogrom was and had lived in fear of it much of his life, like most Russian Jews. But actually to experience one? Just twenty years old, Jacob realized that in a few minutes he would probably be dead.

It was then that the two wooden doors of the synagogue burst inward, and two Cossacks rode in on their horses. Jacob saw one of the Cossacks aim his rifle at the rear of the room. Jacob turned to see his father pulling the two silver cases containing the Torah scrolls from the sanctuary.

"No!" Jacob howled, starting to run toward the Cossack. The rifle barked. Jacob again turned and saw his father stumbling to the floor, the Torah cases spilling from his arms. Simultaneously, the second Cossack threw a burning torch at the wooden pews.

Now the first Cossack, grinning, was galloping directly at Jacob. The young Jew with the wispy black beard and the long black coat saw the rifle aimed at his face. He ran back to the organ, ducking. The rifle fired just as he dived, literally, behind the organ. So terrified that he was acting by instinct, he pushed the organ toward the horse. The heavy instrument creaked on its casters; then there was a thud and a crash. Jacob saw the horse stumble against the organ and fall, throwing the surprised Cossack onto the floor.

"Dirty kike!" yelled the other Cossack, who was still mounted. He had pulled a tin can of gasoline from his saddlebag and emptied its contents on the flame, making of one side of the synagogue an instant inferno. Now the smoke and fire were causing his horse to shy and giving Jacob the extra seconds that saved his life. He ran toward the rear of the synagogue. He stopped beside his father, stooped and stared in horror at the bleeding bullet hole in the back of his skull. Numbly realizing his father was dead, he started to reach for the Torah scrolls when he heard the hoof-beats of the horse clattering across the floor toward him. This Cossack, as fiercely bearded as Ilya Rubenstein and howling like a maniac, had shouldered his rifle and held his saber raised in his right hand, ready to decapitate Jacob.

It had been less than a minute since the Cossacks had burst into the small synagogue; the action had been so galvanic, so fierce, so fast, Jacob was still in a state of confusion and disbelief. But as the horse clattered toward him—now less than ten feet away—his feet thought for him. He raced to the rear door, flung it open and ran out into the snowy field behind the burning building, slamming the door behind.

Run for your life, he thought. *Run for your life! The woods! If I can make the woods ...*

The cold air bit at his thin, sweating face as he ran. The woods were a field away, and the snow made it twice as hard for him to run, but he ran, his tall, skinny body straining for life.

He heard a shot. Not stopping, he looked back. The Cossack had opened the door, led his horse out and fired. He missed. *Keep running!* The Cossack remounted; the horse was galloping after him.

Keep running!

Another shot, and something bit his thigh. He fell forward into the snow, putting his hand on his leg; blood was already matting his trousers. He rolled over and sat up, staring at the Cossack galloping toward him.

He's going to shoot me ... in the face ... he's going to kill me. ...

In his panic he tried to get up again, but his wounded leg failed him and he fell backward into the snow. Something bruised his back. Chattering with fear and cold, sweating, aching from the bullet wound, he put his right hand under him and felt the rock.

Again the Cossack was less than ten feet away, roaring toward him, an express train of death, aiming the rifle with both hands, the superb horseman keeping his balance on the huge steed by the strength of his knees.

Jacob hoisted himself up and threw the rock with all his might.

To his complete amazement, the rock hit the Cossack's forehead, and the man fell from the horse.

Then silence, except for the distant shots in Gorodna.

Slowly, Jacob got to his feet. The horse had stopped and was sniffing its unconscious master. Jacob limped through the snow to the Cossack. Then he reached down and picked up the rifle.

It was the first time in his young life he had ever held a gun. He looked at it, then at the Cossack, then at the village he had spent all his life in. Gorodna was burning; the Cossacks had done their job well. Flames and smoke roiled to the cold blue sky. It seemed impossible: impossible that his father was dead, impossible that in less than five minutes his whole life had been changed.

There were tears in his brown eyes as he aimed the rifle at the Cossack's chest. Tears of sorrow, of rage, of hate. Why had it happened? What had his father done—Ilya Rubenstein, a gentle, music-loving man who had never harmed anyone in his life?

"You bastard!" he said, in Yiddish. Then he repeated it in Russian, forgetting that the language made no difference to the unconscious man.

He started to squeeze the trigger, then realized he couldn't do it. To murder an unconscious man in cold blood? To *kill* someone—even one of his father's murderers?

Then, suddenly, he did it.

The rifle fired, recoiled; the Cossack twitched; the horse whinnied and jumped.

Jacob Rubenstein stared at the blood expanding on the Cossack's chest.

I killed a man.

Then, shouldering the rifle, he limped to the horse, grabbed its reins, put his left foot in the stirrup and painfully mounted.

I killed a man, my father is dead, Gorodna is burning. . . . Oh God, what do I do now?

Digging his left foot into the horse, he started galloping toward the woods. Just before entering them he took one look back at his burning past. Then, forward into the woods.

Chapter 2

His destination was Hamburg, Germany; he had heard other Jews speak of it as the exit port for America. His decision to attempt the arduous journey was made not entirely on the spur of the moment. Jacob had thought about emigrating from Russia many times, but thinking and doing were different things. His greatest tie to Gorodna had been his love for his father, and now that that tie had been dramatically severed, the spur to Jacob's emigration was savagely applied. All that aside, he now had no choice but to leave Russia. He had murdered a Cossack. He had no way of knowing whether the murder could ever be attributed to him, but he wasn't waiting to find out. He assumed that if he were caught, he would be executed.

He traveled with fear and by night. During the day, he and his horse hid in the woods. Tearing a makeshift bandage from the bottom of his coat, he bound his thigh wound. The bullet had gone through the flesh, and he figured that since the wound had stopped bleeding, it was not serious as long as infection didn't set in. A worse problem was food, and for the first two days he starved, too afraid to shoot game because of the possibility the noise would attract attention. At night he stole hay from barns for his horse, but on the third day, hunger overcame caution and he shot a rabbit for himself.

Clumsily cleaning it with the Cossack's bayonet, he cooked it over a twig fire and gnawed ravenously, wondering how far he had come and how far he had to go. Using the North Star as a guide, he was traveling in a northwesterly direction, aware that he had to get out of not only Russia but Poland as well before he was safe. Poland was part of Russia. He figured he was lucky if he covered fifteen miles a night, and wondered if he would ever make the border.

But he kept going.

The fact that he had no money nor any way to pay the fare to America bothered him less than the urgent need to keep going, to get out of Russia. He would survive somehow. His mother, who had died of tuberculosis when he was twelve, had worried about money—or the lack of it—all her life, but Jacob had inherited his father's more casual attitude toward material things. Ilya had been a dreamer—"lazy," some of his neighbors had called him, although he had worked hard enough at his tinsmith's trade. But Ilya's heart had been in music. His only son had inherited his love of music.

Maybe I can play the piano to earn my passage, Jacob thought as he rode through the dark forests of Russia toward that vague dream, America.

It took him almost two weeks to cross the Ukraine to the Polish border, then another three weeks to cross Poland to the German border. The rigors of this exhausting odyssey stripped him of twenty pounds, so that as he crouched in the bushes near the border patrol station, the already skinny young man looked cadaverous. It was after midnight and it was raining hard. The sign by the station bearing the double-eagle arms of the Romanoffs proclaimed in four languages—Russian, Polish, French and German—that the traveler was leaving the domain of the Russian Tsar. Jacob had seen many photographs of the pleasant, weak face of Nicholas II and his beautiful Empress Alexandra. He hated Nicholas, whom he thought of as the Jew-Killer.

Already he was thinking of his new "President," the man he thought of as Fyodor Roosevelt.

The two border guards were dozing in their lonely patrol station, probably drunk on vodka. It would be easy to walk his horse through the neighboring field into Germany.

He waded through the puddles back to the horse and took its bridle. The horse whinnied. Jacob froze, staring back at the dimly lit patrol station.

The guards were still dozing.

Thanking God for the narcotic power of vodka, Jacob walked his horse across the border.

There was no fanfare, no excitement. There was nothing but rain.

But soaked, filthy and hungry as he was, Jacob's heart was singing.

He was free.

The ticket-seller at the Hamburg office of the Hamburg-Amerikanische Paketfahrt Aktiengesellschaft looked through his pince-nez at the young man on the other side of the counter and thought three words automatically: Jew. Russian. Broke.

"Was wollen Sie?" he said curtly.

"How much ticket to America?" asked Jacob, wrestling with the English language.

The ticket agent's fat face registered surprise.

"You speak English?" he asked in his own accented English.

"Leetle," said Jacob. "I speak no German. How much ticket?"

"I assume you want steerage. The steerage ticket to New York via Queenstown is twenty dollars."

Handsome beggar, thought the agent. *Or he might be if he'd shave off that ratty Jew beard and put on some weight.*

"Office across street say fifteen dollar," Jacob said.

The agent's face became glacial.

"The Norddeutscher line offers inferior facilities to Hamburg American."

Jacob shrugged.

"I go cheap."

He left the line, and a fat woman from Bavaria waddled up to the counter. The truth was that Jacob had no money at all, but he had wanted to test the waters at both the major Hamburg shipping offices before trying to find work, in order to know how much money he would need.

"Wait!" said the agent.

Jacob turned and came back. The Bavarian woman glared at him.

"All right," said the agent, lowering his voice. "Fifteen dollars."

Jacob was satisfied. Now he knew he needed fifteen dollars for either shipping company.

"Is truth," he said, "I have no money."

"*Kein geld?*" The agent's face got red. "Then why are you wasting my time?"

"I *work* my way across. I play piano . . ."

"We *have* piano players! Dozens of them! Get out of here! *Nächst, bitte.*"

"*Please!* I *got* to get to America! I wait tables . . ."

"Get out!"

Jacob left the window. He looked numb and felt bilious.

He hadn't eaten in three days.

But he thanked God his father had forced him to study English, French and Italian. Ilya's career with the opera company had given him a fluency in foreign languages that he had wanted his son to share. Jacob's French was passable, and his Italian and English were rudimentary. But the little English he knew gave him a leg up over the other emigrants to America, most of whom spoke no English at all. Having traveled so far and gotten out of Russia, Jacob now thought himself halfway to America. He was fiercely determined to become a "Yawn-kee," as American—whatever that was—as possible, and of course part of that process would be to conquer the English language.

He was intelligent, and, thanks to his musical talent, he suspected he had a good ear for language. He determined that the first thing he would buy when he got some money would be an English textbook.

The first thing, that is, after he bought his passage.

But right now, he had nothing.

And he was *hungry*.

* * *

The overly rouged woman in the window yawned as she looked out at the dirty young man in the ragged coat who stood in the foggy street staring at her. The woman in the window wore a moth-eaten eighteenth-century "Marquise" costume that revealed, if it did not totally expose, her breasts, which she had squeezed together until they almost spilled over the dirty ruching of her bodice. *Wouldn't you like to lick my tits, you horny little Jew,* she thought as she leaned forward slightly to wiggle at him. Jacob's eyes bulged. It was eleven at night, and he was in the Reeperbahn, the notorious red-light district near Hamburg's docks. The streets were almost empty, with an occasional drunken sailor weaving past the windows of the houses in which the whores, most of them as bored as the one Jacob was staring at, displayed their blowsy charms.

Now she slowly turned around, and Jacob gaped. The back of her eighteenth-century dress was cut open, exposing her bare pink buttocks and fat legs. Jacob couldn't hear through the glass, but the whore blew a fart at him. Then, laughing, she sat down on her pink ottoman to finish her beer.

Jacob continued down the wet street. Fog and drizzle were everywhere, and he shuddered at the clammy cold, the rain dripping off his sharp nose. Although he'd had hundreds of erotic dreams, from which he had awakened to find he had stained his nightshirt, technically he was a virgin. There had been plenty of marriageable girls in Gorodna, but the unfortunate fact was that most of them had been plain, and Jacob's romantic life had been almost nonexistent. He wanted women, and the whores in the windows with their tacky, ludicrous come-ons excited him, filling his scrawny body with a desire that ached almost as much as his hunger. Three windows down from the "Marquise" was a fat blonde in dirty underclothes who rubbed her crotch when she saw him. The gesture was so vulgar it shocked him almost as much as the Marquise's bare bottom; but he felt himself getting stiff.

He leaned against a wet lamppost, feeling dizzy and nauseated from hunger, and the whore giggled.

It was then he heard the piano music.

It was unlike any music he had ever heard before. It was tinkly, bouncy, tuneful and joyous. It coiled around his eardrums, foglike, and filled him with delight. It was coming from a few doors farther down the street. He started toward it, drawn as if by a delicious cooking smell.

The door was marked No. 19. Jacob twisted the bell and waited. After a moment a small wooden window opened and a heavily made-up woman peered out. Then the window slammed and the door was opened. The sagging, overdressed madam glared at Jacob and snarled something in German.

"Die Musik," said Jacob, pointing past her at the direction the music was coming from. *"La musique.* The music."

Then he pointed to his ear. The madam saw little prospect of profit from the ragged young man, but, shrugging, she let him enter, and slammed the door behind him. They were in a small entrance hall with a blue-glass lantern hanging from the cracked ceiling. The madam held up a curtain and Jacob ducked through into a large room whose gaudy Wilhelmine splendor widened his eyes. Fringe was everywhere: on ottomans, plush sofas, dangling from silk-ruffled lampshades. Over the cheap rose wallpaper hung oval, wood-framed photographs of buxom girls in various stages of undress, some of them fondling their breasts. On the floor was a frayed rug with several wine stains; at one end of it, a dog had had an "accident" that had never quite come out. A series of closed doors indicated the "action" rooms, and a hallway led to the rear and more beds. Several whores were lounging about, listening to the piano player. He was sitting at the upright playing ragtime, smoking a cigar, wearing a pink-striped shirt with blue garters on the sleeves, sporting a tilted bowler, wearing tight checked pants and spats on his shoes, humming to the music.

He was the first black man Jacob had ever seen.

But it was the music that drew him to the side of the piano, where he stared with fascination at the fast black fingers.

When the piano player saw the dripping Russian, he stopped playing.

"Who the hell are you?" said Roscoe Haines, taking the cigar out of his mouth. He repeated the question to the madam in German. She shrugged.

"This music is . . . different," said Jacob. *"Krasivaya.* Beautiful."

"Uh huh. It's called ragtime. It's all the rage back in New York."

"New York? You from New York?"

"That's right. My name's Roscoe Haines. Mention my name on West a Hundred-and-tenth Street, but please don't tell 'em where I am." He grinned and winked. Jacob guessed he was about thirty. "What's your name? You ain't no kraut, I can tell that."

"I Jacob Rubenstein, from Russia. I go to New York."

"Well now, ain't that grand. A real live emigrant. I bet you think them streets is paved with gold. Listen, Jacob Rubenstein, take it from a man who's been there: The only thing the streets of New York is paved with is dog shit."

This was too much English for Jacob, but he wasn't listening anyway. He was looking longingly at the keyboard.

"I play piano," he said. "I *good* play. I used to play organ in synagogue."

Roscoe laughed as he stood up.

"Well, this sure as hell ain't no synagogue, but feel free. These whores is bored with me. Maybe you can stick a firecracker under 'em. I've played in the best whorehouses in Paris and Amsterdam, and I can tell you this hole is a definite step *down.* You want a sandwich? You look mighty peaky."

Jacob nodded enthusiastically as he sat down on the piano stool.

"Hey, Greta," Roscoe yelled at one of the lounging whores. "You fat strudel, get off your ass and get *ein* sandwich *mit Fleisch für der Junge. Und ein Bier.*"

Greta got up to waddle out of the room as Jacob rubbed his hands together a moment. If nothing else, the whorehouse was warm.

Then he began playing. He played the tune Roscoe had been playing. Moreover, he played it the *way* Roscoe had been playing. The black man from New York picked his beer stein off the top of the piano and took a long gulp.

"You *are* good," he said over the music. "And you mean to tell me you never played ragtime before?"

Jacob shook his head. "Is *fun!*" he exclaimed. Then he launched into a series of variations on the theme. They were so inventive, so rich, so bouncy that two whores got up and started dancing together around the room. Even the surly madam looked less surly and started tapping her feet.

25

"Listen to him!" exclaimed Roscoe in awed tones. "He picks it right up! Why, man, if I closed my eyes, I'd think you was black like me. No white man ever play like that!"

The dancing whores were squealing with glee. Now the door to one of the action rooms opened and an enormously fat tugboat captain stuck his head out to see what was going on.

"Was gibt's?" he said, pulling on his tentlike underpants. Delighted by the music and half-drunk on schnapps, he jigged into the room followed by his near-naked bed partner, and the two started twirling. As Jacob's fingers raced over the keys, inventing delirious, wonderful melodies, the whorehouse took on the air of a madcap carnival.

Then, suddenly, the music stopped, and Jacob slid off the stool onto the rug with a thump. One of the whores screamed, and Roscoe hurried to him, knelt and felt his heart.

"Cognac!" he yelled. *"Schnell!"*

Roscoe was over six feet tall, with huge hands and powerful muscles. Now he easily picked Jacob up off the floor in his arms and started carrying him to the tugboat captain's room.

"This runt don't weigh a hundred twenty pounds," he said as he edged into the small room with the rumpled bed. "Something tells me he's just plain hungry. *Schnell mit der* sandwich!"

He placed him gently on the bed. Greta hurried into the room with the sandwich and a stein of beer. Behind her was the madam with a cognac bottle. Roscoe took the bottle, cradled Jacob's head with one hand and force-fed him a sip of the brandy with the other. Jacob gulped, sputtered, twitched, then came to.

"You all right?" asked Roscoe, sitting on the bed next to him as the whores crowded the room.

Jacob nodded weakly.

"Here, eat this." He took the sandwich from the plate and gave it to Jacob, who started to devour it like a starved dog.

Roscoe watched him. "Now," he said, "I can *assume* you ain't one of the Rockefellers. And judgin' from them rags you got on, you ain't no grand duke, neither. So how you gonna pay your way to New York? Even steerage takes *something.*"

"I try ..." said Jacob between munches, "... get job. Maybe ... play piano ... in whorehouse?"

"Huh. All Roscoe Haines needs is competition like *you*

around. No, sir, we're gonna get you out of Hamburg *fast.*" He stood up. "Let me tell you something: America's not my favorite country by a long shot, which is why I'm in Europe where a black man ain't *necessarily* a nigger. But if a kid as talented as you wants to go to New York"—he took off his bowler hat—"ain't no way he's not gonna get there."

He pulled a fistful of coins from his pocket and dropped them in the hat. Then he turned to the whores.

"Okay, girls," he said, "cough up. Entertainment tax. *Geld! Der Junge geht nach Amerika. Geben Sie!* Come on! Passin' the hat for the piano player."

As the whores pulled their purses from their corsets, Jacob finished the sandwich, licked his dirty fingers, and watched the miracle of the Reepersbahn with amazement. He had understood only about half of Roscoe's English. But he understood all his kindness.

The prow of the liner *Kronprinz Friedrich* loomed high over Jacob's head four mornings later as he stood on the Hamburg dock with Roscoe. The eternal North Sea drizzle didn't dampen Jacob's awe as he stared at the enormous ship with its four tall stacks painted white.

"Is big," he said to Roscoe.

"You got a real gift for original observations."

"You make fun of my English."

"It's hard not to. Now, *Junge,* you got your ticket and you got almost fifty dollars to boot. Man, you're rich!" He grinned. "Compliments of the whores of Hamburg. I'm tellin' you, never saw *those* sausages give money to *no one,* but they sure liked your music. I think one or two of them liked *you,* too, now that I got you to shave off that beard and we got a few pounds on you."

Jacob ran his hand over his clean-shaven cheek. He had had his doubts about shaving his beard—somehow, he now felt less Jewish, and with all his desire to become "American," he wasn't sure that being clean-shaven was exactly, well, kosher. But Roscoe had insisted, telling him that smart New Yorkers were getting rid of their "chinwhiskers." Roscoe had told him so much about New York in the past four days, and Jacob was so grateful to the black man, that he had given in to his request.

"I owe you so much," said Jacob, with touching simplicity and sincerity.

Roscoe put his hand on his shoulder. "Hell, it was fun. We piano players got to stick together. Now, don't lose that address I gave you. When you get to New York, you go look up Abe Shulman. Tell him Roscoe Haines sent you. Abe's a stingy bastard, but he knows good piano playin' when he hears it, and he'll get you a job. Okay, *Junge,* you're on your own. Good luck in the U.S.A.!"

The line of emigrants was starting up the gangway. Jacob grabbed Roscoe's hand and squeezed it.

"Can I write you?" he said.

"Sure. Number nineteen, Reepersbahn. Classiest whorehouse in Hamburg."

"If you come back to America, will you come see me?"

A sad look came into Roscoe's eyes. "Ain't never comin' back to America, *Junge.* Ain't no home for me there. You see what *you* can do with it. Goodbye, now. And good luck."

Impulsively, Roscoe gave him a hug. Then he stepped back into the crowd of relatives and friends, many of whom were wiping their eyes with handkerchiefs as they waved to the boarding emigrants. Jacob got into the line and started up the gangway. When he reached the top he made his way to the rail to look down at the crowd. Spotting Roscoe, he waved at him. Jacob knew there had been a Civil War in America and that the black man there was in a position somewhat akin to the serfs in Russia. Still, he couldn't quite understand why a man as cheerful and talented as Roscoe Haines would never return to his homeland.

The last of the passengers was aboard, and now the gangway was lifted onto the deck. The dockmen quickly unhooked the hawsers, and the heavy lines were brought aboard. The ship's whistle boomed, echoing mournfully in the fog, and the *Kronprinz Friedrich* began to move. As he stood on the deck, waving goodbye to Roscoe and Europe, Jacob's eyes filled with tears. He remembered Gorodna and his father, his mother, his childhood, his friends. All dead now, all gone. Lydia Rupinski, Saul Panev, his neighbors . . . had they all been butchered by the Cossacks? Was he the only Gorodnan to survive the pogrom?

The ship was picking up speed now, and Jacob watched the first twenty years of his life begin to recede.

Then he turned to look at the future: the other emigrants

crowding the deck. Many of them were weeping, too, undoubtedly sharing the same regrets he was. Probably many of them were weeping from fear as well, the fear of the unknown.

But Jacob wasn't afraid. Despite his tears he felt an exhilaration in his heart that tingled his blood.

He was going to the Promised Land.

He was going to America!

Chapter 3

The setting was one of almost sublime beauty. Beneath a gibbous moon stretched the Georgian manor house, set in a two-hundred-acre park, that had been built for the second earl of Wexford by Robert Adam in the eighteenth century. Its classic red brick and stone facade was beautifully balanced, its decoration restrained, its fenestration dignified, the architect having achieved nobility through moderation. The house was surrounded by some of the most beautiful gardens in Ireland, including an artificial lake created by the fifth earl in the 1820's.

Inside Wexford Hall the exterior restraint had been relaxed somewhat, and the sheer gorgeousness of the exuberant decoration had taken the breath away from two hundred years' worth of guests and tourists (for the house was now open to the public every Thursday). A staff of sixty took care of ninety-one rooms, including a ballroom designed by the brothers Adam, an eighty-foot-long picture gallery containing the best collection of Canalettos outside Woburn Abbey, the sculpture gallery holding the famous Barrymore Marbles, the state dining room, the private dining room, the conservatory, the music room, the Green, Vermilion and Mauve salons, the State Bedroom in which Queen Victoria and Prince Albert had bundled on the Royal Visit of 1849, six other guest suites, and the world-famous Roman Bath installed by the "mad" fourth earl. From the richly carved paneled walls hung stately portraits of ten generations of Barrymores, elegant men and women staring at eternity with the supreme self-satisfaction that comes not only with great wealth and impeccable breeding but also from that ultimate ego-booster, physical beauty. For God, as if determined to show how incredibly unfair He can be when He's in the mood, had endowed the Barrymores not only with almost two hundred thousand acres of Ireland's richest land (bringing in an annual income of three hundred thousand 1907 pounds) but also with the smashing good looks of a race of Olympians. There was Roxanne, the third countess, the greatest beauty of her day, who had shocked the world by gambling away the fortune of one husband, Lord Dorrance, then marrying Lord Wexford, only to run off afterward with a stableboy. There was the sixth earl, Rodney, who had been known as the Casanova of London in the 1840's and who had manifested his finely tuned social conscience by evicting over seven hundred of his tenants during the Potato Famine, forcing half of them to emigrate to America and reducing the other half to starvation.

And there was James Tyrone Andrew Strangeways Barrymore, the ninth and incumbent earl of Wexford, who on this particular May night in 1907 was making love to one of his chambermaids in the very bed Queen Victoria had slept in sixty years before. "Jamie" Barrymore was twenty-seven years old, a graduate of Oxford, a Coldstream Guardsman, the second richest man in Ireland, and endowed with the Barrymores' good looks, randiness and sublime indifference to the welfare of his tenants.

He also had a cold.

"God bless!" said Maryanne, his bedmate, as Jamie sat up to sneeze. "If you'd get some heat in this bloody barn, maybe you wouldn't catch cold."

"Why should I heat this 'bloody barn' when I'm only here two weeks out of the year?" sniffed his lordship, reaching to the bed table for his handkerchief. "And you might display a little respect for a house that's been called one of Ireland's treasures."

Maryanne leaned back in the silken sheets and poked her finger at his recently deflated penis. "*That's* Ireland's real treasure." She smiled. "And it's surely gotten a workout tonight. What if I have a baby? Will you adopt him?"

"Of course not."

"Ah, Jamie, what a mean man you are. Now admit it, don't you love me a little?"

Jamie was still blowing his patrician nose in his handkerchief. "I'm *passionate* about you," he said.

"And would you be divorcin' your wife to marry the chambermaid?"

"That's not terribly likely."

"No, I suppose not," she sighed. "But wouldn't I love to be Countess of Wexford. With all me fine clothes and jewels—would you take me to Court, Jamie, and introduce me to the King?"

"Definitely. They might hire you on. I hear Buckingham Palace needs chambermaids."

"Bloody snob," she said, sitting up. She had flaming red hair, milky skin and gorgeous blue-green eyes. She was twenty-two. "I'm fine when you're layin' me, but once you've shot your bolt, I'm Maryanne the chambermaid again, dirt beneath your feet."

"Well, I think you're being a bit melodramatic," sniffed the earl, putting away his handkerchief. "And I *did* buy you that coral brooch."

She smiled and kissed his shoulder. "You *did,* you darlin' man, and I love it. All right, no more fights. And I know what we'll do for your cold."

"What?"

"We'll get dressed and walk down to the lake. It's a gorgeous night, and there's nothing like spring air to chase away germs. Come on, out with you!"

She pinched his side, then got out of the ornate bed to start getting dressed.

Jamie Barrymore admired her nude figure. Maryanne Flaherty was a bit much—a bit too informal for his taste—but there was no denying she was one of the most appetizing girls who had ever worked at Wexford Hall.

He almost wished he didn't have to return to London the next day. But his wife was giving a dinner party two nights hence at their town house on Wilton Crescent, and the Duke and Duchess of York were the guests of honor.

One could hardly ignore royals for a chambermaid.

Denny Flynn was intoxicated by Maryanne Flaherty, but he had also come to hate her. As he stood in a shadowed corner of the upstairs hall, the seventeen-year-old footman raged to think that the gorgeous redheaded chambermaid was in his lordship's bed, rather than his, Denny's. Denny had been smitten by Maryanne's looks since she signed on at Wexford Hall two weeks before, just a few days before his lordship arrived from London for his annual visit. Of course, Maryanne had no time for *him,* a mere footman with a pug nose and freckled face. But how she had thrown herself at his lordship! *It was a disgrace, a bloody disgrace, that any Irish girl could be such a hussy, like a bitch in heat, with the bloodsucking Earl of Wexford! Him who sucks the wealth of Ireland to live high off the hog in London with the filthy limey swells. How could she do it? How could she? And of course he . . . Well, it wasn't long before he had her in his bed and was buying her fancy brooches and shawls. Dear God, was there any justice in the world?*

The door to the State Bedroom opened and Denny squeezed back farther into the shadows as herself and his lordship came out of the room into the hall. Denny's adolescent sexuality almost exploded his brain as he thought of Maryanne rolling in the sheets with that blond stick of wood. He clenched his fists and sweated as he watched the lovers start down the grand staircase, Maryanne—that bitch! That traitor to Ireland!—laughing and chatting.

Oh, dear God, I have to have her, he thought as he tiptoed to the top of the stairs to watch them. *She's Venus herself. I have to have her!*

And herself in bed with that bastard!

Still sweating, he watched as his lordship opened the front doors. Then he and Maryanne walked out into the moonlight, leaving Denny Flynn the only person awake in Wexford Hall.

He rushed down the staircase and hurried into the Vermilion Salon, making his way across the Savonnerie rug, which had been given to the third earl by Louis XV, to one of the tall windows. The room was unlighted, but moonlight splashed across the floor, lapping at the claw feet of the gilded furniture. Denny stood in the window and watched the two lovers stroll through the garden toward the artificial lake. *Is he going to fuck her in the moonlight?* thought Denny, aghast at their debauchery. *Mary, mother of God!*

He hurried back to the front hall and let himself out of the house, running down the stone steps, then out through the garden with its silent statues, undraped goddesses unconcerned by the

32

chilly night air. Running around a topiary bush still crated for winter, he saw the lovers walking toward the lake. *Are they going for a swim?* he thought incredulously. *They must be daft. They'll freeze their asses. Oh, that lovely sweet ass! Maryanne, what I'd give to put me hands on yours . . .*

It was then he saw the three masked men step out from behind the thirty-foot-high rhododendron bushes that had been planted by the "mad" fourth earl in celebration of Waterloo. They rushed the ninth earl, smashed something on the back of his head, then picked him up as he fell to the grass. Denny Flynn froze. *Who in God's name—? Thieves? Kidnappers? Murderers? No, no . . . And she knows them! She's helping them! What is . . .*

Sweet Jesus: Fenians!

Maryanne followed the three masked men who were carrying James Tyrone Andrew Strangeways Barrymore, the ninth earl of Wexford, back around behind the rhododendrons.

A few moments later Denny Flynn heard the snap of a whip and the distant rattle of a carriage. Then he saw the carriage on the lake road, heading west toward Wexford.

Denny Flynn, in a froth of excitement, rushed back into Wexford Hall to awaken Mr. Palmer, his lordship's butler.

Bridget O'Donnell stood with her younger sister, Georgiana, on the Queenstown dock and watched the two policemen who were, in turn, watching the Irish emigrants climb the gangway of the *Kronprinz Friedrich. Keep cool,* thought Bridget. She had washed the red dye out of her hair, returning it to its natural chestnut color, and removed the makeup she had so brazenly worn during her two weeks at Wexford Hall. She had on a straw hat and a plain woolen coat to protect her from the Atlantic wind that had chilled the normally balmy port on the southern coast of Ireland. There was no reason the policemen would connect her with the chambermaid Maryanne Flaherty, although the newspapers had carried descriptions of her. *Damn that brat of a footman, Denny Flynn!* she thought. He had told the police everything. Well, in a few more minutes she would be off Irish soil forever, on her way to New York and safety. It had all been planned in advance, and so far the plan had worked well.

"Do you think Uncle Casey will be meetin' us at Ellis Island?"

asked Georgie, who was nineteen. Georgie had a more fragile beauty than her older sister's. She had the same blue-green eyes, but Georgie's hair was a soft blond. Everyone in Dingle, their home town, said that Bridget took after her late father, who had owned one of the town's few cabs, and Georgie took after her mother, who had died four months ago of consumption. Bridget was fuller, more buxom, and physically more earthy. Georgie, though an inch taller and sturdily built, gave the impression of delicacy.

"And why wouldn't he meet us?" replied Bridget, fighting to hide her nervousness as the line of emigrants moved slowly toward the gangway. *Sweet Mary, I wish this line would move faster!* she thought.

"He sent us money to go second class, but we're goin' steerage," said Georgie.

"Georgie, darlin', I *told* you I wrote him we were comin' steerage to save the money. He'll have had plenty time to get the letter." *Dear God, is that bloody bobby lookin' at me?* She resisted an impulse to turn her face. *Look cool,* she thought. *Only ten feet more and we're on the gangway....*

The headlines had screamed all over Ireland and England the previous day:

EARL OF WEXFORD KIDNAPPED! FENIANS DEMAND
HOME RULE FOR IRELAND AS RANSOM!

She felt more than a pang of sorrow for Jamie, and more than a shudder of guilt at her own conduct. True, it had been for The Cause, but she had acted like a whore. Even worse, she had come to *like* it. Jamie had been a wonderful bed partner. He was a cold-blooded snob, but a superb animal. She cringed to think that she had been tempted to betray the Fenians and become Jamie's official mistress. It would have been nice....

But in the end, it had been the memory of her grandfather that kept her true to The Cause. Jamie was now being held prisoner in a desolate stone hut in the west, outside a village named Ballinrobe in Connaught. He would probably have an unpleasant couple of weeks, but they had sworn to her they wouldn't hurt him, and God knows Jamie *deserved* a little unpleasantness in life, what with his millions and his good looks....

"Do you feel bad leavin' Ireland?" asked Georgie.

"Oh, sure. But I'm lookin' forward to New York. It's goin' to be excitin', Georgie. You'll see."

Sweet, innocent Georgie. She must never know I romped in the sheets with Jamie. Nor must anyone in the family ever know. I'll carry the bloody secret to me grave. . . . Thank God, the gangway! At last! And the bobbies are movin' away.

As she inched up the gangway, she thought of her grandfather. Her dear mother had told her the story many times before she died: how, when she had been a baby, her parents had been evicted from their hut by the estate manager of the sixth earl of Wexford during the Great Famine. How they had suffered so cruelly that Grandmother almost starved to death, and Grandfather *did* die. How Grandmother had eaten grass and even leaves to keep going.

Oh, yes, Bridget owed the Barrymore family more than a kick in the pants. True, it had happened long before Bridget had been born, but time couldn't heal a wound as deep as that. So Jamie and his family could just suffer for a while.

And who knows? It might even get us Home Rule.

"Goodbye, Ireland," Georgie said, in a simple way that yet evidenced her deep sorrow at leaving her homeland.

"Yes, goodbye," echoed Bridget, now halfway up the gangway.

Goodbye and good riddance, she thought.

The emigrants from Hamburg leaned on the rail of the ship watching the Irish board. Standing next to Jacob Rubenstein was a young Italian who had come on board the *Kronprinz Friedrich* that morning, having transferred from a ship that had left Naples four days before. Now he spotted the two O'Donnell sisters and pointed at them.

"*Bellissima,* no?" He grinned at Jacob. The Italian wore a beaten hat, a threadbare jacket, filthy pants and a pair of worn, scruffy shoes. He was nineteen, a strapping *contadino,* or farmer, named Marco Santorelli. Although he badly needed a shave, a haircut and a bath, with his thick black hair and handsome features he was one of the best-looking men Jacob had ever seen.

Now Jacob looked at the O'Donnell sisters and nodded. "*Bellissima, si.*"

"You speak-a English?" asked the Italian.

"I try."

"*Ecco:* I got a book," said Marco proudly, pulling a battered English grammar from his coat pocket and showing it to Jacob. "Great English lady give it to me. She give-a me lessons. English lessons! I speak-a *good,* no?"

Jacob refrained from answering out of politeness, but he was looking at the book with keen interest.

"What English lady?" he asked.

"Mrs. Maud Charteris, the *famosa* actress on-a London stage. She have beautiful villa in Calabria, where I come from. I was-a her gardener. *Very* important!" He grinned. "She teach-a me English. What's-a your name?"

"Jacob Rubenstein."

"I am-a Marco Santorelli. We become-a friends, go to New York-a together, get-a reech. Why not?"

Jacob laughed as he shook Marco's offered hand. "Sure, why not? Do you *really* think we'll get rich?"

Marco shrugged.

"Who knows? Maybe. I sure can't-a get no poorer."

"You and me too." Jacob smiled. "I mean, you and me *both.*"

It was a phrase he had heard Roscoe Haines use several times, and Jacob had stuck it in his mental file drawer of English vocabulary. He as much as Marco wanted to be proud of his English, but both of them had a long way to go.

Marco looked at the O'Donnell sisters, who were passing close to them, edging their way through the crowd toward the fantail of the ship. *The blond one,* he thought. *What a beauty! She reminds me of a . . . a what? A lily, maybe. Something fragile but strong at the same time.*

Georgie noticed the dirty Italian looking at her, but her only thought was that he was good-looking and probably lecherous.

Georgie had not understood why her older sister had decided they should move to America, and in fact she had been rather against the idea at first. But after the ship left Queenstown the excitement of the adventure began to infect her, and even the grubbiness of the steerage quarters failed to dampen her spirits as she began to fantasize about America.

"I've read they've got mountains higher than the Alps," she said to Bridget the first day out as the two girls leaned on the rail, watching the ocean. "And there's a desert worse than the Sahara." She paused to rub her eyes. Bridget noticed it.

"Georgie, darlin', you've got to stop doin' that," she said. "You're just makin' your eyes redder."

"I know, but they itch something dreadful."

"Have you been usin' that eyewash I bought you?"

"Yes, but it doesn't seem to do much good. Anyway, how big do you think America is?"

"They say it's three thousand miles from New York to California."

Which should be big enough to get lost in, she thought.

Chapter 4

Marco remembered.

"Don't end English words with *a*," the English signora had told him. "That's the way wops speak, and you don't want to be a wop. You want to be *Italian.* You want to be *proud* of yourself."

Marco remembered, but in his excitement at meeting Jacob, he had forgotten. Now, as he lay on his upper mattress of the three-tiered steel bunk in the stinking steerage compartment of the *Kronprinz Friedrich,* he mentally kicked himself. *Not "I am-a Marco Santorelli," but "I am." I am. Dio, it is confusing! Dio, this place smells!*

Marco remembered other things, most of all the poverty. During the nineteen years of his life he had known nothing but poverty, the worst kind, the hopeless kind. His family rented a tiny farm in the hot, rocky hills north of Reggio Calabria, not far from the Straits of Messina which separated Italy from Sicily, the Scylla and Charybdis of classic myth. The farm was part of the estate of Principe di Luna, a rich landlord whose family had come from Spain when Calabria was part of the Kingdom of the Two Sicilies. Marco had never seen Principe di Luna, who spent most of his time in London and Naples, but he knew that the Prince's estate agent never forgot a rent day.

The Prince also owned a lovely seaside villa, the Villa d'Oro, which he rented in the winter months to Mrs. Maud Charteris, the famous English actress. Mrs. Charteris, who knew the Prince socially, adored the warm Mezzogiorno sun in January and February, and it was Mrs. Charteris who had spurred Marco to leave Italy.

Marco was smart. When he was a boy he had begged the local priest, Don Polizzi, to teach him to read and write—there were no schools, not even a church school, in the miserably poor area—and the good man had agreed. Becoming literate in itself had set Marco apart, made him slightly "different," and his parents, his two brothers and three sisters had at first viewed his efforts with suspicion. But Marco never shirked his backbreaking work on the farm, and eventually his family's suspicion of his ambition turned to grudging pride; perhaps Marco was the one who would make something of himself.

Then, two years before, he had heard that the Inglesa was looking for someone to do chores at the Villa d'Oro. Something told him la signora Charteris would be useful to know. He applied for the job. Maud Charteris, who at thirty-seven was anything but immune to masculine good looks, took one look at this Calabrian Adonis and hired him on the spot.

Marco was aware that the handsome older woman's interest in him was not entirely spiritual. He was proud of his good looks, and at times displayed a certain southern Italian *maschio* swagger. On the other hand, whatever might have been ticking in Maud's brain, the first year she never made any advances toward him, nor, certainly, did he to her. She had lovers; the villa was often filled with houseguests, including several languid young men from London who, Marco assumed, were bedmates of the star. But Mrs. Charteris always remained a lady, and an elegant one at that. There were no orgies, no drunkenness—at least none that Marco could see from a gardener's limited viewpoint. There were long, lazy lunches on the terrace overlooking the sea. There was sea- and sunbathing on the small beach below the villa, but nothing improper; even the men wore tops to their bathing suits. (It fascinated Marco, whose skin was permanently tanned from farmwork in the blazing Calabrian sun, how the milky-skinned English seemed to adore roasting themselves.)

Then one February day, more than a year ago, when Marco was lugging a heavy terra rosa jardinière filled with pink geraniums to a new position on the terrace, his employer, who was reading a magazine, said to him in her excellent Italian, "Marco, would you like to learn English?"

The young gardener set down the pot, then straightened his perennially sore back to look at the glamorous actress. It was a warm, cloudless day, and Maud was wearing a wide-brimmed yellow hat that matched her flowing chiffon garden dress. She had pale blond hair, exquisite English features and coloring, and dieted herself to a thinness that to Marco was not especially attractive. Marco had a peasant's love of solid women. La signora, in his opinion, needed more curves.

"I don't know, signora," he replied. "I never thought about it."

"It might be useful some day. You strike me as being rather ambitious. If you knew English, you might be able to get a job at one of the tourist hotels up north. The English are rotten tippers, but still you could make some real money. Not that I want to lose you as a gardener."

"Is the signora offering to teach me English?"

"I'm offering to buy you some English grammar books if you're interested. Think about it. You have splendid muscles because you use them. But the brain is like a muscle, and if you don't use it, it won't grow strong."

Marco thought about it. He wasn't sure what the signora's motives were, but his instincts told him learning English could indeed be useful and his brain did indeed need flexing. So the next day he accepted her offer. She bought him English grammars in Reggio Calabria, and Marco began studying them at night, sitting outside his family's one-room stone hut so as not to wake his brothers and sisters and parents with the lantern light. He found learning English difficult, but he hadn't thought it would be easy. He kept at it, and by the time the signora returned to her villa the next winter, Marco knew enough to be able to converse with her.

The actress had seemed delighted with his progress and offered to spend some time with him, coaching him. It was during one of these sessions on the terrace that she had told him not to end words with *a,* not to sound like a "wop." Almost every day for two months Marco spent some time with her, working on his English. Then, at the end of February, during the final session on the terrace, he finally found out what was behind her interest in him.

"As you know, Marco," she said in Italian, putting out one of the cigarettes she smoked too many of, "I'll be returning to London tomorrow. Mr. Maugham has offered me the lead in his new play, *Lady Frederick,* which deals with a love affair between an older woman and a younger man."

She smiled slightly and Marco looked a bit uncomfortable.

"At any rate, if the play is a success, I'll probably tour it— perhaps even to New York. Now, I have a house outside London near Cliveden. It has a lovely little garden—you know how passionate I am about flowers. Of course, the English climate is nothing like Calabria, but I've so admired what you've done here at the villa, I wondered if you'd like to come to England and work for me there? I'd pay all your expenses, needless to say, and would pay you a hundred pounds a year, which I can assure you is a handsome wage. There's a charming little cottage near the house which could be yours. And in time, if you learned to drive you might become my chauffeur as well. I'd buy you a smashing uniform. I think it's important for an actress to have a handsome chauffeur. It makes people talk."

Again she smiled. She opened her gold cigarette case, which she had bought at Chaumet in Paris, and pulled out a Régie. "Do you think you'd be interested, Marco?"

The gardener was studying her. "Is this why the signora wanted me to learn English?"

"Perhaps."

"Pardon me for being rude, signora, but would there be other jobs for me besides gardening and being your driver?"

She handed him her gold lighter and put the Régie in her mouth.

"Perhaps."

Marco studied the lighter a moment, the lighter that had cost more than his father's annual income. Then he stood up to light the cigarette. Their eyes met through the smoke.

"I have to think about it," he said.

"What's to think about? You know there's nothing for you here in Calabria. *Nothing.* Oh, perhaps because you've learned a little English—thanks to *me*—you might get a job as a waiter or bellhop. But the probability is you'll spend the rest of your life being what your father is. I have a feeling you want more out of life than that. I'm offering you that 'more.' "

"The signora wants me to become her gigolo," he said softly. "Not her lover; her gigolo. The signora is very kind, but I have my pride. I am a *man,* not a gigolo."

Again, she exhaled. "Dear God, spare me your tedious peasant morality. You're very good-looking, Marco. Looks may not be everything, but they're enough. You'd be a fool not to use them while you have them."

Marco stood up. "No," he said, sharply. "And you disgust me."

She eyed him coolly. "Very well. You're fired."

"You can't fire me. I quit!"

She laughed. "How noble! And I thought you were smart. It turns out you're nothing but a dumb wop after all."

Glaring at her, he turned and walked off the terrace to go home.

But her words rang in his ears: "There's nothing for you here." "Dumb wop." *Nothing for you here.* Nothing.

It was that night he decided he would go to America.

But now, as he lay on his bunk in the foul-smelling steerage compartment of the *Kronprinz Friedrich,* he was wondering if the signora hadn't been right in calling him dumb.

Being the gardener-chauffeur-gigolo to one of London's greatest stars might not have been very manly, but it must have been better than this stinking hole. And to turn down a hundred pounds a year! He didn't know the exchange rate, but he knew that was a lot of lire. And for what? To garden, which he loved, to drive a fancy car and make love to a beautiful woman?

Shit, Marco, he thought in Italian, *you were an asshole.*

41

Chapter 5

The second day out from Queenstown, the *Kronprinz Friedrich* hit a violent North Atlantic storm. Near hurricane-force winds built up a gigantic wave system—some waves almost fifty feet high—and the liner, though it was, at eight hundred feet, one of the North German Lloyd's biggest, bobbed like a toy before the ominous forces of nature. "Bobbed" would hardly have been the verb used by the terrified emigrants. To them, the ship crashed into giant waves, sending up great curtains of spray, only to rise slowly up on the next wave, lurch over it and then, with the sickening speed of an out-of-control elevator, crash down again into the water. The ship shuddered, creaked and groaned. The emigrants, packed into their airless steerage compartments, cried, whimpered and threw up, as violent seasickness sent many of them staggering to the buckets placed at their disposal by the German crew. For the 221 men crammed into the male steerage (which was at the bottom of the ship near the steering equipment—hence its name), the acrid smell of vomit further fouled the air, which already reeked of body smells. Jacob Rubenstein, whom the storm had terrified as well as nauseated, clung to the steel riser of his bottom bunk and moaned with a sickness worse than anything he had ever known.

"Go outside," called down Marco from the top bunk. "Get fresh air! Eat fish. They got-a . . . they *got* fish in barrel by door. It's good for *stomaco*."

"Fish?" groaned Jacob. The mere thought caused him to crawl out of his bunk and head for the bucket. He reached it just in time to retch. Then, as the ship crashed into what seemed the millionth wave, he got up and weaved toward the door. Maybe Marco was right. Maybe fresh air would help. He certainly couldn't stand the stench inside much longer.

He made his way to the fantail of the ship, which was at the stern and was the only deck steerage passengers were allowed on. As he opened the steel door, the ship lurched violently to port, hit by a secondary wave system, and swung sideways with the same sickening force it had heretofore displayed crashing up and down. Jacob hung on to the door for dear life as a wall of water crashed over the deck, causing the one lone passenger on the fantail to be almost washed overboard. Jacob watched as the little man clung desperately to a riser, the foamy water surging past his feet. Then the ship shuddered and slowly began to right itself to starboard, only to recommence its elevator ride as it began climbing the next wave.

Despite the danger, the sea air was a relief and Jacob went out on the deck, clinging to a handrail on the stern bulkhead. It was the middle of the afternoon, but the sky was oyster-gray with swirling clouds. His sole companion, a young man in his early twenties who looked terrified, hurried across the deck to grab the handrail next to Jacob. He was very short, with a homely face and black hair which the water had plastered to his skull. His cheap coat and pants, all drenched, would have marked him steerage even if he hadn't been on the fantail.

He said something to Jacob in Czech, which was sufficiently similar to Russian for Jacob to understand with difficulty. "I almost went over!"

"I saw," replied Jacob in Russian. "It's dangerous out here."

"I know, but it's better than steerage. What's your name?"

"Jacob Rubenstein."

"I'm Tomas Banicek."

"From Bohemia?"

"Yes. A farm village thirty *versts* outside Prague. You think this ship will make it to New York?"

"If it doesn't, we won't have to worry about getting through Ellis Island."

"Do you have someone meeting you?"

"No. Do you?"

The little Czech nodded. "My cousin. He went to New York six years ago and works in a meat plant. He speaks English now, which is lucky for me. I don't even know one word. Well, I know 'New York' and 'yes' and 'no.' But that's all. If . . ."

He started to say something else, when the ship crashed yet

again into the ocean, sending up such a huge wall of water that it flew over the entire superstructure, dashing the fantail again. Little Tomas Banicek shuddered.

"I'm scared," he said succinctly.

It summed up Jacob's feelings nicely.

Indeed, fear clutched all 407 steerage passengers on the huge German liner. The most immediate fear was of the storm. But though it raged through the night and well into the third day at sea, the storm gradually began to lose force. And as the waves and wind abated, the miserable men, women and children began to clean up the steerage compartments and put some food into their weak stomachs.

By the fourth day, good weather was encountered and the ocean gently swelled, allowing the steerage passengers to crowd out onto the fantail and bask in intermittent sunshine. But though spirits revived somewhat, there was still fear: the fear of Ellis Island and what awaited them in America.

The Irish emigrants like the O'Donnell sisters were lucky because they had no language problem. But the others—with the exception of a few, like Jacob and Marco, who through unusual circumstances had some knowledge of English—were faced with the prospect of settling in a land where they didn't speak the language at all. Moreover, while the majority of them had arranged for someone to meet them at Ellis Island and act as sponsor in the New World, many, like Jacob, knew no one in America, and there were rumors on the ship that without a sponsor a person could be turned back. Other rumors circulated, gathering strength through ignorance and nervousness. It was said that the medical exams were terrifying, that immigrants could be rejected for a crossed eye or a wart. It was whispered that if you couldn't solve complicated mathematical problems, they would send you back to Europe. It was said you had to bribe the officials to get through.

That none of these rumors was true didn't diminish the effect of them on the apprehensive steerage passengers, for the power of the unknown can be tremendous. And although some of them tried to cheer things by singing peasant songs or dancing on the fantail, most of the steerage remained silent and glum.

Going to America was a powerful dream which had impelled

them to uproot their lives. The thought that the whim of an inspector could send them back to Europe—again in steerage—was enough to break their hearts. Ellis Island was two days away, and to many it was beginning to loom like a date with a potential executioner.

The sweet refrain of Franz Lehár's "Vilia" wafted down from the first-class lounge as the Palm Court orchestra entertained the 164 first-class passengers at tea. Jacob, leaning against the rail next to Marco, looked up at a well-dressed first-class lady standing on the promenade deck. She in turn was looking down at him and the other steerage passengers. *What beautiful music,* he thought. Jacob, buried culturally in Gorodna, had never heard the score of *The Merry Widow,* which had swept the capitals of Europe in a whirlwind of success. *And what beautiful clothes!* The world of the rich, so close physically and yet so far out of reach to the emigrants, glittered like a bauble on a Christmas tree. *I can write music as beautiful as that,* he mused. *And someday I will. Someday . . .* but he stopped the thought. He didn't dare to dream of making first class.

But the idea did a merry tap dance in his imagination.

Marco's eyes weren't on first class. They were on the O'Donnell sisters instead.

"Let's go talk to them," he said to Jacob, nudging him with his elbow.

Jacob came out of his first-class reverie. "Who?"

"Those two Irish girls. They is the best-a looking . . ." *No a,* flashed through his mind. "The *best*-looking women on ship! Specially the blonde."

Jacob looked at the girls, who were standing on the other side of the ship, also listening to "Vilia." Indeed, the sinuous melody had entranced all the steerage passengers; they were all listening.

The power of music, mused Jacob.

But he needed no urging to meet the O'Donnell girls, and the two emigrants, neither of whom had shaved since the storm began and whose clothes were by now filthy, made their way through the crowd to Bridget and Georgie.

"Good evening," Marco began.

"Ssh!"

Bridget pointed to the music, and Marco waited till the number was finished. Then, as the orchestra segued to a foxtrot, Marco tried again.

"My name is Marco Santorelli, and this my friend Jacob Rubenstein. How you do?" He took off his battered hat, grabbed Bridget's hand and pumped it so hard the two girls started giggling.

"What's-a funny?" he said, in a huff.

"Nothing," said Bridget. She burst into more giggles.

Marco and Jacob exchanged bewildered looks.

"What *your* name?" Jacob asked, plunging bravely on.

"I'm Georgiana, and . . ." More laughter.

"I'm Bridget O'Donnell."

The two sisters managed to stifle their merriment.

"We saw you come 'board ship at Queenstown," said Marco. "Very lovely Irish ladies. Very beautiful."

Bridget giggled again, but Georgie was becoming more serious. These two would-be swains might have looked a bit ludicrous in their battered clothes, but they were certainly attractive. And the Italian! *Mary, mother of God, what a stunner!*

There was an awkward silence. Marco looked up at the first-class lounge where some of the passengers were dancing. Then he looked at Georgie.

"My English lady friend, Mrs. Charteris, the great stage star, she tell me that dance called a two-step. You know two-step?"

"*You* know Mrs. Charteris?" said Bridget disbelievingly.

Marco swelled with importance.

"*Great* friend. She teach-a me English!"

The girls exchanged looks, as if to say *she didn't do a very good job.*

"How did you know Mrs. Charteris?"

Marco unswelled slightly. "I was her gardener." Then, quickly, "We dance, yes?"

"But I don't know how . . ." began Georgie.

"Neither do I," interrupted Marco, grabbing her and beginning to dance. "But we learn—quick!"

And he started twirling her around the deck. The other steerage passengers quickly backed out of their way, amazed—if not aghast—that anyone in steerage would have the nerve to ape first class. Jacob, dazed by Marco's chutzpah, watched as the two young people danced awkwardly, Georgie yelping several times as Marco stepped on her feet, and Marco gamely saying, *"Scusi! Scusi!"* It was funny, but it was also rather wonderful. Jacob turned to Bridget, deciding that a display of his scanty French might up-class him a bit.

"Voulez-vous danser?" he asked, making an awkward bow.

Again, Bridget giggled. "Why not?" she replied gaily, and off they went, twirling around the fantail in a merry makeshift two-step, Jacob's natural rhythmic sense and musical ear picking the step up quickly.

Tom Banicek was watching. Now he turned to a plump Lithuanian girl in a babushka and pointed, first to her, then to him. The girl blushed, looked at her enormous mother standing next to her who shook her head in a vigorous no. Tom grabbed the girl's hand and pulled her onto the makeshift dance floor, where he, too, started twirling, ignoring the mother's shouts of disapproval. Other emigrants started dancing too. As if momentarily defying their fears, the poor Europeans turned the fantail into a Vauxhall Gardens and forgot their worries with a release of their natural high spirits.

Some of the first-class passengers, seeing the ragged dancers below, came out to the promenade deck to watch.

"I *do* think they're trying the two-step," exclaimed a prominent Fifth Avenue hostess, who was returning from an antique-buying binge in central Europe. "How deliciously quaint!"

"I'm amazed they can do anything beyond the polka," said her companion, the American-born Princess von Hohenlohe, who was returning home from Berlin to visit her steel magnate father in Pittsburgh.

And the emigrants danced on.

"You got friends in America?" asked Jacob as he swooped around the deck.

"You're holding me too tight," said Bridget, sticking her tongue out at the Princess von Hohenlohe, who looked shocked.

"Sorry."

"Our Uncle Casey is meeting us. He owns a lorry company in Brooklyn."

"Where Brooklyn?"

"I don't know. Somewhere near New York."

"What means 'lorry'?"

"Well, I think they call it a truck in the States."

"What means 'truck'?"

Sweet Mary, does he know anything? she thought.

"It's like a big automobile. Do you know what an automobile is?"

"Oh, sure!" Jacob grinned proudly. "So your uncle rich man?"

"Oh, no. But he's well off."

"That good for you. You lucky. I know nobody."

"Nobody?"

"Nobody but Marco. And now you."

Again he smiled.

He's really rather sweet, thought Bridget. *But does he stink!*

"Someday, *I* write songs," said Jacob.

"Oh? You're a composer?"

"Not yet. But someday."

Someday.

Bridget stuck her tongue out again at the Princess von Hohenlohe.

And the emigrants danced on.

Chapter 6

On the fourth night, the ship encountered rough weather again off Cape Race. Although it was not as fierce as the previous storm, it was worse for the steerage passengers because the captain roped all the outside doors, preventing anyone from going on deck. The captain had discovered that the fantail door had not been secured in the previous storm, whether from neglect or on purpose, to allow the steerage passengers to get air, no one knew. The result was that the emigrants were now imprisoned in the steerage compartments. Again seasickness struck; again buckets were filled.

The pounding of the nearby engines combined with the crashing of the ship to make sleep unthinkable. Since there were only four toilets and showers available to the male passengers—and they were at the other end of the ship—few of the men had been able to bathe or change clothes since Queenstown, and the others were now ripe. Furthermore, most of them were unused to indoor plumbing anyway and had taken to relieving themselves in buckets or even in their pants, so that the smell of urine and excrement made the compartment almost unlivable. Marco seemed immune to seasickness, but the stench made him miserable. Jacob again was violently ill and wondered if he would survive the night. Tom Banicek dreamed of his little family farm outside Prague and wondered if he might not have been better off staying in Bohemia after all.

The main food supply for the steerage passengers was herring. Barrels filled with the fish were placed outside the door to the compartment, and the passengers had been told that eating the herring was a cure for seasickness. At Marco's repeated urging, Jacob agreed to eat one. Marco brought him the fish. Jacob took one bite and threw up on his mattress.

The memory of herring would last him all of his life.

On the sixth night, calm seas had returned and Jacob and Marco stood on the fantail, leaning on the rail and watching the lights of Long Island glide by as the *Kronprinz Friedrich* neared Ambrose Channel.

"America," said Marco, and there was awe and wonder in his voice. "I didn't think we'd ever get here."

"What you going to do?" asked Jacob.

"I don't know. They say there's work for Italians in building. And stonecutting. Maybe I get job like that. I'm-a ... *I'm* strong. But I'd like to use my brain. I don't want to be a dumb wop."

"What means 'wop'?"

"Mrs. Charteris use that word. It's a bad word for 'Italian.' "

"I bet they have bad word for 'Jew,' too," said Jacob, watching the distant lights, envying the people living in those houses, people who were already Americans.

"What are you gonna do?" asked Marco.

"I have name of music publisher on Tin Pan Alley. That some

sort of street where they write songs. I go to him and play piano. Maybe he give me job."

"You is lucky."

"*Lucky?!*" Jacob snickered.

"We good friends," said Marco. "You want we stay together and-a help each other? We got nobody else."

Jacob smiled. He had grown fond of the Italian. "Sure. We help each other."

They shook hands. Then Marco laughed and shouted at the distant lights, "Hey, America! Wake up! Marco and Jacob's comin' tomorrow. We gonna take over country and be *important!*"

They both laughed. The lights twinkled sleepily.

America remained silent.

"There it is," said a mother in Greek the next morning.

"It must be *huge!*" exclaimed the Lithuanian girl Tom Banicek had danced with.

"It's the biggest thing I've ever seen," said a Hungarian.

They were all standing on the ship's fantail, staring at the Statue of Liberty. The ship had dropped anchor in the Narrows, placed in quarantine pending clearance, and medical teams had come aboard. As they gave perfunctory medical examinations to the first- and second-class passengers and made sure the ship was not infested with lice and that there was no epidemic aboard—something unlikely with a liner as well-known as the *Kronprinz Friedrich*—the steerage passengers had nothing to do but wait and gawk at New York.

But some of them were crying as they saw the Statue of Liberty.

It was, after all, a dream come true.

At a few minutes past noon on May 23, 1907, the *Kronprinz Friedrich* cleared quarantine and began standing into New York harbor. Two hours later, it docked at Pier 63 in the North River, and the first- and second-class passengers began to disembark. At the same time, one of the ship's officers and three of the crew came onto the fantail and began distributing cards marked with the number 12.

"You vill pin zese cards to your coats!" shouted the officer through a megaphone, speaking English despite the fact that three quarters of his audience couldn't understand it. "You vill stay aboard tonight, und tomorrow morning you vill be taken in a boat to Ellis Island. At zee Reception Center you vill stay togezzer und pass zroo zee inspectors togezzer. You vill carry your baggage viz you."

Then he repeated it in German, which even fewer understood.

"Wait a minute!" yelled Bridget."Why are the first-class passengers getting off?"

"Zey have already been cleared in qvarantine. Steerage must go zroo Ellis Island."

"Of all the unfair—!" Bridget snorted to her sister. "What do they think *we* have? Lice?"

"A lot of them do," whispered Georgie.

"I'll admit a lot of them are dirty, but *still*."

"We should have come second class. Uncle Casey sent us . . ."

"Oh, Georgie, be quiet!"

But Bridget had to admit to herself her younger sister might be right.

She also began to realize something that had never occurred to her: America was hot. The temperature was 86 degrees and it was a humid, sultry afternoon.

In Dingle, when it went over 70 degrees, it was considered a heat wave.

At eight the next morning a lighter appeared and the immigrants began climbing down an accommodation ladder, their cards on their lapels, carrying their bundles, their tattered bags and packages. Tom Banicek carried a sheet in which he had his feather bed (the peasants from eastern Europe in particular seemed fanatically attached to their feather beds; Tom had seen dozens of others in the steerage compartments), a photograph of his family, two clean shirts and a crucifix his mother had given him. Tom's reason for leaving Bohemia had been simple: not only to escape the peasant life of his ancestors but to escape conscription into the Austro-Hungarian Imperial Army. The life of a private in the army was notoriously brutal, and Tom's family had wholeheartedly agreed with him when he said he was thinking of going to America. His cousin, Vodya the meat-packer, had sent him fifty dollars, telling him that, contrary to rumor, you didn't *have* to have twenty-five dollars to get through Ellis Island but having money certainly helped. So as the little Bohemian stepped into the crowded boat, he felt his chances were as good as any to pass.

Jacob still had forty dollars of the money Roscoe had collected for him from the Hamburg whores, so even though he had no luggage at all, he too felt reasonably confident.

Marco had a paper-wrapped package that contained his entire wardrobe (one shirt and three pairs of socks), his mother's rosary and a home-cured salami. He had the equivalent of about forty dollars in lire, all that was left of the money he had earned working for Maud Charteris, so he, too, saw no reason why America wouldn't welcome him with open arms.

When the lighter was full, the boat started across the bay for Ellis Island. In a few minutes the immigrants could see the big, vaguely Romanesque Reception Center with its four towers. The building lay low in the water (the island had originally been a sandbar) and a number of ferries and barges were tied up by its side in the ferry basin. It was another humid day, promising to get hot, and behind the island the New Jersey docks shimmered in the distance. No one spoke.

But everyone knew this was going to be one of the most important days of their lives.

PART II
The New World

Chapter 7

The passengers from the *Kronprinz Friedrich* had been lined up four abreast under the canopy that stretched from the entrance of the Reception Center all the way out to the ferry landing, and the shade gave welcome respite from the hot sun. A Jewish pushcart vendor was near the line, hawking, "Bananas! Box lunches for twenty-five cents! Ham sandwich and a banana, twenty-five cents!"

"What means 'banana'?" Jacob asked Marco.

"Banana? You never see a *banana*?"

"No."

"It's a fruit. It's good. Here: I buy you one. Hey, you! Two bananas. You take lire?"

"Sure," said the vendor. "I take anything."

The transaction made, Marco handed Jacob the banana. "It's sweet, good. You see," he coaxed.

Jacob stared at the exotic object. He was so famished from his days of seasickness that before Marco could instruct him in the Fine Art of Banana Eating, he bit the top off, peel and all.

"No, no, *cretino*! You gotta peel it first. See? Like this."

Jacob, red with embarrassment, spit out the banana, then watched as Marco peeled the fruit.

After he had finished his banana Jacob said, "It was good. Thanks."

"Our first meal in America." Marco grinned triumphantly.

The line moved slowly on.

* * *

Inside the Reception Center the long line of immigrants moved up the central stairs to the Great Hall. This vast room, two hundred feet long and one hundred feet wide, with a fifty-six-foot-high ceiling, was the main registration and examination hall on the island. On the ground floor were baggage handling facilities, railroad ticket offices, food sales counters and moneychangers. The Immigration Service employees wore dark uniforms that frightened many of the immigrants, who mistook them for army officers; to most of the Europeans, any army officer was potentially dangerous. Nurses and other employees bustled about. It was a busy day. Over four thousand immigrants were expected. The flood tide from Europe was at its peak, and the ships from Hamburg, Liverpool, Piraeus and Naples never seemed to stop coming.

It took two hours of excruciating boredom for Bridget and Georgie to get as far as the bottom of the steps. When they did reach them, they began to hear screams from upstairs.

"It's the eye exam," said Georgie nervously. "I hear they turn your eyelid upside down with a buttonhook."

"What in the world for?"

"Who knows? Dear God, and you know how I hate to have *anything* in my eyes!"

"Well, it can't be *that* bad."

"Says *you*."

Jacob and Marco had almost reached the top of the stairs, and now they saw that the huge room, packed with people, was divided by a series of steel bars into a sort of maze, designed to guide the immigrants through the intricacies of the various inspection stations. Two doctors were at the very top of the stairs, watching the immigrants as they ascended, looking for obviously diseased or crippled people who would be marked with chalk on their coats for further inspection later on. The system, while perhaps rather cruel, was necessitated by the enormous number of people going through; the average medical exam lasted less than two minutes. The disadvantage was that it was a system controlled to a certain degree by whim: If one of the inspectors saw a crooked back or a vacant facial expression, he could reject the immigrant out of hand for tuberculosis, say, or simplemindedness. That 80 percent of the immigrants did in fact pass indicates that the inspectors were, in general, humane. But many of the 20 percent who did not pass returned to Europe bitter in the thought that they might have been rejected because one of the inspectors on that particular day had a cold or a hangover or just felt generally surly. It was the capriciousness of the system that caused so many tears on Ellis Island.

When Marco reached the top, he squeezed into a single file.

"Do you speak English?" asked the first doctor.

"Yes."

"Open your mouth."

Marco obeyed. The doctor checked his teeth.

"What's two and two?"

"Four," replied Marco.

"Move on."

Thinking *that* was easy, Marco moved on toward the second inspection team.

"You speak English?"

"A little," said Jacob.

"I see you limp slightly. Something wrong with your leg?"

"No."

He began to sweat. The wound from the Cossack's bullet had long since healed, but sometimes it ached a bit and he favored the leg. Of all days, today it had been aching.

The doctor marked something on his coat.

"What that mean?" asked Jacob.

"Your leg will have to be looked at. What's three and three?"

"Six. But nothing *wrong* with my leg!"

"It'll have to be looked at. Move on."

"But nothing—"

"Move *on!*"

Jacob obeyed. Now he was a wreck. Was it possible he would be turned back? He hadn't had a sick day in his life, except for the seasickness on the ship.

Oh God, they can't send me back to Russia, *can they?*

Twenty minutes later, after undergoing the eye exam with the buttonhook—which indeed did hurt—Jacob was sent to one of the inspection rooms to the side of the Great Hall. As he went he passed a high wire fence behind which were kept those immigrants

57

who, for a variety of reasons, were being detained, or in some cases actually deported. Many of the women were weeping, and they all looked so miserable that Jacob's spirits plunged even further.

Oh God, he thought, *don't send me back! Please!*

He entered a small room, immaculately clean, filled with medical furniture. A nice-looking young doctor with sandy hair looked at the chalk mark on his coat.

"There *nothing* wrong with me," Jacob blurted out. "You see! I healthy!"

"Calm down . . ."

"How can I be calm? I can't go back to Russia. They *kill* me!"

The doctor looked surprised, and Jacob realized he should have shut up.

"Why?"

"They kill *all* Jews," he said quickly. "Russians hate Jews."

"Yes, so I hear. Drop your pants, please."

"Huh?"

"Your pants. Drop them."

Nervously, Jacob obeyed. The doctor leaned down to examine the bullet wound.

"What's that?" he said.

"I got shot. Hunting accident."

The doctor looked at him suspiciously. "Hunting? Did a doctor treat it?"

"No. I mean, *yes!* It all right. Honest! No problem! I healthy, make good American. You see."

The doctor straightened. "All right, pull your pants up. What's the real story?"

Jacob quickly pulled up his pants. "I tell truth. Hunting accident in Russia. I healthy. Look: feel muscle. Strong! Healthy! See?"

Jacob was in such an agony of apprehension that Dr. Carl Travers almost laughed.

"Yes, I think you *are* healthy," he said. "And welcome to America. But I'm going to have you deloused." He chalked something else on his coat, then pointed to the door. "Go back to the main hall."

Jacob was staring at him.

"You mean I pass?"

58

"That's right. I have a funny feeling *you* were what they were hunting, but you pass."

Jacob almost pirouetted out of the room.

Georgie groaned as the doctor raised the buttonhook to her right eye.

"Relax," he said. "I won't hurt you."

"Relax? When you might be puttin' out me eye?"

"I won't hurt you."

She tensed. The buttonhook turned the eyelid all the way up. It hurt and terrified her. Then the left eyelid.

Then it was over.

The doctor made a chalk mark on her sleeve, then pointed to the room Jacob was coming out of.

"You'll have to see Dr. Travers."

"What's wrong?" asked Georgie.

"I'm afraid you have trachoma."

Georgie looked behind her at Bridget, then back to the doctor. "What's trachoma?"

"Dr. Travers will explain. Move on, please."

"Bridey, you'll come with me . . . ?"

"Of course, darlin'. Now don't worry."

"Move on, please."

Five minutes later, Carl Travers finished examining her eyes. "I'm afraid I have bad news for you, Miss . . . ?"

"O'Donnell. Georgiana O'Donnell. Doctor, what is trachoma? I've never even heard of it."

"It's a disease of the eye, a form of conjunctivitis. If it's not treated, it can result in blindness."

Georgie put both hands to her mouth.

"Blindness?" she whispered.

"Unfortunately, it is one of the diseases that requires automatic rejection. I'm afraid you can't come to America."

"Dear God—!"

She burst into tears. Bridget hurried to her and hugged her.

"Georgie, darlin', don't *worry*. It's some sort of mistake. This so-called doctor obviously don't know what he's doin'. You *wicked* man!" she blazed at Travers. "Have you no feelin's? You've scared my sister out of her wits."

"I'm sorry, but . . ."

"You're makin' this whole thing up. Trachoma! Whoever heard of such a stupid thing? Georgie, sweetheart, don't worry, we'll get you through. . . ."

"I'm afraid you won't, miss," said the doctor. "The Immigration Service will not allow trachoma victims into the United States."

"But she's not sick. There's nothing wrong with her eyes!"

"There *is*."

"Says you! And what about all those fine ladies and gentlemen in first class? *They* got into America, and you're not going to tell me none of *them* had this . . . what do you call it? Trachoma? I'd bet half of them have *syphilis*!"

She was spitting mad.

"They were checked in quarantine . . ."

"Oh, sure! And you're going to tell me *they* had buttonhooks stuck in their eyes? I wasn't born yesterday."

"Look: I realize how you feel, but there's no use yelling at *me*. You'll have to face the fact that your sister will have to go back to Ireland. And until her passage can be arranged, we'll have to detain her here at Ellis Island. I'm sorry, but those are the rules."

"Back to Ireland?" sobbed Georgie. "Oh my God . . ."

"You bloody bastard!" said Bridget softly to the doctor. Then she kissed Georgie's cheek. "It'll be all right, darlin'," she whispered. "Uncle Casey will fix things."

As Carl Travers went to the door to signal one of the Immigration Service guards to take Georgie to detention, he marveled guiltily at the thought that had just flashed through his brain. Carl was as resolutely "Amurrican" as the immigrants he inspected were "furrin." The son of an upstate New York druggist, Carl had been raised in an atmosphere of small town late-Victorian strictness. Hard work and "getting ahead" had been drummed into him by his ambitious parents. They had paid his way through medical school, and Carl had paid them back with unremitting hard work. He was a good doctor and he was getting ahead. Three years at Ellis Island, and he was already being talked about as the next chief medical examiner. Popular, clean-living, nice-looking, Carl was a sort of Frank Merriwell dime-novel hero.

But Carl had what he considered a flaw, and a tragic one at

that: plain, good old-fashioned, all-American lust. He was always thinking about women. New York, bursting at its seams, teemed with temptation and crawled with maneaters, as prostitutes were called. Carl avoided the whores from fear of catching venereal disease—he knew all too well from his medical training what syphilis could do—but finding a clean woman who could satisfy his ruttiness was not easy, even in New York, and Carl's private life was a sex-starved misery.

As sorry as he felt for Georgie O'Donnell, the deliciously tempting thought had occurred to him to make a deal with one of the beautiful sisters: He'd forget reporting the trachoma in return for . . .

He signaled the guard to come into his office, but he thought that if anyone deserved deportation that day at Ellis Island, it was he.

But my God, how he'd love to lay that Georgie! Or her fiery, hot-tempered gorgeous sister.

"Give me your tired, your poor . . ."

Chapter 8

At the end of the Great Hall, behind a series of desks, sat what some called the inspectors and others the commissioners. Whatever their title, Marco knew they represented the final test. Among the confused stories and rumors he had heard on the *Kronprinz Friedrich* was the Great Dilemma: If you said you had work in America, you could be designated a "contract worker" and sent back to Europe after your job was finished. If you said you had no work, you might be rejected on the grounds you would become a public charge.

And of course the most important thing was to have a sponsor, which Marco didn't have.

I'll lie, he thought, as he nervously faced the inspector at the desk. *I've come all this way. They can't turn me back now. I'll lie!*

"Your name?"

"Marco Santorelli."

"You understand English?"

"Yes, very good English. Very good."

"Do you have a sponsor?"

"Yes. And a job."

"Who is your sponsor?"

Marco straightened slightly, as if to add importance to his statement.

"She great English actress, a Mrs. Maud Charteris. I was-a her gardener in Italy, and she promise me job as gardener here in America."

The inspector, a thin-faced man in a black suit, looked surprised.

"*You* worked for Mrs. Charteris?" he asked.

"Yes. Her gardener. Very great lady. *Famosa* actress."

"Yes, of course. I happen to have seen her three years ago when she played Lady Macbeth here in New York. She's a wonderful actress. Wonderful!"

"Great lady," repeated Marco rather smugly, as if to indicate he actually *knew* the celebrity, giving him a leg up over the inspector.

"I read," continued the inspector, who obviously was a theater buff and found Marco infinitely more interesting than the thousands of other faceless immigrants he boringly processed, "that she's made a great hit in London with *Lady Frederick* and may tour it in America. But I had no idea she planned to *settle* in America."

"Settle?" asked Marco, confused.

"You say she's hiring you as her gardener. I assume she plans to have a garden if she's having a gardener?"

"She buy big farm," said Marco quickly, feeling the rug slipping from under him.

"Where?"

Marco shifted uncomfortably, his knowledge of American geography practically nonexistent.

"Fifth Avenue," he blurted. It was the only place he could think of, but he realized from the look on the inspector's face that his choice had been less than inspired.

"A farm on Fifth Avenue? That's an interesting place to farm. What crop is she planning to raise? Alfalfa?"

"Geraniums," said Marco, too hastily. "The beautiful lady she loves-a geraniums. *I* grow her geraniums in Italy. Big, beautiful *rosa* geraniums! We do same in New York."

Marco was lucky, the inspector was in a benign mood. Besides, the wildness and absurdity of the Italian's story tickled him.

"Welcome to America," he said drily as he stamped Marco's papers. "And good luck with your Fifth Avenue farm. You may pass on to the delousing station."

Marco didn't realize it, but he had been admitted to America on a whim, just as so many other less fortunate immigrants had been rejected on a whim.

Although probably necessary, the delousing of the immigrants was demeaning. Herded into a small room like cattle, Marco, Jacob and a dozen other men stripped, handing their ragged, filthy clothes through a window to an attendant who proceeded to spray the garments. Then another attendant sprayed the bodies and sent the men to shower. Jacob, whose personal sense of cleanliness had been revolted by the conditions in steerage, was so grateful to be able to bathe he almost didn't mind the indignity of the delousing or the smell of the spray. Besides, his thoughts were soaring. The prospect of employment on Tin Pan Alley—no matter how tenuous—had satisfied the same theater-buff inspector who had passed Marco. The two young men had been accepted. Bathed, dressed and deloused, as they made their way down a wire-enclosed ramp to the first floor to take passage back across the bay to Manhattan, they could think only one thought: The Golden Door had opened and they had slipped through.

Vodya Banicek, the twenty-eight-year-old cousin of Tom Banicek who was sponsoring "Little Tom's" entry to America, had bad news for his cousin. But as he waited in the big room on the ground floor of the Reception Center with the dozens of other sponsors, Vodya decided he would not break the news at first. Little Tom had probably had a rough voyage, and this was his first day in America. Give the kid time to adjust. . . .

Then he saw him coming down the ramp from the Great Hall,

his bag of belongings slung over his shoulder. The sponsors had been warned by the guards not to wave at their relatives until the immigrants could identify them. This little game was played to ensure that the immigrants weren't inventing their sponsors. So Vodya waited while Tom showed his papers to the guard, then pointed to him.

The two cousins pushed through the crowd to hug each other and laugh and, in Tom's case, cry a little.

"Welcome, welcome," Vodya kept repeating in Czech.

"I'm so glad to be here!" Tom replied. "So glad . . ."

They left together to take the ferry to Manhattan.

Casey O'Donnell believed in corruption.

The Irishman who had immigrated to New York with his bride, Kathleen, in 1894 had been twenty-one when he came to America. Big, strong, good-looking and affable, he had joined the Irish-dominated police force and quickly become popular. He had a fund of randy jokes and could drink most of his friends under the table. He forged a chain of potentially useful contacts and friendships within the police, but Casey had had no intention of remaining a cop the rest of his life. He, like so many others, had become fascinated by that new toy of the rich, the automobile. But unlike so many others, Casey had had the wits to see the commercial possibilities of the automobile's stepchild, the truck. Cashing in on a number of favors, Casey raised enough money to buy two trucks in 1905. He started hauling chickens and produce into Manhattan from the Long Island farms. Despite bad roads and frequent breakdowns, he was still able to operate so much more quickly than his horse-drawn competition that he had prospered with a speed even he thought incredible. In two years he had enlarged his operation to a fleet of ten trucks, and the profits were staggering. No longer a poor Irishman, Casey was now a prosperous American businessman and a member in good standing of the Irish political machine that wielded so much power in New York. A natural cynic, Casey had no illusions about how things were "managed" in New York. Perhaps a dozen men—most of them unknown to the general public—controlled the city, and to operate in New York one had to make some sort of accommodation with them. The reformers—who had been trying to clean up the city since the

Tweed scandals of forty years before—called this corruption. Casey thought of it as the only way a city the size of New York could be run.

Anyway, if it was corruption, then in Casey's opinion corruption had a lot to be said for it.

Right now, as he stood in the Ellis Island waiting room, surrounded by (in his opinion) "scummy" people, and waited for his two nieces to appear, Casey O'Donnell was in a black mood. He was a man of importance, of position. To have his damned nieces come through Ellis Island, as if they were dirty wops or Slovaks...!

It was then he spotted Bridget, recognizing her by the photograph she had sent him. Even though she was looking flustered, he was struck by her exciting good looks.

She in turn recognized him by the photograph he had sent her, but he was so dapperly dressed in his white suit and Panama hat, she could hardly have missed him in the poorly dressed crowd of sponsors. Besides, Casey O'Donnell was unmissable. At thirty-seven, his Irish good looks coarsened by forty pounds of overweight, he was known to everyone by his red hair, red face and the big wart on the left side of his chin.

After the guard checked her papers, Bridget hurried up to her uncle to hug him.

"Oh, Uncle Casey, thank God you're here!" she said before he had time to say as much as hello. "The bloody rotten doctors say Georgie has a disease I never heard of, and they've put her in detention and say they're goin' to ship her back to Ireland and the whole thing is a bloody mess and you *must* do something about it!"

Her uncle blinked. "What's the disease?"

"Trachoma, or somethin' like that. He says she'll go blind, but I don't believe a word of it."

Casey O'Donnell groaned. "Trachoma! Oh my God ... you know, if you'd come second class like I told you instead of comin' with these trashy steerage passengers, you'd both be in Brooklyn now."

"I know, and it's all my fault, but can you *do* something?"

Casey's orderly mind raced through his connections. Immigration Service ... he didn't know anyone connected with it directly, but Archie O'Malley, who ran the city's docks, would know someone, and Archie was one of Casey's drinking buddies, and Casey was godfather to Archie's second daughter, Maureen. . . .

"Yes, I can do something," he muttered, taking her suitcase. "Come on, let's get over to Brooklyn."

"But wait! I have to tell Georgie. She'll be worried. . . ."

"You can't get back in there *now*. Wait till I have a chance to pull a few strings."

"But . . ."

"Would you do what I *say*?" he almost roared, and Bridget decided she shouldn't push her uncle too far. He looked ready to explode.

Quietly—almost meekly for her—she followed him to the ferry.

Harry Epstein lit a cigarette and surveyed Orchard Street. Harry could usually be found on Orchard Street at about this time of day. Other men in his profession hung around the ferry landing, but Harry knew that the "greenies" who were most ripe for his particular services would want to see something of the city first. They would gawk at the elevated trains, gawk at the washing hanging between the tenements, gawk at the thousands of people milling around the hot streets of the Lower East Side, the push-carts, the yelling kids, the open fire hydrants, the strolling cops. . . . Only after their initial curiosity was satiated would they be ready for Harry, and that's when Harry would be ready for them. Harry, twenty-seven, was himself the son of Russian Jewish immigrants; but Harry had been born in New York. He was an American, he spoke English, and he was savvy. Harry saw nothing wrong in exploiting greenies. His parents had been exploited when they arrived in New York in 1885. Greenhorns, or greenies, as the newly arrived immigrants were scornfully dubbed, were meant to be exploited.

But for appearances' sake, Harry called his profession a service.

He spotted the two young men and pushed his way through the crowd toward them. It wasn't hard to spot greenies. They always looked bewildered and lost, and these two jerks were as bewildered and lost-looking as any he'd seen for months.

"Good afternoon," he said, tipping his straw hat pleasantly.

"Dobry dyen," he added in Russian, figuring the shorter one was from Russia. The other, he wasn't sure of. "My name's Harry Epstein," he continued in Yiddish (just to make sure). "You gentlemen just off the boat?"

"Yes," said Jacob in English.

"That would be the *Kronprinz Friedrich*?" said Harry, switching to English. If they knew even a little English, they couldn't be quite that easy to pluck.

"You're looking for a room?" he went on, walking beside them. "And jobs? I can help you find both. I have a very nice place on Cherry Street—that's not far from here. Very nice and very cheap. You understand cheap?"

"Yes, cheap," said Jacob. "How much is cheap?"

"Three dollars a week. Apiece. You won't find a better deal in Manhattan. You'd like to see it?"

Jacob looked at Marco, who shrugged.

"Why not?"

"Good. This other gentleman is from Russia?"

"Italy," said Marco.

"Ah, *la bella* Italia! Welcome to America. What's your name?"

"Marco Santorelli."

"You look strong, Marco. I think I have a job for you. Two dollars a day working on the docks. Interested? Of course you're interested! You want to work, right? You want to make money? You're lucky, gentlemen. You've found Harry Epstein. I'll get money for you."

He flipped his cigarette into the gutter, where an open hydrant washed it away, with a cigar wrapper and a dog turd.

The smells of the city assaulted their senses: garlic, sauerkraut, hot dogs, horse manure, bagels, blintzes . . . and then, as Harry Epstein led them up the crumbling steps of the four-story tenement on Cherry Street, something worse, something foul: the smell of poverty, of filth, of urine-stained stairs. When they came into the dark, narrow main hall of the building, Marco and Jacob looked at each other in shock as Harry continued his cheerful spiel, for all the world as if he were showing them around Buckingham Palace.

"The nice thing is, gentlemen, everyone here is an immigrant just like yourselves—we'll climb the stairs here, that's right—so you can think of it as a sort of private club."

He chattered away as he led them up the sagging stairs, the walls peeling their ancient, cheap paper. The house had been built before the Civil War, and it had been all downhill ever since.

On the third landing Harry stopped before a paint-peeling door that stood ajar.

"Here we are, gentlemen." He smiled. "Home sweet home."

He pushed open the door, which sagged perilously on its hinges, and gestured grandly at the filthy room inside. The room, eight feet wide and twelve feet long, had one tall, dirty window that opened onto a narrow airshaft, admitting at high noon barely enough sunlight to illuminate the cell in a penumbral glow. The only furnishings were six iron cots, on two of which sat bearded, ragged men. They blinked numbly at the intruders.

The room was fiercely hot and appallingly smelly.

"This is worse than steerage!" sputtered Jacob.

Harry Epstein's smile vanished.

"You can afford the Waldorf?" he said, coolly. "It's four weeks rent in advance. And if you want a job, I take your first week's pay. Take it or leave it."

Jacob and Marco stared at the tiny room and their two would-be roommates. Then they looked at each other.

"We probably won't get anything better at this price," said Marco. "I think we should take it till we get settled. At least it's a roof."

Jacob sighed and reached in his pocket, as Marco pulled out the dollars he had exchanged for his lire on Ellis Island.

"We'll take it," said Jacob sourly.

Harry Epstein held out his hand for the money. "There's a privy in the backyard," he added graciously.

The conditions Marco and Jacob were facing were no worse than those confronting the millions of other immigrants pouring into New York, the majority of whom would take years to climb out of the slums. However, in the great river of time, Marco and Jacob and their contemporaries had a few advantages over later immigrants. The American economy, despite periodic severe depressions, was still growing, and work was available for those who wanted it—although at low wages. Furthermore, Marco and Jacob could complain about their living conditions, but America was still an exciting adventure; the freedom and electricity of New York were exhilarating compared to the despotism of Tsarist Russia and the feudal stagnation of the Mezzogiorno. Most important, both of them truly believed they had a *chance* at something wonderful, that the brass ring *could* be grabbed, or at least snatched at. And if life is a state of mind, this optimistic attitude was the two young men's chief advantage.

Thus, though they spent a miserable, near-sleepless night in the hot, roach-infested Cherry Street tenement, they greeted the next day with excitement. Marco was taken to the West Side docks by Harry Epstein, and Jacob headed uptown to tackle Tin Pan Alley.

The theater then was in a state of physical change. The Times Tower had been opened two years before and the prestige of the new skyscraper had made Times Square respectable and the new center of the theater district. A theater-building boom was under way on Forty-second Street; and the theater, still viewing the cinema as no more than an annoying mosquito, was in its prime, offering dozens of melodramas, operettas, revues, comedies and vaudeville each year to an insatiable public. The greatest stars included the sensationally beautiful Maxine Elliott, whom the painter Whistler had called "The Girl with the Midnight Eyes"; Minnie Maddern Fiske, whose acting was classically restrained and who had popularized Ibsen; Maude Adams, who was enchanting audiences as Peter Pan; and the incomparably lovely Ethel Barrymore, whose warm, throaty voice thousands of star-struck girls were trying to imitate.

The music publishing industry—if "industry" was the applicable term for such a chaotic, bucket-shop business—had followed the march of the theaters uptown from Fourteenth Street; and at ten that morning Jacob walked into a run-down, three-story building on the corner of Forty-first Street and Eighth Avenue, three of whose second-floor windows sported the painted words: SHULMAN MUSIC PUBLISHING COMPANY.

He climbed the wooden stair, listening to the distant discord of several pianos, for the building held six music companies in all. The frosted glass in the door at the top of the stairs also bore the Shulman legend, adding modestly, "Shulman Publishes the World's Greatest Songs." Jacob, in his tieless shirt and ratty suit, realized he was hardly a dandy; still, considering his wretched finances, he thought he looked as good as possible. Since the tenement had no running water except for a pump-sink in the first-floor kitchen, he and Marco had gone to a neighborhood barbershop that morning where, for the classic two bits, they had gotten a shave and a haircut. Now, clutching the letter Roscoe Haines had written for him, Jacob opened the door and went into the office.

It was empty except for a middle-aged secretary-receptionist who was sitting at a wooden desk reading *The Saturday Evening Post* and munching an apple. The desk was behind a wood-balustrade partition; next to the desk was another frosted-glass door through which piano music was playing. There were a half-dozen wooden chairs, several dirty ashtrays, a spittoon; the walls were festooned with the covers of sheet music, presumably "great" songs Abe Shulman had published.

Jacob crossed to the balustrade partition. The secretary, who wore a white, high-collared blouse, the armpits of which were wet, put down her magazine and looked at him. She had the hint of a moustache.

"Yes?"

"I want to see Mr. Shulman. Roscoe Haines sent me. I got letter—see?"

He held out the letter. Crack! The secretary bit into her apple, but ignored the letter.

"What do you want to see Mr. Shulman about?"

"I play piano, write great songs. Roscoe Haines said—"

He stopped, horrified, as a high-pitched voice began screaming in the inner office. He stared at the frosted-glass door as the secretary, obviously used to the screaming, continued to eat her apple.

"Mr. Shulman's a busy man. You'll have to make an appointment."

The screaming had reached a manic pitch. Now the door opened and a fat, sweating man holding a briefcase hurried out, terror on his face.

"I'll *sue!*" screamed the voice. "You stole that tune from me—sell that song and I'll SUE you! You'll never work in the show business again! Get out! *GET OUT!!!*"

The fat songwriter needed no encouragement. He ran across the reception room as a strange man appeared in the door. Abe Shulman was a dwarf, barely four feet tall, a tiny, fire-spitting dynamo in a loud checked suit with a huge cigar in his right hand, the pinkie of which sported a big diamond of dubious origin. He glowered at the vanishing songwriter and delivered a final salvo: "Besides, you're FAT!"

At the door the trembling songwriter shouted back, "You're not exactly John Barrymore, SHORTY!"

Abe Shulman screeched with rage, grabbed a paperweight off his secretary's desk and hurled it with all his strength at the songwriter's head. The man ducked and was out the door.

Crash! The paperweight sailed through the frosted glass of the rapidly closing door, and shards scattered everywhere.

Crack! The secretary bit into her apple again, totally unfazed; she'd seen it all before.

"If that fat bastard shows up again," snarled Abe, glaring at Jacob, "call the dog catcher. Who's this shmuck?"

"My name Jacob Rubenstein. Roscoe Haines told me to see you...."

"Roscoe Haines? Where'd you meet him? He left the country two years ago."

"In a Hamburg whorehouse."

"Oh!" gasped the receptionist.

"Roscoe Haines is a black *gonif*," said Abe curtly. "He owes me a hundred and fifty bucks."

"But he said you'd listen to me play piano...."

"I don't need no piano players." Abe started back into his office, saying to his secretary, "Rosie, get me Harry Erlanger on the phone."

"*Wait!*" yelled Jacob, pushing through the swinging gate of the partition to run after Shulman. "You got to listen to me play. You got to give me job!"

Tiny Abe turned in the door to glare. "I got to do *nothing*," he snorted.

"I play ragtime good, like black man. I write great songs...."

"I ain't got no job!" screamed Abe. "Now get outta here!"

He stormed inside his office, slamming the door. Jacob was stunned. He had wrongly assumed that Roscoe's letter would at least get him a hearing. Now his anger erupted. Oblivious to Rosie the receptionist's yells, he opened the door and charged into the office. The room was small and cluttered with furniture, song sheets, photographs of Abe's writers ... and a beat-up upright piano against one wall. Abe was going around his desk when Jacob charged up behind him, grabbed him with both hands, picked him up and shook him furiously, as if he were a cigar-puffing doll.

"I come to America for *job!*" he howled. "You gotta listen to me play!"

At which point he slammed Abe down on top of the piano, then sat on the piano stool and started playing his variations of "The Maple Leaf Rag." Abe was so stunned by this manhandling, he was speechless, staring at the young immigrant with mouth slightly agape, his cigar drooping comically. He listened for a moment, then regained his speech.

"All right," he yelled over the music. "You want a job, I'll get you a job."

Jacob stopped playing. "Where?" he asked, eagerly.

Abe pulled a card from his wallet and scribbled on it.

"My cousin runs the Half Moon Clam Bar at Coney Island." He handed the card to Jacob. "Give him that, he'll give you a job because you're a *landsman.* Now get the hell *out!*"

Jacob stared at the card. It wasn't what he wanted, but it was work.

Besides, he had the idea Abe Shulman had been more impressed by his piano playing than he had let on.

"Well, it's fixed," said Casey O'Donnell, coming into the front parlor of his Brooklyn home where his gray-haired wife, Kathleen, was sitting with Bridget. "I talked to Archie O'Malley, who talked with someone in the Immigration Service—he wouldn't tell me who. We'll send Georgie back to Ireland, where she'll change ships and come back to New York second class. She won't have any trouble getting through quarantine in second, and of course she won't even *see* Ellis Island. So she should be home in a few weeks."

"Thank heaven," said Bridget. "What a relief!"

"I might add," said her uncle, lighting a cigar, "this wouldn't have happened if you'd followed my instructions."

"Bridget realizes that," said Kathleen, a handsome woman who was putting on pounds even faster than her husband. "And don't pick on the poor girl. After all, it's her first day in America...."

"I'm not pickin' on her," interrupted Casey. "But this is causin' me a lot of trouble and extra money, too. Bridget, you know your Aunt Kathleen and I are more than happy to take you and Georgie into our home. *More* than happy. Your father was my dear younger brother, and I look on you girls as my own daughters. But I run a tight ship here. And while you're under my roof, I'll expect you to obey me. Is that understood?"

Bridget, sitting very straight on a shawl-draped sofa, tilted her chin a little sharply, a little defiantly.

"That's understood, Uncle Casey," she said. "And we appreciate everything you've done for us."

Casey sat down in an overstuffed chair. The house was large and airy and comfortable, situated in a pleasant Brooklyn neighborhood not far from Prospect Park. But the furnishings were an eyesore. Casey and Kathleen had money, but no idea of taste at all; they bought what others in their up-and-coming class bought, and that was heavy stained-oak furniture with leather arms, dark rugs, vitrines filled with ghastly colored glassware, fringe-shaded floor lamps, and on the walls, Bible illustrations featuring an androgynous Jesus so weepy-eyed as to make an atheist out of the Pope. The religious "art" was Kathleen's touch. She never missed a mass, and the greatest triumph of her life (though Casey considered it otherwise) was that their only child, Thomas, was in a seminary training to take orders as a priest.

"As far as Georgie's trachoma goes," Casey went on, "Archie tells me it's serious. But we've got the best doctors in the world here in New York, and when Georgie's back, I'll get her to an eye specialist. So we don't have to be too upset about her goin' blind."

"Well, I won't have to tell you she'll be glad to hear *that,*" said Bridget. "The poor girl was scared silly. And that terrible doctor! I have half a mind to go back to Ellis Island and kick him right where it would hurt the most."

"Bridget!" exclaimed her aunt, who was beginning to sense that her niece from Dingle was not quite the lady she might be.

"He was only doin' his job," said Casey. "His name's Carl

Travers, and Archie tells me he's highly thought of in the service. I might add, we owe a lot to Archie O'Malley. He has a son, Sean, who's your age, a fine young man who's goin' to Fordham Law School. I told Archie you two girls was almost indecently pretty, and he made a note of it, so I wouldn't be surprised if Sean O'Malley might not be payin' us a call soon. I'll expect you to treat him well, Bridget."

Again, her chin tilted slightly.

"Well, I wouldn't spit in his face," she said. "But I heard America was a modern country. I hope you don't expect one of us to go waltzin' down the aisle with whomever, just because his dad was a friend of yours?"

Silence. Casey sucked on his pipe, emitting Strombolian fumes.

"You've got a sweet face, but a fresh tongue, Bridget," he said. "We'll all be gettin' along a lot better if that tongue of yours gets as sweet as your face."

Bridget held her fresh tongue. So far, she was having mixed feelings about her uncle. He was being a bit of a pill, a bit authoritarian for her independent tastes, but the important thing now was that Georgie was going to be all right.

"Can we get word to Georgie?" she said. "I know how she must feel, all alone over there...."

Casey checked his gold pocket watch.

"There's a four-thirty ferry," he said. "I'll take it over and tell her everything. But I don't want *you* goin' along. We'll have to play this close to the chest and not rouse any suspicions about what we're up to. If you ran into Travers, you'd probably spill the beans. So you'll stay home and unpack."

"Casey, you're bein' too mean to the girl," admonished Kathleen. "Come on, darlin'." She smiled at Bridget, standing up from the sofa and extending her hand. "I'll take you upstairs and show you your room. I had new wallpaper put up for you and Georgie. I *do* hope you'll like it. It's a mixed pattern of shamrocks and roses. I thought it would remind you of the old country."

"It sounds lovely, Aunt Kathleen," lied Bridget, standing up.

"You *do* like our house? Your uncle and I had so much fun decorating it. Of course Casey grumbled about the bills, but that's his way, and the furniture is the best Sloane's had to offer. So solid and sturdy ... I hope you come to love it as much as we do."

74

Bridget hugged her buxom aunt. Kathleen's taste wasn't much, but Bridget felt she was a warmhearted woman, and one she could come to love.

"I know I will," she said. "And it's so excitin' bein' in Brooklyn! Can you imagine, I had no idea Brooklyn was part of New York City? I thought it was another state or . . ."

She stopped, staring at the headline of the afternoon paper that was on the table next to her uncle's chair. *Jamie!* she thought. *Sweet Jesus, Jamie! But they* swore *they wouldn't hurt him. . . .*

"Is something wrong?" asked Kathleen.

Bridget tore her eyes away from the headline. *Act natural!* she thought. *Don't let them see . . .*

"Oh, no." She forced a smile. "Nothing at all."

Her aunt took her hand and led her to the front hall to climb the stairs, chattering away about the house and life in Brooklyn in general. Bridget pretended to listen, but her thoughts were on that incredible headline:

FENIANS MURDER IRISH NOBLEMAN! EARL OF WEXFORD
FOUND WITH BULLET THROUGH BRAIN!

"And you'll love Father Flynn," Kathleen was saying as she climbed the stairs. "He's our priest. Such a fine young man! Everyone at Saint Joseph's loves him. He's raisin' funds for a new stained-glass window, and your uncle and I gave a hundred dollars to it."

Bridget wasn't thinking about stained-glass windows. She was remembering Jamie's hot kisses, and the warm feel of his body, a body now cold and stiff and decaying with death.

"You're sure you're all right, dear?" asked her aunt, stopping at the top of the stairs to look at Bridget's white face.

Again, she forced a smile. "Oh, I'm fine," she said.

The truth was, she was so shocked and horrified, she felt physically ill.

Marco sweated as he pushed the wheelbarrow full of facing stone up the wooden ramp to the scaffold where Luigi Gammi, the ill-tempered mason, was working on the facade of the new office building at First Avenue and Twenty-fifth Street. The summer sun blasted down on him, matting his black hair with sweat, which the handkerchief tied around his forehead kept out of his eyes.

Dio! he thought. *This is worse than Calabria, worse than the farm....*

Reaching the scaffold, he started unloading the wheelbarrow, stone by heavy stone.

"Why don't they use a pulley?" he said in Italian to the mason.

Luigi Gammi was a fast worker and a man of few words.

"Because you're cheaper."

I'm cheaper than what it would cost to put up a pulley? marveled Marco. It was his first day on the construction job. His job on the docks had lasted two weeks, terminating in a fistfight with one of the stevedores who had called him a wop. Marco had won the fight and lost the job.

"Get moving," growled Gammi.

It's goddamned slavery! thought Marco, his anger mounting. *Worse than Calabria ... why did I come to this rotten country?*

His muscles aching, he started back down the ramp to get a new load of stones. If he, Marco Santorelli, was cheaper than a pulley, then something was wrong with Marco Santorelli.

It's got to be better than this, he thought, with desperation. *It's got to!*

Dr. Owen Titus Moore examined the eye, which was bloodshot and teary. He saw the damage to the cornea.

"The light hurts your eyes?" he said to Georgie O'Donnell. The neatly dressed blond Irish girl was trembling. In the two weeks since she found out at Ellis Island that she had trachoma, "blind fear" had taken on a new meaning to Georgie.

"Yes," she answered. "I've had to start wearin' tinted glasses. And my eyes are always waterin'."

"You have lacrimation. Your tear ducts have been infected by the bacteria."

"Is a bacteria a germ?"

"That's right. Trachoma is extremely infectious."

I know, she thought. *I know now!* The trip back to Ireland from Ellis Island, then the return to New York second class, had been a lonely nightmare. Her eyes had rapidly grown worse. Her uncle had gotten her into America—that had been a relief—but now, her second day in New York, as she sat in Dr. Moore's office, she screwed up her courage to ask the question that had haunted her since that terrible morning at the Reception Center.

"Doctor," she said, quietly, "am I goin' blind?"

Dr. Moore was a fat man with a kindly manner. But he knew kind lies only caused later agony.

"I would like to tell you I can cure you," he said, "but I can't. You have a very advanced case, Miss O'Donnell. Your corneas have already suffered damage."

"You're sayin' *yes?*" she whispered.

"Yes. There is nothing we can do to save your sight."

Blindness! Never to see again the sun, the rain, the flowers of spring, the dead leaves of autumn, Bridget's face ... To be helpless, to spend a life with a cane, feeling one's way around familiar rooms and not daring to go into strange rooms ... Never to be able to see a play or read a book or newspaper ...

The panic inside her turned to hysteria as she realized she had just been sentenced to a lifetime of blackness.

Chapter 9

Jacob pushed his way through the kitchen door of the Half Moon Clam Bar at Coney Island, balancing on his shoulder a tray with eight orders of Manhattan clam chowder for table six. It was eight-thirty at night on the second Wednesday in September, 1909. The weather was still warm and Coney Island had been packed all day, so that the Half Moon was doing booming business; every table was full. The big room with the vaulted ceiling representing a trellised bower entwined with fake ivy was open to the beach, and a light sea breeze stirred the smoky air. The clientele was well-dressed, for Coney Island was still a reasonably fashionable resort, and the Half Moon's good seafood and excellent French fries attracted their share of swells (along with some not-so-swells).

"Hey, Rubenstein," said the owner, Saul Shulman, signaling Jacob. The sweating, harassed waiter hauled the heavy tray to the bar.

"Yes sir?"

"My cousin's at table twelve. He wants you to wait on him so he won't have to tip."

Thanks a lot, thought Jacob. He hurried to table six, glancing at twelve to see tiny Abe Shulman sitting with two showgirls half again his height, and a thin young man. The party was sharing a bottle of Rhine wine, compliments of Saul. Jacob served the chowder, then weaved through the crowded tables to twelve. He had been a waiter for more than two years now, working at the Half Moon during the summer season, then transferring to another seafood house Saul Shulman owned in lower Manhattan for the winter months. The pay was miserable and the work exhausting, but the tips weren't bad. Most important, Jacob was no longer a stranger in a strange land. He knew his way around New York now, and if his command of English still left much to be desired, he could at least speak and understand well enough to handle most of the quotidian situations of life, and prided himself that he was becoming constantly more fluent. Every once in a while he even dreamed in English, though his erotic dreams remained stubbornly Yiddish.

"Good evening, Mr. Shulman," he said.

Abe, dressed in a ludicrous (on him) white suit, looked up.

"It's the shmuck," he said cheerfully. "This is the guy I told you about," he said to the young man opposite him. "Two years off the boat and he's writing songs for me. Not bad tunes, but the lyrics? *Vay iz mir!* He rhymed *'shiksa'* with 'cement mixer' and 'else' with 'wedding bells'—how about it?" The dwarf was cackling. "The shmuck thinks 'bells' is pronounced 'bellsse'! A *Yiddisher kop* trying to write English lyrics—can you believe it?" And his cackling turned to coughs as he choked on his cigar smoke.

Jacob was slowly burning.

"It's a good lyric!" he exclaimed. "And my English is a lot better."

Abe shrugged. "It's getting better, I'll admit, but it still stinks. You got something, kid, though it may not be talent. Al, meet the next Harry Von Tilzer—according to *him*—Jacob Rubenstein. Jacob, this is Al Jolson. He's a singer with style—what you could use some of."

The word *singer* brought Jacob to instant attention. He hurried around the table to shake Jolson's hand.

"You got to hear one of my songs some day, Mr. Jilson," he said.

"Jolson, shmuck!" rasped Abe. "You got to admit the kid's a hustler."

Al Jolson's sharp, hungry eyes studied the thin young waiter. Jolson, not yet a star, was planning to invade New York soon and was already planting ads in the trade papers warning the New York managers: "Watch me, boys! I'm coming east! Signed, Al Jolson." Now he said, "I'd love to hear a song where they rhyme *'shiksa'* with 'cement mixer.'"

" 'No One Else But Elsie,' " said Jacob. "My best song. I *told* you, Mr. Shulman, you should publish it."

"It's a lousy song, shmuck, but sing it for Al. He needs a laugh. Then get us the menus. I'm starving."

"Sing it *here*?"

"Sure, why not? There's a piano in the corner. If my cousin complains, tell him to stuff it."

Suddenly, Jacob realized that this was Abe Shulman's oblique way of auditioning him for Jolson. For almost a year Jacob had been submitting songs he had written to Shulman—songs he wrote at night on the Half Moon's tinkly piano after the restaurant was closed, writing on music paper he bought with his tips—and the dwarf music publisher had done nothing but ridicule his efforts. Now he recognized that maybe Abe had seen something in the songs after all and had brought Jolson to hear one, all the while deriding the "shmuck" to protect himself if Jolson was unimpressed.

Jolson, never reluctant to grasp an opportunity to advertise himself, stood up and raised his arms.

"Ladies and gentlemen," he shouted, "my name's Al Jolson— Al *Jolson*—and I'm a singer, and we've got a waiter here who's a musical genius. Are you listening?"

He waited for the hubbub to die down. The fifty or so diners turned to see what was going on.

"What's your name?" he whispered to Jacob.

"Jacob Rubenstein."

"His name's Jacob Rubenstein, he's a new American, and he's written a great song called 'What's Wrong With Elsie.' "

"No, no, 'No One Else But Elsie.' "

"Sorry. 'No One Else But Elsie.' Let's give the kid a hand!"

He began applauding and the diners joined in halfheartedly. Jacob, fighting down his terror, hurried across the big room. *Oh God, oh God, they're going to hate it ... my voice stinks ... Oh God, what am I doing?*

He lifted the keyboard cover, sat down on the stool and struck a nervous dominant chord.

Expectant silence.

He begin singing, to a very bouncy tune:

"I've got myself the cutest little *shiksa*.
She's pretty as a picture
And sweet as apple pie.
But my heart's churning like a cement mixer
'Cause something tells me Elsie
Has got another guy.
Say!
No one else but Elsie is my girl friend,
But Elsie fell in love with someone else.
You ought to see how fast she'll change the subject
When I try to mention wedding bells.
She's got a red-hot pepper
And she sees him on the sly.
If I ever meet that shlepper—*oy!*
I'll punch him in the eye!
Say!
No one else but Elsie is my girl friend,
But Elsie's got a boyfriend
(I fear he is a *goy*-friend)
Elsie fell in love with someone else!"

He ended with a flourish, then tensed, waiting.

Silence. A few subdued snickers. A few mutters: "Did you hear that accent?" "What's *shiksa* mean?" "It's a Jewish word, my dear. Immigrants, you know." Some applause from one table that was Jewish and appreciated the song, but otherwise the cruelest blow to a creative person: indifference. The diners went back to their seafood, the conversation picked up again, and Jacob, still sitting at the piano, slowly died.

He stood up, trying to look nonchalant, but the rejection hurt more than he could have imagined. The dream of becoming a published songwriter had sustained him for two miserable years. Suddenly, he'd had his chance, and nothing had happened.

"So?" hissed Saul Shulman, hurrying over from the bar. "You're a waiter, not an entertainer."

"Mr. Shulman, your cousin told me to sing—"

"My cousin don't own this joint; *I* do! He gets free wine from me and a third off the check—what more does he want? Blood? Get back to work."

"Yes, sir."

He took a handful of menus and brought them to Abe's table, silently handing them out, eyes glued to Abe's and Al Jolson's faces, waiting for a reaction.

"What do you recommend, shmuck?" asked Abe, studying the menu. "The last time I was here, I got a rotten oyster."

Say something! screamed Jacob's brain. *Say it wasn't bad!*

The girl on Abe's right, a stunning blonde, giggled and said, "This time you got a rotten song."

Abe fixed her with his eyes. "Since when are you a music critic?"

"Well, it *was* pretty awful," she said. Then she sang the first line, cruelly mocking Jacob's accent: "No one else but Elsie is my girl friend . . . ," rolling her eyes.

"I thought it was a clever opening for a song," said Jolson, making Jacob a fan for life. "And I liked the tune a lot. These goddam anti-Semites didn't like it because it's got Yiddish words in it—they think it's Second Avenue. Don't listen to Abe, kid. I say you got talent. Keep at it. It's all work, you know. And persistence. That may sound shmaltzy, but it's true."

"The trouble is, Mr. Jolson," said Jacob, "I got all these tunes in my head and ideas for songs, but I don't know English good enough. I know 'bells' doesn't rhyme with 'else.' I mean, I know it *now*. But . . ."

"Go to school," interrupted Jolson.

"How? When? What do I pay with?"

Abe Shulman put down his cigar and his menu and pulled his wallet from his white coat.

"There's a place on Fourteenth Street and Sixth Avenue called the Acme Language School. Here's fifty bucks. Call it an advance. Take one of their morning courses, learn English and write me a hit song."

He handed the cash to Jacob, who took it, fingering the money with awe.

"Acne?"

"No, shmuck, that's pimples. Ac*me*. And change your name. Jacob Rubenstein's too Jewish. Makes you sound like a pants cutter. Call yourself Jake Rubin."

"That's *not* Jewish?" laughed Jolson.

"It's better than Jacob. Jacob sounds like something out of the goddam Bible. Okay, Jake, what do you recommend tonight?"

He was in a daze.

"Uh . . . no one's sent back the chowder."

The four diners laughed at his limp recommendation, but Jake Rubin didn't care. Abe Shulman had invested in him. Abe was on his side after all!

Jake Rubin had a new name and a new hope.

Marco's tongue licked the stiff nipples of the young whore's breasts as Renata wrapped her legs around his naked hips. She was eighteen, blond as a Botticelli Venus, plump, with beautiful skin, and she had been tricking on the streets of the Tenderloin district since she was fifteen. One of eight children of a barber from Turin, she had rebelled against the poverty of her home by running away. Generally, her attitude toward sex was that it was a source of income; but when she had met Marco at a bar two months earlier, she was so attracted to him that she didn't charge. He had been coming to her Sixth Avenue second-floor room at least one night a week since, bringing two bottles of cheap Chianti, getting half-drunk, making fierce love to her, then complaining about his job with the construction company. Her physical attraction to him was almost canceled by his sourness. One night she had actually said to him, "Marco, why don't you shut up and just fuck me?"—which had at least gotten a laugh out of him.

Tonight he was, as usual, half drunk and rutty. He licked her breasts, then kissed his way up to her mouth. She often teased him about the size of his penis and had nicknamed it Vesuvius, which also made him laugh. Now she felt Vesuvius ease into her. His kisses became hotter, and she felt all the strength of his young body as he thrust into her. Renata, who could be noisy when she was enjoying it, began to moan. Then Vesuvius erupted.

"God!" she said. "I wish all my customers fucked like you."

The Sixth Avenue el roared by her window and Marco yelled over the noise: "You should be so lucky!"

She pushed him off. "Conceited ape," she said, and he laughed.

She got out of bed to go douche herself in the porcelain basin. He watched her from the bed, lazily scratching his hairy chest and thinking it was lucky he was born good-looking, because he couldn't afford to pay for such wonderful sex.

"I'm hungry," she said in Italian, the language they always used with each other. "Take me out for a sandwich?"

"No. I'm broke."

"Why, you cheap bastard! I let you lay me for free, and you won't even buy me a sandwich? Jesus Christ, I ought to . . ."

"All right, I'll buy you a sandwich."

"Don't do me any favors."

She started getting dressed, sitting on the bed to pull on her lisle stockings.

"You know, Marco, you think you're God's gift to women, but you're really a pain in the ass to put up with. Listening to you bitch about your job all night isn't a girl's idea of heaven."

"Have I bitched tonight?"

"No, but you will. I know the routine. God, do I know it! 'I'm too smart to be hauling stones,' 'I'm tired of being called a dumb wop,' and so on, and so on. Christ, if you don't like the job, why don't you quit?"

"You got two hundred dollars to loan me?"

She got off the bed, looking at him. "Are you crazy? If I *had* two hundred dollars, I wouldn't loan it to *you,* of all people. Besides, what do you want with two hundred dollars?"

"I want to buy a truck. I saw a used one for sale today on the West Side for a hundred fifty dollars. It was in good shape, and for fifty dollars more I figure I could put it in first-class shape—new paint job, the works." For the first time since she'd met him, she saw enthusiasm in his young face. "Listen, Renata, you say I bitch a lot. You bet your ass I bitch! I didn't come to America to push a goddam wheelbarrow. I came here to *be* somebody! And you know how you get to be somebody? By being your own boss."

"The big news," she said, buttoning her yellow blouse.

"All right, laugh at me—but I'm smart. Too smart to be doing the work I'm doing. On the boat, there were two Irish sisters named O'Donnell, and their uncle owns a trucking company over in Brooklyn. His trucks deliver stone to building sites, and he's *rolling* in money. A couple of years in the business, and he's rich. Why the hell can't *I* do that?"

"It's a free country."

"Except I haven't got two hundred dollars. Shit!" He got off the bed to pull on his underwear. "I'm sick of living the way I do. That hole Jake and I live in . . . cockroaches, no privacy . . . Christ, I lived better back in Italy! I—"

"Oh Marco, I've *heard* all this. And if you think two hundred dollars is going to solve all your problems, why don't you borrow it?"

"No bank will loan me . . ."

"Not banks," she interrupted. "Go to a loan shark."

"Oh, sure. Pay fifty percent interest, and if I go broke, they kill me."

"Well, then go out and *steal* two hundred."

Marco was buttoning his shirt.

"Anyway," added Renata, "if you want a loan shark, I know one."

He looked at her. She was attaching her fake gold earbobs.

"Who?" he asked softly.

"He's one of my clients." She turned and smiled at him. "He's cute, and he fucks almost as good as you. But I make *him* pay."

The Piccolo Mondo Bar was in Little Italy, and the next evening Marco went in and made his way through the crowd. "I'm looking for Sandro Albertini," he said to the bartender.

"In the back."

The air was smoky, and Sweet Caporal cigarette posters shared the wall with an extremely ill-painted mural of the Bay of Naples. Two wood-blade fans turned sluggishly from the tin ceiling. Marco went to a door marked Private and knocked. After a moment the door was opened by a man who weighed at least 250 pounds and whose smashed nose advertised his former profession. He looked at Marco.

"I want to see Albertini about a loan," said Marco. "Renata sent me."

The ex-fighter said nothing. He stepped aside, and Marco went into the room.

"The Russian language," said the middle-aged teacher with the pince-nez set severely on her nose, "has no definite article—no 'the.' Therefore, the most common mistake Russians make in English is to forget 'the.' For example . . ." She picked up the textbook from her desk. Jake Rubin, sitting in the third row in a class of students, watched. "I am picking up *the* book. Behind me is *the* blackboard. On *the* right wall are *the* windows. Outside on *the* street, *the* sun is shining. This is *the* Acme Language School. Now: Mr. Rubin."

Jake stood up. "Yes, ma'am."

The teacher held up a sheet of paper. "What am I holding up?"

"*The* shit of paper."

The teacher, Miss Tavistock, who had learned Russian during her eight-year stint in St. Petersburg as governess to the children of the Grand Duke Alexei, blanched.

"*Sheet,* Mr. Rubin. The *sheet* of paper."

"The *sheet* of paper."

"It is very important that you do not use the *other* pronunciation. That is a *very* vulgar word in English. Now, the other common error concerns the verb 'to be.' This verb, oddly enough, doesn't exist in Russian. In Russian we say *Ya rad*—'I happy.' In English we say 'I *am* happy.' Or 'I *am* hungry,' or 'You *are* thirsty.' Now, Mr. Rubin, give us a sentence using the verb 'to be' twice."

Jake thought. "I *am* happy," he began, "to work at Coney Island because there *is* a lovely bitch."

"Beach!" howled Miss Tavistock. "Ee-ee-ee-ee!"

"Beach!" Jake howled back, totally confused. "Ee-ee-ee-ee-EE!"

Oh God, he thought, *will I ever learn? But I will. I must!*

* * *

85

West Fourteenth Street was thronged with New Yorkers. It was a glorious autumn morning; the heat had been broken by a Canadian air mass, and the New York air, which foreign visitors compared to champagne, seemed to crackle with pleasure. A few blocks away from the Acme Language School, D. W. Griffith was directing Little Mary in a two-reel comedy, neither knowing that within a decade he would be the most famous film director in the world and she would be America's Sweetheart, earning over a million dollars a year. Gloria Swanson was ten years old and living with her parents in a house on the Key West Army Base. In the White House, an extra-large bathtub had been installed for the extra-large new President, William Howard Taft. In England, Edward VII was enjoying the last year of his life and reign, and in Russia the Tsarina Alexandra was having tea with Rasputin while the latter's future assassin, the fabulously rich Prince Felix Yusupov, was dancing with a Coldstream Guardsman in a country estate outside London. In Vienna the heir to the Austro-Hungarian throne, the Archduke Franz Ferdinand, was sulking because the Emperor Franz Joseph would not allow Franz Ferdinand's morganatic wife, Countess Sophie Chotek, to sit in the royal box at the opera. Also in Vienna, Mahler's Ninth Symphony was first performed, as was Strauss's *Elektra,* and Freud was lecturing. In Switzerland, Lenin published *Materialism and Empirio-Criticism,* while in Detroit, Henry Ford had just introduced the Model T. The third Grand Prix motorcar race in France had been won by a German, Lautenschlager, who drove his 120-horsepower Mercedes at 68.9 mph. Blériot flew the English Channel in a monoplane, Peary reached the North Pole, Ehrlich prepared Salvarsan as a cure for syphilis, Rachmaninoff was touring America playing his wildly popular Second Piano Concerto (the third movement main theme of which he had been accused of stealing from his Russian doctor), and Dorothy Rothschild—who would later become Dorothy Parker—was attending a convent in Manhattan, hating her father for being Jewish.

And Jake Rubin was trying to master the language of Shakespeare so he could write lyrics for the tunes that kept dancing in his head.

As he came out of the Acme Language School, he heard a loud *hoo-gah, hoo-gah.* It was the horn of a gleaming white truck parked at the curb, and Marco was in the open cab waving to him.

Jake hurried over.

"How do you like it?" said Marco.

"Whose is it?"

"Mine! Look at the side."

Jake looked to see Santorelli Trucking Company painted in black letters.

"Get in—I'll take you for a ride."

Jake climbed in. Marco shifted, and the truck roared and rumbled into Fourteenth Street.

"Where'd you get the money?" Jake shouted over the noise.

"Found an investor. Isn't this great? I can clear twenty dollars a day bringing in food from Long Island!"

"Look OUT—!"

Marco swerved to miss a car that had pulled in front of him. Then, laughing at the thrill, he headed west across town, weaving in and out of the traffic as Jake hung on for dear life.

"Marco, slow down!" he yelled.

"Why? This thing will do forty miles an hour!"

The accident happened at Tenth Avenue. Marco's left front tire blew, the truck went out of control and was sideswiped by an Oldsmobile, sending the truck into a spin. Its side smashed into a lamppost. Neither Marco nor Jake was hurt, but as they climbed out to survey the smashed body, it took no expert to know that the truck was dead.

Sandro Albertini was twenty-nine, neat, well-dressed, nice-looking and a sadist. As he sat at his desk watching Marco squirm, he could almost smell the man's fear, and it gave him pleasure.

"So the truck's ruined," he said in Italian. "One day, and the truck's ruined. You're stupid, Santorelli. Even worse, you're un-lucky."

"Give me another chance," said Marco. "Loan me another two hundred . . ."

"Why? So you can lose that, too? *I'm* not stupid."

"But I can't pay you the first two hundred unless I can get another truck. I quit my construction job—you *got* to give me an-other chance!"

"Fuck off, Santorelli. You're a loser."

He signaled Paolo. The ex-prizefighter, who was standing behind Marco, pulled a blackjack from his pocket and smashed it on the back of Marco's skull.

"Give him a half hour on the radiator," said Albertini. "Maybe that will give him some brains."

When Marco revived, his head screaming with pain, he found he was in a dirty cellar room, shirtless, his arms tied to a steam radiator, his mouth gagged. Paolo was turning the radiator on.

"You gonna be deep-fried," he said in English, flashing a grin that showed two front teeth were missing, "like-a calamari."

He burped a laugh, then crossed the room to sit on a battered wooden chair and watch. The ancient radiator hissed and banged as the heat began to rise. Marco's back, pressed against the iron ribs, began to feel the heat, tepid at first, then hotting with a speed that might have cheered the tenants upstairs but filled him with terror. Paolo lit a cigar, stamped his foot on a cockroach and continued to watch.

"The boss, he don't like losers," he said, conversationally. "He think you a number-one loser. You real dumb guinea."

Again the smile.

The radiator was hot now. Marco strained away from it. The ropes were loose enough so that he could remove the skin of his back from contact with the stinging iron, but when he did so, his arms were pressed even harder against the sides of the radiator, and the skin of his arms was slowly being cooked. The pain was excruciating. The fierce heat was causing the sweat to pour out of him, dehydrating him swiftly. He bit against the gag, gurgling with genuine agony, pulling, pulling, pulling away from the radiator. . . .

"You got-a fifteen minutes more," smiled Paolo, looking at his watch. "You havin' fun?"

Just before he passed out from the pain, Marco's brain screamed *I'm not a loser! I'm not DUMB!*

They rolled him out of the car into an alley near the East River, tossing his shirt after him, then drove off. It was nine that night, and the good weather of the morning had turned to a cool drizzle. He lay on the pavement, stretching his arms out to catch the rain. The burns on his inner arms were scabbing, and he knew he would bear the scars the rest of his life. His head still ached from the blackjack, and the pain nauseated him. *Some day I'll pay them back,* he thought. *Some day I'll be important and pay those bastards back....*

After a while, he sat up. He tied his soaked shirt around his neck and pulled himself to his feet. He was still so weak, he had to lean against the brick wall to steady himself. *America,* he thought. *Oh shit, America ... "Give me your tired, your poor" ... Shit, shit, shit ...*

He limped out of the alley, rain dripping off him, and started to walk back to Cherry Street. As his brain slowly geared up, he wondered what he would do now. He had no money, no truck, nothing.

It was then he saw the poster on the wall. It read:

DANIEL FROHMAN PRESENTS
THE FAMOUS STAR OF THE LONDON STAGE
MRS. MAUD CHARTERIS
IN
W. SOMERSET MAUGHAM'S HIT PLAY
LADY FREDERICK
BELVEDERE THEATER
Broadway and 43rd Street
Matinees Wed. & Sat.
Curtain Time: 8:30 P.M.

Suddenly, Marco knew what he was going to do next.

Chapter 10

She told herself over and over again that she really was innocent of Jamie's murder, but she couldn't quite make herself believe it.

As the days melted into weeks and months, the shock of the murder numbed, but the guilt grew. In retrospect, she knew she had either been a fool or blind to the realities of Irish political terrorism to think that the possibility of violence hadn't existed from the very beginning. True, the Earl of Wexford represented all the unfairness of what she considered the English "occupation" of Ireland. True, Jamie's family had caused suffering to her own forebears. But symbols of oppression were one thing; human flesh was another. She had slept with Jamie, and the thought that she had caused his violent death—no matter how indirectly and innocently—haunted her. The fact that she had to keep her involvement a secret made it even worse. She longed to tell someone, especially Georgie, but she didn't dare. Besides, Georgie had problems of her own, adjusting to her blindness.

Nevertheless, life had gone on. Her uncle Casey had paid for Bridget's tuition at a secretarial school in Manhattan, since Bridget decided she wanted a career for at least a few years before settling into domesticity. Gradually the sisters became fond of their uncle, who, despite his initial gruffness, was a generous man apparently determined to do everything he could for his nieces, especially Georgie. Both Casey and Kathleen had pushed young men on Bridget, but she had not evidenced much interest in the gentlemen callers who flocked to the house in Brooklyn, attracted by her good looks. Bridget had her typing and shorthand. As far as Georgie was concerned, though her spirits were slowly improving, they all feared that the beautiful younger sister's blindness might prevent her ever experiencing the normal joys of love and marriage. Bridget, however, was eminently marriageable. But Sean O'Malley, whom both Casey and Kathleen were promoting, turned out to be—in Bridget's opinion—a "good-looking nincompoop"; and Casey began grumbling to his wife in private that Bridget was too damned choosy, which meant that he thought she was too independent for a woman. Despite the growing national pressure for votes for women, Casey O'Donnell had a distinctly old-world, Victorian view of the opposite sex.

Bridget was no militant feminist, but one of the most exciting things about New York to her was the relative freedom of American women compared to the near-feudal status of women back in Dingle. She loved exploring Brooklyn and Manhattan on her own, and it was in a Greenwich Village bookshop that she met for the second time Dr. Carl Travers. It was a late Saturday afternoon; he was leafing through a Henry James novel when he spotted her on the other side of the shop. She was wearing a tweed suit and looked so beautiful that he ignored his first thought—which was that she would be anything but delighted to see him—and came up beside her.

"How's America been treating you?" he asked, tipping his hat.

She turned and stared at him.

"You!" she exclaimed. "It's been treatin' me very decent, no thanks to you. I'm amazed you have the nerve to speak to me."

"So am I." He smiled. "And your sister? How's she?"

Be careful, she thought. "I have no interest in talkin' to you about anything," she said. "Please leave me be."

"I realize you don't have a very high opinion of me, but I'd like to improve it if I could."

"Why?"

"Let's say I owe you at least a dinner."

"The nerve!" she exclaimed. "You think I'd have dinner with *you,* after the way you treated my sister? I'd sooner have dinner with the Devil himself! Now, I'll thank you to be lettin' me alone, before I call a cop."

"I was only doing my job," he said, rather testily.

She relented a little. "Well, maybe I'm bein' a bit hard on you. But do you have any idea what it's like goin' through that cow barn you call Ellis Island?"

"I have a very good idea. I'm there every day, and believe me, to have to tell someone they can't come to America is no fun. But you'll have to admit the government has to have *some* control over who they let in."

"I'll admit it, though I don't like it."

"Then how about dinner?"

She suppressed a laugh. "You're a very determined young man, aren't you?"

"Determined enough. I live three blocks from here, so I know this neighborhood. There's a great Italian restaurant on Thompson Street. Do you like spaghetti?"

"I don't know. I've never had it. There aren't many Italian restaurants in Ireland."

He smiled. "You have a point. How about it?"

She hesitated. He seemed so pleasant and so totally different from her memory of him on Ellis Island that it was difficult to continue thinking of him as an ogre.

"Well, I shouldn't," she finally said. "What I *should* do is slam this book over your head. But I suppose I've reached that time of life where I should taste spaghetti."

He accompanied her out of the bookstore, wondering if she was a virgin.

"I assume you're not married?" she said twenty minutes later, after they were seated at the checkered-cloth-covered corner table.

"I'm not married," he replied. "But I'd very much like to be."

"Well, you're not bad-lookin' and I imagine you make a decent salary. If you're so anxious for a wife, I suppose there's a woman somewhere foolish enough to accept you."

He unfolded his napkin, and she noticed a troubled look flit across his face.

"It's not quite that easy."

"Why? In a city this big?"

"Then let's say I haven't found the right foolish woman yet. How about you? Have you found love in America?"

She laughed. "Well, my uncle and aunt are surely tryin' to fob me off on someone, but so far I've kept romance at bay. I'm in secretarial school, you see, and plan to have a fine career for myself. Time enough for marriage later on."

"I'm impressed. You can type and take shorthand?"

"I can indeed, and very good at it, too. I finish the course in two weeks and then the school will arrange job interviews for me. A really good secretary can make decent money these days."

"So I hear." He opened the menu, then said with over-forced casualness, "Coincidentally enough, I'm looking for a secretary."

She looked surprised. "To work with you *there*? On Ellis Island?"

"Yes. I've just been made chief medical examiner, and I'll have a lot of administrative work to do. I'll need someone very good to help me. It might be a bonus to have someone who knows firsthand what it's like to have gone through the cow barn, as you called it." He looked up from the menu. "Do you think you might consider it?"

She opened her menu slowly.

"Perhaps I might," she answered.

They looked at each other with new interest.

Chapter 11

She had eight living nieces and nephews, but everybody in Hawksville, West Virginia, called Edna Hopkins "Aunt Edna." It was a term of affection, because despite a sharp tongue, Aunt Edna was a good woman and a funny woman. She lived a life almost identical to her great-grandmother's a hundred years before. The farmhouse she lived in with her husband, Ward, and their daughter, Ardella, had been hand-built by her grandfather shortly after the Civil War, and little had been altered since except to add the "new" wood stove Aunt Edna had bought in 1904. The house, like most houses of the mountain people, was a four-room log cabin with a tall stone chimney at one end and a comfortable porch in front where Aunt Edna liked to rock as she worked on her quilts or her darning or any of the hundred other chores that filled her life and kept her essentially an extremely happy woman.

She had inherited her house and twenty-two acres from her father debt-free, so despite the fact that she seldom saw much cash and had neither electricity nor a telephone, Aunt Edna was considered by local standards well-off, though by the standards of a rich city-dweller she was a desperately poor hillbilly. But Aunt Edna didn't need cash or electricity or phones. Like generations of her ancestors, she was practically self-sufficient. She had her own cow, she raised chickens and hogs, in the summer she planted a huge vegetable garden, she made most of her own clothes as well as her daughter's, she churned her own butter, made her own soap out of "store-bought" lye, wove her own baskets, caned the seats of her own chairs, and once a year changed the straw stuffing of her own mattresses. She was always busy and never bored. For entertainment, she had the spectacular views of the Appalachians from her porch, the gossip of her friends and relatives, the raising of her lovely daughter, the growing of her flowers in tin pails and cracked pots, and the Bible. She had never traveled farther than fifteen miles from her home, knew practically nothing of the rest of the world and didn't care. The rest of the world wasn't important to Aunt Edna. At forty-six, she was healthy, strong, and though her face was wrinkled and her hair graying, she still retained whispers of her good looks.

The one bane of her existence was that she had married a coal miner. Aunt Edna hated the nearby Staunton Coal Company with all her considerable guts. In Aunt Edna's opinion, Montague Staunton, the multimillionaire owner of the mines, was close to being the Devil incarnate. And the constant possibility of her husband being killed in the mines did little to raise her estimation of coal mining as a profession. "But what could I do about it?" she often said to her cronies. "Dammit, Ward Hopkins was good-lookin' and I fell for him. Didn't have the brains to marry a farmer." Her speech was neither southern nor midwestern but distinctly "mountain," peppered with words like *souse* (the meat of a hog's head) that hadn't been heard anywhere outside Appalachia since the eighteenth century.

The only thing Aunt Edna feared—besides the death of her husband—was snakes. Aunt Edna would have laughed at the idea, but she was really a rather remarkable American.

Nearby Hawksville was the closest thing to a city Aunt Edna had ever seen, though in reality it was a village with one main street and less than a thousand inhabitants. It had a general store, a post office, a one-room bank and a white Baptist Church. Its three-room school was the entire school system for the town, and Ardella—or Della, as everyone called her—had graduated from it the previous June. Every Saturday, Aunt Edna hitched up her buggy and rode into Hawksville to shop and "socialize." Every Sunday, Aunt Edna, Ward and Della put on their best clothes and rode into Hawksville for church. One October Sunday in 1909, as everyone was coming out of the church after the service, Aunt Edna was socializing as usual with her friends when Sam and Ann Fuller came over to her. As Sam, a fellow-miner, talked with Ward, Ann said, "Aunt Edna, have you met our roomer?"

Aunt Edna looked at the short young man in the cheap suit.

"No, but I've heerd about him," she said. "Ain't this the feller from *Bo*-hemia?"

"Yes. He's been with us about two years now. Tom, this is Aunt Edna Hopkins. His English ain't so good," she added, rather apologetically.

Tom Banicek shook hands stiffly, saying, "Glad to meet you."

"And this is her daughter, Della. Della, Tom Banicek."

As they shook hands, Aunt Edna's eyes squinted slightly with suspicion. She didn't like the way the little feller from *Bo*-hemia was eying her daughter.

The tree-covered Appalachian hills were gorgeous in their autumn foliage, so breathtaking that the ugliness of the tipple, railroad sidings, offices and sheds of the Staunton Coal Company were an affront to God and nature. A small river, the Shepaug, meandered past the coal company down farther into the valley where the forty shacks of the company town lined the muddy street. The shacks, built and owned by the company, had no plumbing; the miners and their families were forced to draw their water from communal faucets on the street and to do their laundry in the Shepaug. The shacks were all depressingly alike, with corrugated tin roofs; their floor plan was monumentally uninspired and calculated to give as little comfort as possible. One main room served as living room, dining room and kitchen, two other small rooms were bedrooms, and that was it. The privies were in back, and the sole source of heat was a stove burning, naturally, Staunton coal.

The life and death of the town was regulated by the mine whistle. Its blasts signaled the different shifts, and its repeated blasts signaled one of the catastrophes that occurred all too frequently and made coal mining in 1909 one of the most dangerous and badly paid jobs in America.

The company town was called, originally enough, Staunton, and it was to Staunton that Tom Banicek had come two years before. There had been no work for him in New York after he left Ellis Island, so he had signed a contract in the recruiting office several coal companies maintained near the ferry landing for the purpose of hiring cheap immigrant labor. Reading and speaking no English, he didn't know what he signed. His cousin, Vodya the meat-packer, had gone with him to act as interpreter and Vodya had warned him that the pay was incredibly low—sixty-two cents a ton—and that there was a clause in the Staunton contract stating that the miner was subject to instant dismissal if he advocated in public or private joining a union. But Tom was desperate, and he signed. The company gave him a one-way train ticket west, and the little Czech immigrant had come to Staunton, where he moved into the shack of Sam and Ann Fuller, becoming Sam's apprentice in the mines. Small and overcrowded as the shacks were, it was common practice to rent a bed to unmarried miners, so Tom was sharing one of the bedrooms with the Fullers' two young sons.

Sam Fuller was thirty-three, the tall, lanky fifth son of a Kentucky farmer. He had been in the mines twelve years and hated it. He hated Monty Staunton as much as Aunt Edna did, calling him a Bible-quoting, hypocritical son of a bitch who made millions off the misery of his miners. Monty Staunton was also head of the American Mineowners Association, based in Charleston, and was almost fanatical in his opposition to the unionization of the mines. The miserable living conditions and low pay in the West Virginia mines made conditions ripe for unionization; but thanks to the implacable opposition of the owners, led by Monty Staunton, and the armed guards who were everywhere, no union organizer had been able to penetrate the mines, and the miners, terrified of losing their jobs if they so much as discussed the union, suffered in silence.

In such a sulphurous situation an explosion was bound to occur, and the first round of what was later to be called the Great West Virginia War began on the Saturday after Tom Banicek met Aunt Edna and Della.

Sam and Tom had been working one of the rooms, as the mining chambers were called, in the Number 5 Mine. Both wearing open-flame headlamps, Sam would pick the coal from the seam and Tom would load the car, then push it on its rails to the weighing station. They worked in constant danger of death: A pocket of methane gas could be ignited by their headlamps; the coal cars could come loose or derail, crushing their pushers; or a cave-in could entomb them alive. But the dangers of their job gave the miners a certain perverse pride, a bravado that enabled them to mentally thumb their noses at the world. It also forged deep friendships beneath the earth. The miners might occasionally squabble up top, as they called the surface. But "down here" there existed a solid fraternity of commonality.

And what every miner knew, but seldom bothered to say, was that whoever betrayed that fraternity was a dead man.

The distant whistle was heard. Sam and Tom pushed the last car to the weighing station; then they and the other men on the shift squeezed themselves into the carrier that would haul them up a three-hundred-foot diagonal shaft to the surface. When they emerged from the mine entrance, almost totally black with coal dust, Tom filled his lungs with the clean, cold air, and Sam said, "Ready for a laugh? It's payday." And they went to the office to line up.

Forty-five minutes later they began the walk home. They walked in silence, but Tom knew what his friend was thinking. Every payday the same scene was repeated with slight variation, and today was no different. When they came into the main room of the shack they found Ann Fuller, a gaunt woman whose once-handsome face was already wrinkled at age thirty, standing at the stove stirring a pot of stew. Ted and Bill Fuller, six and five respectively, were sitting on the bare wood floor playing with four lead soldiers their father had given them the previous Christmas. Sam pulled some money from his pocket and slammed it on the wooden table.

"Six dollars and twenty cents," he said. "Two weeks' pay after deductions. It's a good thing you married me for my looks and not my money."

Ann said nothing, continuing to stir the stew as she stared at the coins. Sam began to take off his clothes to step into the tin tub Ann had already filled with water, where he would scrub the coal dust off his body.

Sometimes he wondered if the coal dust hadn't permeated his soul.

Monty Staunton might have been an ogre to his miners, but the millions he sweated out of them he spent with a certain panache. He lived four miles from the mines in a large, columned, southern plantation-style mansion called Belle Meade, set amid splendid lawns and lush gardens. Belle Meade was a showplace, and Belle Meade Farms raised some of the finest thoroughbreds in the country. Monty's mother had been a Randolph from Virginia, and in 1896 he had married a second cousin, Christine Randolph, so he was related to half the aristocracy of the Old South who happily traveled to the many barbecues, hunts and balls he was constantly throwing. As a member of the class of 1892 at Princeton, he had contributed several million dollars to his alma mater and supported the football team almost single-handedly, so he had excellent connections with the eastern Establishment as well. The governor of West Virginia was another cousin, to whose election campaign he had contributed a hefty fifty thousand dollars, and he owned the most important newspaper in Charleston, so Monty was a Power in the state—in his opinion, *the* Power. A big man who had been handsome until he lost his hair and his waistline, he liked Maryland rye whiskey, women, horses, hunting, fine clothes and elegant automobiles. A Philistine to his patrician fingertips, he hated anything even remotely cultural. He had a "good ol' boy" Southern accent, was a backslapper, could be loud, was a born bully, and his lovely wife had come to loathe him and drink on the sly.

On this particular evening, he was entertaining at Belle Meade the Episcopal bishop of Charleston, the editor of his Charleston newspaper, and West Virginia's senior senator. They and their wives had just sat down to the gleamingly polished English yew table with the magnificent pair of Paul Storr silver candelabra made in London in 1810. Two gorgeous K'ang Hsi *famille rose* vases stood on the sideboard; above them hung a George Stubbs painting of the Duke of Beaufort's favorite stallion. Opposite the Duke's horse hung two lovely Randolph family portraits. Over the marble mantel hung a Rembrandt Peale portrait of George Washington. On the wide-plank floor was a green and ivory Savonnerie rug; Christine Staunton's diamond necklace from Tiffany glittered from the two dozen candles flickering in the Charles X crystal and gilt chandelier.

"O Lord," Monty intoned at the head of the table, "thank Thee for all Thy gifts. Thank Thee for Thy bounty in this beautiful land, for the freedom Thou hast given America, for our health and for our wonderful friends and for this food we are about to eat."

Thank Thee, he thought, *for my net worth of forty-two million.*

I wish he'd shut up so I can have my wine, thought Christine.

"Amen."

"Amen," chorused the table.

"All right," boomed Monty with Falstaffian bonhommie, "let's eat!"

Two bows scraped across the fiddle strings, and a lively reel began. Every Saturday night the miners and their families gathered in the redwood hall owned by the company to dance, socialize and get drunk. The company encouraged the practice, lent the hall for nothing and even paid for the fiddlers; it was Monty's idea, his little fling at paternalism. Since there was absolutely nothing else to do in Staunton, the miners came to drink themselves into oblivion and temporarily forget the misery of their lives.

"I hope that boarder of yours ain't gettin' no ideas about my Della," said Aunt Edna to Ann Fuller, who was sitting beside her on the women's side of the room. Aunt Edna didn't like to come to these dances because she didn't like coming to Staunton; but Ward liked to drink with his fellow miners, and it gave Della an opportunity to dance, so Aunt Edna acquiesced and brought along some knitting. But she wasn't too happy about Tom Banicek dancing with her daughter.

"Tom's a fine young man," Ann said.

"He's a furriner who can barely speak the King's English, that's what he is. *Bo*-hemia! Whoever heard of *Bo*-hemia? And he's no beauty, neither. He's shorter than Della. Has he got any brains in his head?"

"Oh, I think Tom's got a good head. It's just been hard for him, having to learn English. He's a hard worker, though, and he's wonderful with Ted and Bill. You could do worse, Aunt Edna," she added slyly.

Aunt Edna wrinkled her nose. "Just let him try to come around courtin' my Della. If nothing else, he's a miner. Lord knows *I've* had twenty years married to a miner, and that's enough for one family. What's going on over there?"

Ann looked across the dance floor to the men's side of the hall, where the miners were sitting at tables drinking. One of them had stood up and was shouting.

"It's Sam!" exclaimed Ann.

"He's got drunk early tonight."

In fact, Sam was loaded. Now he weaved up onto the stage and silenced the fiddlers.

"Listen, everybody!" he shouted, almost losing his balance.

"Sam, get off there!" yelled his wife, but Sam ignored her.

"Listen!" he repeated. "We're . . ." He drunkenly searched for words. "We're fools. No, no, we're worse. We're *slaves*. Might as well be niggers. We . . ." Again he stopped as the alcohol assaulted his brain. He waved his hands in a helpless manner. "I got paid six dollars and twenty cents today. Six *dollars!*" He started to giggle drunkenly. "For two weeks' work! Isn't that . . . Can you believe that? Course, I owed groceries to the company store, and I owed rent on the company house, and the company doctor charged for the house call when my son had a fever, and . . ." Again he waved his hands. "Six dollars and twenty cents. That's crazy! For what we do, that's *crazy!* But how can we fight that son of a bitch, Monty Staunton? He's rich, he's got power. . . . Who are we? Nothing. But if we had a union . . ."

"Sam, shut *up!*"

Sam, still weaving, looked at his wife and smiled. "That's my Annie," he said, pointing. "I love my Annie. I'd love to buy her something pretty . . . but . . ." He stopped and suddenly all his bitterness and rage flashed across his lean face. "We should get us an organizer from Pittsburgh," he shouted. "And until we do, we're nothing but *slaves!*"

Silence as his angry words echoed around the room. Tom and Della were standing on the dance floor, listening. Now Tom whispered, "He's right."

"Yes," Della whispered back, "but that little speech may cost him his job."

They came at dawn the next morning.

Tom, in his bed, heard the loud knocks on the door. He got up and looked out, shivering in his nightshirt. Ann, her flannel bathrobe wrapped around her, was hurrying from her bedroom. Now she opened the front door. Tom recognized the man in the dark suit and bowler hat outside. It was Bill Fargo, the head of the company security forces and Monty Staunton's right-hand man.

"Mrs. Fuller," he said, tipping his bowler with a politeness that was ludicrous under the circumstances, "I'm Bill Fargo."

"I know who you are," she replied. "What's the matter?"

"The matter is, your husband is fired. I'm afraid you folks will have to vacate this house. By noon today."

The Appalachian wind moaned around the corners of the shack. Ann's face was stony.

"Why was he fired?" she asked.

"For advocating a union. It's in his contract, you know. Noon today. You've got five hours. I suggest you start packing your things."

Again he tipped his hat. Then he walked away.

Ann closed the door. Slowly she turned and leaned against it. Tears started running down her cheeks. Tom came into the room. She looked at her young boarder from *Bo*-hemia.

"I knew it would happen someday," was all she said.

Then she went in to try to waken her still-drunk husband.

PART III
That Raggedy Ragtime Music Man of Mine

Chapter 12

The elegantly dressed audience that had filled the Belvedere Theater now rose to its feet, cheering and applauding the great star as
she went into a deep curtsy. Then, aping Sarah Bernhardt's famous curtain-call gesture, Maud Charteris came out of the curtsy,
straightened, put both her hands to her mouth in a kissing gesture,
then slowly stretched her arms out wide in front of her as if embracing the audience. They loved it. They loved her regal beauty.
In an elegant age, they loved her elegance.

Maud Charteris had glamour and great presence. She was
making the then-enormous sum of two thousand dollars a week for
starring in *Lady Frederick*. She had the passionate love of thousands of stagestruck New Yorkers.

I've got the world at my feet, and I'm only thirty-nine, she
thought triumphantly as she stepped back into the set and the
fringed curtain lowered in front of her.

The world at my feet.

Her dresser, Vivian, was removing her wig when the theater
callboy appeared at her dressing room door.

"There's a man at the stage door who wants to see you, Mrs.
Charteris," the boy said. "He don't look like no gent. In fact, he
looks like a bum. But he says he knows you."

"A *bum?*" Maud said incredulously, looking at him in her
mirror.

"He's got a wop name. Santorelli, I think. Says he was your
gardener in Italy."

Marco! Her mind flashed back to the Villa d'Oro in Calabria. Lazy, sun-drenched afternoons on the terrace over the sea. And handsome Marco . . .

"Show him in, Teddy," she said. "Vivian, darling, Senator Ogden is in his car in front of the theater. Would you go out and tell him I'll be a few minutes late?"

"Yes, ma'am."

When she was alone Maud stepped behind a screen to put on her delphinium-blue evening gown. One of the richest men in New York, Senator Phipps Ogden, was taking her to a champagne supper at Delmonico's. She liked the love-sick senator, and the allure of all those Yankee millions was appealing, but he could wait awhile. She was extremely curious to see Marco again and find out what had happened to him after two years in America.

She was also rather surprised by how excited she was.

But her first reaction when he came into the room was slight disappointment. He did in fact look like a bum. His cheap suit was dirty, the battered hat he held in his hand might have been stolen from a horse, he needed a shave, his hair was matted . . . he looked like a wop bum.

"Well, Marco," she said, coming out from behind the screen, "it looks as if you haven't exactly conquered the New World yet. But it's nice to see you again. How's your English coming along?"

"Better all the time, signora. Your lessons helped me a lot."

"I'm delighted to hear it." She came over to him and examined him more closely, her eyes moving slowly from his scruffy shoes up his body, finally resting on his face. *He needs a bath,* she thought, *but my God, he's the sexiest man I've ever seen.*

"Did you see the play?" she asked.

"I couldn't buy a ticket. I have no money."

"Yes, of course. That's fairly obvious." She hesitated. "Well then?"

She could tell he was going through a private misery.

"The signora once offered me a job," he finally said, agonizing over every word. "Do you remember?"

"Oh, yes."

"Well, I   I need a job . . . now."

Their eyes locked.

"I see. You're not quite so proud these days."

"I can't afford to be proud."

She smiled slightly, then went to the dressing table, opened her purse and took out some money.

"Here's fifty dollars," she said, bringing it to him. "Buy yourself some decent clothes, take a bath, then come see me in my suite at the Waldorf tomorrow morning. Make it ten o'clock. Then we'll discuss things."

Marco looked at the money, then looked at Maud. He was disgusted with himself. He forced out two words: "Thank you." Then he left the dressing room.

Maud Charteris was still smiling.

Her suite on the fifth floor of the Waldorf-Astoria Hotel overlooked Thirty-fourth Street and Fifth Avenue and, on the diagonally opposite corner, the handsome new B. Altman department store. From her windows she could see visible evidence of one of the greatest innovations of her age: Fifth Avenue already had more cars than horses. But other innovations were delivering the coup de grâce to the tenacious nineteenth century nine years into the twentieth. Four months before, Maud had met at a house party in a chateau outside Paris a twenty-five-year-old failed actress with a bad reputation. The girl, the illegitimate daughter of a peddler, was then living with a rich French horse breeder named Étienne Balsan and was already mocking the pompous fashions of the rich with their aigrettes, elaborate dresses and huge cartwheel hats by dressing more like a schoolgirl than a "lady." Her little white collars and sporty clothes had impressed Maud so much she had bought a few design sketches from the young Gabrielle Chanel, never dreaming that fifteen years later the woman would revolutionize twentieth-century fashion and throw the final shovelful of dirt into the grave of the nineteenth.

Maud was wearing one of these schoolgirly dresses now as she sat at a table in the living room of her lavish suite, drinking coffee and eying Marco, who stood in front of her looking awkward and nervous in the new suit he had bought with her money.

"So you didn't like the docks, and you wrecked your truck," she said, stirring her coffee. "So far, your life in America hasn't been what I'd call an inspiring saga. But I rather admire the fact that you *tried* to start a business. At least it shows you have ambition, which I always suspected. And now you're ready to peddle your manly charms for what I believe the Americans call a grub-stake?"

"If I had five hundred dollars . . ."

"Yes, I know: You could start a trucking empire. And what makes you think whatever you have is worth five hundred dollars?"

He shrugged.

"You realize," she went on, "I'm not some ancient hag who has to pay for love. I'm a world-famous star, and I've had—and have—plenty of men in my life. Men with culture and breeding, too, not peasant boys with no manners who would embarrass me socially."

"But the signora suggested it . . ."

"Oh, I know. The signora propositioned you. I suppose the signora has a weakness for Italians. Just what mad scheme did you have in mind?"

Again he shrugged. "Whatever the signora wants . . ."

She drummed her manicured nails on the table, considering it. "You know, Marco, if we go through with this sordid little ar-rangement, you'll end up hating me. You're hating yourself now for coming here. Oh, don't deny it—I can tell. You may have the equipment for a gigolo, but you don't have the personality for it—which I also rather admire. It makes you much more interesting. I loathe easy men and hate lounge lizards. There's something deli-ciously earthy about you."

"I'm glad the signora finds me interesting."

"Don't get snotty on me. If I buy you, I buy you *polite*. The question is whether I buy you."

"You're not making this easy," he said, beginning to get angry. He felt like a steak in a butcher shop.

"Why should I? I hold the trumps—money being the biggest trump card in life. Oh, I know how you feel, Marco. I've been in your position many times, in managers' offices where I had to ped-dle *my* charms to get parts I wanted. It's a man's world, and I've had to fight men all my life to get where I am. The fight has made me a bit hard, a bit cynical, but that's all right, too."

She opened her purse and pulled out her gold cigarette case and the lighter from Chaumet. She took a cigarette from the case, put it in her mouth, then extended the lighter to Marco. He remembered. He took it and lit her cigarette. She exhaled and continued.

"My father, improbably enough, is a country vicar in Lincolnshire who disowned me when I went into the theater. He called it a harlot's profession. Even now he refuses to talk to me. My husband, the dashing Edmond Charteris, used to get drunk and beat me. Then, five years ago, he took all my money and went to Brazil with a Russian ballerina. Then there have been all those managers who, shall we say, 'used' me, just as I used them. I've fought men all my life. But now the situation is slightly different. Now, here in this room with you and me, it's a woman's world, isn't it? If I were a vindictive type, I'd say this moment is rather delicious." Again, she sucked on the cigarette. "And I'm a vindictive type. Take off your clothes, Marco."

His eyes widened. "What . . ."

"Take off your clothes. I never buy merchandise until I've seen it. I want to see *you*."

"No!"

"Oh? The famous male pride? It's all right for women to strip for men so they can ogle and drool, but it's not all right the other way around? Very well, keep your clothes on. And good luck with your trucking empire."

"You're trying to humiliate me!"

She smiled. "Of course I am. That's part of the pleasure. Goodbye, Marco."

He stared at her, furious. *Money,* he thought. *Money! She's got it and I can get it from her. Money—I've got to have money!*

Slowly, he took off his coat. Then he loosened his tie and began unbuttoning his shirt. She watched, fascinated, smoking. When he was standing in the middle of the room, totally naked, she put out her cigarette, got up and slowly walked around him, examining him.

"You're magnificently put together," she said. "But wherever did you get those hideous scars on your arms?"

"I borrowed some money from a loan shark. When I couldn't pay him back, he tied me to a radiator."

"Good God, how Inquisitorial! Are you serious?"

"He was."

"Well, you were stupid to go to a loan shark. You should have come to me first."

"I didn't think of it. I'm not so sure I'm better off dealing with you."

"But of course you are, dear boy. Of course you are. You know, I especially like your back. I've always been partial to men's backs, and yours is sensational. So smooth and nicely tapered . . ." She ran her hand lightly down his back, then caressed his buttocks. "And I'm *mad* for your ass!"

"Drooling?" asked Marco drily.

"Definitely," she whispered, kissing his shoulder. "I think we're in business."

Three mornings later he ran two at a time up the sagging steps of the Cherry Street tenement and burst into his room. Jake sat up in bed, rubbing his eyes.

"Marco! Where've you been?"

"Come on, we're getting out of this hole. Get dressed."

"But you've been gone three days . . . ?"

"No questions. Come on, let's go! We're moving out."

"To where?"

"You see. Come on!"

Forty minutes later Marco unlocked the door of the ground-floor apartment of the handsome town house on St. Luke's Place in Greenwich Village, and the two young immigrants walked into the large, empty living room. It had a high ceiling, and two south-facing tall windows overlooked the park across the street and let in floods of sunlight. There was a fireplace with a handsome wood mantel. To the rear, two open doors led into another big room overlooking a small garden at the back of the house.

Jake looked around. "Whose is it?" he asked.

"Mine," replied Marco. "Ours! Come on, I give you a tour. This back room used to be the dining room—see the nice garden?—and look at this kitchen! Brand-new gas stove, icebox, sink with running water—everything! And, Jake, you won't believe this: a bathroom. Look! See? A toilet, a tub, a sink—no more privies!"

He grinned triumphantly as Jake stared at the white-tiled bathroom off the kitchen.

"But this place must cost a fortune," Jake said.

"Fifty dollars a month. I already signed the lease with the owner, a nice old lady who lives upstairs. Isn't it beautiful? *Bello*, eh?"

Jake was staring at him, staring at the new, well-cut dark-blue suit.

"Where'd you get the money?" he asked.

"What do you care? I pay the rent, then when you sell a song, you pay me back. Jake, we're *not* going back to that rathole on Cherry Street. We're gonna live like *Americans*."

Jake was shaking his head. "I can't let you do that for me. . . ."

"Why not? We're friends, aren't we?"

"Sure, but . . . Marco, where'd you get the money?"

The young Italian sighed. "All right, I tell you. I go see Mrs. Charteris. I think you used to laugh at me when I talked about her, but she . . . well, she liked me. You know? And, uh . . . well, what the hell, now I'm her boyfriend."

Jake looked shocked. "You mean, she *paid* you for . . . ?"

"Look: it's our secret, okay? But I tell you the truth. She's *crazy* for me. She moan and groan . . . she go crazy, like an old bitch in heat. I've been in her hotel suite for the last three days. . . . Look: see? She give me this." He pulled a gold cigarette case from his jacket pocket. "She bought it for me at Tiffany, and I don't even smoke. Solid gold! Look inside: see? 'To Marco, My Young God.' How 'bout it? She buy me this suit at Brooks-a Brothers, lots of shirts, shoes . . . She *crazy* for me! And look: I got a checkbook. She open account for me in a bank. I'm gonna buy two new trucks, be a big success! How 'bout it?"

Silence. Marco replaced the checkbook and the cigarette case.

"I know what you think," he said quietly. "I'm a gigolo. And you're right. I'm not proud of it. In fact, I'm sort of ashamed of it. But Jake, God gave you talent to write songs. God didn't give me much except women like to look at me, and I fuck good. I'm-a crazy not to use it, right? Back in Italy, the young men do it with rich women, so I figure, what the hell, Marco, do it in New York and get out of the slums."

He looked rather sheepishly at Jake. "You, uh . . . still my friend?"

Jake started snickering.

"What's so funny?"

"I think it's wonderful." Jake laughed. "And I'm *glad* we're leaving Cherry Street."

"Then you'll move with me?"

"Are you crazy? *Sure* I will! I just wish some rich old woman would pay *me*."

Now they both were laughing and pumping each others' hands.

Chapter 13

"Penny for your thoughts."

Bridget O'Donnell had been leaning on the rail of the balcony overlooking the Great Hall of the Ellis Island Reception Center. Now she turned to see Carl Travers standing beside her.

"Oh, I was just watchin' the immigrants," she said, "thinkin' about the day *I* came through this place. And wonderin' how each of them will do in America. Just think of the millions of stories they'll have to tell their children."

"Will you have dinner with me tonight?" he asked softly.

She sighed. "Doctor . . ."

"Carl," he corrected.

"*Doctor* Travers over here, if you don't mind. Carl in New York. I don't want the staff to start gossipin' about us."

"Will you have dinner? At my place. I'm not a bad cook. Really."

"Well, you've been tryin' long enough to lure me up to your apartment. I suppose the only way to shut you up is to go. But no funny business, mind!"

"No funny business."

She had been working for him on Ellis Island for a month, and Carl Travers was hopelessly in love with her.

All he could think about was funny business.

* * *

He lived on the second floor of a delightful Victorian brick house on Grove Steet, just off Sheridan Square. The double front doors had wonderful curlicue designs etched in the smoked glass, and the parlor ceiling swirled with plaster decoration. Upstairs, he rented two furnished rooms which were filled, if not overflowing, with books.

"I see you like to read," she said as she came in.

"I love it. Books are the most important thing in my life after medicine. And you."

He locked the door, then took her in his arms, kissing her.

"Let me take off my hat!" she protested, pushing him gently away.

"Bridget, I love you."

"Go on with you! If you was Irish, I'd say you were full of blarney."

She put her hat on a table and he helped her off with her coat.

"It's not blarney. Being with you every day in the office, I . . ."

"Shh." She put her finger over his mouth. "You're a dear man, and I'm fond of you. I don't want you makin' a fool of yourself."

She walked over to the window. "You've got a nice view," she said, looking down on Grove Street. "I like Greenwich Village. It's charmin', and you can forget you're in such a big city."

He came up behind her and put his hands on her arms.

"Will you spend the night?" he whispered.

"Go on with you! I'm a decent girl."

"Then will you marry me?"

She turned around and studied his face. "You're serious, aren't you?" she said softly.

"Very serious."

She went to the small table and sat down in a wooden chair. She thought a while. Then she looked up at him.

"Since you're gettin' so serious," she said, "I think you must know something about me that no one else knows. Will you swear on your sacred word you'll keep it a secret?"

He looked surprised. "Well, I suppose . . ."

"No supposin'. Swear."

"All right, I swear."

She began rubbing her hands together nervously, remembering Jamie. She had wanted to tell someone for so long. Though she was trying to keep Carl at a distance, in fact she was a lot more than just fond of him. If he was really serious about marriage, then now was the time to put his love to the test.

Tears welled in her eyes as she said, "In Ireland, I'm wanted for murder."

The eyes of the chief medical examiner of Ellis Island almost popped out. He lowered himself into a chair.

"Who . . . did you kill?"

"Oh, it wasn't me. *I* couldn't kill anybody. Some men I knew in Dingle—they were Fenians, and I won't tell you their names—wanted to do something against the British, and they figured if they kidnapped one of the big English landlords, they might force Westminster into grantin' Home Rule. Well, they picked the Earl of Wexford because he was so bloody rich and well-connected. They knew Jamie was fond of women, and they asked me if I'd help them. They swore they'd never harm a hair of his head, and I was stupid enough to believe them. Georgie and I were plannin' to come to America anyway, so I figured it would be my last little fling for dear old Ireland."

"How did you help them?"

She looked at him rather defiantly. "A moment ago I told you I was a decent girl. Well, I'm not. I became Jamie's mistress."

Lucky Jamie, thought Carl Travers.

"The problem was," she went on, "I became fond of him. Oh, he was a snob and a bit of a stiff, but . . . well, he knew what he was doin' in bed. Then they kidnapped him, and I came here. And a few days later I read in the paper they'd killed him." The tears started flowing, genuine tears. "I *swear* I'd never have done it if I thought they'd hurt him. But I was a damned fool and believed them. If the British could ever get their hands on me, they'd surely hang me." She wiped her cheeks. "So: Now that you know I'm a wanted criminal and a bit of a whore, do you still want to marry me?"

He stood up, crossed the room, knelt beside her and took her hand. "If you become Mrs. Carl Travers," he whispered, "you'll be an American and at least they can never deport you."

Bridget blinked with surprise. She had never thought of that.

* * *

Phipps Ogden had served the state of New York in the Senate for two terms and before that had been a partner of J. P. Morgan. He had entered politics not out of any lust for power, but because public service, as he thought of it, had been a family tradition for generations. His father had been the ambassador to the Court of St. James's in the first Cleveland administration, his grandfather had been Millard Fillmore's Secretary of State, and his great-great-grandfather had signed the Declaration of Independence. The Ogdens had grown rich with America, starting out in the shipping business, then branching into banking. But Phipps's grandfather had made them super-rich, thanks to his hobby of buying Manhattan real estate before the Civil War, when the upper half of the island was still farmland. The result was that Phipps owned fat chunks of the Upper East Side, and his real estate brought him an annual income over two million dollars. Tall, patricianly handsome, with silver hair, well-dressed, decent if rather humorless, cultivated, a leader of New York society, Phipps had met Maud Charteris in London two years before and had been smitten by her then, while his wife was still living. Now a widower, Phipps at fifty-six was behaving, since Maud's opening on Broadway, like a schoolboy with a crush, a bona fide stage-door Johnny.

"Phipps!" exclaimed Maud, opening the door to her Waldorf suite. "What in the world . . . ?"

"I know I didn't phone," he said, coming into the room and handing her the dozen roses he carried, "but you've been avoiding me, and I missed you."

"Darling, the roses are lovely, but I've had a cold. . . ."

"Maud, you're the most beautiful woman on the New York stage and England's greatest actress . . ."

"I couldn't agree more."

". . . but you're a bad liar. A friend of mine saw you in Brooks Brothers the other morning with an extremely good-looking young man. Ergo, you can't have a cold, and you're avoiding me. By the way, I brought you a little get-well present, even if you don't have a cold."

She put the roses in a vase, then took from him the long, black velvet box marked Cartier. She opened it and drank in the diamond and ruby bracelet.

"You *do* know the way to my heart," she said, lifting the bracelet out. "It's lovely."

"Here, let me clip it on."

Marco, in the adjoining bedroom, pulled on his underpants and tiptoed to the door to peek out. He watched Phipps attaching the bracelet. Then he watched them kiss.

"Thank you, darling," said Maud. "I *love* extravagant presents."

"Now: Who was the young man?"

"Oh dear," she said, stalling for time as she went to a table to get a cigarette. She and Marco had been making love when the bell rang. "I *do* hope you're not going to be tediously jealous?"

"When the woman I love is seen in public with a man described to me as half her age, I become tediously curious."

"That's not very gallant," she said, admiring the bracelet as she held up her cigarette. He lit it.

"I agree. Who is he?"

"His name is Marco Santorelli, and he used to be my gardener at my villa in Calabria. He wanted to come to America, so I helped teach him some English. Last week he came to the theater and told me he was absolutely broke. I felt sorry for him—he's really very sweet—so I bought him some clothes and loaned him some money to help him out. The defendant pleads not guilty."

Phipps hesitated.

"You bought him clothes at *Brooks Brothers*?"

"Well, darling, you told me it was the best men's store in New York. I'm not in the habit of shopping in bargain basements."

He smiled and kissed her hand.

"Then the defendant *is* not guilty. I'm sorry, Maud. Will you forgive me?"

"I don't know. You've been very dreary, very Georges-Feydeau-French-farcey. I'm amazed you didn't charge into my bedroom and look for my lover under the bed."

Marco, listening behind the bedroom door, marveled at her coolness. There was no denying that Maud knew how to handle an unexpected situation.

Phipps was laughing. "The handsome young Italian lover, hiding under the bed," he said. "It's wonderful!"

Marco looked at the bed and shrugged. *He* didn't think it was so wonderful.

"At any rate, let me take you to lunch," the senator was saying. "Then you'll forgive me."

"Oh, I forgive you anyway. But lunch sounds nice. Go down to the Peacock Alley and wait for me while I bathe and change...."

"Can't I wait here?"

She smiled slyly. "Oh, no, darling. Then my young Italian lover who's hiding in the bedroom couldn't get out."

Phipps Ogden went into gales of laughter. "You're right! I'll go downstairs so ... what's his name?"

"Marco."

"So Marco can pull up his pants and sneak out!"

Marco thought the man was easily amused. When Phipps had left, Maud returned to the bedroom, admiring the bracelet.

"Who's he?" asked Marco.

"My rich senator. Look, Marco: Isn't this bracelet fabulous? I bet it cost ten thousand if it cost a penny."

Marco stared at the flashing jewels. "And it's not even Christmas," he muttered.

"To the very rich, it's Christmas all year long." She walked over to the bed, saying, "Phipps is a dear, but he has a bad sense of timing. He couldn't have come at a worse moment." She lay down on the bed and opened her red silk kimono, revealing her plump, naked breasts, smooth belly, wide hips and long legs. She smiled at Marco and opened her arms.

"My young Italian lover may now finish what he started before Phipps interrupted."

Marco scratched his chin. "Maybe the Italian lover isn't in the mood now," he said.

Maud had grown used to his occasional sulkiness. She knew that their relationship bothered him, and the fact that he had pride appealed to her. For all the casual amorality of the situation, she had come rather to respect him as well as desire him, which had surprised her. She knew he churned with ambition. She watched him watch her, seeing how she ate, how she dressed, listening to her excellent, stage-trained English, learning, learning.... Marco wanted a lot more out of life than being a gigolo. The thought had occurred to her that it might be pleasant and interesting to help him get it, though she wasn't yet sure just what form the help would take.

Meanwhile, she decided not to force him. And she certainly wasn't going to beg.

"All right," she said, getting up. "I'm not in the mood either, come to think of it."

Which rather surprised Marco.

Chapter 14

"Al Jolson thinks you've got something, kid," said Abe Shulman to Jake. "He phoned me from Rochester the other day and mentioned you. He thinks I should help you out."

"You already have, Mr. Shulman."

" 'Abe.' 'Mr. Shulman' makes me feel old. And don't thank me. I hate thanks. What I want out of you is hit songs, and so far I ain't getting them. I think you've got to get into the business, kid. You know what a song plugger is?"

"No."

"Christ, you *are* a shmuck. When I publish a song, you take the music around to music stores and play it for the owners so they'll buy the music, understand? And you play it to singers, too, so they'll sing the song—got it? That's *really* important. I'll pay you thirty-five dollars a week. So quit that lousy waiting job and tell my cousin he's a cheap son of a bitch and he can shove his rotten clam bar up his ass. Then he'll offer you a raise. The only thing he understands is hostility."

The new job came at a good time for Jake. He had been becoming "blue," as he thought of it, waiting tables; but now he was in the show business, and anything was possible. He had finished his course at the Acme Language School, but not his studies. He had bought books on the English language and had devoted a good deal of his free time to poring over them. The result was that he was coming to know more about English than most Americans. He knew such exotica, for example, as the fact that the African words *yaw kay,* meaning "all right," had been transformed by the American slaves into okay. He still spoke with an accent, but a much less laughable one, and his excellent ear was refining his speech all the time. Most immigrants stayed, either through choice or necessity, in ethnic ghettos speaking their native language to each other and wrestling with English only when they had to. Thus they were doomed never to speak English correctly, and it would be their children—or even their grandchildren—who would finally "melt" linguistically. But thanks to Marco's windfall and his generosity, both men were living in an "American" neighborhood—one of their neighbors on St. Luke's Place was the young Jimmy Walker, who would one day be mayor of the city— so they were both becoming American much faster than most of their contemporaries.

It was only occasionally that Jake would reflect that he had not gone to a synagogue once since he left Russia. He was becoming American with a vengeance.

She was twenty-three, stunning, the daughter of a streetcar conductor from Flushing, New York, fiercely ambitious to become a singing star, and she billed herself Sweet Nellie Byfield, the Thrush from Flushing. (" 'Sweet,' shit," Abe had snorted when he filled Jake in on her. "I hear she can be an impossible bitch.") Her act was "shmaltz," in Abe's word, but she had a following among the rich because she did have a lovely voice and was undeniably beautiful. As Jake stood in the rear of the Cavendish Club watching her sing "After the Ball Is Over" to twenty tables of half-loaded stockbrokers, he knew Abe was only partially right. Her act was shmaltz and her voice was lovely, but she was more than beautiful: She was the blond personification of every erotic *shiksa* fantasy Jake had ever had—and he'd had a lot. In her lovely white dress, floppy white hat and white parasol, Nellie Byfield took the young Jew's breath away.

The Cavendish Club was a high-class "smoker" where businessmen could escape from their wives, get good food, throw parties or conventions and get drunk. It was darkly paneled, and the walls were hung with sporting prints, mooseheads and oil portraits of prominent members, one of whom was Teddy Roosevelt. The first three floors of the Stanford White-designed clubhouse on

East Forty-seventh Street were bars, libraries and poolrooms, but the top floor was the grillroom and White had built a small stage at one end for entertainments. Nellie had been appearing at the Cavendish for four months, singing twice nightly with a six-piece orchestra. For this she received $300 a week, which was good pay. But Nellie was bored and restless. The Cavendish Club was classy, but it wasn't Broadway.

Sweet Nellie Byfield wanted Broadway so much she could taste it. But so far her agent, William Morris, had kept her in clubs, telling her she wasn't ready for Broadway. "Ready?" she had screamed at him the previous week. "When will I be ready? When I'm eighty?" Sweet Nellie did have a temper.

She was taking off her stage makeup in her tiny dressing room when she heard a knock on the door. She yelled, "Come in," and in her mirror saw the door open and a thin young man in a cheap suit enter.

"Miss Byfield, my name's Jake Rubin, and I'm with the Shulman Music Publishing Company...."

"Abe Shulman's a crude dwarf," she interrupted, "and I wouldn't sing one of his songs if he published Franz Schubert."

Jake's mouth dropped slightly open.

"Well ... uh ... You know, you've got a beautiful voice, but your repertoire is a bit dated. I mean, 'After the Ball' is fifteen years old. Now, I've got a new song here by Farley Beaumont called 'You're My Cutie-Ootie Sweet Patootie' ..."

"You're kidding. That's a song title?"

"Yes, and it's got a terrific tune. Very catchy and fast! I'd love to play it for you."

She turned around to look at him. "You're wasting your time," she said. "I've got a class act. I don't sing trash."

"But ..."

"You're wasting your time," she repeated. "*And* mine. Now please go."

"But, Miss Byfield ..."

"I said go."

He stood a moment, drinking her in with eyes that were almost comically hungry.

"Well, thanks a lot, Miss Byfield," he finally said. "But you're going to hear more from me."

"With my rotten luck, I probably will. Close the door—there's a draft."

Still watching her, he slowly closed the door.

"I told you she's a bitch," said Abe the next morning in his office. "So forget her. She thinks she's a goddam duchess."

"No, I don't think I should forget her," Jake replied. "She's bored with her act—I really felt that last night, listening to her—and I think if I could just get her to listen to 'Sweet Patootie," she'd go crazy for it and really put it over. That's a lot of money she's singing to."

"Yeah, I know."

Abe thought a moment, then pulled a roll of bills from his pocket and peeled off a twenty. "Here," he said. "Give this to the orchestra leader."

"Why?"

"Oy vay iz mir, is this one a shmuck. *Bribe* him, stupid!"

Events distant in time and place affect all our lives. On March 1, 1881, as Tsar Alexander II drove through the streets of St. Petersburg, a Nihilist tossed a bomb under his carriage. The explosion destroyed the carriage and wounded the horses and one of the Tsar's Cossack escorts, but Alexander himself was unhurt. Stepping out of the shattered carriage, the Tsar was speaking to the wounded man when a second Nihilist ran up, shouting, "It's too early to thank God!" and threw another bomb, which blew up directly between the Tsar's feet. His legs were torn away, his stomach ripped open and his face mutilated. He was taken to the Winter Palace, where he died shortly after, surrounded by horrified members of the imperial family, some of whom had been ice-skating when the bombs had been thrown.

The gory assassination of Alexander II unleashed a savage wave of pogroms against the Jews, for many of the Nihilists were Jewish. The pogroms in turn prompted many panic-stricken Jews to emigrate, most of them to America. Jake Rubin had come to America because of a pogrom, but in 1882 a pack peddler named David Szemanski had fled the border town of Shervient in Tsarist Lithuania because of the savage pogroms there, then made his way to England and, later, America. When asked his name at Castle Garden, David had said, "Duvvid Szemanski fun Shervient," which the immigration official wrote down as "David Shubert." The newly renamed David Shubert had gone on to Syracuse, New York, where he later fathered three sons: Sam, Jacob (or J. J.) and Levi (or Lee). In 1900 these three brothers—young, ambitious and fascinated by the theater—had invaded New York with fifteen thousand dollars in borrowed money. By 1909 the Shubert Brothers (or the Messrs. Shubert, as they billed themselves) owned fourteen theaters in New York, had produced over fifty shows in nine years, and were well on their way to dominating the American theater. In one of their shows a song had been introduced by the popular Nora Bayes—"Shine On, Harvest Moon." It became a great hit, and on this night at the Cavendish Club, Sweet Nellie Byfield, the Thrush of Flushing, came onstage to the strains of "Shine On, Harvest Moon." Needless to say, Nellie wasn't thinking of the assassination of Alexander II when she came onstage; but the night's events would not have happened the way they did if a bomb hadn't been thrown in St. Petersburg twenty-eight years before.

She was wearing a low-cut red velvet dress and a lot of paste diamonds, with an aigrette in her hair. She opened her mouth to start the song when, to her complete astonishment, the orchestra stopped and began a totally new song. She was staring down at the orchestra leader when she heard someone from the other side of the stage start to sing "You're My Cutie-Ootie Sweet Patootie." She looked to see Jake Rubin coming onstage, singing the song in his wretched voice. He shoved the sheet music in her hand and pointed to the opening bars. Not knowing what else to do, Nellie began singing the song with him, smiling nervously at the audience as if this was all part of the act. The tune was bouncy and cute. When she and Jake had finished one chorus, he made a sweeping bow to her, then hurried offstage, leaving Nellie to reprise the song. When she finished, the members of the Cavendish Club went wild. Sweet Nellie had given them something new, and they obviously loved it. Flushed with excitement, smiling, Nellie curtsied, then left the stage. Jake, grinning triumphantly, was standing in the wings.

"See? What did I tell you?" he exclaimed. "They loved it! It's new and bouncy, not shmaltzy like 'After the Ball.' They loved it!"

She rolled up the sheet music, then slapped his face with it, hard.

"Don't you *ever* surprise me again!" she said, adding viciously as she threw "Cutie-Ootie Sweet Patootie" on the floor: "You pushy little kike!"

Jake, holding his smarting cheek, watched her as she walked back to her dressing room. If she had stuck ten knives into him, she couldn't have hurt him more.

The anti-Semitism of Alexander II's Russia was alive and well and living in New York City.

Chapter 15

Despite the millions of sermons preached during the Victorian and Edwardian ages about the sin of greed and the danger of wealth, few people then had any illusions about poverty. It stank. Furthermore, the general attitude, sanctioned by many preachers, was that if you were poor, it was your own fault. After all, wasn't Horatio Alger what America was all about? Thus it was fairly easy for Marco to rationalize his relationship with Maud. If a woman had sold her body for money, he would have instantly labeled her a whore. But—although he realized the gigolo was not exactly a revered figure in American society, and he still had qualms of guilt—he told himself he was more a clever business man ... not exactly a Horatio Alger hero, perhaps, but he had gotten himself out of Cherry Street, and wasn't that the important thing? He had known poverty all his life, and he hated it. Maud's bankroll had bought him two new trucks, which he kept in a garage on Varick Street; he had hired another driver—an Italian named Gino—and within several weeks, the Santorelli Trucking Company was doing good business. He was making honest money, he had a snappy wardrobe, a nice apartment in a good neighborhood, and if he might not qualify for the Good Ethics Award of 1909, what the hell.

He was even making inroads into Casey O'Donnell's territory;

thus it came as a bit of a surprise one Saturday afternoon as he was walking home from the Varick Street garage when he turned a corner and almost bumped into Georgie and Bridget O'Donnell.

"Hey!" he said, stopping. "Remember me?"

Bridget looked at him. "You were on the ship," she said. "You danced on the deck with my sister."

"Sure!" Marco grinned. "Marco Santorelli's the name. How are you girls liking America?"

"Oh, it's fine," said Bridget.

"We're shopping for furniture for Bridget's new home," said Georgie. "She's getting married next week and will be movin' in to a place on Grove Street."

"Then we'll be neighbors. I'm on St. Luke's Place. Say, you won't believe this, but I'm in the same business as your uncle. Santorelli Trucking Company: That's *me*."

He swelled his chest a bit, in a cock-of-the-walk manner.

"Well now, that's very impressive," said Bridget, who was amused by him. "You're lookin' good, Mr. Santorelli. It's obvious America agrees with you. And I'm glad we'll be neighbors."

Marco was looking at Georgie's eyes, trying to understand why they were so strange.

"How 'bout you, miss? Are you getting married?"

"I'm afraid I have no time for men."

"No time? Why?"

"I've been learnin' Braille."

"What's Braille?"

"A system of reading for the blind."

The realization that this lovely young blonde couldn't see struck Marco with tremendous force. "I ... didn't know ..." he stammered, embarrassed.

She was wearing a plain brown skirt and a matching jacket over a white blouse; her hair was neatly pinned up in a gentle roll under a smart felt hat. Now she reached out to touch his sleeve.

"Do you mind?" she asked with a smile. "I think I remember your face."

He froze as she stepped up to him and put her fingers on his left cheek. Then, gently, she ran them over his nose, his lips, his jawline and, finally, his eyes. His heart turned over at her delicate touch.

124

"Now I remember you," she said, removing her hand. In fact, the handsome Italian's face became vivid in the blackness of her world. "And don't feel embarrassed. I've gotten used to it."

Marco looked at Bridget, who nodded her head slightly as if to say, It's all right. She really *is* used to it.

"You know," he said, "I've forgotten your name."

"Georgie. It's short for Georgiana."

Georgie. Nice. Georgie, the blind lily.

He had a brilliant idea. "Do you like the movies?" he asked.

She stiffened slightly. "Well, *hardly* . . ."

"No, no—don't get mad. I'd like to take you to one. I could tell you the story. I could be your eyes!"

Georgie's smile was pure delight.

"What a darlin' idea!" she exclaimed. Then she reached for Bridget's hand. "Oh, Bridget, do you think Aunt Kathleen would let me?"

"Why not? You're twenty-one. It's time you went to a movie . . . with a man," she added, eying Marco appreciatively.

Marco, like many immigrants, had become a passionate patron of the nickelodeons (*odeon* was the Greek word for theater) because it was cheap entertainment and was all visual, which enabled him to relax from the struggle with English and just watch.

"*The Curse of the Purple Mask* is playing at Hale's on Sheridan Square," he said. "And there's a cowboy movie with it. Want to go tonight? I'm crazy for cowboy movies. You'll like them too. Lots of horses galloping, lots of shooting . . . bang bang! Kill those crazy Indians!"

Georgie started laughing. Suddenly, her world seemed less dark.

"But Georgie, darlin', you hardly *know* this man," said Kathleen O'Donnell as she sat at the dining-room table in her Brooklyn house. "You met him on the boat comin' over, then you bump into him on the street—and now he's takin' you to a movie? I think it's rather pushy of him, if you ask me. And him bein' an Italian! Well, you *know* those Italians have no morals when it comes to women."

Georgie, dressed in one of her best and prettiest dresses, was seated opposite her aunt, drinking a cup of tea.

"Well, Aunt Kathleen, there's not much he can do to me in a nickelodeon."

"Oh, isn't there, now! I've heard what goes on in some of those places. Kissin' and whatnot in the dark. Not a proper place for a well-brought-up girl like yourself."

"Everybody's goin' to the movies these days. It's not like when you were young and gentlemen callers had to sit in the parlor. Now, you mustn't worry. I can take care of myself."

"But he's *Italian*!"

"So's the Pope."

"You'll hold your tongue! And your uncle's not goin' to be pleased when he hears about this. This Santorell—whatever his name is—he's a competitor, you know."

"I know. And when Uncle Casey gets back from Detroit, I'll tell him all Marco's business secrets." The front doorbell rang, and her face lit up. "There he is! Is my hair all right?"

Kathleen got up to lead her niece through the house.

"Yes. You look like a dream—more's the pity. Italians! Well, I want to meet this Mr. Marco myself and tell him if he lays a finger on my niece, there'll be the Devil to pay!"

But for all her clucking and suspicions of Marco, in fact Kathleen was pleased for Georgie; at least a man was interested in her, and her excitement about going to the movie was so palpable that Kathleen didn't have the heart to refuse or insist on a chaperone. Her natural clannishness had been intensified by Georgie's blindness, which had broken Kathleen's heart. She knew how much Georgie had depended on Bridget to adapt to her new, sightless world; and now with Bridget leaving the house next week, there would be a great void in Georgie's life. So maybe, even though Marco was Italian ... *maybe* it was good for Georgie to have someone new in her life.

But when she opened the front door and looked at him, her first thought was *he's too handsome to be decent. And that suit! Where'd a truck driver get a suit like that? It must have cost a fortune.*

"Good evening," said Marco with a smile, his hat in his hand. "Are you Mrs. O'Donnell?"

"That I am," said Kathleen, with notable lack of warmth. "And I want you to know, I'm only lettin' Georgie go out with you because she wants so much to go to a nickelodeon. And you won't be stayin' out too late!"

"We'll be back by midnight," said Georgie, holding out her hand for Marco to take.

"Midnight, my foot! You'll be back by ten or I'll know the reason why!" Then she simmered down. "Pleased to meet you, Mr. Santorelli," she grumped. "But you'll be takin' care of my Georgie, mind."

He was leading her down the steps.

"I'll be taking care of her," he said. And he led her down the walk to help her into his truck. They started to drive into Manhattan.

"You look beautiful," he said.

"Thank you."

"I really think you'll like the movies."

"I can hardly wait!"

The nickelodeon craze had swept the big cities of America with the force of a tornado. In the four years since 1905, when *The Great Train Robbery* had invented the movie with a plot, over three thousand nickelodeons had opened. Chicago had three hundred, Pittsburgh over one hundred, and ex-furriers and junk dealers like Louis B. Mayer were jumping into the business to make a fast fortune. Most nickelodeons were converted stores, and since 200 seats required a theater license costing $500 a year, the "cheapie" houses limited their seating to 199. A screen, a projector and perhaps a piano player (a fillip then coming into vogue) and you were in business. And since two million Americans were pouring into the nickelodeons every day, you were in a very big business indeed.

"The Purple Mask is coming after Helen with a knife," whispered Marco. They were in the back row of Hale's, by the right aisle. The tiny theater was jammed, and the piano player was mangling the storm music from Liszt's "Les Préludes."

Georgie was breathless, seeing the movie through Marco's whispers.

"Now he's about to plunge it into her back . . . wait! He hears something! He turns, listens . . . I think it's got to be the detective . . . *Dio,* no, it's the Chinese opium dealer . . . the Purple Mask slinks back . . . he's hiding behind a curtain . . . hey, it's wonderful! The Chink thinks he's got Helen all to himself . . . he's coming up behind her . . . he's untying her gag . . ."

"Why?"

"I think he wants to kiss her. He's an old lecher . . . oh boy, here comes the Purple Mask again . . . he raises his knife above the Chink's back . . . he *plunges* it. Wow! The Chink is gasping, falling to his knees . . . the Purple Mask knifes him again and *again* . . . the Chink is dying. . . ."

Georgie's hands were gripping the arms of her seat. Now she felt Marco's hand on hers.

"Wait . . . the Chink's two sons have come in the opium den . . . they see their father . . . they draw their knives and start toward the Purple Mask . . ."

"Is Helen still tied to the chair?"

"Yes . . . one of the sons picks up one of those things they burn coal in . . ."

"A brazier," coached Georgie, who was loving the warmth of his hand.

"Now he throws it at the Purple Mask . . . he ducks and it goes into the curtain . . . oh boy, the curtain's on fire! The Purple Mask is getting out . . . the Chinks run after him . . . oh boy, oh boy, the whole place is burning!"

"Is someone going to save Helen?"

"I don't know . . . *Dio,* the flames are right next to her chair . . . she's terrified, struggling to break her ropes . . . *Someone* save Helen!"

"Marco, I can't *stand* it!"

"Damn."

"What's wrong?"

"It's the end of the episode. We'll have to wait till next week to find out."

"Those awful people! I want to know *now!*"

"Okay, here comes the cowboy movie. It's called *Arizona.* Having fun?"

She smiled in the dark.

"I'm having the time of my life," she whispered, and she was.

"So the streets haven't turned out to be paved with gold?" said Roscoe Haines.

"Not yet," replied Jake.

They were drinking beer in a Harlem bar. Roscoe had returned to the States from Hamburg to be with his sick mother and had contacted Jake through the Shulman office.

"I suppose I can't complain," Jake went on. "I have a job and I'm living in a nice apartment—thanks to Marco. God, I owe him so much back rent. . . . Anyway, it could be worse."

He dipped a pretzel in his beer. Being the only white in the bar made him feel a little conspicuous, but Roscoe had told him he, a black man, couldn't get into a white bar. Harlem, which a few years before had been an all-white, middle-class section of the city, was turning black with an explosive speed that was causing ugly racial tensions all over the city and pioneering a pattern that would last for generations.

"Writing any good songs?" Roscoe asked.

"I'm writing a lot of songs, but I guess none of them is any good. At least, Abe says they stink."

"Let me tell you something about Abe Shulman: He only bets on sure things. He's never published an unknown songwriter in his life. He lets someone else gamble on the unknowns, then he steals them away. You're wasting your time with Abe. Take your songs to another publisher."

"Well, that doesn't seem very fair. After all, he did give me a job."

"So what? And what's fair? Have you tried to get a singer to sing one of your songs? I mean a professional."

"I don't have time to plug my own songs. Abe pays me to plug his."

"What are you, his slave? Tell him to fuck himself, man!"

"Sure. I *did* mail 'Raggedy Ragtime Music Man' to Nora Bayes, but she sent it back unopened."

"What's 'Raggedy Ragtime Music Man'?"

"My Song Number Thirty-six."

"Play me Song Number Thirty-six."

Jake looked around. It was nine in the morning, and the long, narrow bar was practically empty. Halfway down the room was a woebegone upright, its lid ringed with beer stains.

"It's not very good," said Jake, picking up his beer glass.

Roscoe studied his face. "What's wrong?" he said. "Your music too good for a nigger?"

Jake, startled, looked at him. "Of course not! Why would you say that? I just told you, the song's no good. . . ."

"Why don't you let me be the judge of that? After all, I helped you get to this goddam country. You owe me a song, at least."

Jake wiped his mouth with his sleeve, then went over to the piano and sat down. "I wrote it with Nora Bayes in mind," he said.

He started playing and singing as Roscoe listened from the bar.

> "Some women fall in love with millionaires;
> Others to society aspire.
> Well, my man's no patrician,
> He's just a poor musician,
> But when he plays me ragtime, he sets my heart on fire!
> Oh, I fell in love with a raggedy ragtime music man
> Who's something of a genius at the keys.
> I'll admit he's underweight
> And his bank account's not great;
> But he's rich as Rockefeller when he's at the eighty-eight!
> His right hand's playing octaves
> While his left hand pounds the bass.
> His ragtime rhythm rocks the house
> And brings a smile upon my face.
> My mother says he's no good, and we'll probably starve,
> But nonetheless those wedding bells will chime.
> I'll be glad to share my house key
> With my sweet ragtime Tchaikowsky
> When I wed that raggedy ragtime music man of mine!"

The fat black bartender, who was wiping glasses on his dirty apron, laughed.

"I like it!" he exclaimed. "That's a good tune, kid. What'd you think, Roscoe? Ain't he good?"

"Anyone who can rhyme 'house key' with 'Tchaikowsky' has got to be some kind of crazy genius."

"I know it's Tchai*kov*sky," said Jake defensively, "but Americans seem to pronounce it Tchai*kow*sky. . . ."

"Don't apologize," said Roscoe, going to the piano. "Would you object to a black singer singing that song?"

Jake looked up at him. "Are you kidding? A *pink* singer can sing it! A *purple* one!"

"Come on. You're going to play that for Flora Mitchum."

"Who's Flora Mitchum?" he asked, getting up from the piano and hurrying after Roscoe.

"Just the best colored singer in New York," replied Roscoe, tossing a silver dollar on the bar, then winking back at Jake. "Who also happens to be my new gal friend."

The next night, as he sat beside Roscoe in the second-rate vaudeville house watching a third-rate juggling act, Jake felt a strange tension. Like most first-rate talents, even in his worst moments of frustration and despair there had been a voice in the back of his brain whispering, *You* are *good. You have something to give the world, and the world will love you for it. You* are *good!*

Now the same voice was whispering, *Tonight! Something wonderful is going to happen tonight!*

They were in the first row of the balcony, because the balcony was the only place where Roscoe could sit. Below them, the packed, all-white orchestra section was registering its boredom with the juggling disaster by hisses, coughs and whistles. The white jugglers sweated their way through their act, then raced off to tepid applause. Two uniformed ushers changed the placards at either side of the proscenium. The new cards read FLORA MITCHUM, THE SULTRY SEPIA SONGSTRESS. The piano in the pit rolled an introductory arpeggio, and Flora stepped through the curtains.

The audience gave her a big hand. She was a tall woman with a great figure, cocoa-butter skin and big eyes that flashed personality and sex. She wore a red feathered hat, a red silk bolero and a long black skirt that was slit almost to her crotch, revealing two extremely sexy legs in black net stockings, with black high-heeled pumps. She had no props. Sticking one sensational leg out, she started singing, *very* sultrily:

> "Some women fall in love with millionaires;
> Others to society aspire."

Then she started prancing around the stage, snapping her fingers to the wonderful beat of the song, giving it all her body language as she belted out:

> "Well, my man's no patrician,
> He's just a poor musician,

131

But when he plays me ragtime,
He sets my heart on fire!"

Jake was sitting up, electrified. When he had met Flora the
day before, she had loved the song, but she hadn't sung it for him.
Now he heard *her* version. She belted it to the rafters and brought
the song to fantastic life. When she came to the last three lines,
the beat slowed, the drummer banged every beat, and Flora threw
her whole body into every syllable:

"I'll be glad to share my house key
With my sweet ragtime Tchaikowsky . . ."

Then the last line, fast, up and brassy:

"When I wed that raggedy ragtime music man of mine!"

The audience went crazy for her and the song and shouted for
an encore.

She sang it three times in all.

"It's gonna be a hit!" Roscoe shouted over the applause.
"You're gonna be rich!"

Jake Rubin, the thin immigrant Jew who had fled a Russian
pogrom and gone through Ellis Island, sat straight, listening to the
applause without moving, clutching his white fists tightly, his eyes
wide with excitement as he sniffed the heady fragrance of success.

I told you it would happen, whispered the voice in his brain. *I*
told *you.*

PART IV
A Violent
Appalachian Spring

Chapter 16

Della Hopkins finally persuaded her mother, Aunt Edna, to ask Tom Banicek to dinner, but it took her a month to do it.

"What are you so interested in him fer?" said Aunt Edna.

"I've never met anyone from Europe. He'd be interesting to talk to."

"But he cain't *talk*."

"Well, he can talk *some*. I feel sorry for him, Momma. It must be terrible to have to learn another language."

"Huh."

"And he might come in handy when you kill the hog next week."

"Huh." Aunt Edna was on the front porch, stirring a kettle of homemade soap, a soupy mixture of water, lye and bacon grease. "What do you think he'd like to eat?"

"I read in school that Europeans eat a lot of game, like we do."

"Think he'd like a coon stew?"

Della smiled. "Couldn't help but like *your* coon stew, Momma. It's the best in West Virginia."

"Well, I'll tell your daddy to ask him—*if* he agrees to help us kill the hog."

Della looked pleased. Momma was stubborn; you had to work on her.

But she usually came round in the end.

Ward Hopkins wasn't a blockader—which was the local name for men who made moonshine whiskey—but he knew several, and when Tom Banicek came to dinner, Ward had a bottle of "ruckus juice" on hand to offer his guest an Appalachian cocktail.

"It ain't popskull," he said as he poured the corn whiskey into a glass. "It won't give you no headache. But it'll make you feel good, and that's the important thing."

They were in the parlor of the log cabin, and in the big stone fireplace a green hickory fire was burning, green hickory being in Ward's opinion the best wood for burning. One of Aunt Edna's quilts hung on a log wall (for insulation as well as decoration) and one of her hooked rugs was on the pine floor. Her tintyped parents stared sternly from another wall. The furniture had all been made by her grandfather and still provided solid comfort after forty years.

"What do they drink in Bohemia?" asked Ward, handing Tom the glass.

"Beer," he replied.

He took an exploratory sip of the ruckus juice. The 100-proof whiskey was searingly strong, but aromatic and tasty. After swallowing it, Tom grinned. "Is good," he said.

"Best corn squeezin' in the county," replied Ward. "What made you leave Bohemia?"

"I didn't want to serve in army. Emperor Franz Joseph make all young men serve in army long time. Officers no good. They beat you up, treat you like dirt."

"Hell," said Ward, "you get treated like dirt here, in the mines."

"Is true." Tom grinned. "But here, I got choice. I can always leave. Besides, is not so bad. Many nice things here. Is beautiful country, beautiful girls ... like Della."

Ward drained his glass, wondering if this little squirt was falling in love with his daughter.

"There's a full moon tonight," said Aunt Edna as the four of them sat around the kitchen table eating her raccoon stew, "and it's goin' to go down to near freezin'. That's the best time to kill a hog."

"What does moon have to do with it?" asked Tom, who was sitting opposite Della.

"You got to kill a hog when the moon's full. If you wait till the moon's shrinkin', the meat'll shrink. Sounds crazy, but it's true.

I've been fattin' this hog up for three weeks on corn. He'll be good and sweet, you'll see. That hog'll give us good eatin' all winter. They got hogs in *Bo*-hemia?"

"Beg pardon?"

Aunt Edna sniffed impatiently. *Rutty little skunk,* she thought. *He can't take his eyes off Della.*

"I *said,* they got hogs in *Bo*-hemia?"

"Oh . . . yes. Lots of hogs."

He's going to be trouble, thought Aunt Edna. *I can feel it in my bones. Damn! Another miner!*

Bill Fargo's office was on the second floor of the Staunton Coal Company's executive office building. Fargo's office was next door to Monty Staunton's baronial suite, but Fargo's was modest in size, almost Spartan in decor, and gave no hint of its tenant's power in the company. Fargo liked it that way. At forty-two, he was shrewd enough not to compete with his boss, Monty, in flash.

On a spring morning in 1910, he was leaning back in his desk chair, picking his crooked teeth with a toothpick and listening to Sam Fuller.

"My wife's expecting a baby, Mr. Fargo," Sam was saying. The lanky coal miner was standing in front of Fargo's desk. "I know I made a mistake last fall, but I was with the company twelve years, I'm a good miner, and it's just not *fair* what you've done to me. Firing me was one thing, but hell's bells, you've blacklisted me! I can't get a job nowhere, and we're broke. Dead broke! You got to give me another chance."

Bill Fargo put his feet on his desk and continued picking his teeth. "I don't have to do a goddam thing for you, Fuller. You advocated a union. You knew what it said in your contract—"

"I was drunk. Drunk out of mind! You can't hold against a man what he says when he's drunk."

"In vino veritas."

"Huh?"

"That's Latin for when you're drunk, you say the truth. You're not going to tell me you're *against* the union?"

Sam shifted uncomfortably.

"Well, I'm not *against* it. But if you hired me back, I sure as hell wouldn't make the same mistake twice. *I have to have money!"*

He almost shouted it. Fargo took his feet off the desk and swung around in his chair to look out the window at the mountains of coal and slag. It was a beautiful day, and the trees were budding. But only weeds grew near the mine.

"There's a lot of unrest right now," Fargo said, "and Mr. Staunton knows it. A *lot* of unrest. We like to keep things quiet here, you know."

Silence. Sam was watching him, wondering what he was getting at.

"I might be willing to hire you back," Fargo finally said. "I'd give you your house back, and of course the company would pay all your wife's medical expenses. Yes, I might do that."

You son of a bitch, thought Sam. *Are you torturing me?*

Fargo turned back to look at him. "If I did that, Fuller, what would you do for me?"

Sam looked surprised. "Well ... what do you mean?"

"Would you turn informer?" Fargo asked quietly. "Would you tell me who's causing all this unrest?"

Sam stiffened.

"I can tell you that now: You are. The mines are unsafe, the pay's rotten ..."

"*Your* pay could be good, Fuller. I'd make it worth your while to tell me what I want to know. Say, fifty dollars a month put in the bank for you. Plus no rent deductions on your house. It could add up to a lot."

Sam started sweating.

"What kind of a man do you think I am?" he said softly.

"A desperate man."

Fargo began picking his teeth again.

The next Sunday afternoon Tom Banicek and Della Hopkins were walking through a field alongside the Shepaug River.

"Maybe things are changing," said Della. "I mean, the company hiring back Sam Fuller after they'd blacklisted him. Maybe things are getting better."

"Maybe," said Tom. "I'm glad for Sam and Ann. They was good to me, when I came here. They nice people."

"Ann told Mother they almost starved in Pittsburgh while Sam was looking for work. Can you imagine?"

"Mr. Staunton knows all heads of big companies. Not just coal companies—steel companies. Everything. They send man's name around, no one will hire him. That's not fair."

"To say the least." Della sighed. She was wearing a white blouse and gray skirt, with a small boater on her head. "Well, let's not talk about Monty Staunton. Why spoil a Sunday? Oh look, Tom: Indian paintbrush!"

She stooped to pick a tiny red wild flower, then held it up for Tom's inspection. "Isn't it pretty?" she said.

"What's it called?"

"Indian paintbrush. At least that's what we call it around here. It comes in all different colors."

"It's color of your eyes," Tom said.

"Red?"

She laughed. He had an unusual sense of humor which, combined with his mangled English, often made her laugh.

"Bloodshot," he said, pointing to her eyes. "You still got cold?"

"Oh, just a sniffle. But are my eyes really bloodshot?"

"A little. Let me look close. . . ."

He came closer, pretending to inspect her eyes. Then his hands were on her waist, and his mouth against hers. They kissed awhile. They had been kissing for months and were both dying to go further. Now she tried to disentangle herself.

"Tom, don't . . ."

"Della, I love you."

"And I love you, but Mother would kill me. . . ."

"It not wrong to kiss. . . ."

"Tell that to Mother."

"Then let's get married."

She looked at him with surprise while a squirrel chittered at them from a tree.

An hour later Aunt Edna sat in her rocking chair and glared at the young couple.

"I *knew* it!" she said. "You two want to get hitched. . . . Della, he don't even speak English."

"Oh, Momma, what's the difference?" said Della, who was holding Tom's hand. "We love each other."

Aunt Edna looked at her husband. Ward was sitting in his chair by the fire. They were in the parlor, and the kerosene lamps threw a soft glow on the log walls.

"What do you think, Ward?" asked Aunt Edna.

"I think Tom's a good man," replied her husband. "If Della loves him, that's good enough for me."

Aunt Edna looked at Tom. "Ain't you a Catholic?" she asked, saying "Catholic" as she would "rattlesnake."

"Yes, but I been to Baptist Church a few times. We get married in Baptist Church."

"You give up your religion mighty easy."

Tom replied with simple dignity, "Della is important thing, not religion. I love your daughter very much. I don't have a lot to give her, but all I have is hers forever."

Aunt Edna rocked a moment.

"This farm will go to her—you know that? Twenty-two acres. It's been in my family since Colonial days. You wouldn't be after the farm, would you?"

"Mother!" exclaimed Della.

"You keep quiet. Look me in the eyes, boy. You marryin' Della for this farm?"

"No. I marry Della because I love her."

Rock, rock.

"Oh, all right," she finally said. "Come here and kiss me." They broke into smiles. Tom came to her and kissed her.

"Thank you," he said.

"I *knew* I'd end up with you as a son-in-law. I *knew* it! Damn!" And they all started laughing.

Ten days after Tom and Della were married in the Baptist Church in Hawksville, on April 21, 1910, Ward Hopkins opened a seam of coal in a room 312 feet down in the Number 6 Mine. His open-flame headlamp ignited the methane gas that had been freed by his pickaxe. The room exploded in flame. Ward Hopkins was killed instantly.

"My father-in-law not killed," said Tom Banicek that night in Aunt Edna's parlor. "He was *murdered*. Murdered by the company!"

The room was filled with miners and their families. Aunt Edna sat in her chair, her wrinkled face numb with grief and shock. Della stood beside her.

"We all know we should have safety lamps," continued Tom, "not open-flame lamps. We all know there should be ventilation shafts in mines, because danger of gas is always there. We get paid little enough as is; why should we have to risk our lives too?"

"You're right, Tom," said one of the miners standing next to Sam Fuller. "But what can we do about it?"

"Since we can't even talk about union, we can at least send a delegation to Mr. Staunton, can't we? And demand safety lamps?"

Silence. Tom looked around the room.

"We got to say *something,*" he added. "Is no one else to talk for us. We got to do it ourselves."

"That's easy for you to say, Tom," said Sam Fuller. "You and Della got your own home here. The rest of us . . . well, I know how it is to be kicked out of my home, and it's no fun."

The other miners murmured agreement.

"Then," said Tom, "what if *I* am delegation?"

No one said no.

Monty Staunton pulled the cork out of the bottle of rye whiskey, took a long guzzle, then poured some of it over Gladys's bare breasts. Burping loudly, he leaned over and licked the whiskey off.

"Glory be to God," he said, "you got the purtiest tits in West Virginia, Gladie."

"Why, thank you, Monty, honey," replied the plump whore in her hillbilly drawl. "That's real sweet of you to say."

"And that pussy of yours! Goddam, every time I even *think* of it, my pecker gets hard as a beanpole."

"Well, honey, that's what my pussy's here for: to give you a hard-on."

"Making love to you's like praying to God, you know what I mean? It's so beautiful, it's like when I'm talking to God."

"Monty, honey, that's one of the most beautiful things I ever heard anyone say. It's real poetic."

"Thank you, Gladie. I mean it."

There was a knock at the door.

"Monty, you got a phone call," a voice said. "It's Bill Fargo."

Monty sat up in bed, scratched his fat stomach and looked at Gladys's clock.

"It's after midnight!" he bawled.

"He says it's important."

"Shit," he muttered. He kissed Gladys, then got out of bed and pulled on his pants. "Be back in a while, honey. You work on that bottle while I'm gone, but don't drink it all."

He went downstairs. The brothel on the outskirts of Charleston was owned by a Mrs. Henderson, a thin and rather prim-looking widow who kept her house and girls clean. Now Monty went into her office and took the phone.

"Yes?"

"Mr. Staunton, we've got a little problem here over that explosion this morning."

Monty sat on the edge of the desk. "Well?"

"My informer, Sam Fuller, came to my house a half-hour ago. A lot of miners met in Hopkins's farm tonight. Hopkins's son-in-law, a bohunk named Banicek, said the company had murdered his father-in-law."

"Why?"

"Because of the open-flame lamp. Banicek's made himself a one-man delegation. He's coming to my office in the morning to ask the company to buy safety lamps and install ventilation shafts."

"What's his name?"

"Banicek. Shall I blacklist him?"

Monty scratched his chest. "No, don't fire him. Tell him the company agrees. We'll order the safety lamps tomorrow. As for the ventilation shafts, put him off on that. Goddam shafts would cost a fortune. Tell him we'll have to make studies. Send a letter to the Hopkins woman with a check for five hundred dollars and the company's condolences. That'll shut Banicek up."

"Do you think this is wise, Mr. Staunton? It may set a precedent."

"It's time we bought safety lamps. I'm not running a slave camp, Fargo. I'm running a company."

"Yes, Mr. Staunton."

142

"But keep an eye on Banicek."

Monty hung up, then went back upstairs to Gladys's room. The whore was sitting up in bed. Monty looked at her breasts and smiled.

"Glory be to God, Gladie. You've got the purtiest tits in West Virginia."

Despite his sewer-mouth love patter, Monty's attitude toward women was quintessentially Victorian. Like Théophile Gautier, who prided himself on being able to solve complicated mathematical problems while having sex, and Gustave Flaubert, who smoked cigars during the act of love, Monty considered women objects to be conquered (and totted up on his mental scoreboard), not human beings. Real women, he once said to Mrs. Henderson, were no more to him than a sofa on which lay the woman of his dreams. To relieve his physical itch, he could just as well—and much more economically—have made love to a cantaloupe.

"Sam, where have you been?"

Sam Fuller had just come into the bedroom of his company house. The lamp by the bed was lit, and his wife was sitting up.

"You know where I've been," said Sam, taking off his jacket. "I went for a walk. You shouldn't have waited up."

He sat on the edge of the bed to unlace his high black shoes.

"You've been taking quite a few midnight walks lately," said Ann in a cool voice. "Are you cheating on me?"

He looked at her. "Oh, sure. I'm having a hot affair with Sarah Finley."

"I'm in no mood for jokes, Sam. You've never taken midnight walks before."

"After a shift in the mine, it's nice to get some fresh air. Put out the lamp and go to sleep."

"No. I want to talk. No man that's been blacklisted by the company has ever been hired back except you. I know you said they made an exception because of your twelve years with them, but *why* did they make an exception? They never have for anyone else."

"How the hell do I know?" He pulled off his pants. "Now put out that damned lamp. I'm tired."

She lowered her voice. "Sam, I love you. You're a good husband. I want you to tell me the truth: Have you turned fink?"

He stared at her. "What a helluva thing to say to your husband!"

"Have you?"

"Of course not!"

She pulled a worn Bible from under her pillow and held it out.

"Will you swear on the Good Book?" she asked.

He hesitated. She saw the fear in his eyes.

"Sam," she whispered, "how *could* you?"

He buried his face in his hands.

"I *had* to," he finally whispered. "We had nothing, Annie. I had to."

Still holding the Bible, she got out of bed and put on her bathrobe. She went to the door.

"I'll sleep with the boys tonight," she said. "In the morning, I'll take them to Aunt Jane's in Hawksville. If you're a smart man, you'll come with us."

He looked at her. "There's no work in Hawksville. There's no work anywhere."

"Sam, I won't tell anyone what you've done because I love you. But if you keep on informing, they'll find out sooner or later. And they'll kill you, Sam. Don't fool yourself. They'll kill you." She opened the door and added, "God help me for saying this, but I wouldn't blame them for doing it."

She left the room.

For the first time in his life, Sam Fuller felt terror in his heart.

Chapter 17

Part of Monty's personality was gelled in a perpetual adolescence, and his childishness manifested itself in a penchant for dressing up in costume. Twice a year he and Christine threw a big masked ball at Belle Meade, and ten days after he distributed the safety lamps to the miners (thereby, he thought, shutting them up), he played host to eighty revelers at the big plantation house. Christine favored romantic costumes—one year she had dressed as Mme. du Barry, this year as the Empress Eugénie—but Monty went for "wild and woolly" stuff, and was wearing a Buffalo Bill costume replete with two six-shooters as he romped around his ballroom in a spur-jingling Virginia reel. A ten-piece orchestra from Charleston provided the music; white-jacketed black waiters were ubiquitous with silver trays of champagne, wine and whiskey; and in the dining room the polished yew table groaned under a fabulous buffet featuring smoked hams, roasts, galantines of duck, beaten biscuits, chickens, salads, cheeses, bowls of fruit, and Monty's favorite dish—which he could gorge on until his stomach almost burst—cottage-fried potatoes. Already, in certain aristocratic circles in England and France, the cult of Slimhood was being enshrined as a new religion; but in West Virginia a certain embonpoint was deemed natural after thirty-five, and no one would have dreamed of denying themselves the pleasures of the table to maintain a seemingly unhealthy thinness. Consequently, the guests stuffed themselves. Christine passed out from wine at midnight and had to be carried to her room upstairs. Monty had a prodigious capacity for booze, but by three the lights in even his brain were snuffing out. By four the house was quiet except for the yawning black servants, who had the job of cleaning up after the bacchanal.

Two miles away, in the company town, the miners on the dawn shift were dragging themselves out of their beds for another day in the netherworld of the mines.

"Who says Number Six is hot?" growled Monty the next morning at ten. He was sitting up in his enormous mahogany bed nursing a savage hangover. Two bicarbonates of soda and four aspirin had so far done little to abate the pounding in his head.

"The miners," replied Fargo, who was standing by the bed, hat in hand. "They say Number Six is filling with gas. They refuse to work in it. They say it could blow up at any moment."

"Damn."

"They're blaming the company."

Monty shot him an angry look. "I suppose it's *my* fault coal mines have gas pockets?"

145

"They say that if the company put in ventilation shafts . . ."

"Who's 'they'?" yelled Monty. "Don't give me this 'they' shit. There's always *one* man. Who is he?"

"Banicek."

Monty threw off his sheet and got out of bed.

"That little bohunk turd—didn't I give him the safety lamps? I was *good* to him. I didn't fire him, and now he's causing trouble again. . . ." He was suddenly dizzy from the hangover. He closed his eyes a moment, sitting back down on the bed. Then, more calmly: "How bad is it?"

"The mine's hot. It could blow."

"Shit."

He lay back down again, his head splitting.

"All right, close it. We'll wait four or five days to see if it cools off."

"What about Banicek?" Fargo asked.

"What about him?"

"We told him the company was making studies about installing ventilation shafts. He asked how far the studies had come along and when the shafts would be installed. What'll I tell him?"

"Tell him if he wants to keep his job, he'd better shut his fucking mouth."

Silence. Monty glared at Fargo. "Well?"

"I'm not sure we can do that anymore, Mr. Staunton."

"Why the hell not? It's my mine, isn't it?"

"Banicek doesn't say much—his English is pretty lousy—but what he says, the miners are beginning to listen to. He's a quiet little guy with guts. I think we'd be well advised to handle him carefully. At least, right now."

"That's the first time I ever heard *you* say anything like that."

"I'm just trying to avoid trouble. We could have blacklisted Banicek before . . ."

"I know," Monty interrupted curtly. He didn't like Fargo hinting that he'd made a mistake. "Then what do you recommend?"

"That we stall him. Tell him the studies aren't ready yet. Wait till the mine cools off—*if* it cools off. Play it low-key. For the time being."

Monty didn't like his right-hand man; there was something

146

cold-bloodedly inhuman about Fargo that forbade friendship. But he respected his instincts when it came to handling the miners. And Fargo *had* warned him about Banicek. . . .

"All right," Monty said, "we'll play it your way—for the time being."

Goddam hangover, he thought.

Goddam miners.

Bill Fargo was an Appalachian version of Lenin. He had grown up in an atmosphere of poverty and passionate piety as one of six children of a Kentucky preacher. His father's daily Bible readings and the savage beatings he administered for even the slightest infraction of "God's Law" had given the boy a loathing of the Christian religion that blossomed into a virulent atheism. By age twenty, Bill had concluded that Jesus was a pious fraud, and that if the meek had not inherited the earth in the almost two thousand years since Jesus had predicted they would, it was highly likely Jesus had been dead wrong. Like Lenin, Fargo believed the only meaning of life was the unending struggle between the weak and the strong, with the strong always winning. Thus, he decided, he would be strong.

A homely man with thinning black hair, Fargo neither smoked nor drank, but he read voraciously—not for pleasure, but on the theory that knowledge was power. He was reading in the living room of his pleasant house on the outskirts of Hawksville when he heard his bell ring.

"I'll get it," he said to his wife. He got up and went to the front door, turning on the porch light. He opened the door. The porch was empty. He reached inside and turned off the light, then went out on the porch.

"Fuller?" he whispered. "It's all right."

He saw the dark figure of Sam Fuller weaving up the porch steps. He smelled the cheap booze.

"Are you drunk?"

"A little."

"You're an asshole to get drunk. With your mouth, you might tell half the county you're on my payroll."

"I'm not on your payroll anymore," Sam slurred. "My wife found out and she's left me. My Annie . . ."

147

He leaned against the porch rail and started weeping. A look of disgust came over Fargo's face.

"For Chrissake, stop blubbering."

"I love my Annie. . . ."

"Love her on your time, not mine. And you know damned well you're not quitting me. You quit me and I'll pass word to the miners in fifteen minutes that you finked on them. . . ."

Suddenly, with a howl of rage, Sam leaped on him, throwing Fargo back against the house. He started strangling him, banging his head against the house, raging, "I hate you, you son of a bitch! I hate you and your fucking company and that bastard Monty Staunton and your goddam coal mines. . . . I HATE YOU!"

He stopped. Still sobbing, he let Fargo go. The older man slumped down to the porch. The porch light came on and Ethel Fargo opened the door.

"What's going on—?" She saw Sam, saw her husband, and she screamed. "Bill! Oh God, what'd you *do?*"

Screaming, she hurried onto the porch and knelt beside Fargo. Sam backed away. "I hope I killed him," he said. Then he turned and ran down the porch steps into the night as Ethel Fargo continued to scream.

A quarter-mile away, on the other side of Hawksville, Ann Fuller was rocking on the front porch of her aunt's house when she heard someone in the bushes at the end of the porch whisper, "Annie!"

She stopped rocking.

"Who is it?"

"Me, Sam."

"Go away."

"*Please,* I've got to talk to you! I'm in trouble."

She hesitated, then walked off the porch and around to the side of the house.

"You're drunk," she said.

"I know. Listen: I . . . I quit. I'm not going to fink anymore. I just told Fargo. I . . . we'll leave the valley, Annie. We'll go somewhere and start all over. All right? Will you go with me, Annie?"

"I don't know. I'll have to think about it."

"You love me, don't you?"

"I used to. I don't know if I do anymore. I don't know if I can love a fink."

He took her hand. "I miss you, Annie. You don't know how I miss you. Do you miss me?"

She didn't answer. He pulled her into his arms and started kissing her, hungrily. She pushed him away.

"*Damn* you!" she snarled.

"I'm your husband," he yelled. "I've got *rights!*"

"Keep your voice down. . . ."

"I don't give a damn who hears. I'm your husband, I've stopped finking and I demand my goddam *rights!*"

Silence, except for the crickets.

"You fool," she whispered, backing away. "The Turners next door . . ."

"Annie, I've *quit.* I'm not working for Fargo anymore! Come home, Annie. Please come home."

"We'll talk about it when you're sober. Now *go home.*"

"Tonight! I want you tonight!"

"No."

She walked back to the front porch. Sam pulled the bottle from his hip pocket and took a long drink.

Then he stumbled to the street and started the walk back to the company town, mumbling "Annie . . . Annie . . ." over and over to himself.

They were waiting for him.

When he came into his house and lit the lamp, the four men, black hoods over their heads, were in the room.

Sam looked at them drunkenly.

"Fargo told us you've been finking," said one hood. "Is it true?"

Sam backed toward the door.

"I've quit," he said. "Honest to God, I've quit. . . ."

The men pulled out butcher knives.

Sam turned, jerked open the door and ran into a knife that pierced his bowels. The three hooded men on the porch dragged him back inside and closed the door. Sam, clutching his bloody belly, kneeling on the floor, watched them come toward him.

"I'm one of *you,*" he whispered. "I quit . . . I'm one of *you.* . . ."

They slit his throat. When he was dead, they pulled off his pants and castrated him. Then, leaving his corpse in a spreading lake of blood, they turned off the lamp and left the house.

To the miners, justice had been done.

Chapter 18

To Tom Banicek, it was the wrong kind of justice. The next night, he, Della and Aunt Edna were eating in the kitchen of the farmhouse.

"We kill each other," he said, chewing on a chicken leg, "but we don't fight the company."

"I agree with you there," said Aunt Edna, "but if you ask me, Sam Fuller got what he deserved."

"Sam was my friend," said Tom. "I worked with him. He would never fink if he not forced to. And if company was fair, they not *need* finks. Murder never right."

"Well, maybe. Della, put on the coffee."

"Yes, Momma."

She was halfway to the stove when the house was shaken hard enough to rattle the dishes.

"What's *that*?" gasped Aunt Edna. Then the sound waves reached the house and they heard the distant boom.

"Number Six!" said Tom, getting up and running to the door. When he looked out, he could see the glow in the sky.

"It blew!"

When he reached the mine twenty minutes later, the entire community was there, watching the flames pour out of the mine entrance.

"Thank God no one was in it," one miner said to him as he joined the crowd. "Jesus, it really went! You ever see anything like that?"

Tom watched the flames, his anger mounting. Then he saw

Monty Staunton's Rolls-Royce pull up and park. Monty's black chauffeur jumped out to hold the door for his employer. Bill Fargo joined Monty, and they started talking.

Tom walked away from the crowd toward Monty. When he reached him, he was literally trembling with rage.

"Mr. Staunton," he yelled, "you a LIAR!"

Monty looked at him. "Who the hell is this jackass?" he asked.

"Banicek," murmured Fargo.

"You say company make studies to put in ventilation shafts. I say you LIE! I say you goddam *lucky* no one in there, cause we been killed like my father-in-law!"

Monty stared at him. The crowd had turned and was staring at him.

"I say you one goddam loudmouthed pipsqueak," Monty shouted back, nastily imitating Tom's tortured English. "And no man calls *me* a liar!"

"Then *show* us studies! *Show* us, instead putting us off. Cause we crazy to go in mines without ventilation shafts. *Crazy!*" He turned to the miners. "You agree? We not work tomorrow unless we *see* studies he talk about?"

No one spoke.

Monty walked past Tom, put his hands on his hips in a belligerent stand and shouted, "Listen! Haven't I always given you men a fair shake?"

"You given us *shit!*" yelled Tom.

"Shut up, pipsqueak. I've dealt fair and square with you, given you decent housing, medical care and the going tonnage rate. . . ."

"Is only 'going' cause there no goddam union!"

Monty turned and smiled at him.

"That's what I was waiting to hear," he cooed. "You're fired, pipsqueak. And you're blacklisted. You'll never get a job anywhere except cleaning *privies.* Can you get that through your dumb bohunk brain? You're *through.*"

Tom said nothing.

"Fargo," said Monty, "get him off company property."

"Yes, Mr. Staunton." He took Tom's arm. "Let's go, pipsqueak."

Tom pushed his hand off. "I go," he yelled to the miners. "But someday I come back with union! Sam Fuller right: we *slaves* without union!"

"Hey, bohunk," laughed Monty. "Why don't you learn English first? It might help if the union could *understand* you."

Tom started to say something, but stopped himself. He realized he had no power. He would get power. It might take years, but he would get it. Then he would return to the valley and fight Monty Staunton on more equal terms. But now he had no power. He turned and walked away.

"Look at our hero!" yelled Monty. "All bark and no bite, I'd say. All right, everybody, go home. The party's over."

"What about the ventilation shafts, Mr. Staunton?" said one miner.

"Yeah, what about them?" said another.

Monty's smile faded.

"We're making studies," he said. "Meanwhile, Mr. Fargo knows all your names. Now, unless you want to be blacklisted like that loudmouth Banicek, I suggest you all go home nice and quiet. All right?"

The miners looked at him. The flames from the mine illuminated him dramatically, and he and his power cast a long shadow.

"Let's go home," said one miner to his wife. "It's no use."

Slowly, they started back toward the company town.

Monty Staunton looked satisfied.

PART V
No One Else But Nellie

Chapter 19

Jake's song "Raggedy Ragtime Man" became not only a hit but a phenomenon. Against Roscoe's advice—for there was a deep-seated antagonism between the black piano player and the Jewish song publisher—Jake gave the song to Abe Shulman to publish, and by the spring of 1910 over two million copies had been sold, making it a publishing miracle. The song was heard everywhere: in clubs, vaudeville, cafés, on street corners, from hurdy-gurdies, at *thés dansants,* and on piano rolls. Over three hundred thousand recordings were sold in a time when the Gramophone was still something of a novelty. The bouncy melody danced into the heart of America, and the young Jewish immigrant found himself a rich man. For Jake Rubin, the streets *had* been paved with gold.

To Jake's shock and disappointment, the song's immense popularity did little to enhance the career of the woman who had introduced it, Flora Mitchum. Jake fought with the record companies to have Flora record the song, but the music tycoons wanted nothing to do with a "colored" singer, and Abe warned him that the sheet music sales could suffer as well if the public suspected it was a "nigger" song. For the first time Jake began to understand the enormity of American racial prejudice against the blacks (there was a popular song called, unbelievably, "If the Man in the Moon Were a Coon," and it was the heyday of "pickaninny" jokes—as well as lynchings), and at last he began to understand why Roscoe had fled that prejudice to Europe. Jake tried to reward Roscoe for his role in launching the song, but Roscoe refused everything except a gold watch. However, at Jake's insistence, Abe arranged for Flora to introduce the song in Paris. Jake paid for a first-class suite on the three-year-old English liner *Mauretania* (burning 1,000 tons of coal a day, her furnaces tended by 324 firemen and trimmers, the *Mauretania* was not only the most beautiful but the fastest ship afloat and would keep the Atlantic blue riband for twenty-two years); and though it was necessary to arrange that the "colored couple" would eat in their suite and not in the Verandah Café or any of the other public dining rooms, in April of 1910 Jake saw them off at the East Fourteenth Street dock.

"Man, first class!" preened Roscoe as he opened the bottle of champagne Jake had brought for the occasion. The three of them were in the living room of the suite, the walls of which were paneled in Tudor linenfold. "This joint looks like Buckingham Palace. God*dam!*"

He filled three glasses and passed them around. He was wearing a tweed suit he had bought for the sailing. "Got my tweeds," he chortled, "got my tuxedo, Flora's got her ballgowns—you know what? The people on this ship gonna think we're peers of the realm. Yessir, they's gonna think we's a duke and a duchess!"

Which tickled him so much, he almost spilled his champagne. He made a sweeping bow to Flora.

"Duchess," he said, "may I have this waltz?"

"Duke," she replied, "you know something? You're too goddam stuffy. You gotta loosen up a little or people gonna think you're a snob."

"Me?" He pointed to his yellow necktie in mock horror. "A *snob?* Duchess, honey, I'm for the *little* people. Yes, ma'am, give that little guy a break. But *meanwhile* ..." and he grinned at Jake, "keep outta my way, *peasants!*"

Now they all three howled. Roscoe drank his champagne, then did a fast time-step around the suite. "We're gonna take Paris by *storm!* Wait'll they see Flora! Wait'll they hear your song, Jake! Hey, man ..." He stopped dancing and confronted Jake. "What's it feel like to be stinkin' rich?"

They both looked at Jake, who smiled.

"It's *wonderful!*" he yelled, and they all three cackled and hooted.

* * *

"Okay," whispered Marco to Georgie, "you remember that Episode Eleven ended with Helen on the mountaintop in an eagle's nest being attacked by a giant eagle?"

"Yes," whispered Georgie. They were back in Hale's on Sheridan Square, where they had come once a week for the last eleven weeks. Since Georgie's initiation into the joys of moviegoing, the nickelodeon had opened a candy and popcorn stand in the lobby, and Georgie's lifelong addiction to buttered popcorn had begun. She held the bag in her lap, and one hand scooped the popcorn while the other squeezed Marco's hand. She listened avidly as her blind world filled with the lurid adventures of that archfiend the Purple Mask and his intrepid adversaries: Helen Broderick, the daughter of a Harvard archaeologist who had discovered the map to an ancient Chinese treasure, and Dick Derring, a detective for the San Francisco vice squad, who was trying to break a vicious ring of Chinese opium dealers and white slavers.

"Here comes the eagle again," whispered Marco. *"Dio,* is he big! Helen's screaming, trying to get out of the nest . . . the eagle swoops down and beats her with his huge wings . . . oh, wow, now he's picked her up with his claws . . . he's carrying her away. It's fantastic! Helen's struggling . . . wait! Look! There's the Purple Mask at the foot of the mountain . . . he sees the eagle . . . he's got a whistle . . . he's whistling to the eagle. The eagle's *trained!"*

"Is he goin' to *drop* Helen?" whispered Georgie, munching furiously.

"No, the eagle's bringing her down to the Purple Mask . . . oh boy, she's his prisoner *again."*

"Is he goin' to torture her again?" asked Georgie, tingling with excitement. So far in the serial, Helen Broderick had been thrown in front of a freight train, dropped from a plane, tied beneath a lethal swinging pendulum, dropped in a snake pit and roasted over an open fire as the Purple Mask tried, with spectacular lack of success, to pry from this rugged virgin the secret of her father's treasure map.

"Yes," hissed Marco. "He's chained her in the basement of his castle. Oh boy, he's ripped her dress open!"

"Oh!" gasped Georgie, almost choking on the popcorn.

"Her back is bare . . . he's picking up a big whip . . . he's going to whip her!"

"Oh *no . . ."*

"He's raising the whip . . ."

"Marco, don't tell me . . ."

"You got to see it. Ah! Here comes Dick Derring . . ."

"How'd he know where she was?"

"He was following the eagle, remember? He attacks the Purple Mask, who's slashing at him with the whip . . ."

"Oh—!"

"Wait . . . the Purple Mask is running out . . . he's throwing a bit switch . . . look! Oh, *Dio* . . ."

"What's happening? What's *happening?*"

"Big steel doors have slammed down . . . Dick and Helen are sealed in . . . oh, *no* . . ."

"Now what?"

"There's a gas . . . it's coming into the room through a pipe . . . it must be poison . . . Dick's choking . . . he's running to Helen . . . he unties her . . . they're both choking on the gas now . . . oh, *no.* He's kissing her. Hey, *cretino!* You gotta get *out* first!"

"I think it's sweet. He loves her."

"When the room's filling with poison gas?"

"Don't you believe in love?"

"Of course I do. I love you. Look! There's the Purple Mask! He's watching them through a window. He's laughing. He's gloating . . . that bastard . . ."

"What did you say?" she whispered.

"The Purple Mask is gloating . . ."

"No, about *me.*"

He brought her hand to his mouth and kissed her palm.

"I love you," he whispered. "I want to *always* love you. I want to take care of you forever. Oh, look!" He released her hand and put his arm around her, pulling her closer to him. Georgie quickly chucked her popcorn bag under her seat. "It's Wong Fu! He's broken into the room where the Purple Mask is. They start fighting . . . now we're back in the other room . . . Dick and Helen can barely breathe . . . they hug each other as they choke on the gas . . . they're going to die . . ."

He kissed her. Georgie sighed with pleasure. Marco and movies were a heavenly combination.

"Look! Wong Fu slugged the Purple Mask and he's fallen back against another switch . . . oh *Dio, Dio,* a big fan is blowing away the poison gas ... Helen and Dick are saved! How about that? I *liked* the fan!"

And he kissed her again.

"Oh, oh ... more trouble! The Purple Mask has thrown another switch ... Aiee! Five daggers have flown out of a wall! Wong Fu looks like a pin cushion! He's dead ... now the Purple Mask runs to the window ... he sees that Dick and Helen have escaped ... oh boy, is he *mad!*"

He loves me, thought Georgie dreamily. *And I love him. I'm in love with a man I can only hear. But I see him! In my mind, I see him. He's so handsome, and he's so kind to me and I love him so much!*

Oh, Georgie, your luck's turned for the better.

"Okay. The Purple Mask has gotten into his car ... and what a car! Now he's roaring down the road after Dick and Helen ... it's a chase, Georgie! And you *love* chases. Look! He's firing out his window at Dick's car! He's blown out a tire! Dick's car is out of control ... oh *Dio, Dio,* it's gone over a cliff!"

Abe Shulman might have been a megalomaniacal midget monster of a man, but he was scrupulously honest with his bookkeeping, and when in May he presented Jake with his third royalty check for forty-three thousand dollars, Jake decided to celebrate by eating out for the first time in his life in a first-class restaurant. It was no minor step. America was coming to the end of a half-century of explosive economic growth; prodigious, tax-free fortunes had been made and were being spent in sybaritic fashion; Fifth Avenue was lined from the Forties to the Nineties with pseudo-French châteaux and fake Rhenish castles; Mrs. Stuyvesant Fish had complained, "We are not rich. We have only a few million"; hundred-thousand-dollar parties were thrown at a time a second butler earned an annual salary of six hundred dollars, and society was taken extremely seriously. Jake was not foolish enough to be a snob, but he had a natural desire to enjoy some of the action. He realized his table manners were atrocious, he knew nothing about food or wine, he knew none of the intricacies of the beau monde, and he was understandably nervous about taking this first step into the terra incognita of high life. But he was determined to try it. He bought himself a dress suit and a top hat, made a reservation for two at Sherry's on Fifth Avenue and Forty-third Street, and invited Marco not only because he was his best friend, but because he figured Marco—who had acquired some polish from Maud Charteris—could warn him off from any horrendous gaffe, like mistaking a finger bowl for a glass of water.

Sherry's was at the height of its palmy glory, and the maître d' led the two well-turned-out young men to a table by the kitchen door that neither of them knew was the worst table in the house. After they were seated and had ordered a bottle of champagne, they looked around the restaurant, which was filled with celebrities and swells, the men all in white tie, the women in evening gowns and aigrettes, weighted down with jewels that must have cost at least five million dollars. Then the enormous menus were handed to them, and the two young men, who three years before had been eating herring in steerage, stared uncomprehendingly at the four pages of French entrées.

"Leave it to me," whispered Marco. "Maud told me she always asks for the specialty."

He put down the menu and locked eyes with the haughty maître d'.

"We'll have the specialty," he said grandly.

"Which one?"

Marco fought down his panic. "Which one you recommend?"

"Why don't you surprise us?" said Jake, coming to the rescue.

The maître d' gave a sniff, then bowed and left. Marco lifted his glass.

"To New York's greatest song writer," he said, adding with a grin, "and New York's best gigolo!"

"Truck driver," corrected Jake, and they both laughed.

She was sitting on the other side of the room at one of Sherry's best tables, dining with her lover, Terry Billings, when she saw them.

"It's him!" exclaimed Nellie Byfield.

"Who?"

"Jake Rubin."

"Who's Jake Rubin?"

"Oh God, Terry, don't you know *anything* except what goes

on in banks? Jake Rubin wrote 'Raggedy Ragtime Man'—and wouldn't you know, *I* called him a pushy kike? I wonder if he remembers . . ."

"I doubt he'd forget *that*."

"No, probably not. Nellie, you *idiot*. Excuse me . . ."

"Where are you going?"

"To say hello to him, of course. You stay here."

She crossed the restaurant, stared at enviously by the women and ogled by the men, her slim white lace dress chic, her blond hair piled in a chignon. Nellie liked being stared at and ogled. When she was a star, she often thought, she would be worshipped. But she wasn't a star yet.

"Mr. Rubin"—she smiled—"do you remember me? Nellie Byfield—the one who was so horrid to you at the Cavendish Club."

Jake and Marco were standing.

"I remember," said Jake flatly.

"Of course you do. And I was so ashamed of my behavior—I behaved terribly. And you were right, of course. I *should* have sung numbers like 'Sweet Patootie' . . . I should have listened to your advice." She smiled meltingly. "Well, don't let me bother you—please sit down. I just wanted to tell you how thrilled I am about your song. You must be the happiest man in New York." She hesitated, then added slyly, "I wish you'd write a song for *me*." More smile. Then, nodding at Marco, she left to return to her table. As he sat down, Jake watched her.

"She's *gorgeous*," said Marco.

Jake nodded, still watching Nellie. He was wondering which was the real Nellie: this ingratiating charmer at Sherry's, or the woman who had slapped his face and called him a "pushy little kike."

Maybe it didn't matter.

Nellie rented a small two-story house in the Murray Hill enclave called Sniffen Court, and the next morning at ten she was drinking coffee in her living room when the bell rang. Moments later her young colored maid, Fanny, carried a long white box in from the entrance hall. "Flowers, Miss Nellie," she said. "You got a new beau? Mr. Terry's too cheap to buy flowers."

161

"Don't talk that way, Fanny. Mr. Terry was nice to you last Christmas."

"You call a ten-dollar tip *nice*? When that man practically *lives* here? Huh. He ought to buy me a diamond ring, all the drinks I fetch him. Who's this from?"

Nellie had opened the box. Inside were a dozen roses and a card. The card read: "I've already written the tune, which you'll hear in a minute. If you'll have dinner with me tonight at Sherry's, I'll show you the lyrics." It was signed Jake Rubin.

The living room was low-ceilinged and furnished like an English country house with bright chintz on the chairs and sofas. A big leaded window looked out on the court, and now the sound of a violin made Nellie look up from the card. Outside the window, a man with a violin was playing a melody.

"That's it!" exclaimed Nellie, jumping up. "The song he wrote for me!"

She hurried around the black grand piano to the window.

"*Who* wrote you a song?" said Fanny, following her.

"Sshh!"

They listened as the lovely melody lapped their eardrums. When he was finished, the violinist made a bow.

"Is *that* romantic," marveled Nellie. "Fanny, run out and give him a dollar—is that romantic! I *love* it. And the song! It's beautiful!"

"Miss Nellie, I ain't got no dollar bill."

"Fanny, get your black ass out there and give the man four quarters! I'll pay you back."

"Yes, Miss Nellie."

As Fanny hurried out of the room, Nellie went to the piano and tried unsuccessfully to pick out Jake's tune.

The little bastard's really hooked, she thought triumphantly. *Really hooked.*

Sweet Nellie Byfield, the Thrush from Flushing, who was currently out of a job, was seeing a possible new avenue to stardom.

Chapter 20

"I received a letter last week from Bernard Shaw," said Maud Charteris as she lay next to Marco in her bed. "Do you know who George Bernard Shaw is?"

"Doesn't he write plays?"

"Bravo. You're coming along very nicely, Marco. I'm proud of you. Anyway, he tells me he's working on a new play for Mrs. Patrick Campbell based on the Pygmalion legend. His hero is a professor of phonetics who, on a bet, takes a Cockney flower girl from Covent Garden, teaches her to speak and act like a lady, then passes her off for a duchess at an embassy ball. He said he's not sure yet how to end it, but it did give me a marvelous idea."

"What?"

She leaned over and kissed his cheek.

"I could educate my Italian gardener and pass him off for an American businessman—or doctor or lawyer or something. Wouldn't that be fun?"

"What are you talking about?"

She got out of bed, put on a peignoir and lit a cigarette. "Some things have happened I haven't told you," she continued. *"Premièrement, Lady Frederick* is closing next week. Secondly, Phipps has asked me to marry him, and I've accepted."

Marco sat up. *"Him?* He could be your father!"

"And I could be your mother, darling. But Phipps is very sweet, he's very social, and he's extremely rich. I mean *extremely*."

"But you're rich. You're a big star!"

"And how long can I be a star? I've said goodbye to forty. I've seen too many stars begin to fade after forty, and I want no part of it. You and I are both outsiders, Marco. You're certainly no gentleman, and I'm no lady. Oh, I speak like a lady and know all the tricks of the trade—after all, I *am* an actress—but secretly, I despise all their ladylike pretensions and taboos. Between you and me, I think half the ladies I know would secretly like to live like me and don't have the nerve to try. But anyway, at my time of life one has to start thinking about security. Phipps is security. He'll also give me an established position in society, and as dear Oscar said, the only people who laugh at society are those who can't get in. But it *does* mean I'll have to give you up, dear boy. My sweetest luxury, my sweetest vice . . ."

She flicked her ash and looked at him with genuine tenderness.

"I was cruel to you at first," she went on. "I humiliated you and treated you like merchandise, and for that I sincerely apologize. The irony is, I've grown quite fond of you. Perhaps 'fond' is a middle-aged euphemism for 'love,' who knows? But at any rate, I don't want to be cruel to you now. I think I've given you a taste of the good life, and I've tried to help your trucking business. . . ."

"Help? You *founded* it! I'd be out on the street if it hadn't been for you. You're the only person who's been good to me in America."

"Well, I'm glad that a relationship that started out rather meretriciously has seemed to blossom into a real friendship. I doubt few preachers would want to write a sermon on our little saga, but there you have it. It's turned out well—against my own predictions—and I want it to end well. I want to send you to school, Marco."

"School?" he said incredulously.

She came back to the bed.

"Darling, you have a good brain. You could be something besides a truck driver, but you need an education. I could give you that, *pay* for it . . ."

"But I'm twenty-three."

"So what?"

"No one goes to school at twenty-three. Besides, I *like* my business. I'm making good money. No, to hell with school. I appreciate your offer, but no thanks."

She looked at him sadly. "Oh Marco," she said, "you're so wrong. If you turn down this offer, you'll be making the greatest mistake of your life."

He gave her a curious look.

"You told me once you resented being called a dumb wop," she continued. "No one calls an educated Italian a wop. So much of the name-calling that goes on in this city is based on *class,* not nationality or race. I'm offering you a ticket to the upper class, Marco. You'll be a fool not to take it. No—you'll be a dumb wop not to take it."

"Then," he said softly, stifling his anger, "I'm a dumb wop."

He got out of bed and started pulling on his clothes.

"And I'm through being your gigolo," he went on. "Go on and marry your rich senator and be a great lady in society! Who wants that anyway? A bunch of boiled shirts—"

"Stuffed shirts," she corrected patiently.

"You were nice to me—sure! You petted me and tried to turn me into your lapdog, and I was *stupid* to let you do it. Marco Santorelli is a *man,* not a lapdog!"

"Dear God," she groaned, "here you go again! I suppose an Italian *always* has to make a scene. All right, I've wounded your pride and I'm sorry. But at least let's part friends. And *think* about my offer."

He buttoned his shirt sulkily. Then a smile pushed its unwilling way onto his mouth.

"I guess I *do* like to make scenes," he admitted. "And we'll part friends."

She came to him. He put his arms around her and kissed her.

"Thanks for everything," he whispered.

"Dear boy," she said, rubbing her fingers over his forehead. "Dear Marco. You were my youth, and now my youth is gone."

He was surprised to see tears in her eyes. He had never seen Maud Charteris cry.

After Episode Twelve of *The Curse of the Purple Mask,* Marco took Georgie for a walk to Washington Square. It was a cool, late May evening, and Georgie was wearing a light coat over her white dress. As usual when she walked with Marco, she held his arm. It had started out because he was her guide, but now it was a gesture of affection as well. She could tell something was bothering him. The loss of her sight had sharpened her other senses, and she could almost feel the tension inside him. He was silent until they reached the square. Then he led her to a bench and they sat down.

"What's botherin' you?" she said softly, putting her hand on his.

"I can't tell you. Oh hell, yes I can. I *want* to tell you. Look, Georgie, I've fallen in love with you. I've had so much fun with you these past weeks, and you ..." he stopped, searching for words. "What I'm trying to say is, you're so wonderful about your blindness, and yet I think I really can ... can help you, and I *want* to help you. I want to be not only your lover, but something *extra*. Do you have any idea of what I'm talking about?"

"If you're tryin' to say I need you, you're absolutely right. I need your eyes, my darlin' Marco. And I need your heart. You know I've come to be crazy about you." She smiled. "And it all happened at the movies."

"But there are things about me you don't know. I'm not Dick Derring, who's pure and brave and never does anything dirty. I'm Marco, and Marco has done something dirty."

She frowned.

"What?"

"There's an English actress ... Mrs. Charteris ..."

"Yes, I remember you mentioned her on the boat. And didn't she just marry Senator Ogden?"

"That's right, two days ago. I was her gardener in Italy, and she made me a sort of proposition ... hell, to be blunt, she wanted me to be her gigolo. I said no there, but when I got to New York and was so broke, I went to her. She's given me a lot of money to make love to her, so you can see what I mean when I say I'm no Dick Derring."

He's Italian, she thought. They think differently ...

"I suppose you think I'm disgusting?" he asked anxiously.

"No," she said. "I don't think the Pope would give you a medal, but I can understand why you did it. But now that she's married ..."

"Oh, don't worry. I'm her *ex*-gigolo now. But here's where I'm really confused. It turns out Maud *likes* me, and she offered to put me through college. I told her no, but ..." He gestured with frustration. "... I keep thinking she was *right,* dammit! It's a tremendous opportunity, and I'm an idiot not to take it."

"Well, of *course* she's right!" exclaimed Georgie. "Oh, there's no doubt about it. She may be a wicked woman, but she's right."

"But what about you and me? What about *you*? Getting an education means *years*. Oh *Dio,* everything was so simple till *this* came up."

"Years? How many years?"

"I don't know. Lots. I have practically no education at all. I could stay the way I am, probably do all right with my truck business ... but she's opened the door to something so much bigger...." He sighed. "I don't know." He took her hand and stood up. "Come on, let's walk some more."

"Marco, you've *got* to do it. Really! We're not talkin' about a ... a snag in our romance; we're talkin' about the most important thing a man can be offered: an education. You've *got* to do it, and if it takes time, so what? It's *worth* it! And I'll always be here, waitin' for you."

He looked at her. "Would you really? Would you wait *years*?"

She smiled. "Oh, you foolish man. Who else do I have to take me to the movies?"

He stopped under a lamppost and took her in his arms.

"Oh, Georgie, Georgie," he whispered, kissing her. "I love you so...."

They kissed for a while. She reveled in his strength and warmth and imagined the love in his eyes that she would never be able to see.

Then he stepped back.

"What an idiot I am!" he exclaimed. "Of *course!* We don't have to wait. We can get married now."

"Married?"

"Why not? We'll get married, and I'll go to school. It's simple after all."

"But ... darlin', I'm thrilled you want to marry me, *believe* me, but ..."

"Do you accept?" he interrupted, taking both her hands. "Say yes, Georgie. You've got to say yes."

"Of *course* I say yes. Do you think I'm crazy?"

He let out a half-laugh, half-whoop of joy and kissed her again. After a moment she pushed him away.

"But could you support both of us?" she said. "I mean, if you're gettin' educated ..."

"Oh hell, I'll borrow the money from Maud. She's rich as Croesus now ..."

"Well, she may pay for *you,* but I have a funny feelin' she wouldn't be too happy payin' for *me*."

"She'll pay," he said softly, "to shut me up, if nothing else.

167

She doesn't want her husband to know about me."

"But that would be blackmail!" she said, shocked.

"Not the way *I'd* do it. No, leave it to me, Georgie. We're going to win the *whole* cake. They've gone to Europe on his yacht for their honeymoon, but when they get back I'll make an arrangement with Maud. And meanwhile, we're getting married."

He took her in his arms again and kissed her, hungrily. But for the first time, the beautiful face Georgie envisioned in her blindness had changed a little.

For the first time, she saw a streak of ugliness.

As Casey O'Donnell's small trucking empire grew, as his political influence waxed, his stomach extended as well. Alarmed by his tighter belts and collars, he tried to fight his weight problem, but his Irish love of whiskey was stronger than his vanity, and instead of losing weight he gave in and bought bigger suits. His red hair was the only thing about him that was thinning.

The morning after Marco's proposal to Georgie in Washington Square, Casey was seated at his cluttered desk in the office of his garage talking on the phone to one of New York's aldermen, when to his surprise, his wife came in. Since Kathleen practically never came to the garage and since she looked to be in a state of mild hysteria, Casey prepared himself for trouble. He motioned her to sit down as he finished his call.

Kathleen, clutching a new leather purse, sat down in one of the plain wooden chairs. The office's sole decorative features were the dozens of framed photographs on the light green walls, pictures of the trucking company's annual picnics, pictures of local politicos (mostly Irish, and all bowler-hatted), a framed commendation to Casey from the Order of Hibernians. The office was as frumpy in its way as Kathleen, who, while always dressing "respectably," as she thought of it, had no pretensions to personal style and looked exactly what she was: a graying-haired, Irish-American housewife. Whatever feminine interest in clothes she had, she had lavished on Georgie. Since Georgie's blindness, her aunt, along with Bridget, had become her dresser, and the fact that Georgie always looked good was a tribute to Kathleen's care and money and Bridget's taste.

The moment Casey hung up the phone, Kathleen pounced.

"Something awful has happened," she burst out. "You've got to stop it, Casey. I won't allow that poor girl to throw her life away!"

"Stop what?"

"Georgie told me this morning, after you left. She slept late because she didn't get home till after midnight. . . . I *knew* there was trouble. I *knew* it!"

"Would you calm *down*?" he roared.

"She wants to marry that dago!"

"Santorelli?" exclaimed Casey, amazed.

"The same. Oh, it was my fault. I shouldn't have let her go out with him, but she was enjoying those movies so . . ." She pulled a handkerchief from her purse to wipe her nose. "She's too young, too innocent. The girl knows nothing about men, and God *knows* what he's done to her! Oh, I can't believe it's happened. . . ."

"Now, wait a minute. There's nothing particularly *wrong* with Santorelli. . . ."

She gaped. "I can't believe I'm hearin' those words!"

"Well, there *isn't*. Maybe it's time Georgie had a husband, particularly now with Bridget gone. And if they're in love . . ."

"Oh!" snorted his wife. "What does that girl know about love? She's never been out with another man in her life. She's *blind,* Casey! She needs to be protected. And this . . . this Italian . . . well, you *know* what they're like. And I'm terrified he's already done something to her. . . ."

Casey looked startled. "Do you think he. . . ?"

Kathleen raised her hands to silence him.

"I *pray* he hasn't, but I fear he may have. Why else this talk about marriage all of a sudden? Oh Casey, you've got to do something. Get rid of him! We'll find Georgie a *decent* husband, a fine Irish lad, but get rid of this awful . . ."

She burst into tears. Casey, who abhorred displays of any emotion except anger, rolled his eyes.

"For God's sake, stop blubbering," he growled.

"But she's like a daughter to me," she wailed. "The poor, helpless thing . . ."

"Georgie's not helpless, and you know it. I think it's amazing how she gets around . . ."

"Whose side are you on?" Kathleen almost screeched. "I

won't have her marryin' that dago! Oh God, *why* those girls came over in steerage . . ."

And she started crying again.

Casey swung slowly around in his swivel chair, his eyes looking at the photos of his political pals, searching for inspiration. When he spotted Archie O'Malley, he suddenly knew what to do. When Casey determined to play, he played rough.

"All right, I'll take care of it," he said. "There's an easy way to get him out of our lives, so quit crying."

"What are you going to do?" she sniffed.

"That's none of your business. Now, get out of here. I have work to do. And *don't* let Georgie know you came to me. I don't want *her* screamin' at me."

Kathleen stood up. "You're a good man, Casey O'Donnell," she said.

"Good, hell," he muttered. "The fact is, Santorelli's been takin' away some of my trucking business."

Archie O'Malley was Casey's friend with connections to the Immigration Service.

In this year of Halley's comet, Mark Twain and Tolstoi died, John Reed was planning to move to Greenwich Village, Diaghilev commissioned *The Firebird* from Stravinski, Sidney Greenstreet was a juvenile on Broadway, Lynn Fontanne was a bit player in *Mr. Preedy and the Countess,* Douglas Fairbanks starred in the hit comedy *The Cub,* and Franklin Roosevelt ran for the state senate in New York. Also, Nellie Byfield gave a small dinner party in her Sniffen Court house that turned out to be a near-disaster.

Aside from her lover, Terry Billings, most of the half-dozen other guests were in the theater: aspiring actors and actresses who chattered endlessly about show business, casting calls, viciously envious of other actors' successes, savoring with sadistic *Schadenfreude* their friends' disasters. It was a well-dressed, good-looking group, and Fanny was passing cocktails in the living room when the doorbell rang.

"That'll be Jake," said Nellie, leaving Terry's side.

"Jake who?" asked the young banker, who was a junior vice-president of the Bank of New York.

"You *always* say 'Jake who.' Jake Rubin, the songwriter."

"You invited *him?*"

"It's *my* party, sweetheart. I'll get the door, Fanny."

She went into the entrance hall and opened the door. There was Jake, looking natty in a tuxedo. He smiled as he held out a bottle of Veuve Clicquot with a ribbon tied around its neck.

"Thanks for asking me," he said.

"I want you to see my house. Oh, Jake, for *me?* Yummy champagne! Thank you."

She closed the door and led him toward the living room.

"I have some *very* pretty actresses here tonight," she said, taking his arm, "so I hope you brought your address book."

"I already got the only address I'm interested in, and that's Sniffen Court."

"Why, Jake, how sweet. But don't let Terry hear that. He's *very* jealous, and can he be mean!" She stopped him at the step leading down to the living room. "Listen, everyone! Here's someone very special who's written the most *beautiful* song for me: Jake Rubin."

She led him around the room, introducing him, finally bringing him to Terry.

"And this is Terry Billings, whom I've told you about," she said. "Terry, Jake Rubin."

Terry, whose slicked black hair was parted down the middle, was leaning on the grand piano. He neither straightened nor stuck out his hand. His narrowly handsome face looked at Jake with all the insolence of St. Paul's-Yale education and a father worth five million dollars.

"Oh, yes, the immigrant," he drawled. "If I'd known you were inviting people off the boat, Nellie, I wouldn't have come. One *does* have one's social standing to think about, after all."

Silence.

"Terry, what a *dumb* thing to say," snapped Nellie. "Get off your high horse and act like a human being, for a change."

"You told me *you* called him a pushy little kike."

"I did and I apologized for it and if you don't behave like a gentleman, I'll ask you to leave!"

Now his insolence was directed toward her. "Oh? And who pays the rent here? Not you, darling. *Me.* I'm not in the habit of being thrown out of my own house."

171

"You son of a bitch!" yelled Nellie, stamping her foot in a rage. "Don't say that in front of my friends!"

He laughed. "Come on, Nellie: Everyone *knows.*"

"Excuse me, Mr. Billings," said Jake, "I think the lady asked you to leave."

He grabbed Terry's arm and pulled him away from the piano.

"Don't grab *me,* Jew boy!" yelled Terry, and he plowed his fist into Jake's stomach, sending him sprawling on the rug. The other guests screamed. Nellie, who was still holding the bottle of Veuve Clicquot, now grabbed it by the neck, raised it over Terry's head and smashed it down on him. He saw it in time to duck, so the bottle crashed on his shoulder instead of his skull, breaking and spraying the champagne everywhere. Terry, howling with rage, grabbed Nellie's wrists and started wrestling with her—for Nellie was spitting mad. Jake, behind them, got to his feet, came up to Terry, jerked him around and smashed his fist into his chin. Terry fell back on the top of the piano, slid across its slick surface like a bowling ball and shot out through the leaded window into Sniffen Court.

After the shattered glass tinkled to silence, Jake and Nellie stared at each other.

"What an evening!" Nellie said, starting to laugh. Jake laughed. Everybody laughed.

"Fanny," called Nellie, "you'd better get a mop and broom."

"Yes, Miss Nellie. I'll go out and sweep up Mr. Terry and put him in the garbage can."

Jake was no longer sexually innocent. He had seduced several of the waitresses at Coney Island, and his new wealth enabled him to go to the city's best and cleanest whorehouse, which was in a private town house on West Forty-fifth Street, next-door to a theatrical boarding house. But Jake was a romantic, which was why he could write beautiful love songs. And as the evening wore on, he began to realize he was falling in love with Nellie. He knew she had a streak of commonness and was not exactly a lady, but this was not unusual in the theater. Besides, he was oblivious to her faults. He couldn't take his eyes off her; she was the physical embodiment of his dream *shiksa.* And he was pleased to observe that Nellie was beginning to have an obvious interest in him.

As the guests were leaving, she whispered to him, "Stay a while." Jake needed no encouraging. He hung around the fireplace while Nellie showed the others out. Then she returned to the living room, smiling at him.

"I liked the way you handled Terry," she said, coming to the chintz sofa and sitting down. "You don't look very strong, but you're full of surprises."

"Will you make up with him?"

She didn't answer for a moment. Then she said, rather slyly, "Perhaps."

"Is it true he was paying the rent?"

"Oh, in a way I suppose you could say that. He gave me money. And I know what you're thinking: I was his mistress. Well, I'd be a fool not to admit it now, wouldn't I?" She smiled at him. "Anyway, he has a wife, which makes it complicated. It's the old story."

"Do you need money? I could loan you some. . . ."

"That's sweet of you, but I'm all right for the time being. I've got something in the bank, and my agent's arranged an audition for me next week with Mr. Ziegfeld—at *last!*—so I'll get by. Of course, if Ziggy doesn't like me . . ." She hesitated. "Why don't you come sit by me? I can't talk to you when you're over there."

He needed no more urging. When he was next to her, he said, "I didn't mean loan. I meant give. Let *me* pay the rent, Nellie. Oh God, that sounds awful. What I mean is, I'm crazy about you!"

She said nothing, knowing that at the moment, silence was the best seducer. He was visibly nervous.

"I know my lyrics are better than my dialogue," he went on, taking her hand, "but I want you, Nellie. More than anything in the world." He kissed her hand; then, meeting no resistance, he took her in his arms and kissed her mouth. She could feel the hunger of his desire, and it rather excited her.

"Miss Nellie—oh, ex*cuse* me!"

Nellie pushed Jake away.

"*Damn* you, Fanny!" she yelled. "I thought you'd left."

Fanny, clutching her purse, was in the hall door, a straw hat on her head.

"I need carfare home, Miss Nellie. Someone stoled my coin purse."

"Oh!" Snorting, Nellie got off the sofa. "Don't give me this 'stoled' crap, you bought yourself a beer!"

"Now don't get mad, Miss Nellie. . . ."

"God! Now I can't find *my* purse. . . ."

"Here," said Jake, going to the door as he pulled out his wallet. "Take a taxi, Fanny. On me."

He gave her five dollars. She stared at the money.

"*Thank* you, Mr. Jake! Miss Nellie, this one's *much* nicer than that cheapskate, Mr. Terry! 'Night, everybody. Sorry I bothered you, Miss Nellie."

And she was gone.

"So much for the passionate love scene," sighed Nellie. "That Fanny . . . sometimes I could strangle her."

"I like her."

"Oh, she means well, I suppose."

They looked at each other.

"It's late," she said, "and I'm tired. Do you want to spend the night?"

It wasn't very romantic, but his heart flew to heaven.

Nellie's language might not have been very ladylike, but she had natural taste and a flair for dressing well. She also was a passionate shopper and kept well abreast of the latest trends in decoration. She knew that five years earlier, an ex-actress named Elsie de Wolfe—the future Lady Mendl—had startled New York taste by decorating the new Colony Club with the light colors and furniture of eighteenth century France, thus banishing to oblivion the brooding, dark, neo-Moorish interiors of the Victorian era. Since then, brightness had swept the country, and Nellie's happy chintzes downstairs were very much in style. Upstairs were two tiny bedrooms and a bath. She had painted the paneled wainscoting white and papered the walls with a big, swirling Art Nouveau pattern, with green, blue and pink tendrils twisting across a white background. In her bedroom a brass bed was covered with a lace spread, and white lace curtains hung over the two dormer windows. The room smelled sweet, thanks to a glass bowl filled with potpourri on the chiffonier.

After Nellie had led Jake into the bedroom, she turned on the bed light and began unpinning her hair. Jake watched silently as she undressed, the soft light kissing her milky flesh as she stood in her white underclothes. Then she sat on the bed, removed her shoes and started rolling off her white stockings. His heart thumped as he drank in her legs.

"I assume," she said, "you don't intend doing it in your dinner jacket? I'm not *quite* that formal."

Realizing he must look like a fool, he began undressing. When they were both in the bed, naked, he began feeling her breasts.

"Nellie, Nellie," he whispered.

She watched him as he felt and kissed her body.

"You're a randy little guy, aren't you?" she whispered.

"Nellie, Nellie . . . Oh God, I love you, Nellie. . . ."

Now he was clasping her head with both hands, kissing her mouth, his hot, thin body pressing against her soft, smooth flesh. *It's true,* she thought. *He hasn't got much technique, but he sure as hell enjoys it.*

"I hope you brought a condom?" she said, somewhat shattering the mood of romance.

He groaned, got off her, ran to his pants and searched through his pockets. She suppressed a giggle at the way he turned his back to her, trying to hide his erection as if there were something wrong about it. When he had found the condom and put it on, he hurried back to bed and climbed on her.

"You're the most beautiful thing in the world, Nellie," he whispered. "This is a beautiful moment for me . . . beautiful . . ."

He really believes it, she thought. *That's rather sweet.*

Three days after Kathleen O'Donnell went to see her husband in his garage, Marco drove his truck into Little West Twelfth Street to deliver a load of Long Island chickens, when two mounted policemen blocked his way. Marco stopped the truck and leaned out to yell, "Get out of the way!"

One of the policemen drew his gun as the other dismounted. He came to Marco's door.

"Get out," he ordered.

"Why? What is this?"

"I'm searching your truck."

"For what?"

"We'll see."

"Wait a minute—"

"Get OUT!"

Whatever it was, the police were serious. Confused and a little nervous, Marco climbed out. The policeman disappeared in the rear of the truck. Marco looked at the other cop, who still had his gun drawn, aimed at him. A small crowd of curious onlookers was gathering. Marco pulled out a handkerchief and wiped his face. It was a warm day, but it wasn't the heat that was making him sweat.

"Here it is," said the first cop, coming out of the truck. He held a burlap sack. He reached in and pulled out a fistful of five-dollar bills.

"The phone tip was right," he said to the other cop. "There must be ten grand in phony bills." He said to Marco, "You're under arrest, mister."

Marco stared at the sack.

"How did that get in my truck?" he said.

"That's what you're gonna tell us. Okay, let's go."

Marco was numb.

The next morning, Jake and an attorney were led into a small, high-ceilinged room in the Tombs.

"Wait here," said a policeman, indicating four chairs around a plain table. It was the only furniture in the room. The two windows looking out on Centre Street were barred.

Jake and the attorney sat down. A moment later, Marco was brought in by another cop. He said, "I didn't do this, Jake. I swear to God I didn't do this."

"I know, Marco. This is your attorney, Millard Whitehead."

They shook hands as the other policeman left. Marco sat down at the table.

"Somebody hid that bag of funny money in my truck, then phoned the cops," he said. "But who? All night I've been trying to think who? Who wants to hurt *me*? It doesn't make any sense! Does it make any sense to you, Jake?"

"No. But obviously somebody wants to get rid of you."

"But this isn't going to work, is it? I know they found the money on my truck, but they have to prove I was printing it, don't they? Or at least that I was going to try and pass it?"

"I'm afraid they don't have to prove anything at all, Mr. Santorelli," said the attorney, "because I doubt very much that your case will ever come to trial."

"Why?"

"You're not an American citizen. Under the existing rules, the Immigration Service can deport you at any time for any reasonable cause. Any hint of criminal activities is reasonable cause. I imagine whoever put that bag in your truck knew this and wanted you deported."

Marco's face went white.

"You mean they can send me back to Italy?" he said, softly.

"They can, and I'm afraid they will."

Marco looked at Jake, panic in his eyes.

"Jake, they can't do this to me! Oh God, after all I've done to get here, they can't send me *back*! Jake, tell me they can't. *Tell* me!"

It killed him not to be able to help his friend, but Jake remained silent.

When Jake, at Marco's instructions, telephoned the news to Georgie, the blind girl became hysterical.

"Deported?" she almost screamed. "But *why?*"

Jake explained.

"But I don't understand," said Georgie. "Who would have done that to him? *Why* ..."

She stopped. She was in the kitchen of her uncle's home. Casey was at work, but Kathleen was in the living room. Suddenly, Georgie knew who and why.

"Where is he now?" she asked.

"They took him on a police boat over to Ellis Island. They're going to hold him in detention there until they can arrange getting him back to Italy. I'm sick about it, but the lawyer I hired says there's nothing we can do. ..."

"Yes ... thank you, Mr. Rubin. ..."

"He told me he'd asked you to marry him. ..."

"Yes, and I'm *going* to. Even if *I* have to go to Italy! Excuse me, Mr. Rubin, I have to talk to my aunt. And thanks for calling."

She hung up. She knew every inch of the kitchen; now, as she had done thousands of times, she felt her way around the familiar counters to the dining room door. Then into the dining room, feel-

177

ing her way down the long sideboard, then walking to the left through the double doors into the living room. Tears were streaming down her face. Kathleen, who was sitting in one of the overstuffed chairs reading the Bible, looked up to see her niece coming toward her. As always, Kathleen was struck by Georgie's beauty. Then she saw the tears.

"Darlin', what's wrong?" she said, putting the Bible on the side table.

"Did you do it?" she said, clutching the back of the sofa. "Did you and Uncle Casey deport Marco?"

"Deport?" exclaimed her aunt. "I know nothing' about deportin' no one. . . ."

"He's been deported. They're sending him back to Italy, the man I love, the man I . . ."

She broke down completely. Kathleen hurried over to her and hugged her.

"Darlin', darlin' . . ." She kissed her.

Georgie pushed her away.

"It was a cruel thing to do. A wicked thing! I've never complained about anything—even about losing my eyes. But the *one* thing I wanted was Marco, and you've taken him away from me."

"But I didn't do it!"

"You didn't like him—admit it!"

"I'll admit I didn't like him—I thought he was wrong for you, and he *is*. The proof is that they're deportin' him—he must have done something wrong, or they wouldn't do it. . . ." She stopped. "Oh my God," she muttered. Kathleen wasn't the smartest woman in the world, and it had taken her a few moments to realize what her husband had done. "Dear Lord, I did get him deported. But I swear I wasn't thinkin' of *that.* . . . Oh, Georgie, forgive me. . . ."

"What did you *do*?"

"When you told me you wanted to marry him, I was half-sick with worryin', and I went to your uncle and told him to get Marco out of your life. But, dear God, I never thought he'd do *this*."

"Then call him and tell him to *un*do it."

"Yes, I suppose I should. . . . Oh, Georgie, darlin', I was only thinkin' of your best interests. . . ."

"*Call* him!"

Her aunt hurried into the kitchen and called Casey's office. When she got him, she said, "What did you do about Marco?"

"I had some phony bills planted on his truck and called the police."

"But they've deported him!"

"I know. That's what you wanted, isn't it? You said, 'Get rid of him.' "

"Dear God, I didn't think you'd take me that literally! Georgie's practically hysterical here. . . . You'd better get him out."

"Dammit," Casey exploded. "Would you make up your bloody mind? I can't get him out now. He's been officially deported. He's like a prisoner. Now, I don't want to hear one more goddam word about Marco Santorelli!"

And he slammed down the phone.

"Oh dear," whispered Kathleen to herself as she hung up. "What have I done?"

She turned to see Georgie standing in the dining room door. "Well?" Georgie said.

"Darlin', it's too late. It can't be undone—he's a prisoner. Oh God, can you ever forgive your meddlin' old fool of an aunt?"

Georgie stood totally still; then she slowly clenched her fists. She said, "Please call me a taxi."

"Where are you goin'?"

"To Ellis Island."

"But you *can't*! You can't see . . ."

"I'm goin' to talk to Marco." She raised her voice. "Now, please call me a taxi!"

Kathleen reached for the phone.

As a rule, Georgie avoided going to unfamiliar places by herself, for obvious reasons. But as she stood at the rail of the ferry, cane in hand, she told herself Ellis Island was not unfamiliar to her. If anything, it was becoming all too familiar, as if the shadow of immigration would never be lifted entirely from the lives of those who went through it. Now she pictured the place in her mind. She remembered the squat buildings set on the tiny island in the bay. She remembered the slow climb up the stairs, the long lines in the Great Hall, the smells and sounds of the thousands of immigrants from all over the world. Most vividly, she remembered her eyelids being turned up by the buttonhook, and that unfamiliar word that had changed her life: trachoma. Now she was returning to Ellis Island for another reason: to save her love.

If possible. When the ferry docked she asked one of the guards to take her to her brother-in-law's office, and she was led into the building, which was again packed with humanity. As she climbed the stairs to the administrative offices, Georgie listened to the voices of the immigrants and wondered what *their* lives would be like in the New World.

Bridget was alone in the office when Georgie came in.

"They've brought Marco here," said Georgie.

"I know," said Bridget, kissing her sister. "They brought him in this morning."

"Where is he?"

"In one of the detention cages over in the west end of the building."

"Can I talk to him?"

"Of course. I'll take you there."

"Bridget," she whispered, "can we get him out? Can Carl?"

"Darlin', there's nothing we can do. I don't blame you for askin', but believe me, there's *nothing* we can do. Come on."

She took her to the detention wing, which was at the very edge of the island. A guard unlocked a steel door, and Bridget, holding Georgie's hand, took her into a long hall. On the right side, tall windows looked to the west across the bay to New Jersey. On the left side of the hall, chain-link fencing rose from the floor to the tall ceiling, and steel walls divided the area into narrow partitions or cubicles, each with a fold-up cot, a sink and a toilet. The windows were open, letting in the breeze, but Georgie could still smell sweat. At the end of the long corridor was another steel door with a sign over it that read FIRE EXIT.

Bridget led her down the hall. Most of the cubicles were empty, but a Greek was snoring on one cot, and a bearded Croat leaned on the fencing of his cubicle with bored resignation, watching the two Irish girls pass.

Marco's cubicle was the next to the last at the end of the corridor. When he saw Georgie he jumped off his cot and ran to the door. He was still wearing the working overalls he had had on when the police picked him up.

"Georgie," he said softly.

She came to his voice, putting her hands against the fencing. He put his hands against hers, and their fingers touched.

"I'll wait down here," said Bridget tactfully, and she walked back down the hall.

"Everything's gone wrong," whispered Georgie. "It was Uncle Casey that did it to you. . . ."

"I know. I figured that out—finally. It doesn't matter. I've got a way to get out."

Georgie blinked with surprise. "How?"

"There's another Italian in the end cage, right next to mine. They're deporting him because he was mixed up in one of the rackets. He's been here a week, and he told me that on summer nights, the night guard opens the fire door and sits outside." He stopped, listening to Bridget's receding footsteps. Then he whispered, "Dino says there's a master key for all these cages. If your sister could get one of those masters, Dino and I can get out—tonight."

"Get out? But where would you go? This is an island. . . ."

"We can *swim*," he whispered. "The water's ten feet past the fire door—we can swim to New Jersey. Dino says a lot of guys have done it. . . ."

"But that's a long swim!"

"Dino says it's about a half-mile, maybe less. I can do it. But we have to have the *key*. Can you get it?"

"But . . ." She hesitated. *Oh, dear God, yes. Get it! Bridget will help. . . .* "But even if you made it, wouldn't they be lookin' for you?"

"Yes, for a while, but I can hide out. And then when Maud gets back from her honeymoon, I'll call her. She'll get the senator to fix it for me with the Immigration Service. But the important thing is to get out of here before they deport me. Can you get the key?"

"Yes. At least, I'll try. . . . Oh, Marco, are you *sure* you can make it? A half-mile's a long way, and I've heard there are bad currents in New York Bay. . . ."

"If I bump into anything, it'll probably be a floating beer bottle. Don't worry. But *get the key!*"

"All right, I'll be back in a while. . . ."

"Georgie . . ."

181

"Yes?"

"I love you."

"Oh, dear God, and I love *you*. Wait for me. . . ."

"I'm not going anywhere."

"Mary, mother of God . . . did I say 'wait'? I must be goin' crazy. . . ."

She turned and called for her sister.

"And you tell him he's *daft* if he tries to swim that bay," said Bridget ten minutes later in the women's washroom, where she had taken Georgie when she asked for someplace private to talk. "The last idiot who tried it floated up four days later, and the fish had made a pretty picture of his face."

Georgie shuddered. "But *some* make it, don't they?"

"Yes, some. A lot of them try. This bloody bay is like a swimmin' meet, and of course we don't have the budget for enough guards to turn it into a *prison,* which it really isn't. The security here is a joke, because it *is* an island. But tell him he's crazy to try and swim. The bay is dangerous."

"He has no choice. He's bein' deported because *our* uncle framed him. Bridget, you've *got* to help him!"

Bridget hesitated. "If Carl found out I'd done it . . ."

"Bridget, it's *me,* Georgie. Your *sister!* I love that man, and you've got to help me save him."

Bridget looked at her, in particular at the sightless eyes, wide with pleading intensity. Bridget couldn't resist her sister—which Georgie knew. Besides, Bridget remembered Maryanne Flaherty and Wexford Hall and Jamie Barrymore. She was certainly no stranger to breaking the law.

Impulsively, she kissed her sister.

"You know I couldn't say no to you," she said. "Sit on the loo while I go get the key." She went to the door and added, "But tell him not to hurt the night guard. He's an old love, and he's due for retirement in a month."

"Marco wouldn't hurt anyone."

Bridget hurried out of the washroom, excited by being once again on the side of, and rooting for, the underdog.

"It's enough to make you turn against female education," said Phipps Ogden to Maud in their suite at the Paris Ritz. "I sent her to Porter Hall outside London, thinking she'd make some nice English contacts, and what happens? Her history teacher turned out to be a Fabian Socialist! So when she came home babbling about the beauties of the Webbs, I transferred her to Mlle. de Cluzy's school at Versailles so she could improve her French. And what happens? Her gym teacher is a supporter of Jean Jaurès, the French Socialist."

Maud smiled. "It's probably just a phase. A lot of young people in England think it's fashionable to be radical."

"I'm not sure how seriously she takes it, but it's damned annoying to be told—as I was—that I was decadent marrying a 'bourgeois' actress."

Maud looked surprised.

"She said that?"

"Yes she did. I thought you should be warned before you meet her."

"Bourgeois? I suppose that's because I do drawing-room comedies. Do you think she'd approve if I did Gorki and Chekhov?"

"She'd probably worship you."

"Anyway, darling, you've told me she's moody, artistic, and now that she's a flaming Marxist. We'll probably get along famously—at least she sounds interesting. Now go down and fetch her."

"You know," said Phipps, rather sadly, "Vanessa used to be a sweet little girl. We were very close—after all, she's my only child. And then . . ." he took a deep breath. "She grew up."

He went to the door. "Well, into the breach!"

Blowing his wife a kiss, he left.

Maud was wearing a simple white lace dress and almost no jewelry; she had purposely underdressed to meet her much-publicized stepdaughter. One reason for their honeymooning in Europe had been for Maud to meet Vanessa, who was touring French museums after graduating from Mlle. de Cluzy's exclusive school for girls at Versailles. And on the same day Marco was planning his escape from Ellis Island, Vanessa had returned to Paris from Lyons. She had checked into the Ritz—a curious address for a Fabian Socialist, as Phipps had sourly remarked (he, of course, was footing the bill).

So far, Maud's marriage had been a smash hit, and anything but socialistic. Phipps's 180-foot yacht, the *North Star,* which had brought them across the Atlantic, was a floating fantasy of luxury. In London they had been wined and dined by the titled and the rich, for Phipps was well-connected socially and Maud was, of course, everyone's favorite star. Phipps had bought her fabulous jewels, expensive knickknacks at Fabergé. . . . Then on to Paris for an orgy of shopping and Vanessa.

It was four in the afternoon. Maud was standing at a window looking out on the Place Vendôme when she heard the door open. She turned to see a girl of twenty come in with her dapper father. Phipps brought her across the room. Vanessa was tall and slender, with a good figure. She had mousy-colored hair that looked rather dirty. Her face was attractive: She had inherited some of her father's good looks, and her blue eyes were lovely. But Maud thought she had no style; the brown dress and depressing brown hat she wore were an embarrassment at the Ritz. Vanessa apparently didn't give a damn how she looked.

"Maud, this is Vanessa," said Phipps.

Maud came to her and kissed both cheeks, noticing that the girl tensed slightly.

"I've heard so much about you," said Maud, with a smile. "I *do* hope we can become friends."

Maud stepped back, and Vanessa inspected her stepmother, whose figure was still that of a woman in her twenties and whose stunning face showed few evidences of middle age.

"I knew you were beautiful," said Vanessa, who had a rather hoarse voice and who spoke with a faint trace of an English accent. "Now I can see why my father fell in love with you."

"That's very kind of you, dear." There was an awkward silence; Vanessa apparently didn't have much else to say. "Well," said Maud, "shall we order tea? The Ritz is the only place in Paris that makes decent tea."

"I don't want any," said Vanessa, "but you and Father have some if you want."

With which, she wandered over to a table, picked up a magazine and started leafing through it. Maud looked at Phipps.

"Van," said her father sharply, "I was under the impression that Mademoiselle de Cluzy taught *manners* . . . at least, that was what I was paying for. The reason we are here is so you and Maud can get to know each other."

"Oh?" She put the magazine down and turned to look at them. "I think we all have to realize that Maud and I probably have very little in common."

"That doesn't mean you can't be polite."

"Now, Phipps," said Maud, placatingly, "we're all probably a little tense at first." She smiled at Vanessa. "I thought perhaps you and I could go shopping tomorrow."

"I hate shopping," said Vanessa. "And as you can tell, I'm not in the least interested in clothes."

My God, thought Maud, *she's got all the winning ways and charm of a giant stingray. . . .*

What Bridget told Georgie was true: The security on Ellis Island was a joke because it wasn't a prison, and the authorities counted on the bay to act as a wall. The night guard in the detention wing was an aging Irishman named Timmy Walsh who every Christmas put on a fake beard and a Santa outfit and distributed presents at a Staten Island orphanage. Promptly at ten that night, "Santa" Walsh, as the other guards nicknamed him, carried a chair down the long hall of the detention cages, unlocked the fire door at the end and carried his chair outside, leaving the fire door open. Soon Marco smelled the smoke of his pipe wafting through the door.

By midnight, he heard his snores.

Dino Farentino, in the next cage, was a nineteen-year-old whose father had been a fisherman in Sorrento and whose mother had brought him to America in 1908. His progress had been all too typical: He joined a street gang, he became a petty thief, other thieves brought him into the world of adult crime, he was caught at trying to shake down a grocery store owner, and he was deported. Wiry, short, with black hair and dark brown eyes, he listened in the dark as Marco unlocked his cage door and slowly swung it open. Santa Walsh kept snoring. Now Marco was unlocking Dino's door.

"Let's go," he whispered in Italian.

The two young men went to the open fire door and looked out. It was a clear, balmy night. Across the bay were the lights of New Jersey. The lights of a freighter twinkled as the big ship passed through the Narrows. Several tugs were pushing a coal barge. Santa Walsh was snoring in his chair by the door.

Marco signaled Dino, and they hurried across the weeded strip of land to the rocky shore ten feet from the door. As they took off their shoes and socks, the waves from the passing tugs slapped the rocks, but otherwise the night was silent.

They waded in.

"My father was a fisherman," Dino whispered. "He told me you can last in the water for hours if you know how to float. The important thing is not to panic."

"And let's stay close to each other. If one gets in trouble . . ."

"Right. Let's go. Good luck."

"Good luck."

They started swimming. The water was cool, and for the first ten minutes they made good progress, though neither of them knew how to swim well. Then Marco felt a surge in the water, and both of them started drifting south.

"It's a current!" yelled Dino. "A strong one . . ."

"So we end up on Staten Island . . ."

"That's too far! Shit . . ."

Marco realized he was right. They had to fight the current or be swept into the middle of the enormous bay. He redoubled his efforts, swimming against the current, but realized he was barely holding his own and was beginning to tire. He unbuttoned his overalls and wriggled out of them to rid himself of their weight. As he kicked them off, some foul-smelling sewage drifted by his face.

"Jesus Christ," he yelled, "I almost swallowed a turd!"

"Yeah, this water's filthy. . . ."

Dino, who was up-current from Marco, was also barely holding his own. Marco looked back. They had come about a hundred feet, and Ellis Island seemed discouragingly near, just as New Jersey seemed frighteningly distant. The swim was turning out to be much harder than he had thought, and he fought down a mounting sense of panic. *Keep going,* he told himself. *Keep going. . . .*

Marco's muscled body had no fat, but for the first time in his life he wished he had some, because he was a "sinker"; he had no natural buoyancy. As his arms and back and lungs began to ache, he tried to float for a moment's rest, but he went immediately under. He stayed under for five seconds, remembering Dino's advice, then pushed his way to the surface again, gasping for air, to find that the current had swept him ten feet farther away from Dino.

"Dio," he muttered, redoubling his efforts, but he realized he was making practically no headway at all because of the current, and neither was Dino. He was beginning to despair when a piece of timber floated by. Grabbing it, he hung on to it to rest his arms while his legs kicked furiously. This enabled him to make some headway, and to his relief, after five minutes he felt the current lessen and realized he had passed it.

It was then he saw the lights of the tug bearing down on them.

"Dino," he yelled, "there's a boat!"

"I see it," Dino yelled back. "Shit, it's coming on fast...."

In fact, the tug was making twelve knots, and in the darkness Marco knew the helmsman would never spot them.

"Yell!" he cried.

Dino started yelling as the tug headed directly for him. Then, suddenly, there were no more yells.

"Dino!" cried Marco, who was kicking furiously to get out of the way of the oncoming tug. It was now so close he could hear the pounding of the engines. He continued yelling, but realized with mounting horror what Dino must have realized: The engine noise drowned him out. *Dio, Dio ...* his adrenaline galvanized every muscle. He was directly in the path of the tug, which was bearing down on him, its prow less than ten feet away. He grabbed the end of the timber and turned directly toward the tug, deciding his best chance was to use the timber as a buffer. In seconds he felt a tremendous jolt that almost lifted him out of the water. Then he let go of the timber and swam with all his strength as he felt the wake of the tug push him away. The chug of the engines roared in his ears. Then it was past.

He realized he was safe.

"Dino!" he yelled again.

Silence.

"Dino!"

He realized Dino wasn't there anymore. And then, with the force of the timber being shoved by the tug, he knew Dino had been killed.

"Oh Jesus—Dino!"

He treaded water, telling himself to save his breath and

strength. Now he was alone. The kid from Sorrento was gone, his body vanished in the waters. Terror clawed at him. Had he been crazy to try it?

But it was too late to turn back. He sank under the water again to relax for a few seconds, shocked into momentary immobility by the swift death of the young Italian. Then he surfaced again, filling his aching lungs with air and looking at New Jersey.

He was halfway there.

He started swimming again, his mind screaming *keep going, keep going.* Another twenty minutes dragged by, and he kept going, but his strength was going too.

I can make it, I can make it. . . .

The shore was nearing. He could see a dark dock now, and he headed for it.

I can make it, I can make it. . . .

It was then the first cramp seized him. He doubled over as pain grabbed his intestines, his head going under water. He panicked as he realized that until the cramp released him, he was trapped underwater. He tried to push his way up, but he was sinking, and he was beginning to choke for air. Then, just as quickly as it had struck, the cramp eased. Marco kicked with all his might, his lungs stabbing with pain. He rose toward the surface, but it seemed an eternity. Just as he started to choke, he broke through the water. He sucked his lungs full of precious, sweet air.

He knew it was now a race between him and the next cramp. He started swimming again. The dock seemed to creep toward him with agonizing slowness, but he thought if he could last twenty more feet, he was there.

I can make it, I can make it. . . .

Each stroke was torture now, each kick a test of will. The swim, which had seemed so easy in concept, was a nightmare in reality.

But there were only ten more feet, perhaps twenty more strokes. . . .

The second cramp hit him with the severity of whiplash. Again he went under, doubling over with pain. Again he panicked as his lungs emptied. Again his fatless body sank into the black water, down, down. . . . *Georgie* . . . The thought struck him that this blackness must be like her sightless world, that she would live

the rest of her days visually at the bottom of the ocean. *Georgie
... I'm going to die ... Georgie ... oh Jesus, give me AIR!*

The cramp eased. He started kicking, pushing his aching arms
against the water as he fought for the surface. *Air, air ... I'm a
second from death ... Air ... keep going ... air ... shit ...*
RISE! GO!

AIR!

He broke through just in time. Gasping, he started again
toward the dock.

When he finally grasped the bottom rung of the dock's ladder,
he thought, *Never again. They'll never throw me out again. I'll
never have to escape again. I'm going to beat this goddam country. I'm going to BEAT IT!*

He stole a pair of blue jeans from a clothesline. He had no
money and no shoes, but he was back in America. Money, he kept
thinking. They don't deport rich people. America is for the rich.
I've got to get money. . . .

He waited till dawn, then walked into Jersey City barefoot,
begged a nickel from a milkman and placed a call to Jake. Two
hours later, Jake pulled up in a taxi and Marco got in. Jake had
brought him clean clothes, his razor and toothbrush and three
hundred dollars. Marco told the cabbie to drive him to a cheap
hotel. "I'll hide out for a couple of weeks until Maud gets back," he
told Jake. "If I'm lucky, they'll think I drowned. And Jake, thanks
for your help. I'll never forget this." He took Jake's hand in both of
his and squeezed it. "You're the best friend I've ever had."

"Listen, this is a tough country we came to," said Jake. "You
helped me; I help you. That's what friends are for."

"I'll *never* forget," Marco repeated.

Money, he thought. *I've got to get rich. . . .*

Chapter 21

It is a curious fact that the man who glorified the American girl and elevated cheesecake to the level of an art form got his first success in show business by presenting the German strong man Sandow. In 1892, Florenz Ziegfeld, Jr., was sent to Europe by his father, Dr. Florenz Ziegfeld, the founder of the Chicago Musical College, to engage the famous German conductor Hans von Bülow to bring his Hamburg orchestra to Chicago the next year as a cultural attraction for the public at the Chicago World's Fair. Though Ziggy came from an intensely musical family, the dapper man with the long nose had little interest in music. To his father's dismay, Ziggy returned not with Hans von Bülow (whose wife, Cosima Liszt, had been seduced by Richard Wagner) but with the Von Bülow Marching Band (another Von Bülow) and Sandow. Ziggy pasted Sandow posters all over Chicago and brought the Hercules onstage wearing nothing but makeup and a strategically placed fig leaf. When Sandow lifted a piano player with one hand and the piano with his other, the crowd went crazy. When clever Ziggy induced the two leaders of Chicago society, Mrs. Potter Palmer and Mrs. George Pullman, to pay three hundred dollars apiece for the privilege of feeling Sandow's biceps, the story made every newspaper in America, and Ziggy's meteoric show business career—which was to prove a Comstock Lode for Broadway myth spinners—was launched.

His next triumph was to bring the diminutive Polish-French-Jewish chanteuse Anna Held to New York. Ziggy hinted to the press that the beautiful singer with the eighteen-inch waist was "vair-ee naugh-tee," and when Anna sang "Come Play Wiz Me," the temperature of male New Yorkers sizzled. Ziggy dreamed up one of the great publicity stunts of all time: He let it be known that a Brooklyn dairy was suing Miss Held for nonpayment on delivery of fifty cans of milk to her hotel every day. The press, naturally curious why anyone would want that much milk, flocked to her hotel, where they were told Miss Held took milk baths. This sensational news, so redolent of the most decadent days of the Roman Empire, made Anna Held a household word and sent hundreds of American women plunging into their milk-filled bathtubs.

Of course it was all a lie.

Ziggy fell in love with and married his French star. In 1907, he came up with the idea that put him in history books. He realized that if theater was a mirror reflecting its audiences, then the Broadway mirror was sadly distorted. Broadway shows were unsophisticated, the showgirls were bovine, and the sets and costumes tacky. The audience, on the other hand, was sophisticated and elegant. Ziggy decided to focus the mirror. He took over the roof of the New York Theater at Forty-fourth and Broadway and converted it into a simulacrum of a Parisian café, replete with bright awnings, plants and circus-colored canvas screens. At the time, New York theaters closed in the summer because of the heat, but Ziggy announced that his rooftop theater would be cooled by ocean breezes—a lie, because the place was closed in by a glass dome. On an extremely sticky July night, he opened the *Ziegfeld Follies of 1907*. It was a fast-paced revue (Ziggy first used the French spelling) consisting of comedy skits, songs and, of course, girls: sixty-four Anna Held Girls (who would later become the Ziegfeld Girls). The Follies were an instant hit and became an annual institution. Ziggy combed the country for the most beautiful girls he could find, and he found them. By 1910, the name Ziegfeld meant to the American public glamour, fabulous sets and costumes, and—the great showman's favorite word—pulchritude.

This was the extraordinary man who sat at one of the tables in the Jardin de Paris on the roof of the New York Theater one May morning in 1910 and listened to Nellie Byfield sing "By the Light of the Silvery Moon."

"I don't like her voice," said Ziggy to Nellie's agent, William Morris, "but she's beautiful. Ask her if she wants to be one of my chorus girls."

Nellie's response was to burst into tears and run off the stage.

"A chorus girl!" she ranted at Jake an hour later in her Sniffen Court living room. *"Me,* Nellie Byfield! Oh, I've never been so humiliated. Never!"

"Being a Ziegfeld Girl isn't exactly being a 'chorus girl' ..." Jake said, but she cut him off.

"I'm a *star* or I'm nothing!"

"But Nellie, a contract with Ziegfeld is something special. When he signed Fanny Brice, she was so excited she stood in Times Square all day showing her contract to everyone who went by."

"Fanny Brice doesn't have my class," she sniffed, starting to cry again. *"Damn* him! Everyone knows he has a tin ear. How *dare* he not like my voice? Who's Florenz Ziegfeld anyway?"

Jake came over and took her in his arms.

"You've got the most beautiful voice in New York," he soothed. "And I'll make sure it gets heard on Broadway—and in a Ziegfeld production, to boot."

"Oh, sure," she sniffed. "How? Wave a wand?"

"Ziegfeld is producing a new show called *Manhattan Merry-Go-Round.* He's asked me to write the score."

She looked at him. "Jake!" was all she managed to say.

"I'm signing the contract next week. Of course, Abe says Ziegfeld robs his writers blind, but still and all, doing a Ziegfeld show ..."

"Why didn't you *tell* me?" she almost screamed.

"I wanted you to audition on your own first. Now we know he likes your looks, and maybe I can push him a little about liking your voice. You'd be perfect for the lead."

"Oh Jake, I *adore* you!" She started covering his face with kisses. "You're the most wonderful songwriter in the world. I *adore* you."

"Will you marry me?"

She stopped kissing him. "Huh?"

"I said, will you marry me?"

She got up and went over to the piano.

"You're certainly full of surprises this morning."

"Nellie, you know I'm crazy about you.... Look, I bought a ring...."

He pulled a black box from his pocket and brought it to her. He opened it, and she looked at the square-cut diamond.

"Jake, it's beautiful. But . . ."

"But what? Don't you love me, Nellie?"

She hesitated. "I don't know. I . . . I never thought about *marriage*. In the first place, you're Jewish and I'm not. . . ."

"My father would kill me if he heard this, but we don't have to get married in a synagogue. We could have a civil ceremony. Please say yes, Nellie. I'll write you the best songs on Broadway."

"Are you negotiating me, Jake? Is it 'I'll write you the songs *if* you marry me'?"

Now it was his turn to hesitate.

"No," he finally said. "I'll write the songs for you no matter what. You know that. But if you're my wife . . ."

She took the ring out of the box and tried it on her finger. After examining it a moment, she said, "All right. You *are* negotiating me, but what the hell. Let's get married."

His face lit up.

"Nellie!"

He took her in his arms and kissed her.

"It had better be a *wonderful* score," was all she said.

Chapter 22

The north shore of Long Island, which a decade later Scott Fitzgerald would immortalize as East Egg, was already in 1910 being called the Gold Coast. The rich were pouring into the rural area, attracted by the lovely farmland and the magnificent harbors and coves so ideal for their favorite sport, yachting. Phipps Ogden, with his inherited sniff for real-estate trends, had jumped in early, in 1903 buying sixty rolling acres on Lloyd Neck overlooking Cold Spring Harbor and Long Island Sound. He hired the firm of Carrère and Hastings to design him a Georgian mansion, and a French landscape architect to lay out the gardens. Garden Court, as he named the place, rose in majestic splendor, costing over four million dollars exclusive of the furnishings. Situated on a hill overlooking the Sound, the house had a magnificent view of the water; yachtsmen on the Sound in turn saw one of the most imposing facades in America. The architects took their inspiration from Uppark in Sussex, England, which had been built by the first earl of Tankerville in 1690 (and where, at the end of the nineteenth century, H. G. Wells's mother was housekeeper). Garden Court had the same silvery-pink bricks as Uppark, the same restrained and handsome stone carvings as decoration on its pediments; but Carrère and Hastings added a four-columned portico that a purist would have condemned but which nevertheless gave the mansion a grandeur that worked.

On the main floor, a twenty-five-foot-high marble hall bisected the house, opening out to a terrace at the rear and, beyond, the formal gardens that were one of the wonders of the country. Off the central hall was a main salon that would not have looked out of place in Buckingham Palace, a ballroom, a dining room that could comfortably seat sixty, a library containing Phipps's collection of incunabula and his First Folio, a conservatory, a music room replete with a pipe organ, a morning room and the usual kitchen rooms. Upstairs were two master bedroom suites and eight guest apartments, as they were casually called. On the third floor were twenty-five servants' rooms.

As if this were not enough, past the ten-car garage Phipps built a "playhouse," which contained a hundred-foot indoor pool, four indoor tennis courts, two squash courts, a complete gymnasium and an exotic addition copied from baths he had enjoyed on his Scandinavian travels, a sauna. Beyond the playhouse were the stables, for Phipps's daughter, Vanessa, was an avid equestrienne. Then there was the immense greenhouse, and a charming Grecian-style pavilion. On the Sound, a pier serviced Phipps's yacht, which he often moored in Cold Spring Harbor—that is, the steam yacht, the 180-foot *North Star,* which could accommodate sixteen and which had transported Phipps and Maud to Europe on their honeymoon. His sailing yacht, a sleek sixty-foot sloop named the *Sprite,* he moored at the nearby Seawanaka-Corinthian Yacht Club, where his burgee fluttered alongside those of Roosevelts, Vanderbilts and Morgans. To maintain this princely style, Phipps employed almost a hundred people—there were fourteen full-time gardeners alone—which made him something of a one-man industry.

It was this regal establishment that Maud had become the mistress of when she married the senator and became the second Mrs. Ogden; and it was to this Xanadu that Marco came one hot July day in 1910. When he had called Maud the day before from his hideout hotel in Jersey City, he hadn't been sure what his reception would be. After all, he was a potential embarrassment to the new Mrs. Ogden. Furthermore, he had turned down her offer of a paid education—just as, years before in Calabria, he had turned down her offer to hire him as her chauffeur—and now to come back a second time, hat in hand . . . It would certainly be understandable if she told him to go to hell.

On the contrary, she had been delighted to hear from him, and when he said he was having second thoughts about her offer, she had said, "It's about time you got some sense. Come out tomorrow and we'll discuss it."

He walked down the path through formal gardens that were in their full summer glory, gaping at the rose bushes and the splashing fountains, gawking at the immensity of Garden Court, which loomed before him, marveling at this display of enormous wealth. *Do people really live this way?* he wondered, remembering the poverty he had come from, the stench of steerage, the squalor of the Cherry Street tenement. No wonder Maud had married Phipps Ogden so fast!

He felt envy waking in his soul.

The door was opened by Yates, the butler, who was expecting him. He led Marco down the marble central hall, past the pipe organ, the console of which was recessed in a wall, past the Gainsborough portrait of the Duchess of Devonshire, past the Constable landscape, to the library, where he knocked, opened the door and intoned, "Mr. Santorelli."

It was the first time Marco had ever heard his name announced by a butler. He liked the feeling.

He went into the library, taking in quickly the ceiling-high bookshelves encased in elaborately carved walnut and fronted with handsome bronze grills, the rich Persian rug, the leather armchairs by the marble fire, the eighteenth-century standing globe, the Georgian desk with its green leather top, the two small aquarelle landscape sketches by Watteau. Maud and Phipps were standing by the windows, chatting as they looked out on the Sound. Maud turned. She was wearing a white summer dress, and Marco thought that marriage to the multimillionaire seemed to agree with her. She looked wonderful. "Marco," she said, coming to him, her hand extended. "It's good to see you. Phipps, this is Marco."

After she took Marco's hand, she led him to her husband. The senator was wearing white duck trousers and a blue blazer with the Seawanaka-Corinthian Yacht Club burgee stitched on the breast pocket. He looked Marco over for a moment, rather coolly, Marco thought; then he pulled his hand from his pocket and extended it.

"Maud has told me about you," he said, shaking Marco's hand. Marco thought he was forcing his politeness. "She told me about your—shall we say unpleasantness?—with the Immigration Service. I know Casey O'Donnell, who is no friend of mine. He and his Irish hack friends are mixed up with half the trashy deals in New York. I wouldn't put it past him to pull a stunt like the one he pulled on you. Happily, the head of the Immigration Service is a friend of mine, and I'm sure I can straighten things out with him."

"That would be wonderful, sir," said Marco.

"Yates will show you your room," said Maud.

"My room?"

"Of course. You can't go back to your apartment until Phipps has got you 'unported,' or whatever the word is, so you might as well stay here. Don't worry, there's *plenty* of room. And then, too, we must discuss your education. Lunch is at one. We'll see you then."

"Yes . . . thank you." He turned to Phipps, who was still watching him. "And it's been nice meeting you, sir."

Phipps said nothing until Marco had left the library. Then he lit a cigarette.

"An interesting young man," he remarked casually. "And extremely good-looking."

"Yes, isn't he? Marco's a definite pleasure to look at."

"Is that why you've taken so much interest in him? Because you like to look at him?"

"Perhaps. I probably wouldn't if he were a hunchback."

"Was he your lover?"

Maud looked surprised. "What a crude suggestion!"

"*Was* he?"

She smiled. "I think we're about to have our first quarrel. How delicious! Yes, if you must know, he was. I hope you're not going to get pompous."

"And you expect me to educate your former lover? I think you're expecting a bit much, Maud. I know there have been many men in your life—I'm no idiot. But if I have to start educating them, even *I* may go broke."

She laughed as she came to him.

"Darling, you *are* a funny man! No, you don't have to educate them, *or* him. I'll pay for it. But be nice to him. He's really a sweet thing, and he reminds me of Italy and glorious sunshine and a lot of things I love. So be nice to him. Will you?"

She took his hand.

"I will if I don't have to worry about you and him doing something behind my back. This isn't Europe, you know, and it's certainly not Italy. This is America. I'm a politician and I have to keep up a clean front for the voters. Will I have to worry about him?"

She kissed his cheek.

"No. I've got you now. And don't worry: I like being Mrs. Phipps Ogden, the wife of New York's senior—and most dashing—senator." She smoothed his lapel. "I have no intention of losing you. But I would like to help Marco. Let's say I've made him my private charity project. And think of all those millions of Italian voters who are pouring into New York. Don't you think they'd vote for a senator who had had the decency to take in a poor Italian immigrant?"

Phipps laughed. "Maud, I should make you my campaign manager. All right, I'll be good to Marco. There's a cram school outside Philadelphia that could get him ready for college in a couple of years if he has any brains and is willing to work day and night. I'll call the headmaster and see if we can get Marco in. You know, I should be terribly annoyed with you for corrupting young gardeners."

"Are you?"

"Yes."

He took her in his arms and kissed her, passionately.

"Don't do it again," he whispered, "or I'll kill you. You're *mine*, Maud. God damn you, you've bewitched me."

She purred.

True to his bargain with Nellie, Jake launched a campaign to get her the lead role in *Manhattan Merry-Go-Round*, but it was no easy task. Ziegfeld admitted Nellie had the looks, but he was stubborn about her voice and no amount of pleading or cajoling on Jake's part seemed to move him. Meanwhile, Jake coached Nellie, teaching her the songs as he wrote them. The gossamer plot of the show dealt with a pretty trapeze artist who went through a series of romantic entanglements, finally having to choose between a handsome lion tamer and a Fifth Avenue playboy. Jake persuaded Nellie to hire a circus performer to teach her the rudiments of trapezery so she could wow Ziggy if and when her moment came. She obeyed, but Ziggy remained adamant. The truth was, he wanted the part to go to his mistress, the beautiful, if feckless, Lillian Lorraine. But a week before rehearsals began, Lillian decamped with a handsome millionaire—thus proving that life can be like musical comedy plots—plunging Ziggy into despair but forcing him to find a replacement. There was Jake, with Nellie in tow. He brought her to Ziggy's suite in the Ansonia wrapped in a cloak. When she removed her cloak to reveal herself in a trapeze costume, Ziggy took one look at her sensational legs and began to see the light.

Nellie got the part. Rehearsals went amazingly smoothly, and the word along Broadway was that *Merry-Go-Round* was going to be a smash and that Jake Rubin's score was one of the best in years. Opening night was September 22, 1910, at the Maxine Elliott Theater. The auguries continued good: opening night sold out, sublime fall weather; the cast's hopes were high. Then, one hour before curtain time, Nellie became hysterical.

"I can't do it!" she cried in her dressing room, which Jake had filled with flowers for the occasion. "I'll be *awful!*"

Jake hugged her.

"Nellie, it's just nerves. . . ."

"I *know* it's nerves! Of *course* I'm nervous. *Everybody's* nervous opening night. But I have *reason* to be. Oh God, I can't remember the words. . . . Jake, I can't do it. I *can't!* I'll be awful. . . ."

She sobbed on his shoulder. Abe Shulman, his hands in his pockets, rolled his eyes.

"Oy," was all he said.

"I'm going to be sick . . ." she gasped, pushing Jake away and running to the bathroom. She slammed the door and they heard her retching.

"She's going to be wonderful," said Jake, rubbing his hands nervously. "I know she is. . . . It's just nerves. . . ."

"Oy."

More retching.

"The great Broadway star," said Abe, "tossing her bagels. It's elegant as all shit."

Jake turned on him. "You might be more sympathetic!"

Abe shrugged. "I've seen this opening night crap before. Don't worry, Nellie will be all right. She's a killer. She'll kill *you* if you don't watch out."

"What do you mean?"

Again Abe shrugged. "She's got you wrapped around her pinkie. You follow her around with your tongue hanging out, like some love-sick puppy. You're a shmuck."

"Goddammit, Abe, mind your own business. . . ." Jake started shouting when the bathroom door reopened, a pale Nellie emerged, and Jake turned to her. "Nellie, honey, are you all right?"

"I'm fine," she said, coolly. She sat down at her dressing table and looked at herself in the mirror. Slowly, she picked up a puff and began powdering her nose. "I'm going to be wonderful tonight," she said. "Tonight's going to be a night they'll talk about for years."

Abe looked at Jake and nodded, as if to say, See? Did I tell you? She's a killer.

Nellie's crystal ball was clear. People did talk about that night for years. The show was a smash. The audience laughed at the silly plot, adored Jake's music and lyrics, and fell in love with Nellie, who gave the performance of her life. Jake stood in the wings applauding and cheering, watching Nellie take one curtain call after another. He was drunk with Nellie, and tonight his intoxication was at its peak. As proud as he was of his own achievement, the fact that the woman he worshiped had been made a star singing his songs made him almost burst. Jake was flying.

Afterward, Ziggy took the entire cast, crew and orchestra to Jack Rumsey's 60 Club in the Astor Hotel on Times Square. The 60 Club was restricted to people in the theater, and to be invited to join it meant you had arrived in show business. The club had a grand staircase which actresses used to make dramatic entrances (and, often, drunken exits), and as Jake led Nellie down the stair, she basked in the applause that greeted her.

"It's happened," she said to Jake. "I'm a star!"

"Don't let it go to your head," kidded Jake.

"Why not?" she replied, and she wasn't kidding.

Now the money was rolling in. With Nellie's success, Ziggy generously doubled her salary to $1500 a week; Jake's royalties brought him almost twice that much, and it was all tax-free. Nellie, the passionate shopper, went on a spree, buying herself a floor-length sable coat and a Pierce Arrow town car which, on a whim, she had painted white. Jake, more conservative, banked his money and began pressing Nellie to live up to her end of the bargain and set a date for the wedding. Nellie dragged her feet, dreaming up excuses that drove Jake to the edge of despair; to make her his wife had become a fixation. Finally, a month after the opening night, he confronted her in her Sniffen Court living room.

"You're cheating me, Nellie," he said, "and I don't understand why. Are you trying to tell me you don't want to marry me?"

She sighed. "All right, it's time we had this out in the open. I'll admit I haven't been fair to you. The trouble is, you say you want a lot of children. Jake, I don't want to have any—at least for a long time."

"No children?" he said, disbelievingly. "Why? Don't you like them?"

"Not particularly. I'm not the maternal type. And it would mean getting fat and ugly. . . . Jake, I'm on top now! I'm a star. It's what I've dreamed of all my life. It would kill me to have to give it all up, just so I could have some red-faced, bawling brat."

He sat next to her.

"You wouldn't be permanently fat, and you could never be ugly. All we're talking about is maybe three or four months away from the stage—it's crazy to say you're giving it up. Other actresses have children."

"See? I *knew* you'd say that. I just don't want children, period. I saw what it did to my mother, who had eight. She was an old woman by the time she was thirty and dead by thirty-seven."

"Who's talking about *eight*? I'm talking about two or three."

He slipped his arm around her waist and pulled her to him to kiss her. After a moment she said, "All right: *one*. After *Merry-Go-Round* closes, we'll have one baby. But that's it, Jake. I'm not going to turn into a baby-factory for *any* man."

"You might like it."

"Don't get your hopes up. Is that a deal, Jake? *One?*"

He hesitated. "If I say yes, can we set a date to get married?"

"We can get married tomorrow as far as I'm concerned."

"Then I say yes."

He knew he could talk her into more later on. The important thing now was to get married. Despite the glamorous, loose-morals show world he had become a part of, Jake was still extremely old-world and conservative. In his bones, he felt his sleeping with Nellie was wrong.

He didn't want a mistress; he wanted a wife.

"Shmuck," said Abe Shulman the next day in his office. "Why marry her when you're already sleeping with her?"

Jake tried to hold his temper.

"Abe, two things have got to change if you and I are going to stay in business. First, you have to stop calling me a shmuck. This shmuck is now the hottest songwriter on Broadway. Second, you have to start treating Nellie with respect. I know you don't like her, but she's going to be my wife."

Abe sucked on his cigar. "All right, you're not a shmuck. But let me tell you something as a friend, Jake. You're making a mistake marrying a *shiksa*. Marry one of your own kind."

Jake's face turned red, not from anger but from embarrassment. He might have retained his old-world morality, but he knew he had betrayed his religion.

"That's crazy," he mumbled.

"What's so crazy?"

"This isn't the old world, this is the *new*. I'm an American—or at least I will be. I can marry anyone I want. Nellie and I have agreed to have a civil ceremony."

Abe flicked his cigar ash. "America's a little over a hundred years old," he said. "We Jews have been around five thousand years."

"So what? I'm in love with Nellie! I don't care *what* church she goes to. My God, Abe, you're a worse bigot than the Tsar—except you're a bigot in reverse."

"Have it your way." Abe shrugged. "But five thousand years is a long time to throw out the window."

"I don't know what you're talking about," growled Jake.

But he knew.

They were married November tenth in the 60 Club, and Jake, who paid for everything, made it lavish. Nellie's streetcar-conductor father and her seven siblings gawked at the show business celebrities, the cases of champagne and the five-foot-high wedding cake topped by a treble clef sign made out of icing. Nellie looked beautiful in a spectacular wedding dress Ziggy had had designed for her which included a twelve-foot-long veil that one of the waiters stepped on and almost pulled off. Jake—still thin but not quite so hungry-looking anymore—came close to dashing in a trim suit of tails. His wedding present to his bride was a diamond and pearl necklace with a ruby clasp. Included among the hundred guests were Fanny Brice, Victor Herbert, Lillian Lorraine, the Castles, Ethel and John Barrymore, Nora Bayes, the playwright Ned Sheldon, Diamond Jim Brady and Lillian Russell.

As Jake kissed his bride, he told himself he was the luckiest man in the world.

But a five-thousand-year-old voice whispered in his mind, *Shmuck, you've made a mistake.*

PART VI
Vanessa

Chapter 23

The seventeen-year-old boy in the football jersey tossed the pass to Pete Johnson, who ran down the field and caught it.

"Not bad!" yelled Eddie Forbes, who was also seventeen and whose father owned the Forbes Oil Equipment Company of Altoona, Pennsylvania. Eddie had flunked out of Choate. Pete Johnson, whose father was a real-estate developer in Chicago, had flunked out of Exeter.

Now Pete threw the football back to Eddie, who ran to catch the pass. It was five o'clock of an October afternoon. The small campus of Bryant Academy, north of Philadelphia, was resplendent in its autumn foliage, the red and gold leaves framing the six brick buildings that comprised the physical facilities of the private cram school where a faculty of eighteen masters tried to stuff enough learning into the heads of the fifty-three students for them to get into college. A few of the boys were genuinely stupid. Most of them, like Eddie and Pete, were fun-loving athletes who had no interest in books and whose fathers' fortunes guaranteed them a secure future, at the same time depriving them of any incentive to learn. Their parents considered Bryant a place to keep them out of trouble. The boys considered Bryant a place to try to cause trouble. No one took it very seriously.

Eddie fumbled the ball. As he picked it up, he saw a man in a sweater carrying his books toward his dormitory. Eddie knew this was one student who *did* take Bryant seriously.

"Hey, Marco," he yelled, tossing him the football. "You

catch-a the football, eh? You play Americano game, no?"

Marco saw the ball sailing toward him. He tried to catch it with his one free hand, but failed. The ball bounced on the ground and hit a tree.

"Throw it back, Marco," yelled Eddie. "Be a good dago. Throw it back."

"We give-a you extra spaghetti for dinner," yelled Pete Johnson. They both laughed.

Marco put his books on the ground, went over to the tree, picked up the ball and threw it to Eddie.

"Not bad!" yelled Eddie, jumping to catch it. "You got a pretty good arm. Can you kick? Try a kick."

He kicked the football back to Marco, who caught it.

"Kick! Go on! All-American game, football. You gotta learn how to kick."

Marco, who had watched a few games on the campus, tried to imitate what he had seen. He held the football out, dropped it, then kicked. The ball went straight up over his head into the tree, where it bounced around in the branches, then fell back down, narrowly missing his head. Eddie and Pete howled with laughter.

"Hey! What-a goes up gotta come-a down, eh, Marco?"

Marco said nothing. He threw the ball back, picked up his books and continued on to his dormitory.

Wise-ass little shits, he thought.

"Hey Eddie," yelled Pete, "why do Italians start school when they're twenty-two?"

"Because it takes them two years to learn how to walk and twenty years to learn how to push a pushcart."

More howls of laughter.

The little shits. I'd like to kill them.

Besides, it's a dumb joke.

Marco took Bryant seriously because now he had made the great commitment of his life: After having failed at everything he tried in America, he was going to get an education or die trying. Besides, he owed his best efforts to Phipps Ogden. To Marco's surprise, the senator had insisted on footing the bills for his education, buying him clothes and books and throwing in a generous pocket-money allowance to boot. Admittedly, the money meant nothing to Phipps. In his more cynical moments, Marco wondered if perhaps this wasn't the easiest, most gentlemanly way for Phipps to get the younger man out of his—and Maud's—life. Whatever his motives, Phipps had been generous, and Marco had no intention of letting him down, or himself either. Being so much older than the other students made him feel self-conscious and a little ridiculous, and their unending taunts burned him, but he told himself to ignore it all. He'd have the last laugh when he got into a college—something these ball-tossing cretins would probably never achieve (not that they cared).

Further, he found he enjoyed studying. The challenge of books was waking up his unused mind. In the seven weeks he had been at Bryant, he was beginning to feel he was making progress. The faculty—in particular the supportive headmaster, Dr. Hill—took an interest in his unusual case, and when they saw that Marco meant business, they psychologically pitched in on his side. After hundreds of spoiled rich kids, an Italian peasant who had come through Ellis Island and was now trying to get into college was a refreshing change. Everyone wanted Marco to make it.

Everyone except his classmates.

He missed Georgie. As soon as his problems with Immigration had been cleared up by Phipps and it was safe for him to contact Georgie, he had called her to tell her where he was and that he was all right. Georgie had been sick with worry for his safety, because Dino's body had floated ashore; he had been almost sliced in two by the tug's propellor. When Marco told her what Phipps was doing for him, they both agreed that Bryant Academy and marriage were incompatible, and Georgie urged him again to get the education; she would wait for him. Intellectually, he knew she was right, but his heart hated to leave her. The years of schooling yawned before him, coldly and rather forbiddingly. He wanted Georgie, physically and emotionally. He missed the fun of taking her to the movies more than he imagined possible. He loved her, loved being with her, and it took all his concentration to push her out of his thoughts as he studied. At night he lay awake thinking of Georgie and wondering if he wouldn't be happier driving trucks, coming home at night to the woman he loved.

But then he remembered swimming away from Ellis Island, and his determination to acquire the security of money reasserted itself.

He and Georgie and love would have to wait.

Two nights after the football incident, Marco was struggling with math problems in his small room. It had turned unseasonably warm, and his window was open. Since he had never had any math at all, the math teacher, Mr. Higgins, was giving him a crash course, trying to get him through basic arithmetic, geometry and algebra all in one year—no easy task, admittedly, and one that Marco was finding particularly difficult. He was wrestling with long division when he heard an organ-grinder outside his window. Then two voices started bawling "Santa Lucia."

Marco got up from his desk and went to the window. His room was on the second floor. On the lawn below, Eddie Forbes and Pete Johnson were singing, Pete grinding the organ. Both had tied red bandanas around their throats. A dozen other students were with them. When they spotted Marco in the window, they started cheering and clapping, chanting: "Garibaldi, tutti-frutti, mama mia! Garibaldi, tutti-frutti, mama mia!"

Marco slammed the window shut, returned to his desk and tried to focus his mind on long division. *Ignore them,* he told himself. But the music and noise couldn't be ignored.

Pushing his book away, he went back to the window and threw it open.

"Goddammit, shut *up!*" he roared.

"Garibaldi, tutti-frutti, mama mia! Garibaldi, tutti-frutti, mama mia!"

"You cretins don't give a damn about college, but *I* do!"

"Garibaldi, tutti-frutti, mama mia! Garibaldi, tutti-frutti, mama mia!"

Again he slammed the window and sat down on his cot, grinding his teeth with frustration.

Keep cool, he told himself. *Be smart. You're smarter than they are. Think of a way to shut them up. There must be a way . . .*

Suddenly, it occurred to him.

The next Saturday he walked to the nearby village and bought himself a football and a pair of football shoes. He tramped into the woods till he found a clearing. He put on the football shoes, stood up and kicked the football.

I'll beat the little bastards at their own game, he told himself.

208

All it takes is determination, and by Christ, have I got determi-nation!

Four afternoons later he went to the school's football field, where the varsity team was practicing. He watched until the squad took a break. Then he walked over to Pete Johnson. Point-ing to the football, he said in a grotesque Italian accent, "Ees-a great American game, no?"

Pete laughed. *"Si, signor."*

"I try-a keek once?"

"Sure, go ahead. Just don't lose the ball in a tree."

Marco walked onto the field and picked up the ball. He went to the thirty-yard line as Pete shouted, "Hey, guys, it's the great Roman football star!" The rest of the team turned to watch. Marco faced the goal, then kicked. The ball sailed beautifully into the air and went between the goal posts.

The boys stared in amazement. Marco walked off the field.

"It's sort of a dumb game," he commented to Pete.

"Hey, wait a minute! Marco—that was fantastic. Wait a min-ute!"

Marco smiled to himself as he continued walking, ignoring their shouts.

The next day the coach asked him to join the squad. Marco declined, telling him his studies were more important than foot-ball.

The coach could hardly believe his ears.

Chapter 24

The dining room at Garden Court was almost unbelievably sump-tuous. The entire room had been transported from France—where it had been designed in 1756 for a château near Cahors—and in-stalled in the Long Island house of Phipps Ogden. The cream and gilt paneling was delicately carved with a curvilinear motif of shells, plant tendrils and birds which framed the four tall mirrors and the overdoors, eighteenth-century copies of Raphael's paintings in the Vatican Apartments. In front of each of the four mirrors was a gilt and marble-topped console table with a huge white and blue Ming vase on top. The elaborately carved ceiling arched thirty feet over the parquet floor, and a crystal chandelier still burned candles, Phipps having refused to electrify it. Four window bays, facing the mirrors, looked over Long Island Sound, and on Thanksgiving Day that year, snow flurries were swirling over the water as the five guests of Phipps and Maud sat down for a turkey dinner that was as American as the dining room was French.

The guests were Phipps's older sister, Edwina Vaughn, and her archaeologist husband, Dr. Emmet Vaughn; Vanessa; the Comte de Saint-Denis, a young French aristocrat whom Phipps and Maud were trying to get Vanessa interested in; and Marco, who had been asked to Garden Court for the Thanksgiving holiday. Four footmen served the turkey, the creamed onions, the mashed potatoes, the peas, the buttered carrots, the hot biscuits and the chestnut stuffing; they also poured the Louis Roederer Cristal. But even the excellent champagne failed to put much fizz into the lunch. The Comte de Saint-Denis's English was mangled to the point of absurdity, and Vanessa said hardly a word, sneaking glances across the table at Marco, to whom she had been introduced before lunch. Finally, Edwina Vaughn, who was gray-haired, tweedy and matronly, turned to Marco and said in her formidably upper-class accent, "Do you ride?"

Marco looked at her, completely taken aback.

"No," he said, "but I used to plow."

Maud laughed as Edwina cleared her throat.

"Yes, of course. How silly of me. But so many of us *do* ride around here. Vanessa, for instance, is almost inseparable from her horse." Edwina turned to François-Marie Hubert de Longueville, the Comte de Saint-Denis, who was in the house mainly with the hope of snagging Vanessa's fortune. "François, you must get Vanessa to show you some of her clay figurines. She's really *terribly* artistic." The count was looking so blank that she switched to north-shore Long Island French. *"Ma nièce est une femme sculpteur."*

"Ah!" said François, finally seeing the conversational light. He turned to Vanessa. "You are like Rodin?"

"Hardly."

"I would like to see."

"Phipps has built her a little studio in the playhouse," said Edwina. "Her figurines are so charming. Vanessa, dear, take François out after lunch and show him."

"My studio is very private," said Vanessa. "I prefer to keep it that way."

"Oh well, the poor child is modest," said Edwina, giving up on Vanessa. "But she *really* is gifted."

Marco noticed Vanessa sneaking curious glances at him across the table.

"We hear in Washington," said Maud, "that President Taft has put on more weight. One would think that a country as powerful as America deserves an attractive President."

"I fear your political views are rather superficial, Maud," said Edwina. "I'll take Taft over Teddy any day. Just imagine: a Roosevelt—and a *neighbor!*—attacking big business! Shocking."

"Don't you think big business deserves to be attacked, Aunt Edwina?" asked Vanessa, putting down her fork. "After all, most big businessmen are greedy pigs who don't care that millions of the poor live in obscene slums." She looked at Marco. "Father told me that you came from the slums. Tell Aunt Edwina what they were like."

"Van," said her father, "I don't think Thanksgiving lunch is an appropriate time to discuss the slums."

"But why not? We have everything to give thanks for. The poor have nothing. I think we should spend at least a *few* minutes thinking about them. It might do us some good. Tell them, Marco. Tell them about the slums."

Tense silence. All eyes were on Marco.

"The only thing I'll say about the slums," he remarked, "is that they're a good place to get away from."

"But that's not *describing* them," she insisted. "Tell us about the stench and the filth and the cockroaches. . . ."

"Oh," groaned Edwina.

"VAN!" Her father almost shouted. "That's enough! If you're so in love with the slums, go *live* in them. I'll be delighted to pay your rent. Meanwhile, we are *trying* to enjoy our meal."

"All right, Father. But we can't just *ignore* the poor."

The lunch continued. Edwina, desperate to make conversation, turned to the Frenchman.

"Do *you* ride, François?"

"I beg your pardon?" François had understood practically nothing of what Vanessa said.

"*Chevauchez-vous?*"

He smiled. "Ah! Horse! *Oui,* I like to ride."

Marco was eying Vanessa, thinking she was a very strange girl indeed.

After lunch, coffee was poured in the drawing room.

"Do you show your sculptures to *no* one?" Marco asked Vanessa as he brought her a cup.

She hesitated. "Well, just to *certain* people." She added in a whisper, "I can't stand François, but if *you'd* like to see them, I'll show you."

"I'd like to very much."

"Then come out to the playhouse after I leave. My studio's at the far end of the pool."

The playhouse, thought Marco. *Sounds like fun.*

The playhouse was, like everything in Phipps's world, out of human scale: the indoor pool was Olympic-sized and surrounded by Roman statues of undraped goddesses, while at one end a big marble frog squirted water out of its mouth into the pool. As Marco walked down the side, an idea began nibbling at his brain. It was an idea he didn't like, but it fascinated him....

Vanessa opened the door of her studio when he knocked. She smiled at him.

"Come in. This used to be a potting shed, but when Father built the greenhouse, he let me have this. Not that he approves of my sculpting—he really doesn't. But then he disapproves of a lot of things I do and say."

Marco followed her into the room. On one side was a big, paned window with a simple white café curtain over the lower half. There was a long wooden shelf across the opposite wall on which were several clay animal figures, a pile of sculpting clay, burins, sketch pads and a gas burner with a tin coffeepot on it.

"I love to sketch," she said. "I spend hours out here."

"Then this is more than a hobby?"

"Oh, it's a *passion*. I want to be a professional sculptress one day. But it takes a lot of hard work. I go into the city twice a week to take life classes, and I'm studying anatomy." She hesitated. "I hope I didn't embarrass you at lunch, asking you to talk about the slums."

"You didn't embarrass *me,* but you embarrassed everyone else."

"Oh, well, it's good for them. I love Father, but politically he's a mossback and a tool of the big business interests. He needs to be shaken up every once in a while."

"I think there's more to it than that. I think you enjoy the attention."

She laughed. "Oh, well, I suppose there's a little of that, too. You're very observant." She hesitated. "May I ask you a rude question?"

"Sure."

"Why is Maud so interested in you?"

She leaned back against the shelf, watching him.

"I used to work for her in Italy."

"Yes, I know." She ran her eyes up and down him. "I don't particularly like her, but I've made my peace with her because she makes Father happy, and that's the important thing. Do you mind if I ask you a *really* rude question?"

"Go ahead."

"Did she ever . . . well, do you think she was ever interested in you romantically?"

"Maud? Of course not. She's a lady. I'm a nobody."

"Ladies have been interested in nobodies before. I read about a very rich woman last week—*terribly* social, my dear—who ran off with her groom."

Marco shrugged. "That happens. But not Maud."

"Well, then, I misjudged her. Anyway, here are some of my animal figures. They're very simple, but I love animals. Here's a rabbit I did."

She handed him the figurine, which was well done. He inspected it.

"It's very good."

"No it's not, but it's a start. This is a dog I did, which is much better. Are you staying here the entire weekend?"

"Well, I'm going into New York tonight to take a friend of mine to the movies. She's blind, and I tell her the plots."

"What a wonderful thing to do!"

"We both love the movies."

"Well, I don't. It's just another way to exploit the poor."

He couldn't believe his ears.

"*Exploit* them? Are you crazy? They *love* them!"

"Well ..." She backed off. "You wouldn't understand."

"Why wouldn't I? I was poor. I still am."

She looked a little embarrassed. "You must resent us very much," she said.

"Why would I resent you? Your father's paying for my education."

"But I mean ... Father has so much ... *too* much, in my opinion. That really doesn't bother you?"

"No."

She looked baffled, then shook her head.

"Maybe I could learn a lot from you." She hesitated. "Will you be coming here Christmas?"

"I don't know. Nobody's said anything about it."

"Oh, you *must* come Christmas, because Father always takes his Christmas cruise on the *North Star*. And while I don't approve of yachts, I have to admit it's a lot of fun."

"Where does he go?"

"Down to the islands. You know, the Bahamas, Jamaica. It's gorgeous. We live on the yacht and swim and fish. . . . You'd love it. I'll tell Father to invite you, if you promise to come."

Marco was inspecting the clay dog.

"Oh, I'll come," he said. "I'd love to. Who wouldn't?"

So much for Georgie this Christmas, he thought. *Marco, you shit.*

Roscoe Haines felt like a human being in France, for the French considered black people exotics rather than inferiors. Flora had been a great success in Paris singing Jake's songs, and she and Roscoe were hired by the owner of a small boîte called Le Chat Qui Rit. Roscoe played, Flora sang and the black couple packed them in. They rented an apartment on the Left Bank,

214

began learning French, and after several months Roscoe said, "You know something? You boss me around so much, you might as well be my wife."

Flora looked at him.

"Was that some sort of half-ass proposal?"

He grinned. "That proposal was *full* ass."

They took a week off for a honeymoon, rented a car and drove out into the Seine Valley northwest of Paris where, outside Les Andelys, their employer owned a charming millhouse, which he lent them. The mill had been built before the French Revolution and was situated beside a stream that turned the mill wheel, then splashed merrily over a low dam on its way to the nearby Seine.

"If this ain't rural charm," said Roscoe, getting out of the car, "ain't nothin' ever gonna be."

The flowered fields by the stream, the herd of cows, the small stone château on the opposite side of the road: In truth, it was all lovely beyond belief, and on their second day Flora prepared a picnic, which they ate in the field opposite the mill, drinking Muscadet and tossing bread crusts at the cows.

"This is livin'," said Roscoe as he lay back in the grass.

"Is it?" said Flora, sticking the empty wine bottle back in the wicker picnic basket.

He looked at her.

"What's wrong with *you*? Fields, cows, millhouse, good wine—what more do you want?"

"I miss New York."

He looked disgusted. "Don't start *that* again."

"Well, I do. How long are we going to stay in Paris? We don't make any plans; we just drift."

"There's a lot to be said for driftin'."

"And you've said it *all*! Now that we're married, I think it's time we started making some plans."

"Phew! I *knew* I shouldn't have proposed. Honey, you can plan all you want, but nothin's gonna get Roscoe Haines back to New York. I like *la belle France*."

She gave him a dry look as she put the rest of the picnic back in the basket.

"We'll see," was all she said.

* * *

The millhouse had a Pleyel spinet whose date of manufacture, painted on the inside, was 1854. It was out of tune, but on the third day of their honeymoon Flora heard Roscoe picking out a melody. She came from the kitchen into the low-ceilinged living room, where Roscoe was seated at the Pleyel.

"What's that you're playing?" she asked.

"Do you like it?"

"It's sort of catchy. Is it yours?"

"Uh huh."

She came over to the piano.

"Roscoe, why don't you ever write these things down? Some of your tunes are good."

He turned to her, putting his arms around her waist.

"Cause, A, I ain't got no lyricist. And B, this is our honeymoon, and I don't work on my honeymoon."

"We could find you a lyricist."

He pinched her, then got up to go over to the window and look out at the mill wheel. She watched him for a moment.

"Well?" she said. "We *could* find you a lyricist, particularly if we went back to New York."

He laughed. "Boy, you don't miss a chance, do you? No thanks, baby. I'll leave the songwritin' to Jake Rubin. He's got the talent."

"But so do you! At least you should *try.*"

He turned on her. "Hey, Flora, baby, you're forgettin' we're *black* folk. We're shiftless and lazy and no-good, so don't try and reform *me.*"

"Well, *I'm* not shiftless and lazy and no-good!" she said angrily. "But you sure as hell could get the shiftless and lazy prize *this* week. The problem with you is you use your color as an *excuse.* If you'd stop bein' a black man and start bein' a human bein', you just might surprise yourself!"

And she stormed back into the kitchen, leaving Roscoe alone, a look of amazement on his face.

"Shit," he muttered.

After a moment he wandered back to the piano. He stood in front of it, staring at the keyboard.

But he didn't sit down.

Chapter 25

Phipps's luxurious yacht, the *North Star,* embarked for the Caribbean the morning of December 10 with a party of five: Phipps, Maud, Phipps's sister Edwina, Vanessa and Marco. No sooner did the yacht leave Long Island Sound than it hit rough seas. Edwina had come along to join her husband, who was on a dig in the Yucatan, and she was the first to retire to her cabin with, as she called it, *mal de mer.* She was soon followed by Phipps and Maud; but Marco, whose immunity to seasickness had been proven on the *Kronprinz Friedrich,* felt no discomfort and he was free to explore the floating private palace.

It was certainly a far cry from steerage. Built six years before by the Belfast firm of Harland and Wolff—who were beginning work on the White Star Line's opulent liner *Titanic*—the *North Star* incorporated the best and most up-to-date engineering and equipment. Its sleek white hull, two masts and single stack gave it a look of almost rakish elegance, and its two engines could make eighteen knots. Carrying 270 tons of coal, it could steam nonstop for 5,500 nautical miles, enabling Phipps to go anywhere in the world. Its gleaming galley was run by a fat, bearded Lyonnais named Edmond Castre, who had trained under the great Escoffier himself, and whose staff of six could prepare anything from simple beach picnics to elaborate eight-course banquets. Its temperature-controlled wine bin stored a thousand bottles of wine, including fifty bottles of 1894 Château d'Yquem, Phipps's favorite, and two hundred bottles of Louis Roederer Cristal. Its main saloon was paneled in Circassian walnut; its dining room was furnished with Louis XV reproductions; its library, containing five hundred books, had a marble mantel over a fake fireplace; and its ten staterooms ranged from the magnificent (Phipps's and Maud's) to the simple (Marco's). The yacht had cost a million and a half 1904 dollars, and its annual maintenance was fifty thousand dollars. Its crew of twenty was captained by a Bostonian named Forbes McIntyre.

After Marco had explored these marvels, he went out on deck to lean on the rail and watch the ocean. It was a cold day with a rough wind whipping the Atlantic, but the *North Star* handled well, and its bow sliced through the waves with a minimum of pitching. They were four miles off New Jersey, and Marco was remembering his swim from Ellis Island, when he was joined by Vanessa. She had on a tweed coat and had tied a plaid scarf over her head. She leaned on the rail next to him and said, "You don't get seasick?"

"No."

"Me either. I love it when it's rough like this. The ocean seems so alive and beautiful." She hesitated. "You know, I'm terribly glad you came along on this cruise, because you can be a great help to me.'

"How?"

"Well, I've been doing a lot of thinking, and I've realized I'm in a rather unique position. You know, Father has been in the Senate three terms and he has a lot of seniority, which counts there. He's due to be the next chairman of the Foreign Relations Committee, which is a pretty powerful position. Politics is all a state of mind, and Father's state of mind is very much to the right, which I guess is natural, considering his age. But if you and I worked on him during this cruise—you know, you talk to him about the slums and the terrible conditions of the poor, and I tried to open his mind a *little* to the advanced thinking I encountered in Europe . . . well, maybe we could move him a little to the left. And *think* what effect that would have on the country! If Phipps Ogden moved to the left, with his power and connections . . . well, maybe the Senate might move a little to the left, and then maybe the House . . . do you see what I mean? We could do a lot of *good*."

She turned to look at him, holding on to her flapping scarf, and he could see she was serious.

"Well," he said, "do you mind if I give you a little advice?"

"Please do."

"I don't think the way to do it is to talk about cockroaches at the dinner table."

"You're probably right."

"I think you have to stop trying to shock everybody for the fun of it, and just talk politics naturally. But I don't know how much help *I'd* be. I don't know anything about politics. I'm still trying to memorize the Presidents."

"But it would help me to have your moral support. All Maud will talk about is the latest fashions, and Edwina will talk about horses. . . . It's so wonderful *your* being here, because you know what life is really like out there. You've been poor. You have no idea how I admire you for what you went through."

He looked at her, thinking, *Jesus Christ, she's in love with my poverty!*

"I'll give you moral support up to a point," he said. "But you have to understand I can't antagonize your father. He's paying my way through school. Without him, I'd be back on the streets."

She frowned. "You're right. I keep forgetting . . ." She studied his face. "You mustn't fall in love with all this, you know."

"All what?"

"Father's world. The *North Star,* Garden Court . . . It's all beautiful, of course, but it's wrong. When I inherit it, I'm going to give half of everything away to the poor."

"Good." He grinned. "Then I'll get a piece of the pie."

She laughed. "Oh, you're not going to be poor—I can tell. I think you're terribly smart, Marco. Anyway, are we allies?"

"I hope we can be more than that."

Her eyes widened slightly, and he saw something in them that might have been fear, or curiosity, or excitement—or all three.

But Vanessa had all the zeal of the convert, without any sense of timing or tact. And despite Marco's admonition to move subtly, the next evening at dinner—after the seas had abated and the others recovered their appetites—she interrupted a discussion on bridge with a petulant, "Can't anyone talk about something *interesting?*"

All eyes turned to her.

"Like what?" growled her father. "Art?"

"Yes, art! Or the suffragists . . . Maud, what's your position on votes for women?"

"The subject bores me exquisitely," she said. "I believe

women should operate the way they have all through history: by their wits, if they have any."

"Hear hear!" approved Phipps.

"If women become men's equals, there'll be no more romance in the world...."

"Romance?" interrupted Vanessa. "Where's the romance in the slums? What's romantic about slaving in sweatshops?"

"Here we go," groaned her father.

"But these things must be discussed!" she exclaimed. "Here we sit on this million-dollar yacht while immigrant women are working under appalling conditions for pennies an hour. And *you* talk about bridge!"

Phipps threw down his napkin.

"Vanessa, I am fully prepared to tell the captain to put into Roanoke or *wherever* and let you off this million-dollar yacht which seems to bother your conscience so. All you have to do is mention the word *slums* once more. Believe me, I'm *serious*. This is my vacation, and I get enough talk about the damned slums in the Senate! Do you understand?"

"But, Father, it's *important!*"

He leaned forward. "My *happiness* is important!" he practically hissed.

Vanessa stood up. "I think you're all selfish troglodytes!" she burst out, and she ran out of the room onto the deck.

"Good God," said Phipps, picking up his napkin, "I wish the girl had never learned how to *read*."

"Excuse me, sir," said Marco, "but maybe *I* could talk to her."

Phipps looked at him. "Yes," he said, thoughtfully, "that's a good idea.... Yes, Marco, *you* talk to her. You're her age.... I'd appreciate it."

Marco stood up. "Excuse me," he said politely. Then he went out on deck.

After he left the dining room no one spoke for a moment. Then Phipps turned to Maud and said, "You know, he's a very civilized young man. He may be able to do something with her."

"He's also," said Maud, cutting into her *quenelles de brochet,* "a very handsome young man." She smiled suggestively at Phipps.

"Yes," he said. "Yes, he is ..." He looked at the door to the deck, thinking, *By God, that's what she needs: a good-looking dago!*

Marco and Vanessa, mused Maud. *What an interesting combination . . . and why not? It would be good for both of them, and it would keep Marco around indefinitely, which I enjoy. . . .*

How clever of Marco! I've underestimated the dear boy. . . .

Outside, the seas and wind had calmed as the *North Star* continued south, but it was still cold and when he came up to Vanessa by the starboard rail, he took off his coat and put it around her shoulders.

"Do you want to catch pneumonia?" he said.

"Would anyone care if I did?" she replied, hugging the coat around her.

"That's ridiculous."

"No it's not. Oh, I know what you're going to tell me: I shouldn't have made a scene. I should have talked about bridge or golf or something stupid. . . . I know. You're right. I've never fit in, and I probably never will. That's another reason I'm glad you've come along."

"Why?"

She turned to him. "You're an outsider, like me."

He looked at her a moment, her face faintly illuminated by a cloud-masked quarter moon. He wondered how in the world she could consider herself an outsider. Then he took her in his arms and kissed her. She didn't resist for a while. Then she pushed him away.

"We shouldn't have done that," she whispered.

"Why not? I liked it."

"Yes, it was nice, but I don't know much about kissing . . . or love . . ."

"Then it's time you found out."

He took her again, kissed her again. This time she put up no resistance, but he felt her trembling against him.

"Relax," he whispered, stroking her hair. "Relax . . ."

"Yes, I want to relax. . . ."

He thought it was a curious thing to say.

"You're not afraid of me, are you?"

"No . . . I don't think so. . . ."

She wriggled out of his arms and took off his coat.

"I have to go to bed."

She handed him his coat, gave him a searching look, then

hurried back down the deck toward her stateroom. He put on his coat, watching her.

He heard footsteps behind him and turned to see Phipps walking toward him. Phipps, who dressed for dinner even at sea. Tall, distinguished Phipps, smoking a postprandial pipe.

"How did it go with Van?" he asked, leaning on the rail next to Marco.

"I calmed her down. I think she listens to me."

"Good." Phipps said nothing for a moment, watching the reflection of the moon flash periodically on the water.

"She's a good girl," he said finally. "But she's got a bee in her bonnet about the problems of the world. In a way, I suppose I admire her . . . but it's hard to live with." He turned to Marco. "She's never shown much interest in men," he went on. "She's young, she's been in girls' schools . . . that's to be expected. Do you think she has any interest in you?"

Marco stuck his hands in his pockets. "I don't know."

Phipps smiled. "I hope she does," he said. "Good night, Marco."

He continued walking down the deck, puffing his pipe.

Upon the death of his elderly landlady, Carl Travers, prompted by Bridget's first pregnancy, had bought the Grove Street town house from his landlady's estate. He and Bridget took over the entire three floors of the house; and on Christmas Eve of 1910 they gave a party, inviting Casey and Kathleen, Georgie and a dozen friends to drink eggnog and sing carols around Bridget's gaudy tree. The first-floor drawing room of the old house had a high ceiling with elaborate Victorian plaster coving and a wonderful plaster plaque around the chandelier; and the nineteenth-century ambience of the house combined with the heavy snowfall outside to give the festive Noel a proper Dickensian flavor.

After they had finished "Hark, the Herald Angels Sing" for the second time, Bridget brought her sister a cup of eggnog. Georgie, sitting on a plush sofa, was wearing a dark green dress Bridget had picked out for her, and the carols and eggnog and general bonhommie had put her in a beamish mood.

"I've got a young man who's dyin' to meet you," said Bridget, sitting next to her. "He works for a publishin' house, and he's not bad-lookin'. He's been eyin' you all evenin', but he's a tad shy, poor lad. I'm goin' to bring him over ..."

"Bridget," said Georgie, smiling, "will you ever give up?"

"Well, there's no harm meetin' other young men. And I don't see our fine Italian friend here this evenin'! Him off on the senator's yacht, gallivantin' around the Caribbean ..."

"I *told* him to go. It's good for him to know the senator better. Besides, he needs a vacation, after what he's been through."

Bridget sniffed. "Maybe. But why didn't he invite you?"

"How could he? It's not his yacht."

"Oh, Georgie, you silly girl! I know you're crazy about him, but you know nothin' about men."

Georgie groped for her sister's hand. Bridget took it and squeezed it.

"Don't you understand?" Georgie said. "I *trust* him."

Bridget sighed, but said nothing.

Dio, dio! The Purple Mask has got Helen in his clutches! He's tying her to a chair! No, *wait:* Dick Derring! He has a gun! The Purple Mask sees him ... he runs to the wall and pulls a switch ... Aiee! Dick falls through a trapdoor into a pool filled with *sharks!*

I trust him, she thought. *He loves me as much as I love him. I trust him.*

A little after midnight on the third night of the cruise—the night before the *North Star* was to make a landfall at Bermuda—Marco slipped out of his stateroom and closed the door. He was barefoot, wearing a pair of white duck slacks and a horizontally-striped crew shirt. He listened a moment, hearing nothing but the muffled pounding of the yacht's powerful engines. Then he started down the deck. Reaching the door of Vanessa's stateroom, he paused again. All the ports were dark; everyone was asleep.

He knocked lightly on the door, then opened it and slipped inside. He closed the door softly behind him. A bed light was turned on by Vanessa; she was sitting up.

"What do you want?" she whispered, pulling the sheet up over her chest.

"Ssh."

He came to her bed and sat on it, next to her. She was watching him, fear in her eyes. He reached out and put his hand on her cheek. It calmed her a little. Slowly, he leaned toward her and put his mouth against hers. Then, continuing to kiss her, he gently pulled the sheet down, revealing her lovely bare shoulders crossed by the thin strips of white satin that held up her nightgown. As he went on kissing her, his right hand pulled the left strip over her shoulder. Then the right strip.

"Don't," she whispered, pulling away from him.

He tugged off her covers and climbed in beside her, taking her in his arms.

"I love you," he whispered. "You're everything I've ever dreamed of." *Oh, you liar,* he thought. *It's Georgie I love, not this one. But all that money . . .*

"Marco, don't . . ."

He pulled her nightgown down, baring her breasts. He started kissing them.

"Oh God," she whispered, closing her eyes.

"Say you love me," he kept murmuring between kisses. "Say you love me. . . ."

"I don't know . . . I've never been in love. . . ."

He slowly sucked her right nipple as his hand slid down her stomach. Then he was rubbing her vagina through her nightgown. She began to moan.

"Say you *love* me," he repeated, this time insistently.

"Oh God, *yes.* I love you. I love you, Marco!"

Her voice was so loud with excitement, he shut her up with a kiss as he thought, *Oh God, if this were only Georgie! How can I do this to Georgie? Except it's the money, the goddam money, so much money . . .*

He got out of bed and pulled off his shirt. She eyed his magnificently muscled torso.

"Take off your nightgown," he said.

She obeyed as he unbuttoned his slacks and dropped them to the floor. He wore no underwear. Naked, he turned out the light and got in bed, pulling her body to his and starting to make love to her.

"Relax," he whispered. He turned her gently on her back, then straddled her.

He kneaded her breasts a moment. Then he went into her, ever so gently. She cried out as he ruptured her hymen.

224

"Sshh . . ."

Then, very slowly, his midsection began its rhythmic crescendo.

When she came, Marco winced, because her cry would have awakened the dead.

The next morning the *North Star* dropped anchor in Hamilton harbor, Bermuda. The weather was balmy, and Marco was in the dining room, devouring a monstrous breakfast, when Maud joined him. She was wearing a handsome khaki skirt and matching jacket and seemed in high spirits as she sat opposite Marco.

"Good morning," she said. "Isn't the weather divine? Just orange juice and tea, please," she said to the steward. Then she turned back to Marco as she unfolded her napkin. "We're lunching with Lord and Lady Despard today. He owns a healthy percentage of the Kimberley mine and is a client of Phipps's law firm. Phipps says his house is charming . . . he owns a little island in Somerset bay. He has a swimming pool, so bring your swimsuit. Thank you," she said with a smile to the steward, who served her her fresh-squeezed orange juice and tea, then retired to the galley.

When they were alone, Maud lowered her voice.

"Phipps and I were wakened by the *most* peculiar noise last night," she said, with a slight smile. "It came from dear Vanessa's cabin. You slyboots."

Marco munched his third piece of toast, watching her, saying nothing. Maud sipped her orange juice.

"Well," she went on, "once we were awake, we couldn't get back to sleep, so we had a talk about Vanessa. Phipps is terribly worried about her—all this radical nonsense she's picked up. . . . He feels strongly that she should settle down with a husband and have children. The problem is, she's never had any interest in men. Of course, she's immature, but still . . ."

Marco buttered a fourth piece of toast.

"Naturally," she went on, "there are plenty of eligible suitors around who would jump to marry her. She *is* one of the richest heiresses currently on the market. But Phipps rather disapproves of arranged marriages. Phipps, dear man, believes in love. Well, it will be interesting to see how things turn out, won't it?"

225

She finished her orange juice as Marco bit into his toast. Their eyes were locked.

"I remember a marvelous Italian proverb," she continued. "How does it go? *Se il sedere avesse soldi. . . ?*"

"*. . . si chiamerebbe 'Don Sedere.'*" Marco finished.

"That's it! Such charming folk-wisdom. 'If one's rear end had money, it would be called *"Sir* Rear End."' You Italians have such a *practical* view of life."

She sipped her tea, which she drank without sugar.

Chapter 26

The letter was postmarked Jamaica and dated January 2, 1911, though it didn't reach Georgie until a week later.

"There's a letter for you from Marco," said Kathleen as she brought the mail into the living room. Georgie, who was reading a Braille edition of *Quo Vadis?*, said, "Read it to me!" and her face was beaming.

Kathleen opened the envelope as she sat down.

"It's from Jamaica," she said. "Not a bad life that one leads. 'My dearest Georgie,'" she began, reading ahead a moment to herself. The opening sentence alarmed her so much, she read the rest of the short letter in order to be able to cushion Georgie.

"Read it!" said Georgie, eagerly.

Dear God, thought Kathleen. *The bastard! The cold-blooded bastard!*

She took a deep breath. "Darlin'," she said, "you have to be brave."

"Why? What's wrong?"

"He's a rotten man, and we'll find someone better for you."

Georgie's face turned white.

"What is it?" she whispered.

"He's marryin' the senator's daughter. He says he fell in love

226

with her, but I don't believe a word of it. He's after her money...."

She stopped. Georgie had risen out of her chair. She wobbled a little, then reached out till she felt the table to support herself. Kathleen got up and hurried to her, taking her in her arms.

"My poor darlin'," she said, hugging her. "There'll be others better than him...."

"Don't feel *sorry* for me!" Georgie almost screamed, pushing her aunt away. "I'm goin' to be all right. Just don't feel *sorry* ..."

She headed for the stairs, feeling her way along the furniture. Kathleen watched her, tears in her eyes.

"I'll be all right," Georgie kept repeating as she reached the stairs in the front hall. "I'll be all right...."

She started up the stairs, but on the third step she stopped. She sank down and sat on the stair. She leaned her head in her hands and started sobbing with the high, keening sound of a broken heart.

They were married on June 5, 1911. The weather was glorious, and the gardens at Garden Court were bursting with late-spring exuberance. Peonies were everywhere, and since they were Maud's favorite flower, she filled the house with them: white, pink and blood-red. The effect was spectacular.

Promptly at noon the Wedding March was played on the pipe organ in the central hall, and Vanessa started down the marble stair, escorted by her father. The bride looked extremely pretty in a white satin gown with an enormous veil. When they reached the bottom of the stairs they crossed the hall to the vast ballroom, which was filled with over a hundred guests sitting on gilt ballroom chairs. Maud, wearing a champagne lace dress with a big ruby and diamond brooch, watched her husband and stepdaughter walk down the white satin runner with satisfaction. Things had turned out nicely.

At the altar stood the groom and his best man, Jake Rubin, both in cutaways. Nellie, three months pregnant, was among the guests, drinking in the splendors of Garden Court with wide eyes; it was difficult for the daughter of a streetcar conductor to comprehend wealth on such a vast scale as Phipps Ogden's. After the ceremony the guests went outside, where a big green-and-white-striped awning had been set up on the front lawn overlooking the Sound. Fifteen round tables, each set for eight, were beneath the awning, and the guests seated themselves for a lunch of caviar, Dover sole and roast beef. Rivers of champagne flowed and, for the beefeaters, Lafite Rothschild '98. At one-thirty, the groom— by now a bit bleary-eyed from the bubbly—and the bride cut the seven-foot-high cake. Toasts were drunk; more champagne flowed. At ten past two, the bride went upstairs to change for her honeymoon, which was to be a ten-day cruise to Maine on the *North Star,* at the end of which the happy couple would spend the rest of the summer at Phipps's twenty-eight-room Newport "cottage," Stoney Brook Farm, where tutors would continue to stuff book-learning into the groom's head.

The groom, by now weaving a bit, carried a glass of claret into the house. He spotted Jake in the drawing room looking at an enormous oil painting.

"It's a Titian," burped Marco, coming into the room. "Tiziano. A good wop painter. Maud told me it cost a million bucks. And over there's a Raphael Madonna—another wop painter. Pretty fancy wops, wouldn't you say, Jake?"

And he laughed.

"This place is incredible," said Jake in awed tones. "I can't *believe* it."

Marco shrugged drunkenly.

"It's not much, but it's home," he said. "So what do you think, Jake? Four years off the *Kronprinz Friedrich,* and you're the best songwriter in America and I'm the best stud. Not bad, wouldn't you say?" He waved his hand toward the French doors leading out to the lawn. "You see all those important people out there?" he went on. "All those politicians and millionaires and whatnot? You know what they've been thinking all day? They've been thinking, 'Vanessa Ogden bought herself a good-looking wop who'll keep her happy in bed.' *That's* what they're thinking, Jake, but they're *wrong.*" He grinned gleefully and leaned toward Jake, lowering his voice. "I went after Vanessa," he whispered. "In Italy we say, *La pera matura cade sola,* which means 'the ripe fruit will fall by itself.' But Vanessa wasn't quite ripe enough, so I gave her a little push, you know? And she fell right into my lap."

He drank more wine.

"You'd better go easy on that stuff," cautioned Jake.

"Why? I'm rich. To hell with everything! To hell with love . . ." He stopped, staring at the fireplace. "To hell with Georgie O'Donnell . . . goddam, she must hate my guts today."

Suddenly, swiftly, fiercely, he threw the wineglass into the fireplace. It smashed on an eighteenth-century French andiron.

Then the groom weaved upstairs to change for his honeymoon on the yacht.

PART VII
Murder

Chapter 27

The rich world of Phipps Ogden received its first seismic tremor with the introduction of the federal income tax in 1913 and its second tremor with the federal estate tax in 1916. But to Jake and Marco's fellow-steerage passenger on the *Kronprinz Friedrich,* Tom Banicek, the American class structure seemed as formidable in 1916 as it had in 1907. After being fired by Monty Staunton, Tom had left his wife on her mother's farm and gone to Pittsburgh to try to find work. But there he encountered the blacklist, the same blacklist that had reduced Sam Fuller to such desperation that he turned informer. Now Tom's name was on every list, and there was no work for him anywhere.

He finally got a job as a street sweeper to keep alive, but the little Czech's stubborn nature was aroused: The system wasn't going to beat him, no matter how powerful it seemed. Fortunately, by now a network of blacklisted men had come into being. Tom met a certain Serb socialist named Josip Nardo who had been blacklisted by the steel companies and had gone to work for the Wobblies, as the International Workers of the World were known. Nardo in turn introduced him to a burly ex-miner named Joe Haines, who worked for the miners' union. Joe liked Tom and got him a job with the union. The pay was minute, but there was enough for Tom to rent a room in a respectable boardinghouse and bring Della up from Staunton.

During the next six years, Tom slowly rose in the union hierarchy. He also became a father, siring two boys, Stanislaus and

Ward. By 1915 they were able to rent a small house in a working-class district of Pittsburgh. And one morning in September 1916, Della was hanging some clothes up to dry in her backyard when she heard a car horn honking in front of the house.

The paint-peeling clapboard house had four rooms and was on a tiny lot, but the place was immaculate and the neighborhood generally quiet, so that the horn-blowing was annoying. Then she heard a familiar voice yell, "Della, come out front!"

Putting down her wicker laundry basket, she hurried around the house. Parked in the street was a Model T Ford, and her husband was at the wheel, waving at her.

"Tom, stop making all that noise," she said as she came up to the car. "And where'd you get the Ford?"

"It's ours!" he exclaimed. "Get in. I'll take you for a ride."

"What do you mean 'ours'?"

"I bought it from Phil Stone at the office. Ninety bucks, and it's only got sixteen thousand miles."

"Where'd you get ninety dollars?" she asked. The price of a brand-new Tin Lizzie in 1916 was $360.

"I've been saving it—it's my secret. And would you stop asking dumb questions and get in? This is the most beautiful car in Pittsburgh—no, America!—and it's all *ours,* Della!"

She had rarely seen him looking so happy. She knew he was car-crazy and had dreamed of owning one for years. Despite her horror at the thought of spending so much money, she wasn't about to spoil his triumph. She climbed in beside him and looked at the dashboard.

"You know how to drive it?" she asked.

"Just watch." He shifted gears and the Model T chugged away from the curb. "I've taken a ten-day vacation, so we're packing up the kids and driving down to the farm. Send Aunt Edna a telegram. Wait till she sees *this*!"

"Show-off!" laughed Della. Then she leaned over and kissed his cheek. "Tom, it's beautiful."

"The most beautiful car in America," he repeated proudly.

For Tom Banicek, the early years of struggle were finally paying off: He owned his little hunk of the American Dream.

The next morning at dawn they packed the two boys in the back seat and started for West Virginia. It was only 120 miles to

Hawksville, but travel in 1916 was a risk-filled adventure and they were allotting themselves a full day to get there. The cement roads gave out outside Pittsburgh, and they bumped along the dirt roads of the buggy era. Luckily they were dry; to get stuck in the mud was one of the worst hazards of travel. But gas was cheap, the Tin Lizzie a remarkably tough car, and the thrill of free mobility the homely little flivver was giving to millions of poor Americans more than made up for the inconveniences of flat tires and broken axles. America was in love with the Model T, and Tom was in love with his. As he bounced over ruts—in one place he had to drive through a field when the road inexplicably gave out altogether— he smoked Camels and sang and commented on the beauties of the countryside, and his wife fell in love with him all over again.

They arrived at the farm at five that afternoon, dirty, dusty, tired, but happy. Aunt Edna greeted them with kisses and was suitably impressed by the car, telling Tom that someone had opened a garage in Hawksville. Then they all went inside the farmhouse to eat a delicious supper of Aunt Edna's Brunswick stew, cracklin' bread, corn pone, cabbage and a gooseberry pie for dessert. They talked family matters, in particular Stan's series of earaches the previous winter.

"You had earaches when you was five," Aunt Edna said to Della. "You do the same thing to Stan that I did to you."

"What's that?"

"You take a spoonful of your pee—"

"Momma!"

"Do you want to know or not? I say, you take a spoonful of your pee, you warm it, then you put some drops into his bad ear. Nothing wrong with pee. It's part of the body, God made it, and it cures earaches. You listen to your mother and you won't have to pay no doctor bills. Pass the corn pone, Tom." He did. "Stan will be all right," Aunt Edna went on. "He's a good-lookin' boy. Takes after you, Della."

"Thank goodness," said Tom with a smile.

"Well, your looks was never your long suit," said Aunt Edna, bluntly.

"I think he's very handsome." Della smiled and took his hand.

"There's no accountin' for taste. When's that union of yours gonna do somethin' with the Staunton mines?"

Tom took another piece of cracklin' bread. "One of these days," he said.

Aunt Edna snorted. "You've been sayin' that for years. What's wrong with your people? God knows, if *any* mines need unionizin', it's these. That Bible-quotin' murderer Monty Staunton ought to be *first* on your list!"

"Monty Staunton is first on my list, but he's not first on the union's. The union wants to stay out of West Virginia for the time being. The owners here are the toughest in the country, and we want to build our strength nationwide before we tackle Monty Staunton."

"He's a murderer," said Aunt Edna, softly. "He murdered my husband. His mines are still dangerous, and there'll be *more* murders. Your union may know what it's doing, but every man who gets killed in Monty Staunton's mines will be on their conscience. And I'll tell you something else, Tom: The miners are losin' faith in the union. Every day you wait is gonna make it that much harder for you."

Tom didn't answer.

"I know we both have a lot of bad memories about this valley," said Della that night as she lay next to Tom in bed. "But I still think of it as my home. It's good to be home again."

"Pittsburgh is *my* home," said Tom.

"Do you hate it here?"

"Oh no. The land here is beautiful—you couldn't hate that. But I hate Monty Staunton."

"Do you think Mother's right about the union? I mean, that every day they wait to come in here makes it that much harder?"

"Your mother's right about pretty near everything. She's right about this, too."

They didn't speak for a while, lying in the wooden bed with ropes instead of springs, and a straw-stuffed mattress. Della had forgotten how sweet straw mattresses smelled. She was remembering her childhood when she felt Tom take her hand.

"I love you," he said, softly and tenderly. He always said it before making love to her, and the wonderful thing was that he al-

236

ways made it sound genuine, never just a ritual or formula. Tom loved his wife with a love that was simple and pure.

He was the nicest man she had ever known, but she knew he also was tough. As he began making love to her, she had no doubt that some day he would tackle Monty Staunton. Whether or not he would win, she wasn't so sure.

The next morning Tom walked from the farm to the top of the neighboring hill, where he stood awhile, looking down at the mines and the company town. A warm wind almost blew his cap off.

Someday, he thought. Someday soon.

Chapter 28

On April 6, 1917, the United States declared war on Germany, finally entering the senseless three-year-old conflict that was slaughtering millions and destroying Europe for reasons no one any longer quite understood. President Wilson said America would fight to make the world "safe for democracy," which was accepted by most Americans, including Tom Banicek, who, despite the faults of the country he had immigrated to, loved America. He tried to join up, but was rejected because of spots on his lungs, a condition he was unaware of and which he probably had contracted in the mines. Tom was disappointed, but his union superiors weren't; they needed him. For America's entry into the war brought about a savage wave of mining-company repression against the miners. And the death of a twelve-year-old boy was to bring the Great West Virginia War to its bloody climax.

His name was Alfie Davis, he was the son of a miner named Llewellyn Davis, and he worked in the breaking room at the Staunton Mining Company. The breaking room was an iron shed near the mine entrance where children were employed for ten cents an hour to remove shale from the coal moving on conveyer belts to the breaking machines, which reduced the raw coal to manageable size. It was March 3, 1918, and the temperature was 12 degrees. The shed was heated by one small stove and the interior temperature was below freezing. The two dozen "breaking boys" wore mittens, coats and scarves, but Alfie Davis was already sneezing when he reported for work at eight that morning.

By six that night, when he left the breaking room to walk home through the snow, he was coughing and his nose was running. When he came into his house, his mother took one look at him and knew he was seriously ill. She put him to bed immediately and fed him hot soup. By the next morning, his fever was 103 degrees, and the company doctor diagnosed it as pneumonia.

By the next afternoon, Alfie Davis was dead.

His father, Llewellyn, was a bald giant of a Welshman who had emigrated from Wales in the nineties and had worked for the Staunton mines eighteen years. He had four sons, of whom Alfie was the youngest and favorite. When Llewellyn saw the doctor close the eyes of the frail blond boy, his reaction was as much rage as sorrow.

"Eighteen years," he muttered. "Eighteen years in the goddam mines, and this is what I get."

He left the tiny bedroom and went into the main room of the company-owned house. His wife, Sarah, got up from the chair next to the bed and hurried into the next room. What she saw frightened her. Lew Davis was taking his shotgun off its wall brackets.

"Lew, what are you going to do?"

He put two cartridges in the gun.

"Revenge my son's death."

She tried to stop him, but he shoved her away and went out into the night with the shotgun.

Monty and Christine Staunton took their seats in the dining room at Belle Meade. With them was Charlotte, their daughter, and her husband, a Charleston doctor named Howard Bennet.

"O Lord," intoned Monty, closing his eyes, "we thank Thee for Thy many blessings. We ask Thy special blessing for our country in this time of trial, and ask Thy protection for our many brave American boys in uniform who are fighting the wicked, satanic

Germans on French soil. We ask Thy special protection for Thy servant, Montgomery Staunton, Junior, who is flying in France. And we ask Thee to bless this food. Amen."

"Amen," chorused the others. And the servants passed the first course.

"I got a letter from Monty today," said Christine, taking a healthy slug of her Meursault. "He was in Paris on leave. He says Paris is quiet and the French are filling the theaters and restaurants. One would think the French could at least take *war* seriously."

"He's shot down nine Germans," said Monty proudly, as he dived into his consommé. "The Kaiser doesn't have a chance with Monty over there."

"Of course I worry," Christine continued. "It just all seems so dangerous."

"What to do you think war is?" Monty boomed down the table. "Safe? Of *course* it's dangerous. That's what makes it fun."

"I don't think getting killed would be much fun," sniffed Christine, finishing her wine and eying the white-jacketed, white-gloved black servant standing by the sideboard, where the wine bottle rested in a silver cooler. "And if Monty were hurt . . . well, I just don't want to think about it."

"Monty will come through all right," said her husband. "That boy's got guts. Besides, he's lucky. Luck runs in the family."

The footman was refilling Christine's wineglass when they heard the noise outside the dining-room door. As they all turned, the double doors burst open and Lew Davis entered the room holding his shotgun. Monty's black butler was behind him, yelling, "Mr. Staunton, he done pushed his way in. . . ."

"You killed my son!" roared the miner, aiming the shotgun down the table at Monty's surprised face. "An eye for an eye!"

Just as he fired, the footman standing next to Christine swung the bottle of Meursault at Davis's arm. The shotgun blasted, but in the air, biting a huge chunk out of the plaster ceiling. Christine screamed, Monty ducked, the plaster crashed down on the yew table, and the butler jumped the miner from behind.

There was a fight, but the two servants, Howard Bennet and Monty finally subdued the raging miner while Christine phoned the police.

"Open another bottle of wine," she gasped after making the phone call. "My nerves! I need some wine. Oh God, a crazy man!"

After the police took Lew Davis to book him for attempted murder, Monty sank down on his knees in front of his family, clasped his hands in prayer, closed his eyes and said, "O God, thank Thee for protecting me from this lunatic. Thy protection proves to me the righteousness of my ways. I have always been Thy faithful servant, and Thou knowest I always will be. But I just wanted Thee to know I *especially* appreciate what Thou didst for me tonight, and I won't forget it, Lord. No, sir, I won't forget. Amen."

He got to his feet and gave his butler and the footman who had saved his life twenty dollars apiece.

The next morning Aunt Edna drove her buggy into Hawksville to Dale's filling station, which had the nearest telephone, and made a collect call to her son-in-law in his Pittsburgh office.

"Lew Davis broke into Belle Meade last night and took a potshot at Monty Staunton," she said. "Unfortunately, he missed him, but you know he don't stand a chance with any court around here."

"I know. But why did he do such a crazy thing?"

"Because his boy who worked in the breaking room died of pneumonia. They ain't got no heat in that place. I'm telling you, Tom, one of you union boys better get down here and help him. Lew ain't got a nickel for lawyers, and this is the perfect chance for the union to start looking good around here."

Tom thought a moment.

"You're right," he said. "I'll be there tomorrow."

Late the next afternoon, the sheriff let Tom into Lew's cell in the Hawksville jail. Davis was sitting on his cot, huddled in his coat, for the jail was freezing.

"Lew, I'm Tom Banicek. Remember me?"

"I remember."

"I'm with the union now. It sent me down here to help you get legal representation."

"You're wasting your time, Banicek. I ain't got a chance around here. Staunton's got these judges in his pocket. Besides, I did it and I'm glad. I'm only sorry I missed the bastard."

"I understand, Lew. But the point is, you've got to have a lawyer. Now, if you can't pay for one, the union has a legal contingency fund. . . ."

"Get outta here with your goddam union!" exclaimed Lew. "Don't give me this shit about legal funds—the union's in Staunton's pocket too. Christ, don't you think we *know*? The owners pay you guys off."

"That's not true."

"Ain't it? Then why don't the union come into the valley? Why do you stay in Pittsburgh?"

"Because we need to be *strong* before we tackle the West Virginia mines."

Lew Davis looked at him with contempt. "Tell that to my dead son," he said. Then he added, "Go on, get outta here. I don't want your help. Let 'em send me to jail. Jail couldn't be worse than the mines."

Tom hesitated. "If you change your mind, I'll be at my mother-in-law's."

Then he went to the cell door and signaled the sheriff.

"Around here, the union's about as popular as the clap," said Tom that night as he sat at his mother-in-law's kitchen table.

"Tom!" exclaimed Della. She was feeding the two boys.

"Sorry. But it's true."

"I told you so," said Aunt Edna. "The miners feel betrayed by everyone. They don't think anyone cares about 'em, and maybe it's true."

"*I* care," said Tom.

"Then what are you gonna do?"

"Talk to the union tomorrow. Convince Joe Haines it's time we organized the Staunton Coal Company."

Aunt Edna smiled. Della looked worried.

"Tom," she said, "Joe Haines knows what he's doing. He has a national strategy. Now you know Monty Staunton's the worst of a bad lot, and if the union gets defeated here, it's going to be bad for the cause all over the country."

"I know," said Tom. "But the union isn't going to get defeated here."

Little Stan Banicek banged his spoon against his bowl for more soup.

Chapter 29

In 1872 a red-brick Victorian Gothic mansion was built on the main street of Charleston. This brooding, vaguely sinister pile was paid for by a group of local businessmen who called themselves the Jeremy Bentham Society (they were admirers of the English economist), and the Jeremy Bentham Club soon became the most exclusive men's club in town. It was in the darkly paneled library of this club that Monty Staunton addressed ten men sitting in leather chairs.

"Gentlemen," he said, "I've called this meeting because there's a union man in my valley."

He paused for a moment to add drama to his statement.

"His name is Tom Banicek," he went on, "a Czech immigrant who used to work for me until I blacklisted him for troublemaking. He was foolish enough—or perhaps brazen is the word—to ask to rent the company hall to address the miners. Of course we told him to go to hell, but he's passed out leaflets that he's holding an organizing meeting outside the hall."

"You'll stop him, of course," said Ludwell Tyson, president of the Tyson Coal Company.

"Oh, yes, we'll stop him. But he's a determined little bugger, and he'll just go somewhere else. Now, gentlemen, I think we have to be realistic about our situation. We mineowners are out of whack with the times. The union movement is gaining strength all over the country. It's possible I should let Banicek organize my company, which would give the union a big toehold in West Virginia. Your mines would be the next to be unionized, and I doubt you'd be able to prevent it happening. That's one way of viewing the situation."

"Hell's bells, Monty," snorted Tyson, "you mean you're going to give up without a fight?"

"I didn't say that. What I'm trying to make all of you realize is that if one of us cracks, all of us go. I'm going to fight Banicek with everything at my disposal, but you men better back me up all the way."

"You know damned well we will! We've kept the union out of the state for twenty years, and I say we can keep it out for twenty years more!"

Monty smiled. "Well, I was hoping you'd say that, Ludwell. But this time is going to be harder. However, we have one big advantage: the war. President Wilson is on our side. He told me last month at the White House that the war effort requires we produce as much coal as possible and that the government will do anything we ask to prevent coal production from being interrupted. In other words, we got a carte blanche from Washington. And thanks to that attack on me by that lunatic Davis, the general public thinks the miners are a bunch of radicals. So I think we're in a position to act forcefully. It's a war, gentlemen, between them and us, and in war, blood gets spilled. And a war has to be fought with weapons. After we say a little prayer together, I'm going to show you pictures of a new weapon I've designed that's going to scare the shit out of Tom Banicek and the miners." He smiled. "And the beautiful thing is, the government and the country is going to be on our side because we're doing the patriotic thing: We're producing coal to make the world safe for democracy."

"Whatever the hell *that* means," said Tyson. "What's this secret weapon? You going to gas 'em?"

"No, it's something Bill Fargo and I have been working on for several months. We had them built in a garage here in Charleston. They're sort of versions of those tanks they're using in France, but Bill and I call them 'death vehicles.'" He grinned. "They're spooky! But first, the prayer."

He closed his eyes and addressed the brass chandelier. "O Lord, give us Thy support in this righteous struggle against the enemies of private property...."

I'm a general! he thought gleefully. *I'm a goddam general!*

"Neither I nor the union is endorsing what Lew Davis did to Mr. Staunton," Tom said the next morning. He was standing on the steps of the company hall, speaking through a megaphone to a crowd of almost a hundred miners and their wives. It was a cold, gray day, but the crowd ignored the weather; they were eager to hear what Tom was saying.

"We don't believe there is any place for violence in the American labor movement," he went on. "But, by God, the frustration that made Lew take down his shotgun was real! The miserable working conditions that killed his young son are real! And the need to improve these conditions is real! I say the *only* way—I repeat, the *only* way—to improve these conditions is through organization. . . ."

He stopped. Everyone had heard the noise: the rumble of motors. Now they turned to see a convoy heading for them. It consisted of two open trucks filled with dark-suited, bowler-hatted Pinkerton men carrying rifles. And then, the two "death vehicles." They were indeed spooky. They looked in fact like tanks, except they had wheels instead of treads and had obviously been built on truck chassis. They were steel-plated, had no windows, and on top of each was a moveable turret with a machine gun sticking through the opening.

The convoy halted twenty feet from the company hall, and Bill Fargo, who was riding in one of the trucks, yelled through a megaphone: "You're on company property. Return to your homes!"

"You go to hell!" Tom yelled back. "Are you going to tell me the *air* is company property? As long as I'm not in your buildings . . ."

"You're on company *land*," Fargo interrupted, and the gun turrets turned and aimed at Tom. "If you people don't disperse, you'll lose your jobs and your homes."

"It's the same old threat," Tom shouted, wondering if Fargo had the nerve to fire. "I say it's time we show management they can't treat us like criminals! They can't aim guns at us as if we were slaves. . . ."

He was interrupted by the chatter of machine-gun fire. Though the bullets were aimed over their heads, the fierce rat-tat-tat was nevertheless terrifying. Many of the women screamed.

After the burst was finished, Tom said, "All right, I'm going back to my mother-in-law's farm to finish what I have to say. Any of you who happen to think—like I do—that this is a free country where free speech is guaranteed by the Constitution are welcome to follow me out to Edna's."

He walked off the steps and started down the street. The miners watched him.

"I'm with Banicek," shouted one of them, and he started after Tom.

"So am I!" shouted another, and then another until the whole crowd was walking down the street behind the little Czech. Tom was looking pleased. Someone started chanting, "Strike! Strike! Strike!" and the rest quickly took it up. "Strike! Strike! Strike!" The harsh word shrilled the air defiantly.

Bill Fargo, having lost his audience, looked a bit confused.

Della was bathing the two boys in a tub when she heard the shouts of "Strike! Strike! Strike!" Aunt Edna ran to the window. "Glory be to God!" she exclaimed. "That runt of a husband of yours has done it!"

Della hurried to the front door and looked out. Tom was crossing the field followed by the shouting crowd. As he neared the house he stopped and raised his hands for silence—which he got.

"All right, we're free agents here," he said. "You're all yelling 'Strike.' Are you serious?"

"YES!" came the roared reply.

"In the past, they've always beaten us by threatening to take away our homes. There's only one way to beat that: You've got to give up your homes first."

He paused to let the impact of that set in.

"If you're serious about fighting the company," he went on, "I'll get the union to get us tents, food and medical supplies. We can set up a tent city right here on my mother-in-law's land, and there isn't a damned thing the company can do about it. So I say, go back home and pack whatever you'll need to survive—blankets, clothes, pots, pans, kettles and so forth. When I get the tents, I'll send word and you can move out here. Until you get the word, just carry on as usual. But when we're ready for 'em, we'll strike—and we'll *win*! Are you willing to do it?"

A pause, then shouts of "Yes!" "We're with you, Tom!"

"All right, go home, and I'll call the union."

At the farmhouse door, Aunt Edna said to Della, "He's sure as hell stirrin' things up. It's about time."

Tom, his face excited, came to the door and kissed his wife.

"This time we're going all the way," he exclaimed.

"Will the union back you?" asked Della.

Tom grinned as he headed for his Model T.

"If they don't, we'll start a new union."

And he climbed in the car.

While he was talking to Joe Haines on the phone in Dale's filling station in Hawksville, a truck pulled up behind his Model T and parked. Bill Fargo and four of his men climbed out. The street was almost empty, but when the few pedestrians saw what was happening, they scattered. Fargo's men attacked the Model T with crowbars. They smashed the windshield and headlights, ripped the canvas top, battered the fenders and punctured the tires.

When Tom came out of the filling station and saw his beloved car demolished, he went crazy.

"BASTARDS!" he howled, running at them.

He didn't stand a chance.

They beat him into unconsciousness and left him in the gutter, bloody and almost as demolished as his car.

"That'll teach the little fuck," said Bill Fargo as he climbed in the truck.

Chapter 30

But it didn't teach him.

Farley Dale phoned the town doctor, who came to give Tom first aid. Then, taking him to his office, he bandaged his sprained left wrist, and cleaned and bandaged the other cuts and bruises. When he was done, Tom looked like a survivor of the trenches in France, but he would live. Farley Dale said he'd work on the Model T and loaned him a truck to get back to Edna's. When Tom came in the farmhouse door, Della looked at his bandages and gasped, "What happened?"

"Bill Fargo," he said, sinking wearily into a chair. "He and his boys beat me up. It's all right."

"All *right?* You look like a bomb explosion!"

"Joe Haines is sending the tents tomorrow by truck. That's the important thing: The union's backing me."

Della came to him and kissed him. *"You're* the important thing," she said.

He forced a smile.

"Hell," he said, "we Baniceks are tough little bohunks. But the car's a mess. It's one thing to beat *me* up. But anyone who beats up a man's car has got no ..." He thought a moment, then said, rather to his surprise, "... class."

Monty Staunton stood next to his Rolls-Royce and looked down at the tent city in the field below. The weather had turned pleasant, and dozens of the miners and their families were sitting, standing or walking, some of them stirring pots boiling over open fires. There were a hundred tents.

"The strike's in its third week, Mr. Staunton," said Bill Fargo, who was standing next to him. "I'd say they're dug in for the long haul."

Monty looked ready to spit.

"Tell Banicek I want to talk to him," he said, starting around the front of the car. "Bring him to Belle Meade."

That night, Tom—his wrist still bandaged, but the other bandages gone and his face returned almost to normal—sat down at the yew table in the dining room of Belle Meade. Sitting opposite him was Monty. For a moment the two men eyed each other. Then Monty said softly, "What do you want, son?"

"A union contract," was Tom's reply.

"You may have heard there's a war on. It's vitally important that the government gets coal. You're a patriot, aren't you? You don't want to hurt the government of the United States?"

"I love this country, but my men aren't going to dig coal without a union contract."

" 'My' men," said Monty. "Well, that's interesting. You smoke?"

"Camels."

"I mean cigars?" He pulled a leather case from his coat pocket and held it across the table. "Have a Villar y Villar, 1911—a fabulous year. After the krauts torpedoed the *Lusitania,* I ordered two hundred. You never know, they might invade Cuba. Can you imagine those dumb sauerkrauts trying to rule the *Cubans*?"

He laughed as he clipped his cigar and lighted it. Then he passed the paraphernalia to Tom, who also lighted up. Monty watched him like a hawk.

"It's good," said Tom, exhaling.

"Should be. Cost three bucks apiece. You know, you're a likable fellow. It kills me to say it, but I admire your guts. Bill Fargo tells me you stood right up to my death vehicles. . . ." He chuckled. *"Love* that name! 'Death vehicles' sounds like something out of the funny papers, doesn't it? Of course . . ." He exhaled and smiled. ". . . They *do* kill people. You've got a couple of kids, I understand?"

"That's right. Two boys, Stanislaus and Ward."

"Stanislaus—is that a Czech name?"

"It is the name of the patron saint of the village where I was born."

"Uh huh. You going to send Stanislaus and Ward to college someday? Give them advantages you never had?"

"I hope to."

"College is expensive, you know. Real expensive. And you have to buy them nice clothes and maybe a car so the gals will go for them. . . . It all takes money. *Lots* of money. Where you going to get that kind of money, Tom?"

"Maybe I'll rob a bank."

Monty snorted a laugh. "Hell, it's easier than that, son. A lot easier. *I* could take care of your kids' education. Hell, I could get them into Princeton, if you wanted. That's my college, and I give 'em enough money . . . they'd take your boys if I told them to. I could do a lot for your boys. I could do a lot for *you,* if you cooperated. I could set you up real good, Tom. Maybe buy you a little business somewhere. What would you think of that?"

"Mr. Staunton, if you're trying to bribe me . . ."

"Oh hell, come on, Tom! This is no bribe, this is a business proposition. Now, I'm willing to admit you're costing me a helluva lot of money. So I got two choices: I either try and kill you—which I tried—or I make a settlement with you. Listen, you like cars, right? And my boys wrecked your Model T? I'm willing to replace it with any car you want up to five thousand bucks. Now, that's no bribe; that's a fair and square *offer.* What do you say?"

248

"No."

Monty's face darkened. He leaned forward.

"Every man's got a price," he said quietly. "What's yours?"

"A union contract."

"I'll sweeten the pot. I'm willing to give your men—since you call them yours—a twenty percent across-the-board wage hike. *Twenty* percent. I'll install ventilating fans, increase safety precautions—hell, I'll give you everything the union wants. *Plus.* I'll send your boys to college and buy you a five-thousand-dollar car. Now, you can't say *that's* not fair, can you?"

Tom hesitated. "Well . . ."

Monty saw the crack in the armor. He stood up.

"Look, don't give me an answer now. You go back to your wife and talk it over with her. There's no reason we can't work this out like sensible men, is there?"

Tom also stood up.

"What do you have against the union?" he asked. "I mean, if you're willing to give what the union wants . . ."

"I'll tell you, Tom, it's real simple. This company has always been *my* company, and the miners have been *my* miners. Now all of a sudden you're calling them *your* miners. That's what I have against the union."

Tom looked at him. For the first time, he began to understand what made Monty Staunton tick.

That night at the farmhouse, Tom, Aunt Edna and Della were seated around the fire.

"He's got something up his sleeve," said Aunt Edna. "I don't believe Monty Staunton is gonna give a twenty percent raise. I just don't believe it."

"What do you think, Tom?" asked Della.

"I think Monty Staunton's a lot smarter than I gave him credit for," said Tom. "And his offer's genuine. I believe that." He looked at Stan and Ward who were playing on the floor. "He's making it awfully hard for me to say no."

"Did he offer *you* something, Tom?" asked Aunt Edna.

"He said he'd put the boys through college. Pay all the expenses. He offered me other things, too, but *that* was tempting."

"Get behind me, Satan!" said Aunt Edna.

"Exactly. Then of course it's possible the timing is bad for us.

The country's at war, so do we want coal miners to look like traitors?"

"That war's mighty convenient for Monty Staunton," said Aunt Edna. "He and the other mineowners are getting real rich off it."

Tom was still looking at the boys.

"Princeton," he mused. "Isn't that one of those fancy colleges? Can you imagine *my* sons going to Princeton?"

"Probably turn them into sissies," said Aunt Edna.

"What do you think, Della?" asked Tom.

Della rocked slowly.

"It's up to you, Tom."

"No, it's your decision, too. They're *our* sons."

"What if you say no? What will he do then?"

"I don't know. But people might get hurt."

"Then if he's offering everything the union wants, maybe you should consider saying yes."

Tom almost groaned. He could deal with Monty Staunton the son of a bitch. But Monty Staunton the reasonable and generous was pushing him right up against the wall.

Although his miners called Monty a hypocrite, considering his frequent "talks with God" nothing more than theatrical bunk, the man was a true believer and a generous supporter of the church. Thus, when Bill Fargo came into Monty's library at Belle Meade the next evening, he wasn't surprised to see his employer sitting at his desk reading the Bible.

"You wanted to see me, Mr. Staunton?"

Monty looked up from the Scriptures.

"Oh . . . yes, Bill. Sit down."

Bill took a chair in front of the desk. Monty was silent for a moment. Then he made a rather remarkable statement.

"You know, Bill, if you read the Bible—especially the Old Testament—you can't help but come to the conclusion that God is not a particularly nice person."

Since Bill was an atheist, he refrained from comment.

"For instance," Monty went on, "let me read you this from Exodus, chapter twelve, verse twenty-nine and thirty. 'And it came to pass, that at midnight the Lord smote all the firstborn in the land of Egypt, from the firstborn of Pharaoh that sat on his throne unto the firstborn of the captive that was in the dungeon; and all the firstborn of cattle. And Pharaoh rose up in the night, he, and all his servants, and all the Egyptians; and there was a great cry in Egypt: for there was not a house where there was not one dead.' " He looked up from the book. "That's not nice, is it?"

"Hardly."

"Of course, from the viewpoint of the Jews it worked out well. But from the viewpoint of the Egyptians it was a goddam disaster. Right?"

Bill, who had no idea what he was getting at, nodded. "Right."

"If I had been an Egyptian and God had pulled that one on me, I'd have been mad as hell. But you see, Bill, you have to understand how God works. Now, the situation in Egypt was pretty desperate, and God wanted to get things moving, so He had to do something that wasn't exactly nice. The point being that sometimes you have to be cruel for the general good. Wouldn't you agree?"

"Yes."

"And for us right now, the general good means getting the mines working again so we can supply the government with coal. You know, my boy's over in France risking his life every day for this country. And that's why it makes me so goddam mad that these goddam miners won't go back to work—particularly when I've been really reasonable with them. I mean, if I were some sort of monster, it would be one thing; but you know the offer I made Banicek. It was generous. Hell, it was probably crazy on my part, but I want peace in this valley, I want to get the coal to the government, and I want my people to be happy. All right, I've made mistakes in the past—who hasn't? Things are changing fast these days ... changes in attitudes, changes in relationships, and it's hard to keep up with them. But yesterday I tried to wipe the slate clean and make a genuine, bona fide offer that should make everyone happy. And what happens? That little runt turned me down."

He slammed the Bible closed.

"Banicek turned *that* offer down?" said Fargo disbelievingly.

"Yes, sir. He said the union was a matter of principle. Goddam radicals always see *everything* black and white, there's never any gray, no shading, no reasonable compromise. Principle? What's the *point* of the union? Isn't it to get the miners what I'm offering? My God, I don't understand it."

"Then what happens now?"

"Well, we're nowhere unless I take action. Banicek obviously won't budge, and meanwhile no coal is getting dug and the war's going on. I've tried to be nice, Bill. I've tried to be reasonable. They won't respond to that, so I'm forced to be unreasonable. I'm forced to be not nice. It's just like the Lord, Bill: Sometimes you have to be cruel for the general good. I've thought about it, I've prayed, I've talked with the Lord, I've read the Good Book, and I've got a phone call in to the governor to make it all legal."

"I'm sorry, Mr. Staunton, I'm not quite following you. . . ."

Monty leaned forward.

"At dawn tomorrow, Bill, you take those death vehicles into that field and you destroy that tent city. If they won't be reasonable, then by God, *we* won't be reasonable."

"Destroy?" repeated Bill cautiously. "Exactly what do you mean, sir?"

"Take torches and burn the tents. Run the D.V.'s right through them. And if some people get hurt . . . and I'm thinking of *one* person in particular . . . at least we'll have settled once and for all who's boss in this valley. It'll be legal, Bill, don't worry. I'll get the governor to declare a state of wartime emergency. Just *do* it." He put his hand on the Bible. "Unfortunately, there comes a time when you have to be cruel for the general good."

Bill Fargo reflected that it wasn't the first time in history religion and patriotism had been used by the powerful as excuses for death and destruction. Weren't they, in fact, the excuses used by the crowned heads of Europe to start the Great War that was currently slaughtering a generation?

Tom and Della were asleep in each other's arms in the farmhouse when the rat-tat-tat of machine guns awoke them. Tom sat up, rubbing the sleep from his eyes. He could hear distant screaming and, closer, the terrified squawking of Edna's chickens.

"What's that?" murmured Della, also sitting up.

Tom got out of bed and went to the window. He could hardly believe what he saw.

"Monty Staunton's gone *crazy*," he said. "He's gone *crazy!*"

The neighboring field was wreathed in ghostlike early-morning mist, but already a dozen tents were aflame. The death vehicles were rumbling through the tent city like juggernauts, their machine guns firing into the tents, while behind them the Pinkerton men in open trucks flung lighted torches. Miners and their families, most of them in B.V.D.'s and nightshirts, were stumbling out of the tents to flee the deadly invasion. As Tom watched he saw two men and a woman cut down by the hail of bullets.

"Oh God . . ."

He grabbed his pants from the bedpost and pulled them on.

"Tom, you're not going out there?" said Della.

"Somebody has to stop them. They're *killing* people!"

"But not you, Tom! Not *you*—!"

It was too late. Snatching his shirt from a hook, he opened the door and rushed out, throwing the shirt on. Della was out of the bed. Getting her bathrobe, she ran into the parlor. Her mother was coming out of her room.

"What is it—?"

"Tom!"

He was at the front door. He turned to look at her.

"I love you, Della," was all he said. Then he ran outside. She hurried across the room to the door and looked out. The tent city was ablaze, smoke roiling up through the mist. People were running in all directions as the death vehicles continued on their murderous path, in many instances driving into the tents and running over everything in front of them. She had never seen anything so savage.

Tom was running toward the death vehicles, waving his arms frantically, yelling "Stop it! Stop it!" over and over, almost maniacally, as if the slaughter had caused him to go temporarily insane also.

"Come back, Tom!" she cried, tears in her eyes.

She saw one of the death vehicles turn toward her husband. He was running through the tents directly at the machines, as if he alone might be able to stop them. If it was suicidal, it was also brave.

The gun opened fire, chattering furiously. Tom was raked

across the chest. The force of the bullets lifted him momentarily inches off the ground.

Then he fell, face forward.

"Tom!" screamed Della. She started to run out of the house, but her mother grabbed her arm and held her.

"Honey," said Aunt Edna, "it's too late."

Della was sobbing hysterically.

It was all over.

PART VIII
Follies

Chapter 31

The Ziegfeld Follies of 1916 opened in September of that year and starred W. C. Fields, Ina Claire, the black comic Bert Williams, Geraldine Farrar and Nellie Byfield. The motif of the show was Shakespearean, and Nellie played Cleopatra against an enormous set depicting the Sphinx and the Nile. As she sang to Marc Antony the haunting waltz Jake had written for her, called "The Night That We Fell in Love," ten gorgeous Ziegfeld Girls appeared on the bank of the "Nile," parading with their celebrated Ziegfeld Walk a variety of outrageous costumes and gigantic headdresses that had absolutely nothing to do with either Shakespeare or Cleopatra, but which displayed to tempting perfection the fabulous figures of such showgirls as Olive Thomas (who was to die a mysterious death in the Paris Ritz four years later, and whose ghost allegedly haunts the roof of the New Amsterdam Theater to this day) and the haughty, breathtaking Dolores. It was extravagant and a bit silly, but Jake's score was memorable, Nellie was at the peak of her ripe beauty, and the audience loved it. The great showman—now married to the beautiful Billie Burke (who would later achieve immortality as Glinda the Good Witch in *The Wizard of Oz*)—had another triumph on his hands. Ziegfeld owned five Rolls-Royces (each a different color), and his country estate boasted indoor and outdoor swimming pools, a gymnasium, two thousand pigeons, five hundred chickens, four dogs and a monkey. To Ziggy, nothing succeeded like excess.

He threw an opening night party at his suite in the Ansonia, that exuberant Beaux Arts hotel at Broadway and Seventy-third Street, and the place was jammed. The guests stuffed themselves with beluga caviar which was heaped in four silver bowls set in ice, and they swilled Laurent Perrier. Candy, peanuts, and French pastries called *pets de nonnes,* or "nuns' farts" (so named because of their delicacy), were everywhere. Jake was pushed to the grand piano, where at Ziggy's insistence he played his waltz, Nellie standing on top of the piano to sing it and everyone joining in for the chorus. But Jake seemed strangely down, and no amount of begging could get him to play more. Rather, he edged through the crowd to the bedroom, where he closed the door to make a phone call.

"What's wrong with your husband?" Ziggy asked Nellie as she climbed off the piano.

"Oh, Laura's got a cold," she answered. "You know Jake. He's the original worrywart. Every time she sneezes he wants to put her in surgery."

She took a fresh glass of champagne from a passing waiter and changed the subject. Ziggy, who knew how Jake agonized over his daughter, didn't mention Laura further.

The enormous popularity of Jake's songs, which seemed to flow like an artesian well from his talented pen, had made him a millionaire several times over, and a year after marrying Nellie he had bought a handsome Georgian town house on East Sixty-second Street between Madison and Fifth. The five-story building with its pleasant brick facade had been constructed in 1902, so it contained all the modern conveniences: electricity, central heating, telephones and even a small elevator—or lift, as Nellie rather snootily insisted on calling it—which had its own house phone in case one got stuck between floors. Two elaborate wrought-iron and glass double doors were the main entrance and led into a marble-floored foyer with a stair and, behind the stair, the "lift." On the ground floor were the kitchen, pantry and laundry rooms. The second floor held a high-ceilinged double drawing room with French windows overlooking the street, and in the rear, a dining room overlooking the private garden. The third floor had the study-library, two master bedrooms and a tiny room in which Jake locked himself to compose on a black upright. The fourth floor had

Laura's bedroom and playroom; and on the top floor were three servants' rooms which housed Mrs. Fleming, the English nanny, and two maids.

It was to the fourth floor that Jake hurried when he got home from the Ansonia. There he found the pleasant, gray-haired Mrs. Fleming just coming out of Laura's bedroom. She put her finger to her lips as she quietly shut the door.

"She's just dozing off," she whispered.

"How is she?" he whispered back.

"I told you she's much better. Her fever's gone. She's going to be all right, Mr. Rubin. You really mustn't fret so. And there was no need to phone me from the party."

He relaxed a little.

"Do you think I could go in and kiss her good night?"

The matronly nanny smiled. "Well, you shouldn't wake her up, mind; but I don't suppose it could do her any harm. She's always glad to see her father. Go on in—but just a minute. She needs her rest."

"Thank you, Mrs. Fleming."

He opened the door and tiptoed in. The light from the hall revealed a child's fantasy world. The year before, Jake had commissioned Maxfield Parrish to paint murals on the walls of the nursery rooms, and Snow White, Alice, the Mad Hatter, the White Rabbit, the Red Queen, Dorothy and the Wizard of Oz and dozens of other wonderful characters frolicked around the room in an eternal childhood. Jake went to the bed and looked down at his four-and-a-half-year-old daughter.

She had Nellie's blond hair, and there was a vague facial resemblance to Jake. She might have been a pretty child if her head had not been slightly misshapen and too large. Now she opened her eyes and looked at her tuxedoed father.

"Daddy," she said. Her voice was strangely low.

He sat on the bed, leaned over and kissed her. She hugged him, clenching her ill-formed fists.

"Where's Mommy?" she asked.

"Mommy's still at the party," he replied. "The show was a big hit. Your mommy made everybody very happy."

"What's the name of the show?" She had asked the same question at least fifty times in the past month.

"The *Ziegfeld Follies of 1916*," Jake patiently replied.

"What's a follies?"

"Oh . . . something silly. Look, Daddy brought you something good from Mr. Ziegfeld."

He pulled a piece of chocolate candy from his pocket, unwrapped it and put it in her mouth. She chewed it, swallowed it, then said, "Good."

"You're feeling better, Laura. I can tell."

She said nothing.

He kissed her again, then gently removed her arms from around his neck.

"Now go to sleep, honey," he said.

She laid her head on her pillow and closed her eyes.

"I love you, Daddy," she said.

"And your daddy loves you. *Very* much. Good night, darling."

He kissed her again, then stood up and went to the door. Taking a look back, he went out and softly closed the door.

"I think she *is* better," he whispered to Mrs. Fleming, who was waiting in the hall.

"Oh, she'll be bright as a penny in the morning." She smiled.

He stared at her. The nanny turned slightly red, realizing his pain.

"I mean, good as new," she said.

"Good night, Mrs. Fleming."

He walked down the stairs to wait for his wife in the library.

"Ziggy was nice enough to send me home in his Rolls," Nellie said two hours later as she unclasped one of the four diamond bracelets she had worn to the party. Nellie had developed an expensive appetite for jewelry. "Of course, it would have been nicer if my *husband* had brought me home."

"I was worried about Laura," said Jake, who was sitting up in bed.

"Oh, I know. But that's Mrs. Fleming's job, and she's perfectly well qualified to do it. You can't let Laura dominate your life just because she's a half-wit."

Jake winced. "For God's sake, don't you have *any* compassion?"

She turned to look at him.

"Of course I have compassion. But it doesn't help anyone—including Laura—to try and hide the truth behind a lot of fuzzy words."

"But 'half-wit' is so cruel—"

"Oh, all right, she's slow. Does that make you feel better? The point is, she's never going to get better, and we both have to face that fact and adjust our lives to it. It was important for you to be at Ziggy's tonight, and it was rude and silly to run off just because Laura has a cold. If nothing else, it just reminds everybody that our daughter is . . ." she hesitated, ". . . not all there."

She began unbuttoning her light blue chiffon dress with the pink silk rose at the waist. Jake watched her undress. His physical desire for her was as strong as ever, but years of marriage had taught him Nellie had an icicle for a heart. He sometimes wondered if he loved her or was just fascinated by her.

"Anyway," she went on, stepping out of her dress, "I thought the show went fabulously well, but you'd never know we had a hit from Ziggy. He's the most—what's the word?—phlegmatic man I've ever met. Is it 'phlegmatic,' Jake? You're the word expert."

"Yes, phlegmatic. I was proud of you tonight, Nellie."

"Why, thanks, darling. There's no point my telling you your score was terrific—I'd just be repeating what everybody else said. But I'll say it anyway: The music was wonderful. I think the waltz is the loveliest thing you've ever written."

She went into her dressing room to hang up her dress. Her fifteen-foot-long mirrored closet held over eighty different outfits, and the tilted shoe rack held fifty pairs of shoes, each with its custom-made shoe trees carved out of violin wood by an Italian on the Lower East Side. There were drawers filled with silk lingerie made by an order of Belgian nuns on Long Island, a safe for her jewels, and a cedar closet for her six fur coats. Nellie was doing her level best to spend the enormous income she and Jake generated from the theater, and she had absolutely no interest at all in the concept of "whispered wealth." "If you've got it, wear it" was her social philosophy; and if she had ever felt any need to justify herself—which she didn't—she could have said it was expected of her because she was a star.

"I'm exhausted," she yawned as she came back into the bedroom in her white silk nightgown. "And I drank too much bubbly.

I hope I don't have a headache in the morning." She turned out the crystal lamp on her dressing table and went to the bed. The bedroom walls were papered with hand-painted panels she had imported from a dealer in Hong Kong, and exquisite concubines of the Ch'ien Lung Emperor drifted around the walls in an enchanted Chinese garden, at a hundred dollars a panel.

"There's something for you under your pillow," said Jake.

"Well, I was *wondering*," she said, reaching under and pulling out a Cartier box. She opened it. Inside was a diamond brooch in the shape of a butterfly, its eyes emeralds and its two platinum antennae tipped with rubies.

"Oh, darling, it's beautiful!" she enthused, leaning over to kiss him. "Thank you."

"That's for tonight," he said, adding, "there's a card."

She reached under the pillow again and found the envelope. Opening it, she pulled out a card on which was written, "You're the most beautiful star on Broadway. I want another child. Love, Jake."

She frowned, put the brooch and the card on her bed table, turned out her light, and turned on her side, her back to her husband.

"Did you read the card?" he asked, watching her.

"Yes, and I don't want to get into *that* boring conversation again."

"I don't find it boring," he said, his anger mounting.

"We made a pact, Jake: *one* child. I lived up to my end of the bargain. We have Laura. It's not my fault she's damaged goods."

"*Damn* you!" he roared, grabbing her shoulder and turning her toward him. "It's not fair! I want another chance."

"Let go of me! And don't give me any of this shit about another chance—you *had* your chance."

"I ... want ... another ... child."

He was straddling her, shaking her furiously. She tried to push him off.

"Jake, let me alone! Damn you—"

"You've put me off too damned long. Tonight, I'm not going to use a condom...."

"You think I'm going to let you make love to me after *this*?"

"You haven't got any choice!"

He ripped open her nightgown.

"Jake!" she screamed.

He pulled down his pajama pants. Then, as she continued to scream, he pinned her to the bed and went in.

"I warn you," she said, "if you knock me up, I'll go to a doctor. I'm warning you, Jake. You're just wasting your time."

He pulled out of her, released her, crawled over her and off the bed, tugged up his pajama bottoms, then limped to a chair in the corner of the room, curled into it and started to cry.

"Oh Jesus, Nellie," he sobbed, "as good as I am to you, why can't you be good to me?"

"Good to me?" she exclaimed, sitting up and turning the bed light back on. "When you try to *rape* me on my opening goddam night? If that's your idea of being good, I'd hate like hell to see you turn mean."

He looked at her with bloodshot eyes.

"I want a normal kid," he sniffed. "I love Laura till it breaks my heart, but I want a normal kid."

"Then adopt one," she said, getting out of bed and looking at her upper arms. "Damn you, Jake, you bruised me. Well, I suppose makeup will cover it." She came to the chair and looked down at him. "Don't you *ever* get violent with me again," she said, coolly. Then she pointed to his bulging pajama bottoms and said, "God, does that thing ever go limp?"

She walked to the door.

"Where are you going?" he said, sitting up.

"To sleep in the next room. Sleeping in the same bed with Mr. Hyde is too much for my nerves."

And she left the room.

Chapter 32

If there are any universal truths that can be said about mankind, one would seem to be that every society in recorded history has naturally evolved some kind of pecking order; and few pecking orders were more highly evolved than that of New York society in the early years of this century. One of the major complications was that there were *two* societies. One was the gentile society of Phipps Ogden, the Astors, Vanderbilts, Goelets, and such, which had its own rules and taboos. The other was the Jewish society, the "our crowd" of Loebs, Schiffs, Guggenheims, Wertheims and Seligmans, who had *their* own rituals and taboos, many of which were mirror-images of the gentile society. At this pinnacle of moneyed American aristocracy (and by 1916 it had become an aristocracy, albeit one without titles), the two worlds often touched; there was even some intermarriage. Indeed, a visitor from another planet would have had some difficulty telling the two worlds apart. Many of the Jewish grandees even shared their gentile counterparts' anti-Semitism, and despite attendance at synagogues and patronage of "Jewish" charities such as Mount Sinai Hospital, the Henry Street Settlement, and the New York Association for the Blind, the unwritten rule was to be as little "Jewish" as possible. "Jewish" in this sense meant anything even faintly redolent of the Lower East Side, of dirty peddlers in long coats, of knishes and bagels and chicken fat. When Maud told Marco that the basis of most name-calling in New York was class rather than race, she knew whereof she spoke. Thus, when the department store magnate Simon Weiler told his wife, Rebecca, that he had invited Jake Rubin to tea the following afternoon, this imposing, humorless woman, whom one wit had labeled the Jewish Lady Bracknell, looked as if she had just found a large and particularly juicy cockroach in her salad.

"Whatever *for*?" she said, staring down the long dining-room table at her fat, bearded husband, who owned twenty-six department stores across the country and commanded a fortune in excess of fifty million.

"The Liberty Loan Drive," he replied, sipping his Romanée-Conti '09.

"What in the world is a Liberty Loan Drive?"

"As you know, President Wilson is campaigning for reelection on a keep-America-out-of-the-war platform, but my friends at the Treasury think he's whistling in the dark. They think there's an even chance we'll be in the war soon. . . ."

"But my dear Simon," interrupted his wife, "how could *we* fight the Germans? *We* are Germans. I find the idea preposterous."

"Preposterous or not," sighed her patient husband, "they think we'll be fighting soon, and they're already drawing up plans to finance the war. One scheme is to sell what they're calling Liberty Loans to get the public to invest in the government on an unprecedented scale. They've asked me to serve on the New York committee, and one of the ideas is to get Broadway talent to do a musical show to entertain the public's money out of its pocket. I've approached Mr. Rubin to see if he'd be interested in writing the music for such a show, and he's agreed to come discuss it tomorrow. He seems like a pleasant young man."

"But he's from the Lower East Side," huffed Rebecca, who once had been a beauty, but now, at forty-eight, had turned into a gray-haired monument.

"Ah, but now he lives on the *Upper* East Side. In fact, just three blocks from us."

"Still, he's an Ashkenazi."

"Rebecca, you forget that *we* are Ashkenazim."

"We're Germans, not Russians."

"Your knowledge of Jewish history is a bit foggy, my dear. There are Sephardic Jews like the Lazaruses, who came from Spain and Portugal. And there are the rest, who are Ashkenazim, who are Mr. Rubin and, I regret to inform you, us."

"I have no interest in history," she snorted. "I know what I know, and what I know is that we Germans are people of culture and refinement, while the Russian Jews are barely off the boat and rarely bathe. I assume you will not expect me to meet this Mr. Rubin socially?"

"I not only expect it, Rebecca, I insist on it. Mr. Rubin has something our country needs: talent. I will be asking him to volunteer his talent. I will expect you to extend all the hospitality of our house—as if he were one of the Loebs or Schiffs."

"Broadway," she said, contemptuously, wiping her mouth with her damask napkin. "That *hardly* seems the type of entertainment *we*—or the government, for that matter—should get involved with. Why don't you put on a production of *Lohengrin*?"

Again, her husband sighed.

"Because A, Wagner was a German, and Germany is the enemy. And B, the public is bored by opera."

"Did you ever consider that it might be our duty to uplift the public's taste? Heaven knows it could stand uplifting."

"If the public gets too fancy," said Simon Weiler, "they won't come to my department stores, and then *we* won't be able to afford to go to the opera."

Rebecca Weiler stiffened. "That is *not* amusing, Simon," she said. "And I find the remark in rather poor taste."

She rang the crystal bell to summon the servants to clear the first course.

The Weiler town house, at the corner of Sixty-fifth and Fifth, had been built in 1897 in the French Renaissance style and was a grandiose limestone pile of spires, towers, *tourelles,* oriel windows and ornate stone chimneys, all surrounded by a delicate-looking but quite strong wrought-iron fence. The next afternoon at five, Jake, looking well-dressed in a dark suit, astrakhan-collared overcoat and bowler hat, rang the bell, drinking in the architectural fantasies of the Weiler mansion with an appreciative eye. The butler admitted him to the front hall, which surrounded a circular marble fountain, took his coat and hat and led him to the drawing room.

"Mr. Jake Rubin," he announced grandly. Jake's first impression of the mammoth room was gold: It was as if the decorator had been King Midas. The French furniture was gold, the heavily carved console tables were gold, the oil paintings were gold-framed, the high silk draperies were gold, the two chandeliers were gilt—even the autumn sunlight pouring through the Fifth Avenue windows was gold. Simon Weiler, a high-cut double-breasted suit minimizing his paunch, came to Jake and shook his hand.

"Mr. Rubin, it's a pleasure to meet you. And I most appreciate your coming this afternoon."

"It's my honor, sir," said Jake, noticing the girl in the white dress sitting on the sofa next to the formidable lady in mauve with three strands of enormous pearls covering her ample bosom.

"This is my wife," Simon was saying, leading Jake to the woman behind the tea tray. "Rebecca, this is Jake Rubin."

Rebecca held out her hand, forcing a wintry smile.

"My husband and I have seen several of your musical plays, Mr. Rubin," she said. "We enjoy your music, though I must say that sometimes the dialogue is not as tasteful as one would prefer."

"Well, uh, I don't write the dialogue, Mrs. Weiler."

"I'm glad to hear it. And this is our daughter, Violet, who insisted on meeting you." *Why, I can't imagine,* she thought, *though he dresses better than I would have guessed, and he's rather handsome—for an Ashkenazi.*

Violet was aptly named; her eyes were pale violet, which with her auburn hair made an arresting combination. Nineteen, slim, with beautiful skin, she was enchanting. She smiled as she shook Jake's hand.

"My first love is ballet, Mr. Rubin," she said, "but my second is your music. I'm a great fan."

"Thank you," he said.

"Tea, Mr. Rubin?" said Rebecca.

"Uh . . ." He tore his eyes from the daughter to the mother. "Yes, please."

"Lemon or cream?"

"Both. I mean . . . cream, please."

The setting, about as cozy as Buckingham Palace, and Mrs. Weiler, about as chummy as Queen Victoria, were making him nervous and clumsy. When she handed him his cup and saucer, he was so shaky the cup rattled, which of course made him even more nervous. By the time he sat down in the uncomfortably stiff chair, he was feeling clammy. But the girl—what a jewel! Could that old cow be her mother?

Mrs. Weiler began the conversation.

"My husband has apprised me of your kind interest in donating your talents to the government, Mr. Rubin," she began. "If you wrote the score for an entertainment, what kind of show would you have in mind?"

"Well, uh ... I hadn't given it much thought yet. Mr. Weiler called me only a few days ago. I suppose it would be a sort of revue."

"A revue. Something like Mr. Ziegfeld's extravaganzas, one assumes?"

"Perhaps not as ... well, lavish. But songs, of course. And dance numbers. And comedy skits."

"Comedy skits," she repeated. "Of course, nowadays what passes for comedy might less charitably be labeled gutter humor. I'm afraid the age of the epigram is past, unhappily."

"Well," said Jake, desperately trying to make a joke, "Oscar Wilde *is* dead, after all."

An ominous silence, broken only by Jake's rattling teacup.

"We do *not* mention that man's name in this house, Mr. Rubin," intoned Mrs. Weiler, and Jake wished he could die.

Simon Weiler came to the rescue.

"Rebecca," he said, "I think Mr. Rubin is in more of a position to judge what the public likes than we are. After all, he's in show business." He turned to Jake. "So you think a revue would be best? Can you suggest some comedy writers a bit less sensational than Mr. Wilde?"

"Oh, sure. There's Morry Klein—he's great on one-liners. And there's Yuri Kadinsky—his specialty is skits with girlie gags. . . ."

"Girlie gags?" interrupted Mrs. Weiler, her lips curling. "My dear Mr. Rubin, I must remind you that this show will be sponsored by the government of the United States. One assumes there will be dignitaries in the audience—diplomats, senators, perhaps even the President! Surely 'girlie gags' would be grossly inappropriate."

"Doesn't the President like girls?" asked Jake, with fake innocence. He had taken just about enough of Mrs. Weiler.

"That is *hardly* the point. In my opinion, if there are to be any 'comedy skits,' as you call them, it would be more in keeping with the spirit of the occasion to restage scenes from Sheridan, perhaps, or Restoration comedy. Or even Shakespeare. Yes— something from *As You Like It* might be charming, come to think of it. And as far as music is concerned, as a patron of the Metropolitan Opera, I would be sorely disappointed if a few selections from grand opera were not included. I am aware you will be appealing to the mass audience, but surely we cannot afford to ignore those people best prepared to loan the government substantial sums, namely Society?"

Jake's cup was no longer rattling. He had turned to ice.

"I think," he said, standing up, "you've got the wrong composer." He put his cup and saucer on a table. "It's been nice meeting you," he went on. "I won't take up any more of your time. Good afternoon."

"Now, wait a minute," said Simon, standing up. "My wife has got this all wrong. . . ."

"I'm sorry, Mr. Weiler, but I think you're looking for a classier act than mine. If you'd like, I can put you in touch with Signor Puccini. He's a friend of mine."

"Puccini is a friend of *yours?*" gasped Mrs. Weiler.

"Yes," smiled Jake. "I met him when he was in New York a few years ago. He liked one of my songs so much, he insisted I give him an autographed score."

Screw you, lady, he thought as he walked out of the room.

Violet got off the sofa.

"Mother," she said, "you really ought to come out of the fourteenth century."

"Violet! I will not be spoken to that way!"

"I can't *believe* how rude you were to him. I'm going to apologize."

She started across the room.

"There is nothing to apologize for. Puccini, indeed. As if I believed *that* pack of lies! Puccini can't even speak English. I say good riddance to Mr. Rubin."

When Violet came into the entrance hall, the butler was just opening the door.

"Mr. Rubin," she said, hurrying up to him. "I . . . well, I want to apologize for Mother. She didn't mean half the things she said. . . ."

"Didn't she?"

"Well, maybe she did. But anyway . . ." She suddenly felt stupid. "*I* like your music and so does everyone else, and Mother's so stuffy she makes me want to scream and . . . and I wish someone would kick her in the pants!"

He smiled. "I'd be glad to volunteer."

As he walked out of the house, she found herself enchanted by his smile. It was one of the nicest smiles she'd ever seen on a young man.

"Mr. Rubin!" She ran out after him.

He turned. "Yes?"

"I know this will sound . . . well, I realize you probably hate amateur theatricals, but I study ballet with Mme. Levitska above Carnegie Hall and our class is putting on a show tomorrow afternoon and I'm doing the *pas de deux* from *Swan Lake* and . . ." She turned red. ". . . Everybody would be thrilled *silly* if you were there. And I won't be hurt if you say no, but I really *am* good. Well, not *that* good, but . . ."

"Will your mother be there?"

"Yes, but I could save you a seat on the other side of the room. The whole thing's only an hour. I don't think you'd be *too* bored. Well, you probably would. I'm sorry, I shouldn't have asked."

"What time does it start?"

"Five."

"I'll be there—*if* you promise to have a drink with me afterwards."

"A drink? You mean a cocktail?"

"Yes. At the Plaza."

A married man asking me *for a drink?* she thought, her head spinning. *How wildly sophisticated!*

"I'd *love* it," she blurted out. Then she thought of her mother. "But Mother mustn't know . . ."

"If you bring her along, I'll walk out."

"Oh, I wouldn't bring *her*. . . . I know: You leave Mme. Levitska's by yourself; then I'll meet you later at the Plaza. I'll lie to Mother. . . ."

"Good." He smiled. "See you tomorrow."

He started walking home. Violet watched him, thinking, *What an interesting man.*

270

Chapter 33

Jake's emotions were in such turmoil, because of his fight with Nellie and his constant agonizing over his retarded daughter, that meeting the lovely, nubile Violet Weiler was a breath of emotional fresh air. That the girl seemed so impressed by him flattered his ego; and though he thought the chances were probably slim of their relationship being anything but platonic, still the idea of seducing her occurred to him—after all, he wasn't *that* much older than she—and nothing would have kept him away from the recital at Mme. Levitska's, even the prospect of encountering for a second time that dragon, Mrs. Weiler.

Mme. Levitska was a chirpy sparrow of a woman who had once been a favorite of Tsar Alexander III (or so she claimed) and her studio on the fourth floor of Carnegie Hall was a barren room with mirrored walls, a battered grand piano and the inevitable barre. For the recital, a curtain had been strung across the room and folding chairs placed in front of it. Several dozen parents were seated, including the Weilers; but Jake was spared Rebecca, because when she spotted him, after her initial shock, she snubbed him. *Thank God,* thought Jake, and he settled back to study the printed program.

"Messieurs et Mesdames," announced Mme. Levitska as she came through the curtain. "We are proud to present our leetle program of our oh-so-talented leetle pupils."

She sat at the piano and began banging out "The Dance of the Hours." The curtain was tugged open, and eight girls in tutus went through their paces. Although one rather pudgy girl almost knocked over one of her fellow Hours, and none of the pupils would have ever made the Bolshoi, the parents dutifully applauded. Next came Violet and one of the male students, and suddenly there was magic.

Jake sat up. He didn't know enough about ballet to know

whether the dancing was good, technically. But anyone could tell that Violet danced with exceptional grace, and Jake's romantic soul responded strongly to the lush music and the sheer loveliness of the girl. She was delicate poetry in motion, she was innocence, she was purity, she was all the things Jake dreamed of in women, all the things he thought Nellie had been when he first saw her sing on the stage of the Cavendish Club so many years before and which time and experience had so cruelly exposed as illusion. When the *pas de deux* was over he jumped to his feet, yelling "Bravo! Bravo!" and applauding so loudly that Mrs. Weiler glared at him and said to her husband, "Such a vulgar display! Really, that Mr. Rubin has *keine Kultur*. And what in the world is he doing here, anyway?"

"Maybe he's interested in Violet," said Simon, with a mischievous twinkle in his eye. The look of shocked horror on his wife's face was so funny, it almost made up for thirty years of listening to her bombast.

"You were *terrific!*" said Jake forty-five minutes later as Violet joined him in the Champagne Court (which would in time become the Palm Court).

She looked delighted by the compliment.

"Did you really think so? Oh, Mr. Rubin, to hear that from *you* . . . I *was* good, wasn't I? Jim—he's my partner—was scared silly and so was I, but I thought it went awfully well. Mother absolutely roasted me about why you were there."

"What did you tell her?"

"I told her the truth: that I invited you. She got very huffy and said, 'Well! He made a spectacle of himself applauding'; and I said, 'After all, Mother, Mr. Rubin is a professional showman and he recognizes talent when he sees it.' Then she got so nervous thinking maybe I'll want to become a pro and go on the stage, that she shut up."

They both laughed.

"What would you like to drink?"

"Oh, something *very* wicked and strong. To be perfectly honest with you, I've never been out with a married man before, and I'm sure I've compromised my reputation, so I might as well go all the way and get tipsy and fall down on my face in public. What do *you* think I should have?"

"Do you like champagne?"

"I love it."

While he ordered a bottle of champagne, she was looking around the crowded room.

"I'm hoping I'll see someone I know so Mother will hear about this, but I don't recognize a soul. Oh, well, it's probably just as well. I told Mother I was going to Olivia Hamilton's—she's a friend of mine—and if she found out I was *really* out with you, she'd go through the roof. It really was wonderful of you to ask me, Mr. Rubin. This is probably the most exciting thing that's ever happened to me."

"You're kidding."

"No, honestly. Mother guards me like a hawk."

"You mean you don't have any boyfriends?"

She looked surprised. He couldn't take his eyes off her.

"I didn't say *that*," she said. "I'm practically engaged."

His spirits plunged but he tried to look indifferent.

"Oh? To whom?"

"His name's Craig Wertheim. I've known him for years—his family's cottage is next to ours up in the Adirondacks—and he's very nice. He's over in Italy now driving an ambulance. He volunteered, which I thought was terribly brave. Anyway, when he comes back we'll get officially engaged and then married. But meanwhile, I'm going to pack in just as much as I can—which means cocktails with married men. Wait till I tell Olivia! She'll *die* with envy."

The waiter brought the champagne and served it.

"To *Swan Lake*," said Jake.

"To Tchaikovsky, my second favorite composer."

"Who's your first?" asked Jake, not daring to hope.

"Mozart."

"Oh."

They clinked glasses.

"Your wife's so beautiful," she went on. "It must be wonderful being married to a glamorous star. Does she get fan letters?"

"Oh, yes."

"You must be terribly in love."

He ran his finger over the rim of the glass.

"Yes, I suppose I am."

"Suppose? Don't you *know*?"

273

He looked at her sadly.

"No, I don't know. Not anymore."

For the first time she felt a hint of his vulnerability, and it embarrassed her.

"I'm sorry, I didn't mean to . . . pry."

"No, I'm glad you asked."

He looked at her so intently she became nervous, as if realizing she was stumbling into an adult world she knew nothing about.

"I've written a lot of love songs," he went on, "but the funny thing is, I'm not sure I know what love really is. I know what infatuation is, because I used to be infatuated with my wife. But love is supposed to last, isn't it?"

"I think so. I guess I never really thought about it."

"I guess I never did either. Oh, I know love rhymes with 'above' and 'glove' and 'of' and 'shove' and it would make songwriting a lot easier if it rhymed with *more* words. But that's about all I do know about it. Sometimes I wonder if I haven't been peddling dreams all these years in my songs. Or illusions."

She frowned. "What a terrible thought: that love's just an illusion."

"Oh well, I'm probably wrong. I'm wrong about a lot of things these days. But don't let me be a wet blanket. More champagne?"

"Thanks. And you're not a wet blanket. I just think you *feel* things more deeply than most people, and I think that's nice."

And attractive, she thought. *Very attractive.*

When she got home, the butler said, "Your mother wishes to see you in the library, Miss Violet," and she thought: *trouble.* When she came into the library, which was the only room in the baronial house that was remotely cozy, her mother was sitting in a high-backed Renaissance chair doing petit point.

"Where have you been, Violet?" she asked in a soft voice.

"I told you I went to Olivia's," she replied, instantly on the defensive. Rebecca Weiler might not have been the broadest-minded woman in New York, but she was a formidable adversary. It took all of Violet's will to confront her.

"Indeed?" said her mother. "You know, Violet, your father and I have lavished love and affection on you. It wounds me deeply to be repaid by falsehoods. It so happens by sheer coincidence Olivia's mother telephoned me a half hour ago. When I asked her if you had left yet, she said you had never come. Now I would like the *truth,* young lady."

Violet sat down. "The truth is, Mr. Rubin asked me to the Plaza for a cocktail. I knew you'd never let me go, so I lied."

A stormy Wagnerian silence.

"I see. I assume you are aware that Mr. Rubin has a wife?"

"Of course. Oh, Mother, you don't have to go into it. I knew what I was doing, and it's not the end of the world. I *like* him! He's an interesting man. What possible harm could come from my having a cocktail with him?"

"He is a despicable little Russian. . . ."

"He's *not* despicable! If you'd only get to know him a little, you'd find he's charming and sweet and quite intelligent and deep. . . ."

"Deep? A Tin Pan Alley Tunesmith, as I believe the crasser periodicals describe him? And what vast reservoir of Socratic philosophy have you discovered in him? That 'moon' rhymes wth 'June'? Modern life is a *bit* more complex than the lyrics of popular songs would lead us to believe."

Violet sighed. "Mother, you're being impossible."

"I am merely trying to discover what possible reason you could have for jeopardizing your reputation by being seen with this vulgar man in public."

"He's *not* vulgar. He's different, he's new. . . ."

"In my opinion, a mania for novelty is no hallmark of gentle breeding. And need I point out that your behavior is hardly fair to Craig and his parents? While that brave young man is risking his life in Italy for a cause he thinks is noble, you are drinking cocktails at the Plaza with a married man considerably older than yourself. What would Craig think if he knew? What would his parents think?"

"I'm sure Craig would understand, and his parents too. It's not as if I did something *awful.*"

Her mother looked at her suspiciously.

"Awful? And just *what* do you mean by awful?"

Violet squirmed.

"Oh, I don't know. Kissing him . . ."

"Kissing him? I'm amazed such a thought would even occur to you. This man's Broadway vulgarity must be contagious. Did he *try* to kiss you?"

"Of course not. He was a perfect gentleman."

"Then why did you mention it? Oh Violet, you are behaving so foolishly, so selfishly. . . ."

"Oh, all *right*," she said, exasperated. "You win! I'm sorry, and I won't do it again."

"I trust that means you are not contemplating any further clandestine rendezvous with Mr. Rubin?"

"No. I mean, yes. I won't see him again."

"Then I believe we may consign this sordid incident to the oblivion it so richly deserves. There are our kind of people, my dear, and there is everybody else. Craig Wertheim is our kind. Mr. Rubin is definitely everybody else. You may kiss me, child. We are having sole véronique for dinner, which should please you."

"I'm not hungry," she said, getting up and going to the door.

"Violet!" said her mother, sternly. "I *said* you may kiss me."

Violet looked at her defiantly, said nothing, and left the room.

Chapter 34

To a later age, Rebecca Weiler's snobberies would seem laughable, but Jake Rubin took her with dead seriousness. He knew all too well the prejudice against the "Russians," as Russian, Polish and Bohemian Jews were all dubbed, on the part of the established German Jews. The German Jews had come to America in the nineteenth century and had built their fortunes against formidable odds: not only the anti-Semitism of the Christians, but the anti-German-Jews-ism of the established Sephardic Jews. By 1900 the German Jews had "arrived" and were assimilating well into American society. But then, the floodgates had opened and the great tidal wave of poor "Russian" Jews had swept through Ellis

Island, reviving all the old incendiary anti-Semitism, which the German Jews were so afraid could easily be turned against them again. Thus, Jake, who was "Russian," could well understand Mrs. Weiler's abhorrence of him; he represented some vague threat to her own social security, and the merest hint of any romantic interest between her beloved daughter and Jake Rubin was more than enough reason for her to load every cannon she had at her command and declare open warfare.

Just how open the warfare was, Jake found out the next day. He didn't know if he had any romantic interest in Violet, but he was certainly enchanted and intrigued with the beautiful girl, and he called the Weiler house to talk to her. But when the butler heard his name, he froze the line with "Miss Violet is not at home, Mr. Rubin, and will not receive any calls from you in the future." Click.

If it were going to be open warfare, Jake was ready to fire a few guns of his own. He determined to launch a two-pronged attack, one at Violet and the other at her mother. He knew that the German Jews—not only out of humanitarian reasons, but in an attempt to "launder" and "pretty up" the hundreds of thousands of desperately poor Russian Jews who were turning New York into one of the most Jewish cities in the world—had set up a number of philanthropic organizations to improve the lot of the Jewish poor. One of these was the Amalgamated Hebrew Fund, to which the Weilers were heavy contributors and of which Mrs. Weiler was honorary chairwoman. Jake sent off a check for twenty-five thousand dollars to the Amalgamated Hebrew Fund. Like the German Jews, he had mixed motives. He was glad to help alleviate the suffering in the slums from which he had himself so recently escaped.

But he also figured the handsome check could hardly fail to impress Rebecca Weiler.

He then went to Mme. Levitska's ballet studio, where Violet had told him she had a two-hour lesson every day, beginning at ten. Mrs. Weiler might be able to cut off the telephone, but she couldn't keep him away from Mme. Levitska's.

Violet was just finishing her barre exercises when he arrived, and when she saw him, her face first lit up, then looked troubled. He waited in the corner until the lesson was finished. Then she hurried over to him.

277

"Mother found out about last night," she whispered. "There was a terrible scene...."

"I know," he interrupted. "She told you you mustn't see me again."

"How did you know?"

"I guessed." He grinned. "When your butler frosted me on the phone. How about lunch?"

She looked confused. "Well ... Mr. Rubin ..."

"Please—Jake."

"All right, Jake. I don't see much *point* to it. I mean, all it will do will be to get me in more hot water with Mother if she finds out, which she will—Mother finds out everything. It's very sweet of you and I'd love to talk to you more, but I did promise Mother I wouldn't see you again, and, well, I just don't see any *point.*"

"I know a wonderful Chinese restaurant two blocks from here. If you'll have lunch with me there, I'll tell you the point."

She bit her lip.

"You're awful," she said. "I'll meet you downstairs in twenty minutes."

"How did you know I love Chinese food?" she asked a half hour later after they had ordered two from Column A and two from Column B.

"Everybody in show business loves Chinese food."

"I'm not in show business."

"You study ballet."

"That's not show business."

"All right, it's art. But don't you enjoy performing?"

"Oh, *yes.* I think I'm a ham at heart."

"Then you're a performer, and that makes you show business, which is why you like Chinese food. You told me your mother's afraid you'll make a career out of ballet. Have you considered it? In my opinion, you're good enough."

"Oh, I've considered it. Or maybe dreamed about it is more accurate. That's why I left Vassar—so I could spend more time studying here in New York. Besides, Mother thinks two years of college is all a 'lady' needs anyway. But I don't have any illusions about making a career of it. There's no future for American ballerinas, and all the publicity if I tried to go on the stage ... well, as

278

much as I fight with Mother, I wouldn't want to subject her and Father to that. So I'll remain an amateur."

"What kind of publicity?"

"You know—society girls aren't supposed to do that sort of thing. No one would take me seriously anyway."

"Is society that important to you?"

She looked surprised at the question.

"I don't know. I don't *think* so, but I'm used to it, and ... well, it takes a lot of nerve to break the rules. Just as I'm breaking the rules now, having lunch with you in a Chinese restaurant." She puffed herself up and imitated her mother. "Chinese restaurants are not *comme il faut,* my dear."

He smiled. "You do her pretty well."

"Well, I ought to; I've heard her enough. Now, I've come to lunch with you; you have to live up to your end of it."

"Which is?"

"What's the point of this lunch?"

"The point is to get to know you better. That's all. And I enjoy being with you."

She looked troubled.

"But why *me?* I'm not complaining—really!—but I'm just curious. You're a Broadway celebrity who probably has every show-girl in New York fawning over you. What in the world could interest you in *me?* I try and act sophisticated, but I'm really not, and I know it."

He didn't want to tell her yet that he was falling in love with her, for fear of frightening her away; so instead he said, "Let me put it this way: If this were one of my shows, I'd probably have the hero—me—sing a song at this point about how lovely you are, and how sweet and young and inexperienced. And I'd probably tack on a chorus that would say how you're everything my wife isn't, which is why I enjoy being with you so much."

She blushed.

"I think I'd like that song," she said. "But ..."

"But what?"

He could tell she was nervous.

"I don't want to compete with your wife. That's not fair to her—or me, for that matter. I guess what I'm trying to say is ..."

Again she hesitated.

279

"What?"

She confronted him.

"I'm beginning to like you too much to see you anymore."

The waiter served the egg rolls. Jake forked his listlessly, desperately trying to think of a reply. He admired her honesty as much as he disliked his duplicity. As much as he was pleased by her remark, and the fact that she was beginning to feel an involvement with him that was frightening her, he had run up against the brick wall of her innocence and his marriage.

"Then," he finally said, "we can do the simple thing, which would be not to see each other again. Or we can do the complicated thing, which is to fall in love with each other."

"In love?" she marveled. "But I thought you didn't believe in love anymore?"

"When I'm with you, I believe in it."

She savored this a moment, liking it.

"But *love* . . . you and me . . . it's impossible, isn't it? You're married, I'm practically engaged . . . it has to be impossible."

"It's not impossible. But it might be very unpleasant, for both of us—which is why we have to be careful and think things out before we do something we'll regret." He pulled his wallet from his coat and extracted a card. "This is the number of my business phone," he said, handing her the card. "You think about what you want to do, and if you want to see me again, call me on that number. That way, it can be private, just between you and me. I don't want to lure you into anything that might mess up your life; believe me, I respect you too much for that. On the other hand, my life's already a mess, and if anything, you might be able to straighten it out . . . so I'll be hoping you call. Whatever you decide, Violet, you're the loveliest thing that's happened to me in years. And even if we never see each other again, I'll always remember these past few days as something very special and precious."

She looked at the card, then at him.

He really means it, she thought. *Oh Lord, now what do I do? And what does he mean by keeping it "private" and not wanting to lure me into something that will mess up my life?*

If only I knew what he's talking about! Is he talking about making me his mistress? *I don't even know what mistresses do!*

280

Chapter 35

In the first week of June 1916, Marco took his not-quite-five-year-old son, Frank (who was named after Vanessa's maternal grandfather) to Washington to show the handsome black-haired boy the sights of the capital and to visit Phipps. Normally, Phipps would have been on his way to Newport by now, because the senator (who had won reelection to his fourth term in 1912, bucking the Democratic tide that brought Professor Woodrow Wilson into the White House) couldn't stand the humid heat of Washington in the summer. But the pressure of the European War was preventing congressmen from going home; and though Phipps had lost his chairmanship of the Foreign Relations Committee, he was still his party's leading spokesman on foreign affairs and was heading the pro-involvement faction in the Senate, for Phipps was convinced the Germans would win unless America entered the war on the Allied side. So Phipps was still in Washington; and after Marco had shown his son the White House and the Washington Monument, he took him to the Capitol, where they were led to Phipps's office.

Because of Phipps's seniority, he had one of the most prestigious offices in the building, and as Frank came into the high-ceilinged room with the enormous glass-bowled, be-crystaled chandelier that was a holdover from the 1870's, the boy gawked.

"Here he is," exclaimed Phipps, coming around his heavily carved desk and crossing the flowered Axminster carpet to pick his grandson up and kiss him. "Grandpa's pride and joy! How are you, you little rascal?"

Frank hugged him. "I'm fine, Grandpa. Boy, you've got a *big* office. You must be important."

"Oh, I *am*," laughed Phipps. "Nobody makes a move in this town without checking it out with me first."

"That chandelier's funny-looking."

"That chandelier was hung up there forty years ago, and I'm told the contractor charged the Congress twice what it was worth and got away with it. Marco, how are you? It's good to see you."

They shook hands; then Frank was turned over to one of Phipps's aides for a tour of the building. Marco, who was wearing a double-breasted white linen suit, took a chair, saying, "Vanessa sends her love."

"Good," said Phipps, going back behind his desk. "When is she planning to go to Newport?"

"In a couple of weeks. She's working on a new statue, and she's being very secretive about it."

Phipps lit his pipe. "Is she cutting down on her drinking?" he asked quietly.

"Well, she's stopped drinking at lunch. That's something."

Phipps leaned forward. "What's *wrong* with her, Marco? She's gotten so damned moody lately, and now this drinking . . . I don't understand her. She's got a wonderful son, a fine husband, everything in the world she could want, and yet she doesn't seem to enjoy anything except going out to her studio and working on those damned statues. She seems to resent *me,* which I don't quite understand. I know she doesn't agree with my politics, but still and all, I'm her father. The strange thing is, I get along with you, but don't get along with my own daughter. I simply don't understand it."

"Part of the problem is my fault," said Marco. "I've been at Columbia these past four years, so I haven't seen as much of her as I should have. And I haven't had any income, so I've had to depend on Vanessa and you. It's been a mixed-up situation, which has been hard on her. But now I've got my degree and maybe I can start being the head of my household for the first time. Which is one reason I came to Washington."

"What do you mean?"

"I want to go into politics."

Phipps looked surprised. "Politics? You?"

"Why not?"

"But you don't know anything about them."

"I can learn. You can teach me." He stood up. "I want to run against Bill Ryan next fall for the Silk Stocking district. I want to be the first immigrant to be elected to Congress."

"But Ryan's a tough man to beat. He's got the Irish machine behind him, and he's got deals with every crook in the Village...."

"*But*," interrupted Marco, leaning on the desk, "he can't speak Italian. *I* can. The Village is full of Italians who still can barely speak English, but who've been here long enough to get the vote. I'm that one Italian immigrant in a million—or *ten* million—who, thanks to you, has gotten educated, who can speak English almost as well as you, and who has the backing to be able to run for Congress. Ryan doesn't represent those people; he exploits them. I can tell them in their own language that one of their own kind will represent them in Congress, and I think they'll vote for me."

Phipps leaned back in his chair, a smile coming over his face. Patrician that he was, he loved nothing better than a good political fight.

"I like it," he said. "I think I like it a lot. It never occurred to me, but you're a natural. An immigrant in Congress! And why not? Maybe it's time." He got out of his chair, full of enthusiasm. "And, by God, *you're* the man to beat that hack, Ryan. Yes, sir, I *like* it!" He came around the desk and grabbed Marco's hand to shake it. "I'll back you all the way, one hundred percent," he said. "We'll have *two* congressmen in the family! Come on: I want to introduce you to Jerry Foster in Ways and Means. He's the power behind the throne when it comes to picking candidates."

As they left the office, Marco took a quick look around. *This office may be mine one day,* he thought.

The distant artillery shells illuminated the night sky, even though they were so far from Paris their explosions seemed only a muffled thunder. But Flora Mitchum Haines was fascinated. She stood at the double windows of her Left Bank apartment, watching the show, just as thousands of other Parisians were watching.

The door opened, and Roscoe ran into the single room of their third-floor flat. "Baby, I got it," he yelled. "I *got* it!"

She turned from the window. "Rio—?"

"Rio *dee* Janeiro! Ten weeks at the Copacabana Palace Hotel: Roscoe Haines's Jazz Combo, featuring the sultry voice of the world-famous chanteuse, Sexy Flora Mitchum! You know that's gotta sound *dynamite* in Portuguese."

He picked her up and twirled her around the room, kissing her.

"How much?" she asked.

"A thousand a week for the band, three hundred for you. And I hear Rio's cheap. Baby, we're gonna make big bucks. And we're gettin' out of this war *fast*. Hot damn!"

He set her down and went to the bureau.

"This calls for a drink," he said, opening the top drawer and pulling out a bottle of Scotch. "Rio's supposed to be *gorgeous*. Beautiful beaches, the greatest bay in the world ... You know, everything's ass-backwards down there. Summer's winter, and vice versa...."

"That's enough, Roscoe."

He was filling the glass.

"Huh?"

"I *said*, that's enough."

"Shit, baby, this is a celebration!"

"Roscoe, honey, it's gettin' to be that *wakin' up* is a celebration for you. Now, you just pour half *that* into another glass and give it to me. Then stick that bottle back in the drawer."

"Shit."

Nevertheless, he obeyed. He brought her the second glass.

"Cheers!" he said. They clinked glasses and drank.

"We're still runnin', aren't we?" said Flora, looking at him. "When do we stop?"

"You call Rio *runnin'*? You're crazy."

"It's *runnin'*. Oh, you've been good, Roscoe. You put together the best jazz band in Paris, and we've made money. I ain't complainin' 'bout that. But until you're ready to go back to New York and face what you are, you're runnin'."

He threw the glass on the floor, smashing it.

"God *damn* you!" he shouted. Then he slapped her so hard she fell back on the bed. "Bitch!" he howled, leaning over her and slapping her again and again. "You black bitch! Ain't I *never* gonna shut you up?"

She kneed him in the groin. He groaned and fell back, doubling over with pain. Flora sat up, fire in her eyes.

"You'll shut me up when you say to me, 'Flora, I'm a black man who's *proud* of it. And I'm not afraid to go home!' "

He collapsed on the bed, holding his testicles with both hands, and started to sob.

"Ain't no home," he sobbed. "Ain't no home for Roscoe . . ."

"And don't give me none of this self-pity shit!" she yelled at him, hands on her hips. "Now, we'll go to Rio and we'll play ten weeks at the Copa Palace and we'll save our money. But *then* we're goin' home to New York. You understand? New York. *Home!* If Bert Williams can star in the Ziegfeld Follies, then there's somethin' there for you and me."

The effect on Georgie O'Donnell of Marco's betrayal, as her Aunt Kathleen called it, was even more traumatic than the effect of her trachoma-induced blindness. Georgie had learned to live with blindness, but it took her years to learn to live without Marco. Her initial shock at the news he was marrying Vanessa Ogden had turned to despair, then raging hatred, then back again to despair, mixed with bitterness. To the family—especially Casey O'Donnell—Marco's betrayal was more like treachery, especially since it was Bridget and Georgie who had helped him escape from Ellis Island. (Casey conveniently overlooked the fact that he had engineered Marco's deportation in the first place.) Marco became the family villain, and his name was banished from conversation.

But the human heart is complex, and it was Marco's very wickedness that perversely made him all the more desirable to Georgie. She told herself a thousand times he was out of her life forever, and good riddance at that. But the memory of her happiness with him lingered like the fragrance of an exotic, forbidden flower; and the more she forced him out of her mind, the more he sneaked back into her dreams. She was a passionate, highly sexed woman, but now she forced her emotions into a bottle, corked it and told herself she wanted nothing more to do with men. She had been hurt to the point of devastation once, and she would never allow it to happen to her again. She resigned herself to becoming the blind maiden aunt who, as the years passed, the family would whisper about as once having had a tragic romance. She accepted the fact that she was one of life's victims and told herself to make the best of what she had left.

Her uncle was anything but a sentimental man, but his blind niece's sorrow came as close to cracking his heart as anything could, and, being practical, he set about finding her a job that would fill the emptiness in her life. Using his political connections, he got her a position as receptionist at a small library for the blind on Bleecker Street in Greenwich Village. Bridget accompanied Georgie several times back and forth between the library and the Travers home on Grove Street, where it was decided Georgie would live during the week, spending weekends at her uncle and aunt's new house in Irvington. Georgie quickly memorized the three-block route between Grove and Bleecker so that she felt confident navigating the short distance by herself. Her job pleased her and gave her a small income and some sense of independence. She enjoyed living with her sister and Carl and sublimated her maternal instincts by playing with her two young nephews and niece. The years slipped quietly by, and the scar tissue of time slowly covered the wound left by Marco. The ecstasy of romance became something she read about in the Braille novels she devoured as she passed the silent hours at the receptionist's desk at the library.

But Braille novels weren't as exciting as the breathtaking adventures of the Purple Mask, and she still dreamed about Marco's hot kisses in the back row of the nickelodeon.

The orgy of conspicuous consumption that stamped the Gilded Age for all time reached its apogee in the little Rhode Island resort of Newport, where in the last decades of the nineteenth century untold millions were squandered on mammoth marble and stone "cottages." Social wars were fought and energies dissipated during the ten-week summer season to determine who was the most prominent hostess, whose daughter had made the most desirable match—who was, in short, number one. Oblivious to the fact that millions of the poor in the slums, factories and mines of America didn't give a damn who was the leading hostess in Newport, ignoring the rising tide of criticism that regarded a five-million-dollar summer house as an obscenity, the rich squabbled, spent, snubbed and sniped in a grotesque gavotte of social climbing that could only be compared to the hothouse of intrigue that was the Versailles of Louis XIV. Mrs. Cornelius Vanderbilt II—Alice—built The Breakers, a seventy-room, thirty-bathroom Italian Renaissance palace where one had a choice of salt water or fresh in one's bathtub. Her sister-in-law and rival, Mrs. William

Vanderbilt—Alva—built Marble House, where five hundred thousand cubic feet of Italian marble were installed at a cost of seven million dollars. The horses of Oliver Belmont slept on white linen sheets, and Mrs. Pembroke Jones spent three hundred thousand dollars during one season on dinners alone.

Phipps Ogden could hardly have been described as pinchpenny, with his yachts and multimillion-dollar Garden Court, but to his credit, even Phipps was somewhat put off by the callous vulgarity of the Newport excesses. Though he would have hated to admit it, not all of Vanessa's radical attacks on him had fallen on deaf ears, and his voting record in the Senate had squeaked a few inches to the left—or, as one of his Democratic rivals laughed, "to the left of Rutherford B. Hayes." Spending an increasing amount of time in Washington each year, he was certainly more in tune with what was happening in the country than his fellow millionaires. And while his princely style of life remained unchanged, he didn't succumb to the foolish temptation to compete in the Newport cottage-building sweepstakes, contenting himself with the modest—by Newport standards—white house called Stoney Brook Farm that, while it commanded a sweeping view of Narragansett Bay and could hardly be called cramped with its twenty-eight rooms, still would probably have been ignored by bomb-throwing Anarchists when such more highly visible targets as The Breakers were available.

In the last week of June, Phipps was finally able to get away from Washington, traveling to New York in his private railroad car, then picking up Marco and going on to Newport to join Maud, Vanessa and Frank. Phipps, who saw nothing wrong with nepotism, had easily arranged the candidacy for his son-in-law, not only because of his power in the party, but also because no one else was particularly eager to take on the well-entrenched Bill Ryan. Now, Phipps and Marco discussed the details of the campaign, Phipps strongly recommending that Marco hire as his campaign manager a New York reporter named Gene Fairchild. "He's worked for the *World* for years, he knows every reporter in the business and they like him, and he can get you good press coverage. More important, he knows New York politics like the back of his hand. He knows where the bodies are buried, and that can be a help. He drinks too much, but what the hell, most reporters do. I think you'll like him. Shall I set up a meeting?"

"Fine."

"You know, of course, that Bill Ryan's a front for your old friend Casey O'Donnell? Casey's running the Irish machine these days, and when Casey says jump, Bill Ryan somersaults. Since Casey tried to deport you once, I think we can safely assume he's going to play dirty again. It's best to be prepared."

"I know," said Marco, looking out the window of the car and thinking of Casey O'Donnell's niece. He thought of Georgie often, and always with a crushing sense of guilt. He knew how he must have devastated her; Georgie had been the victim, the stepping-stone to the security of Phipps Ogden's world of power and money. He was secure in that world now, and no one would ever deport him again; but he was so miserable with his marriage that he often wondered if he weren't a victim too. One thought that had impelled him to enter the congressional race was the idea that somehow, by taking on Casey O'Donnell's stooge, he might reencounter Georgie. It was probably a foolish thought; what could he possibly say to her—"I'm sorry"? She must hate him with a passion. He wasn't even sure he'd have the nerve to speak to her, as far as that went.

But the thought was there.

They arrived at Newport at three-thirty, and by four-fifteen Marco and his son were pushing off from Phipps's white dock in a small dinghy. It was a blazingly hot day with almost no wind, but Frank dutifully tugged the canvas sail up the mast, then took the helm, waiting patiently for a puff of wind to move them. It was somewhat ironic that Marco, the son of a Calabrian peasant, had fallen in love with yachting, the sport of the rich. But Marco had fallen in love with a lot of rich things, and the past summer he had been passing on to his son what he had learned about boat handling, using the crude dinghy he had put together himself rather than his father-in-law's sloop, *Sprite,* on the theory that a small boat is the best place to learn seamanship.

"We're not getting anywhere, Daddy," said Frank after five minutes of aimless drifting.

"I'll row us out," said Marco. Putting the oars in the locks, he started rowing the dinghy out to catch a breeze. The sun bit into his shoulders, which were already tan, and turned his face even browner.

In his small way, Marco had contributed to the social history of Newport. Used to being sunburned, when he first came to Newport on his honeymoon he had helped popularize the tanned look, with its overtones of athletic fitness. Now, pale faces were out. Even women were shedding their parasols and hitting the beaches, defying the tradition that ladies' complexions should always be pale. Already, in the second year of the Great European War (and four years away from the Constitutional amendment that would give women the vote), the slow, subtle revolution in the attitude of the sexes toward each other was under way. There were strongholds of conservatism, Mrs. Weiler being one of the most bristling fortresses on the moral front line. But in many cosmopolitan circles, young women were beginning to act and look "boyish." The bulky, dresslike bathing costumes of a few years back were being replaced by one-piece bathing suits. The hourglass figure so admired a decade before was giving way to a slimmer, flatter look that was the precursor of the flapper. The ideal of the Victorian maiden had been laughed off the tennis courts by the New Woman, who was independent, athletic, intellectually curious and increasingly sexually aggressive. Though the old taboos were still in force, cracks were beginning to appear. Divorce was becoming accepted. If men could have mistresses and get away with it, some women were beginning to take lovers. As the differences between the sexes blurred, homosexuality began tiptoeing into more and more closets of the rich and not-so-rich. People were beginning to talk about Freud. Many laughed at his theories and called him a crackpot, but still people were becoming conscious of sexuality and were beginning to reexamine the Victorian concept of sin.

Amid the birth pangs of the new morality, one could also discern a new concept of class consciousness taking shape, for the new forces of the twentieth century were not only blurring the sexes but the classes as well. Few people experienced this more personally than Marco, with his meteoric rise from the bottom to the top. After his marriage to Vanessa, the initial reaction of Phipps's gilded friends had been predictable. As Marco had foreseen, they whispered that Vanessa had "bought" him for his ability to keep her happy in bed. Wop, dago, immigrant and peasant were words seldom absent from gossip about him. His attempt to educate himself at the cram school and, later, Columbia University elicited nothing but mocking laughter. "What's he trying to become?" one fop asked. "A gentleman?" One tired joke making the rounds was that his old school tie had a picture of Ellis Island on it.

Marco had lived through enough rejection and name-calling in his poor days to ignore all this. He didn't give a damn what people thought or said. But then the quirky perversity and faddishness of the rich began to change things. Once the butt of crude jokes, Marco slowly became the object of curious interest. Naturally, because of his good looks, it started with the women. As the young men of Newport became increasingly languid and effete, Marco's earthiness which had so attracted Maud began to look better. His slight Italian accent changed from laughable to sexy, and wherever he went in Newport, female eyes followed him hungrily. Hostesses who had once asked him and Vanessa to parties only because they could not snub Phipps Ogden's son-in-law now began to vie with each other to nab him. And as Vanessa's behavior became more and more unbearable, they began to wish they could get Marco alone.

To Marco's amusement, by 1916 he found himself almost the fashion.

"Here comes a breeze," he said to Frank as the sail began to flap. Marco put away the oars, then went aft to sit by his son. "Head out to that buoy; then we'll come about."

"Okay." Frank concentrated on his sailing for a while. Then he asked, "Are you and Mommy going to that big party tonight? The one at Renfrew Hall?"

"That's right."

"Is Mommy going to act funny when she comes home?"

"Frank, don't talk that way about your mother."

"Why? She *does* act funny at night. Then you two fight. . . . I wish you wouldn't fight, Daddy. It scares me."

Marco put his arm around his son and hugged him. Marco adored Frank with all the intensity of an Italian peasant father, and when his son was hurt, he was hurt.

"I wish we wouldn't fight, too," he said. "But don't get scared. We really don't mean anything when we fight."

Like hell, he thought.

"Then why do it?"

Marco sighed. "It's hard to explain. Here's the buoy. Let's come about."

Frank put the tiller to port.

Millicent Renfrew, the Duchess of Dorset, was the daughter of Harley Renfrew, the steel magnate. In 1904, at the height of the American mania for marrying titles, Millie Renfrew followed the path of her sister-Americans Consuelo Vanderbilt, who married the Duke of Marlborough, and May Goelet, who married the Duke of Roxburghe, by marrying Ian Fitzalan Maurice Sackville-Hyde, the fifth duke of Dorset. The duke was twenty-six, reasonably attractive, but stupid and broke. After the wedding, his father-in-law gave him forty thousand shares of Renfrew Steel stock, worth four million dollars, which was the pay-off. The duke and duchess returned to England where, after two years, the duke ran off to Spain with a flamenco dancer. Since Millie couldn't stand her titled husband, his flight was a relief rather than a tragedy. Millie Dorset, as she was known to her friends, climbed on the international carrousel, spending half her time in Europe and half in America; and on this July night, she was giving a ball in her father's Newport palace, Renfrew Hall.

Millie was no beauty but she had a sense of style and fun and had become a bosom pal of Maud Odgen and an unabashed admirer of Marco, so that when the Odgen party arrived, Millie greeted them with enthusiasm.

"Now the party can start," she exclaimed, kissing Maud. "Darling, I love that dress! It makes mine look like a rag."

"An expensive rag," remarked Maud, whose expert eye guessed the price of Millie's heliotrope dress.

"I bought it in Paris before the war, and now it smells of mothballs. But *que faire?* There's that damned war. . . . Phipps, dear, you look divinely handsome as always. And where's that Apollo of a son-in-law of yours? *There* he is! Marco, every time I see you, I wish I were fifteen years younger and twenty times better looking. I *insist* on a dance. Oh, hello, Vanessa."

When she came to Vanessa, the smile dimmed and the enthusiasm became a bit forced. The Duchess of Dorset thought, like everyone else in Newport, that Vanessa's indifference to clothes amounted to *lèse majesté* in the fashion-conscious resort, and the frumpy yellow dress she had on tonight was not only un-flattering, it committed the grievous sin of having been worn the previous season. Furthermore, everyone knew about Vanessa's notorious "views," which were so highly critical of her own class and the conspicuous comsumption in Newport. No one likes criticism, especially the rich; so Vanessa was about as popular as the flu.

It was a two-way street. As Marco escorted her through the marble entrance hall, Vanessa muttered, "God, I dislike that woman."

"Well, don't show it."

She shot her husband a glare.

"I suppose *you* think she's wonderful because she's a duchess and rich."

"I like her because she's fun and likes to dance. And I want you to watch yourself tonight."

"What's that mean?"

"That means don't get drunk. You're not just my wife any-more; you're the wife of a candidate for the United States Con-gress."

"What a laugh *that* is! And if you get elected, are you going to legislate for the poor and downtrodden? For the immigrants *you* got away from as fast as you possibly could? Not jolly likely. You ought to run here in Newport. *They'd* elect you soon enough! Mil-lie Dorset would pass out campaign buttons for you. 'Vote for Marco Santorelli, who not only married rich, but kisses their feet.'"

They had reached the pink marble ballroom, where the or-chestra was playing a tango. Huge sprays of white gladioli in white wicker baskets stood between the four French doors, which were open to the broad terrace and, beyond, the famous Neptune foun-tain with its thirty-foot jet of silvery water. The gardens were hung with Japanese lanterns, and the guests were strolling through the grounds as well as dancing on the terrace and inside, making the whole scene an indoor-outdoor panorama of well-dressed beauty. Marco drank it all in, tuning out as best he could Vanessa's spite, which he had become used to and bored with. Be-sides, he was looking for Celia Bartlett, the beautiful divorcée with whom he was having an affair.

"Shall we tango?" he asked. "Or do you want to get on a soapbox and make a speech?"

"I *hate* the tango."

He looked at her.

"You hate everything," he said. "Why don't you try and *like* something for a change?"

"What's there to like?" And she started walking away from him.

"Where are you going?"

"To the bar."

"Van, you'll be careful ..."

"Oh, shut up."

She walked down the side of the room, past the seated dowagers with their plumes, tiaras and nonstop gossip toward the observatory, where, amidst the palms, a white-clothed bar was set up. Marco watched her a moment, toying with the idea of murder. Then he saw Celia Bartlett come into the ballroom. Celia was everything Vanessa wasn't: elegant, graceful and rather dumb. Vanessa had turned her marriage into warfare; Celia worshipped her handsome Italian lover. Vanessa had locked Marco out of her bedroom; Celia all too happily locked him in.

Marco came up to her.

"Let's dance," he said, taking her in his arms and tangoing onto the crowded dance floor.

"You're upset," said Celia, who was wearing a sensational silver dress which dropped to mid-calf in front, then swept back to a pointed train. Her black pumps had silver buckles. "Is Vanessa acting up again?"

"Vanessa," said Marco, his jaw tightening, "is a royal pain in the ..."

He stopped himself. Celia laughed.

"Ass?" she prompted.

"Ass," he agreed.

They danced on.

"You ought to talk to Vanessa about her clothes," said the Duchess of Dorset as Marco waltzed with her. It was an hour later. "*You* dress so well, just like Phipps, but Vanessa is a total frump."

"She's not interested in clothes."

"Darling, that's painfully obvious, but she *should* be. You're getting to be an important man, and your wife should dress the part. I'm going to talk to Maud, who has such wonderful taste. Maybe the two of us could work on Vanessa. . . ."

She was interrupted by a scream from the bar.

"What in the world—?"

They stopped waltzing. More screams. The orchestra stopped playing, the dancers stopped, the room was filling with murmurs. Marco hurried through the crowd, Millie Dorset in tow. He pushed through the mob at the bar door and saw his wife squirting fizzing champagne from a bottle all over two drenched teen-aged debutantes, who were cowering in a corner of the observatory. Vanessa, who was drunk, was whooping with laughter.

"Damn her," muttered Marco, hurrying into the room and grabbing his wife's arm. "Give me that thing!" He jerked the bottle out of her hand and gave it to one of the bartenders. Vanessa turned to the crowd at the door and yelled, *"Merde! Vous êtes tous merde!"*

Shocked gasps, because everyone there knew enough French to realize she had just told them they were all shit—something even a drunk Vanessa couldn't bring herself to say in English. Marco didn't know French, but the Italian *merda* was close enough for him to catch the drift. He grabbed Vanessa from behind and clamped his hand over her mouth. Immediately she bit his fingers so hard he roared with pain and retracted his hand, which was spouting blood. Vanessa returned to the attack, weaving around the observatory as she yelled, *"Newport, c'est de la merde! Les riches sont de la merde! Et mon mari, c'est la plus grande merde du monde!"*

Her husband, whom she had just called the biggest shit in the world, had had enough. He came up to Vanessa and slugged her on the chin. She fell back into the palms, kayoed.

The crowd burst into gasps and a smattering of applause.

Marco carried her to his car, put her in the back seat, then drove her to Stoney Brook Farm, where he carried her upstairs and put her to bed. When he returned downstairs, Phipps and Maud were just coming into the house.

"Well," said Maud, taking off her gloves, "at least Vanessa

won't have to bother hating Newport parties anymore. She'll never get another invitation in this town."

"Isn't there a clinic in Connecticut where she could take the cure?" asked Marco.

"Yes," said Phipps. "Silver Lake, outside Darien. I had a cousin who was one of its first patients. It worked, too. He hasn't touched a drop since."

"I'm going to call them in the morning. I think Van needs medical help."

When Vanessa woke up the next morning, she had a first-class hangover, and her jaw was sore and black and blue. She sat up, groaning.

"Want a bicarbonate?" asked Marco, who was standing by the bed.

She looked at him blearily. "What happened?" she asked.

"You don't want to know. Do you want a bicarbonate?"

"Yes."

He went into the bathroom, fixed the bicarbonate of soda, and brought it back to her bed. She drank it, then sank back into her pillows. Marco sat beside her.

"Why are you always sniping at me?" he asked. "Do you hate me?"

She turned her head away from him, staring at one of the windows. It was a bright, sunshiny morning.

"I don't know," she said wearily. "What did I do last night?"

"You made an ass of yourself. I had to knock you out to shut you up."

"Is that why my jaw aches?"

"Yes. If I flop as a politician, I may go into boxing." He hesitated. "We have to work this out, Van."

She turned back to look at him.

"What's to work out? You don't love me. Do you think I'm a fool? Why don't you admit you married me for my money?"

"All right, I married you for your money. What the hell *else* would anyone marry you for? You're sullen, spoiled, bitchy, you don't like to make love...." He stopped. "Do you want a divorce?"

She sighed. "No," she said. "We have to think of Frank ... I

295

don't know. . . . " Her eyes started to tear. "I'm so miserable. . . ."

"*Why?*"

"I don't *know!* There are twenty-eight Vanessas rolling around inside of me, and I don't know which one's the real Vanessa. I think that's why I drink. . . ."

She started sobbing. He took her in his arms to comfort her. As much as they fought, he often felt sorry for her, as he felt guilty about the cold-blooded way he had gone after her fortune.

"All right," he said, "we're going to take one thing at a time. I've talked to Dr. Conrad, who runs a clinic outside Darien. Will you go there for a few weeks to get yourself straightened out?"

"Yes," she said, sniffing.

"Then I'll drive you there this morning. Do you feel well enough to get dressed?"

"I suppose . . . Marco, do you love me a *little*?"

"Not last night. I hated you last night."

She straightened. Her eyes were bloodshot from the alcohol and the tears.

"Did you *ever* love me a little?"

He looked at her coolly.

"Do you want the truth?"

"Yes. I'm sick of lies."

"No, I never loved you. I fell in love with an Irish girl I met in steerage, coming to America. Isn't that a laugh? Here I am, married to you, carrying you out of the Duchess of Dorset's ballroom, and all the while I'm in love with a girl I met in steerage? A *blind* girl! I jilted a blind girl who was in love with me to marry *you*."

"And just for the money?"

"Yes, for the money." His voice was bitter. "You romanticize the slums because you've never been in them. I've been in them, and I can tell you, it's *rotten* being poor in America. Ah, but I paid a price—a *big* price—to get out of those slums. The price was *you,* Vanessa. And this stinking, loveless marriage of ours. All right, I'm willing to pay, and I'm willing to do everything I can to make this marriage work. But at least now we know where we stand. Am I right?"

She smiled slightly.

"The funny thing is, everybody loves you, and they all hate me. But *you're* the real son of a bitch." She slapped his face.

"*That's* for last night," she said. "And for *every* night of this filthy marriage!"

He got off the bed. "I'll send the maid up to pack your things," he said. He started toward the door.

"You'll be glad to get rid of me, won't you?" she shouted. "You'd like to lock me up in a loony bin forever and throw away the key. Because I'm in your way now, aren't I? I wasn't in your way five years ago when you wanted my money, but now I'm an inconvenience, aren't I? An embarrassment. Poor Marco, he's so wonderful, but that awful, drunk wife! Well, maybe that's why I get drunk: to make you *squirm!*"

He looked at her from the door.

"You know," he said, "last night I actually thought of murdering you."

"Then why didn't you do it? I wish you *had*. I'd rather be dead than what I am!"

She started sobbing again. He looked at her a moment, then left the room.

Chapter 36

The Women's Christian Temperance Union was the broad national response to the widespread drunkenness of America in 1916 and was the driving force behind the movement toward prohibition. Silver Lake was a much more private, discreet response to boozing in the upper classes. It was a big, New England-style farmhouse on top of a hill that the patients had jokingly dubbed Coffee Hill and which overlooked Silver Lake. Its maximum capacity was twenty patients, its atmosphere was relaxed, and the theory behind it was to isolate the patients from alcohol long enough for them to dry out and build up their physical strength.

On Vanessa's first morning she woke up in her plainly-furnished private room, feeling better already for having no hangover. She washed, got dressed and went downstairs for breakfast. The big low-ceilinged dining room had four round tables seating five each. Vanessa took a seat between a Wall Street stockbroker whose bottle of Scotch a day had ruined his marriage, his liver and his business, and a newspaper publisher from Hartford who had scandalized his family and friends by peeing in the punchbowl at a country club dance. They were friendly, the staff was friendly, the food was good and Vanessa was beginning to enjoy herself when she noticed the strikingly beautiful brunette at the next table eying her. It was a look of such intensity that it made Vanessa slightly nervous. She smiled uncertainly, then went back to her bacon and eggs. But she could feel the woman's eyes still on her.

After breakfast, she left the house to take a stroll down to the lake. The lawn was shaded by ancient elms and lovely white pines, and though it was hot, a breeze stirred the leaves and rustled the pine needles, making the morning summer at its best. Bees and wasps were busily at work, squirrels and chipmunks were scurrying, and she even spotted a ribbon snake asleep on a rock in the sun. Her love of animals and nature added to her sense of peace, and her rebellious nature began to doze.

There was a bench under a pine by the lake, and she sat on it to look at the water. She had been there perhaps five minutes when a low voice behind her said, "Do you mind if I join you?"

Startled, Vanessa turned to see the brunette who had been staring at her at breakfast. She was tall and slender and stunningly beautiful, with ivory skin and those arresting dark eyes. She wore her dark brown hair tight against her head, with softly waving curls framing her face like curtains. She wore lipstick, which Vanessa had never used. She had on a sleeveless tan dress, and wore two curious ivory bracelets on each wrist. Vanessa had no style, but she recognized it when she saw it, and this woman had a very personal flair.

"Please do," said Vanessa.

"My name is Una Marbury," she said, coming around the bench. "Some patients use fake names here to protect themselves, but that's my real name."

"My name is Vanessa Santorelli, and that's real too."

Una sat down beside her.

"Odd—you don't look Italian."

"I'm not. My husband is."

"Oh? You're married?" She looked at Vanessa's left hand and spotted the ring. Then she waved away a fly. "I'm here because of gin. What's your problem?"

Vanessa smiled. "Alcohol. Any form."

"Did you do something *ghastly*?"

"It must have been. No one wanted to talk about it."

"I love ghastly things. I love to take off my clothes at parties."

"*All* your clothes?"

"Well, my dear, there would be no point in taking off one's shoes. I'm obviously a frustrated nudist."

"Apparently you're not so frustrated."

"I have an actress friend who gets absolutely *blotto* and insists on going to the potty with the door open. She says her bowels won't move unless people are watching."

Vanessa looked shocked. "But that's disgusting!"

Una smiled. "Isn't it? I have so many disgusting friends. I absolutely adore them."

"Where do you live?"

"Greenwich Village. I own an art gallery. Oh, I'm terribly Bohemian, my dear. Terribly. My family haven't talked to me for *years,* thank God. They're such awful bores. Father even votes Republican. He absolutely dotes on that *ghastly* Senator Ogden. Can you imagine?"

Vanessa giggled.

"Did I make a joke, my dear?"

"That *ghastly* Senator Ogden is my father."

"Oh, Una, you have made a serious social error. I *hope* you can't stand his politics?"

"Oh, I'm a socialist."

"How *delicious,* my dear. So am I. We'll have *so* much to talk about—thank Heavens! This place is boring beyond belief. All this *ghastly* nature; one *longs* for something artificial."

Vanessa was fascinated.

Chapter 37

The teens were the golden age of American radicalism, and the Emerald City of the radicals was Greenwich Village. Here such publications as *The Masses* and *The Call* glamorized the working-man, attacked the bourgeoisie and the capitalist "exploiters," championed free love and tended the holy flame at the shrine of Marxism. The fact that most of the intellectuals who wrote and read these publications had never been in a mine or a factory and shunned real workers as ignoramuses was beside the point. The point in Greenwich Village was rebellion for its own sake, rebellion in art against realism, in literature against plot, in music against harmony, and in sex against marriage. Most of the bohemians were children of the middle class—John Reed was a Harvard graduate. Many of them were to experience bitter disillusion: Max Eastman, the nudist editor of *The Masses,* was to end up on the extreme right, an editor at—of all places—*Reader's Digest.* But in 1916, communism was still an untested ideal, and bohemianism promised the young the heady excitement of adventure.

The Village of the John Reeds and Una Marburys was what attracted publicity. The other Greenwich Village was the Village of the poor—predominantly Italian—who led their unexciting lives, doing their laundry, running their tiny groceries, fruit stands and shoe-repair shops, the Village of bakers, masons, undertakers and restaurateurs. These were the votes Marco was after. When his candidacy for the congressional seat was announced, the intellectuals in the Village reacted with indifference (what did they care about local politics, when they were out to change the world?) or, in a few instances, a sneer that he was the tool of his rich father-in-law. But word quickly spread among the Italians that one of their own was bidding to represent them in Congress, and the reaction of most Italians was excitement. The fact that an Italian immigrant had managed to marry one of the richest girls in

America caused the men to swell with masculine Italian pride and crack innumerable jokes about the probable size of Marco's penis. The Italian women, who couldn't vote, took one look at his face on the posters that started appearing all over the Village and sighed in chorus, *"Bellissimo."* Early on, it looked as if Marco, at least with the Italians, was going to be a shoo-in.

Financed by Phipps, Marco rented a small, three-story Federal house on tiny Jones Street, between Bleecker and West Fourth, and installed his headquarters on the first two floors while turning the third floor into a *pied-à-terre* which would give him the required residency in the district. He leased office equipment, desks and typewriters, hired three Italian-American girls as secretaries and assistants, and turned the small back room on the ground floor into his office.

But most important, he took Phipps's advice and hired Gene Fairchild as his campaign manager. Gene was forty-three, a bald, skinny chain-smoker who wore bow ties, striped shirts and had a smoker's cough so richly phlegmy that it had been compared to the majestic rumble of a cathedral pipe organ. But Gene knew his politics, and the first thing he told Marco was: "Watch out for two men: Mike Murphy and Sandro Albertini."

"That last name sounds familiar," said Marco.

"Let me tell you a story," said Casey O'Donnell as he leaned back in his desk chair and propped his size eleven black shoes on his desk. "Nine years ago a poor wop comes to New York in steerage. He's got no money, no education and barely speaks English. What would you say is going to happen to him?"

"He'd become a barber," replied Mike Murphy, who was the campaign manager for Congressman William Ryan. They were both in Casey's Brooklyn office. It was a hot morning, and an electric fan hummed in front of one of the open windows. Murphy, who as a young man had worked on the docks, was now, at thirty-eight, beginning to convert his muscles to flab. He had taken off his dark-blue suit jacket and loosened his tie, but there were still blotches of sweat on his shirt. "A barber or a construction worker."

"Right—for ninety-nine percent of wops. But this one's different. He knew Mrs. Charteris, the English actress. Mrs. Charteris is in New York with a play. The wop is young and good-looking. All of a sudden, he's wearing Brooks Brothers suits and has bought himself two trucks. Now, what would you say probably happened?"

Mike Murphy was looking interested. "I'd say he was laying Mrs. Charteris. Are we talking about Santorelli?"

"Who else? Now, the story continues. Mrs. Charteris marries Senator Ogden. Then all of a sudden, the senator becomes interested in our poor wop and sends him to a private school, footin' all the bills. Why?"

Mike Murphy's thick lips curled in a hungry smile. "Two possibilities: Either Santorelli's blackmailing him about being his wife's boyfriend, or he's *still* screwing the wife and she wants to get him educated so he won't embarrass her socially."

"Either way, you've got a nice, smelly stink of a scandal, right? And you know the rest of the story: Santorelli marries the rich daughter, and now he's got the balls to run against Bill Ryan. I hope I don't have to spell out what should be included in some of Bill's speeches? The education of Marco Santorelli ought to make this campaign a joke."

Mike Murphy mopped the sweat from his freckled forehead. "No, Bill won't have to attack him. After all, it's not something we can prove, and it might backfire with the wop voters. Wops admire guys who fuck their way to the top. But we'll let the news out, Casey—don't worry."

Casey took his feet off the desk and sat up.

"This Santorelli clown jilted my niece to marry Ogden's daughter," he said softly. "I don't only want Bill to beat him; I want him to *bury* him."

"We've got *lots* of ways to bury him."

The four men came into the Bay of Naples Saloon at the corner of Perry Street and Seventh Avenue shortly before midnight. The small bar was about to close; a few customers were lingering over their final drinks.

"Hey, Guido!" Mike Murphy smiled as he came up to the bar where the monstrously fat owner was drying glasses. "How's things?"

Guido Martinelli shrugged.

"Not-a bad, Mike. Not-a bad."

Mike looked around the place. Four of Marco's posters were

302

on the wall. Mike's three companions stood behind him.

"We're delivering your beer in the morning, Guido." Mike was also a vice-president of Casey O'Donnell's trucking company.

Guido stopped drying.

"What beer? I didn't order no beer."

Mike turned and nodded at the men. They went to the tables where the drinkers were sitting and said, "Closing time."

"What you mean, 'closing time'?" exclaimed Guido, his fat face turning red. "Hey, what's-a going on here? *I'm-a* owner of this joint!"

"Shaddup," growled Mike.

When the customers had been hustled out the door, the men locked it and pulled the green blinds down. Guido was beginning to sweat.

"What's-a going on, Mike?" he whimpered. "I'm-a good customer. I give-a you no trouble. What's-a going on?"

"Mr. O'Donnell thinks you're not buying enough beer, Guido," said Mike, taking some popcorn from the glass bowl on the bar and putting it in his mouth. "We only delivered two kegs last month. That's not enough business, Guido."

"My customers don't drink that much beer. You know that! They're Italians, they drink wine."

"Yeah, but we don't deliver wine, we deliver beer. That's why you're getting a delivery in the morning."

Guido was rubbing his hands in despair. "You can't do this to me!" he wailed.

"Can't I?"

Mike signaled his goons. One of them jumped over the bar and swept a whole shelf of glasses onto the floor, where they smashed. Guido started trembling.

"That's-a not nice," he wailed.

"No shit, fatso. Now, we don't want to break anything else. You taking the beer?"

"Yeah, sure, I take it. I don't want no trouble, Mike. I take it."

"Good. And another thing: We don't like your politics." He pointed at the posters. The goons tore them off the wall and ripped them.

"That's-a my candidate!" cried Guido. "He's Italian, like-a me!"

"He's a wop and a loser, like you. We'll bring some Bill Ryan

303

posters in the morning with the beer. You'll put Ryan posters up, understand? Then we won't-a have-a no more trouble, *capische*?"

Guido nodded, his chins wiggling.

"Okay, Guido. *Buona sera*. Come on, boys."

They left the saloon. Guido, shaking his head sadly, started sweeping up the broken glass.

"Bastardi," he muttered.

The Blue Grotto Club on Thompson Street was hardly the Village's classiest whorehouse, but it was popular with the Italians because it was affordable. Downstairs was a bar, four quarter slot-machines, and the walls were lined with dark wood benches where the "Johns" would sit drinking and inspecting the girls, who paraded around in various weird outfits, some in gingham rompers with little-girl bows in their hair and on their shoes, others in nothing but black lace underwear and gartered black-net stockings. Some of the girls were Italian, some Canadian, some from the South. Wiggling their hips, they would deliver immortal lines like "Want a good time, honey? I can do it French, baby. You'll love it." Or: "I'll take it front or rear, baby. Your choice. But the mouth's three bucks extra."

Those Johns who bought went upstairs with the girl. There, a Mrs. Cosmatani sat at a little desk in the hall. She would hand over a towel and a metal check to the girl when the customer paid his money—the cheapest trick being two dollars, no frills. Then down the hall they'd go to their assigned room, which was no more than a bed in a cubbyhole. Mrs. Cosmatani enhanced the romantic ambience by keeping up a running monologue: "All right, Number Eight; all right, Number Ten—customers are waiting, don't take all night."

At two in the morning, a well-dressed man in a camel's hair coat entered the Blue Grotto Club, accompanied by an ex-prize-fighter named Paolo. The man went to the bar. The bartender hurried over.

"How's business?" asked Sandro Albertini.

"Fine! Really good tonight, Mr. Albertini."

"What you got for me?"

"Comin' up, Mr. Albertini."

The bartender hurried back to the cash register, opened it, took out an envelope and rushed back.

304

"For you, sir," he said, handing over the envelope. Albertini put it in his coat, then checked his watch.

"There'll be a Mr. Murphy to see me," he said.

"He's already here, Mr. Albertini. He's waiting in the back room. I gave him a beer. Glass-a milk for you, as usual?"

"Yeah. Send it in. Come on, Paolo."

They walked down the bar past the slots and the sluts till they came to a door. Opening it, they went into a small, dimly lit room with a round, felt-covered poker table in the center. Seated at the table was Mike Murphy, smoking a cigar and drinking a beer. He got up and stuck out his hand.

"Glad to see you, Albertini." He smiled.

"Cut the shit," said Albertini, ignoring the hand and sitting down. "What's up?"

Mike sat down again as Paolo closed the door.

"It's the election," said Mike, tapping his cigar. "We're not happy with the Italian vote."

"Who's 'we'? Ryan? O'Donnell?"

Mike shrugged, indicating yes.

"I hear you're squeezing some of the saloon owners," said Albertini. "It's small-time shit, but I don't like it. They can take just so much squeeze."

"We'll be glad to leave the squeeze to you. Can you deliver the Italian vote?"

"Maybe. What's in it for me?"

"We can make sure the cops stay friendly another two years."

There was a knock at the door. Paolo opened it. The bartender handed in a beer tray with a glass of milk on it. Paolo took the tray, closed the door and placed the glass of milk on the poker table. Albertini took a sip.

"That's not enough," he said.

"Plus ten grand cash," Mike replied.

Albertini took another sip of milk, then stood up.

"I'll think about it," he said.

"We'd like an answer soon."

"You'll get an answer when I'm ready to give it. Come on, Paolo."

They left the room.

Mike Murphy took a drag on his cigar, then stood up and dropped the cigar in the glass of milk.

305

Marco was dictating a letter to one of his assistants when the man in the camel's hair coat came into the campaign headquarters on Jones Street. Marco remembered Sandro Albertini, but the loan shark who had risen to become the crime boss of Greenwich Village didn't seem to remember Marco. However, he recognized the candidate from his posters and came over to him.

When he chose, Albertini could be affable. Now he smiled and stuck out his hand.

"Mr. Santorelli?" he said. "My name's Sandro Albertini. I wondered if I could talk to you a few minutes."

Marco stared at the man who had had him tied to the burning radiator so many years before. Then he shook his hand.

"Why not? Come back to my office."

They went to the small room in the back. Albertini kept his coat on even though the office was warm. Marco closed the door, offered him a chair, then sat down behind his desk.

"Maybe you know who I am," said Albertini.

"I know."

"Good. Then I'll get right to the point. I'd like to help you win this election."

"Why? Because I'm Italian?"

"Hell, you could be a Serbo-Croatian for all I care, or a goddam Turk. I want to help you get the Italian vote because your father-in-law's got more power than Casey O'Donnell, and he spends more money in a week than O'Donnell will see in his life."

"I see you're an idealist."

"What?"

"Nothing. I don't need your help, Albertini. I think I've got the Italian voters on my side already."

"Maybe, maybe not. A lot can happen between now and November. I can *guarantee* the Italian vote for you. Let me put it this way: Think of me as insurance."

"How much is this insurance going to cost me?"

"Twenty-five thousand, cash. That's like your father-in-law's heating bill for a month."

"Uh huh. And what if I say no?"

"The other side's already made me the same offer. If you say no, I go with them."

"What kind of guarantee would I have you wouldn't take my money *and* theirs? I know Bill Ryan's kept the police off you, so it's to your advantage to keep things as they are. I'm not a sucker, Albertini."

Albertini was surprised by Marco's guessing his game—he had assumed the young candidate was a brainless pawn of Senator Ogden's—but he managed to conceal it.

"Ask anyone in the Village: My word is my bond."

Marco laughed as he stood up.

"Jesus, you got some nerve using *that* line. You don't remember me, do you?" He took off his coat.

"Why should I remember you?"

"We've met before—a long time ago. I was just off the boat and was trying to raise some cash, so I came to you. You loaned me two hundred dollars to buy a truck, and when I wrecked the truck, you had a goon tie me to a hot radiator for a half hour."

He had rolled up his sleeves. "See these scars? They're my souvenirs. That radiator hurt like hell, Albertini, but even if I didn't owe you for that, I wouldn't play your stinking game. And I'll tell you something else: If I win this election, I'm going to force the cops to clamp down on you, on your whorehouses, your so-called protection racket, your loan sharking—the whole rotten business. I've done my homework on this district and I know what's wrong with it. You've leeched off the poor Italians long enough, and if I win, the joy-ride's going to be over."

Albertini smiled.

"That's a good speech, Santorelli, a real crusading political speech." He stood up. "When I get done with you, you're going to wish you were back on that radiator."

He left the office. Marco sat down and put in a phone call to his father-in-law in Washington.

"Sandro Albertini was just here," he said to Phipps. "He tried to get me to pay him twenty-five thousand to swing the Italian vote. I told him to go to hell. Was that dumb?"

"No, it was smart," said Phipps without hesitation. "You don't need crooks, and you don't want them. But I wouldn't be surprised if he pulls something dirty. I wonder if we should get you a bodyguard."

"I don't want a bodyguard."

"Albertini can play rough."

"I know, but he doesn't scare me."

"That's brave, Marco, but maybe it's not very smart. Will you at least buy a gun? I'm telling you, Albertini's dangerous, and you've got to protect yourself."

Marco remembered the radiator.

"All right," he said, rather reluctantly. "I'll buy a gun."

Chapter 38

The Village being so small, it was probably inevitable they would encounter each other; but the afternoon he did see her, he was amazed by how strongly the sight of her affected him after all those years.

She was returning from the library of the blind to Bridget's house on Grove Street and he was returning from a meeting with Gene Fairchild, when he spotted her crossing West Fourth Street at Sheridan Square. He stopped. Gene Fairchild said, "What's wrong?"

Although she was twenty feet away, Marco motioned to Gene to keep silent. She was wearing a plain white dress with a matching hat. She carried her cane, but she had become so used to the route that she used it only to find curbs. Marco stared at her as she approached him. *The strong lily* ... he remembered thinking those words when he first saw her coming aboard the *Kronprinz Friedrich* at Queenstown so many years before, and she still looked that way. Her beauty was still in its prime, and she walked with a confidence that few blind people managed.

He backed up against a bookstore window as she passed. He had a violent urge to take her hand, to reveal himself to her, to say the magic name, "Georgie." But he did nothing.

"Will you tell me what the hell is happening?" whispered Gene. "You have enough trouble in this election without going crazy on me."

Marco was still watching Georgie. It wasn't until after she had gone inside Bridget's house that he spoke.

"That's Casey O'Donnell's niece," he said.

"No kidding! And she's blind?"

"Yes."

"She's a looker! Do you know her?"

"I used to."

"Why didn't you say hello to her?"

Marco closed his eyes a moment.

"I wish to God I had the nerve to," he said.

Then he opened his eyes.

"Come on."

The two men continued walking back to Marco's campaign headquarters, but Marco wasn't thinking about politics. He was thinking about kissing Georgie in the back row of the nickelodeon, about telling her in excited whispers the adventures of the Purple Mask, about love and betrayal and guilt. Five years before, he had wanted money and power and security more than Georgie.

Now he had the money and security, and was getting the power. But all he wanted at that moment was to hold her hand at the movies.

The blind develop other senses to compensate for their lack of vision, and for several days Georgie had had the vague feeling someone was following her as she walked from Bridget's to the library. She had become aware of the footsteps close behind her. On the third day, she actually stopped and turned. "Is anyone there?" she asked. There were dozens of pedestrians there, and some of them looked at her curiously. But Marco froze and said nothing, telling himself he was acting like a fool, but nevertheless unable either to stop following or to make his presence known to her.

Aware he might be picked up on charges of molestation, he crossed the street. *Talk to her!* screamed his heart.

But what in God's name can I say? moaned his brain.

He knew his obsession with Georgie was taking his concentration off his campaign. For three days he forced her out of his mind. But on the fourth day, he gave up. Telling himself he would speak to her and to hell with the consequences, he left his headquarters before noon, walked around the corner to Bleecker Street and climbed the steps of the small building beside the front door of which was the brass plaque reading LIBRARY FOR THE BLIND. He opened the door and went in.

Five people, three of them elderly, were sitting at the wooden reading tables passing their fingers over the pages of Braille books. Around the walls stood bookshelves and file cabinets. The summer sun poured through the tall windows. Opposite the door, seated at a wooden desk, was Georgie, who was also reading a book with her fingers. She wore a light blue blouse and black skirt.

He came to the desk. She looked up and smiled.

"Yes?"

He started to say something, when his guilt slammed him like a baseball bat. She was so vulnerable, how could he have done the monstrous thing he did to her? He remained silent, staring at her sightless eyes.

Now she was frowning.

"Who *are* you?" she said.

He turned and almost ran out of the library.

"It's Marco," she said that night to her sister. They were in Georgie's second-floor bedroom in the Grove Street house. All through dinner Georgie had been silent and preoccupied. After coffee she asked Bridget to come up to her room with her.

"Marco?" asked Bridget. "What are you talking about?"

"For the past week, someone's been following me," said Georgie, who was sitting on her bed. "Then today, he came into the library. Don't ask me how I know it was the same person—I just *do*. I *sensed* it. And I'm sure it's Marco."

"But why? What does he want?"

"I think he wants to talk to me, but is afraid to. His campaign headquarters is just around the corner from the library.... He must have seen me and followed me...."

She was trembling. Bridget sat on the bed beside her and took her hand.

"Now darlin', you don't *know*. This may be all imagination. God knows, it may be some masher.... I think you should tell the police."

"The *police?* Oh, no. No, it's Marco, and I've got him where I want him. I'll make him *crawl*.... If he's tryin' to make it up to me some way, I'll hurt him worse than he hurt me. *Worse!* Oh, the bloody bastard, the rotten man . . . with his rich wife . . ."

Suddenly she burst into tears. Bridget hugged her as she leaned over, burying her face against Bridget's waist, shaking with sobs.

"Oh, Bridey, I loved him *so*," she sobbed. "I loved him *so* . . ."

Bridget ran her hand over her blond hair.

"Poor darlin'," she whispered. "You still love him, don't you?"

"I don't know . . . I love what he *was* before he hurt me, but people change. I don't know what he's like now. But . . ."

"But what, darlin'?"

She looked up, tears streaming down her face.

"I've tried to . . . to adjust to what I am, to what I'll be the rest of my life. But, Bridey, sometimes I wake up in the middle of the night, and I'm so *lonely*. . . ."

"But darlin', you won't see other men . . ."

"I'm afraid of bein' hurt again—can't you understand? And yet . . . maybe *livin'* is bein' hurt . . . I don't know . . ." She sat up, trying to control herself. "Oh God, if it *is* Marco and he hurts me again, may his soul rot in hell."

They were both naked, standing waist-deep in a forest pool.

Marco moved through the cool water toward her, stretching out his arms, his body aching with desire. She stood still, her blond hair hanging down over her white shoulders, waiting for him. Now he was in front of her. He took her into his arms and began kissing her, running his hands over her back and hips. Georgie began moaning.

"I love you," he was saying. "I love you more than life itself. . . ."

Then he woke up. He was in his bed on the third floor of the Jones Street house. His stomach was covered with sperm.

"Oh God," moaned Marco. "Oh, Georgie."

It was the first wet dream he had had since he was seventeen.

The next morning, Nellie Byfield Rubin, looking sensational in a tight-fitting white suit, carrying a white parasol and wearing a smart white hat with a white egret feather soaring out of it, stepped out of her white limousine as her black chauffeur in the white uniform and smart brown boots held the door. Nellie walked grandly up the three steps of the Federal house on Jones Street, across the front of which was stretched a banner reading SANTORELLI FOR CONGRESS. She went into the first-floor office. The sight of the glamorous star caused the secretaries to stare and brought Gene Fairchild hurrying over to her.

"Miss Byfield," he exclaimed, rather breathlessly. "May I help you?"

Nellie flashed her most irresistible smile. "I'd like to see the candidate. He's a personal friend. Is he in?"

"We're expecting him back any minute . . . he had a meeting over on Perry Street. . . . Will you come back to his office?"

"Thank you."

He led her past the desks toward the rear.

"Miss Byfield, would you autograph something for my son, Edgar? He's one of your greatest fans . . . he's seventeen, and I think he's in love with you."

"How sweet." She smiled. "I'd be glad to."

Gene led her into Marco's small office and held a chair for her. Then he ran around the desk and pulled open one of the drawers to get a sheet of stationery emblazoned MARCO SANTORELLI FOR CONGRESS. Grabbing a pen, he hurried back around the desk. "Here, Miss Byfield . . ."

Nellie, looking as grandly condescending as the Queen Mother opening a charity bazaar, took the pen and scribbled in her fifth-grade scrawl, "To Edgar. Much love, Nellie Byfield."

"There," she said, handing it back.

"Oh boy, he'll go crazy! Thanks a lot!"

"It's my pleasure." She smiled, thinking, *The little creep will probably take that into his bathroom and whack off.*

"Here's Marco now . . ."

She turned to see the candidate come in the door. He was wearing a cord suit and a straw hat. Nellie drank in his dark good looks.

"Nellie," exlaimed Marco, coming over to take her hand. "It's wonderful to see you. How's Jake?"

"He's fine. We're both so excited about your campaign—Jake thinks it's wonderful you may go to Congress. In fact . . ." She opened her purse and pulled out a rolled lead sheet. "Jake wrote a campaign song for you. It's called 'For More Pasta in the Belly, Better Vote for Santorelli.' "

Marco burst into laughter.

"I love it," he exclaimed. "Will you sing it?"

"Well, I read in the paper you're having your first rally next Sunday. I thought maybe it would help you draw a crowd if I sang it at the rally."

"Nellie, that would be wonderful!" He turned to Gene. "Can you get that in tomorrow's papers?"

"I'm on my way!" exclaimed Gene, hurrying out of the office, closing the door behind him.

Marco turned back to Nellie, smiling. "How can I ever thank both of you?" he said. "I owe Jake so much. You two are such great friends."

Nellie stood up. "Perhaps we could have lunch some day," she said softly. "I'd like so much to get to know you better."

Suddenly, sex was swirling around the two like invisible smoke. Marco's smile became frozen.

"Yes, maybe we can . . . maybe after the campaign. I'm pretty tied up until then."

Nellie reached out to smooth an imaginary wrinkle on his lapel.

"Couldn't you untie yourself for one lunch?"

Their eyes met.

"I'll have Gene check my calendar," said Marco.

The phone rang.

"Excuse me." He started around the desk. "Thanks again, Nellie. I really appreciate this."

Her eyes followed him.

"It's my pleasure. What time do you want me Sunday?"

"Gene will give you the details." He picked up the phone. "Hello?"

Nellie let herself out of the room.

When Una Marbury told Vanessa that she was through with her treatment at Silver Lake and was going back to New York, Vanessa checked out of the clinic the next day also, even though she had been there only ten days. But she felt terrific physically, and she had no more interest in alcohol because now she had Una. The beautiful Una, as affected and decadent as she was, cast a spell on Vanessa. Vanessa had never met anyone remotely like her; and her affected way of talking, her bizarre African and Indian jewelry, her theories on art and life, and the exotic world she lived in with its hints of perversions fascinated Vanessa like some glittering crystal that flashed weird, mesmerizing fires.

Realizing she was *persona non grata* in Newport after the fiasco at the Duchess of Dorset's ball (and not really liking Newport anyway), Vanessa returned to Garden Court from where, the very next morning, she took the train into Manhattan, then taxied down to the Village. She got out at the Jefferson Courthouse on Sixth Avenue and crossed the street to the cozy little enclave of tiny houses around a closed court called Patchin Place. Her heart pounding with excitement, Vanessa hurried across the court and knocked on a door bearing a discreet steel plaque which read GALERIE DES SCULPTURES MODERNES.

Una was expecting her. She opened the door saying, "You're early. To be early to anything is a *ghastly* error. Don't repeat it."

"I'm sorry. I . . . oh!"

She looked around the room, which Una had opened up to include the entire first floor of the house. Everything was virgin, sterile white, including the floor, which made an invisible background for the sculptures that stood around the bare room. And what sculptures! Vanessa was aware of the modern art movement, of course, and had seen the sensational Armory Show of 1913 (a year that had also witnessed the uproarious opening of *Le Sacre du Printemps* in Paris; it was as if the artistic world were setting the stage for the war that was to explode the following year). But her innate conservatism had rejected modernism then; it was too much for her to grasp.

But now she approached the first steel abstraction with a new attitude, her mind already expanded by contact with Una.

"What's it called?" she asked, drinking in the object shaped vaguely like a woman's breast.

"It's called 'Promise of Spring,' " replied Una, lighting a cigarette in a ten-inch holder. An Indian belt of silver and turquoise was clipped around her slim waist. "It's by Carol de Witt, my dear. She's extremely—one might almost say ostentatiously—talented.

She's quite, quite beautiful and is convinced she is a vampire. It might very well be true. I've never seen her in the light of day, and she has no mirrors in her apartment. It's quite possible she's dead."

Vanessa was studying the sculpture.

"It's very . . . suggestive," she said.

"Oh my dear, it's erotic. It's quite, quite obscene, and offensively suggestive. It has been only by exercising the fiercest self-control that I have been able not to give in to the temptation of inviting my parents and their vicar to tea to see it. I think Dr. MacDonald would faint dead away. I have never understood how he got through all those 'begats' in the Bible. Do you like it, my dear?"

"Oh, very much."

"Now do you see what I mean by 'suggestion'? So much more can be conveyed by suggestion than by trying to copy nature, which is a tedious thing at best, anyway. Who *cares,* my dear, about a tree? Or, for that matter, a chipmunk? What dear Carol has captured, in my opinion, is the essence of lust. It's *terribly* interesting."

"Is it expensive?"

"Oh, my dear, it is so *crass* to discuss money when we are in the temple of art! It's five hundred dollars."

"I'll take it."

"Do you wish it sent to that *monument* to bad taste, your father's house?"

"Yes, please. Oh, Una, it's all so interesting! It's everything you said it would be: new, exciting, different. . . ."

Una crossed the room to the back where, in a corner, was a small oak chest. She opened it and pulled out a bottle of gin.

"Now that we're sprung from that *ghastly* Silver Lake, my dear, shall we have a drink?"

Vanessa shook her head.

"No, not for me."

"My dear, the good doctor actually *cured* you! A pity. Health is something I'm firmly convinced should be taken in moderation. Too much of a good thing can kill you. Cheers."

She sipped the gin, eying Vanessa, who was wandering around among the sculptures.

"My dear," she said, "has anyone ever told you you're quite, quite attractive?"

Vanessa turned to look at her.

Marco's first major rally was scheduled for a Sunday afternoon so the working-class Italians could attend, and it was held on the steps of Saint Anthony's Church on Sullivan Street, in the very heart of the Italian Village. Luck smiled; it was a beautiful September afternoon. Gene Fairchild had done his job well, and a crowd of over one thousand people—mostly Italian—packed the block, curious to see the Italian son-in-law of one of the richest men in the country. Marco had made a handsome donation to Saint Anthony's, so the local priest, Father Piero Domenici, had agreed to let him use the church and put up a banner in front of it that proclaimed, in Italian and English, MARCO SANTORELLI: ONE OF YOUR OWN FOR CONGRESS! This had done little to further the pastoral career of Father Domenici in the Irish-dominated diocese, but the young Italian priest wanted to support Marco, and also agreed to open the rally with a prayer, which did Marco no harm.

Then Marco announced in Italian through a megaphone, "My friends, I have the honor to introduce the beautiful star of the *Ziegfeld Follies,* Miss Nellie Byfield!"

Nellie got a big hand from the Italians as she came up on the steps of the church. An upright had been placed on the church porch and Jake now took a seat as Marco said: "Miss Byfield's husband is the great Jake Rubin, who is an old and dear friend of mine and who came over to this country from Europe with me in steerage. We went through Ellis Island together, and I guess a lot of you know what *that* feels like." This drew a tremendous response. "Jake has written a campaign song for me, and now Nellie is going to sing it for us."

Jake banged out a quick vamp, then Nellie belted "For More Pasta in the Belly, Better Vote for Santorelli." The English lyrics weren't understood by many of the crowd, but the tune—like all Jake's songs—was so catchy they were soon singing along with Nellie. When it was over, she drew cheers. The rally was becoming a big outdoor party.

Then Marco took center stage again.

"My friends," he said through the megaphone, "my platform is very simple: I want to be the first immigrant congressman in American history. There are millions of us—people like you and me—who have come to this great country in the past twenty years, who have struggled to survive in a world that is totally new, wrestled with a different language, had to take the lowest-paying jobs because we were the newcomers, we were the ones that the established Americans could exploit. Well, it's time we immigrants were represented in the Congress of the United States, and I offer myself to you . . ."

"Is that the way you offered yourself to your mother-in-law?" yelled a man on the edge of the crowd. He was speaking Italian. "Isn't it true she paid you to make love to her? Hey, pretty boy— aren't you a gigolo?"

Gasps and cries from the crowd.

"Tell us about how *you* were exploited when you came to America," yelled another man. "You just *screwed* your way to the top!"

Some raucous laughter. But Marco was way ahead of the hecklers. He had assumed Casey O'Donnell might use this ploy, and he was ready for it. In fact, he welcomed it as a springboard to launch his carefully researched counterattack on Casey and Bill Ryan.

"These are *lies!*" yelled Marco through the megaphone. "These hecklers are being paid by my opponent, Bill Ryan, and *his* boss, Casey O'Donnell! Now, gentlemen, you go back to Casey O'Donnell and tell him I am fully aware of his part-ownership of the Blue Grotto Club, which everyone here knows is a bordello. I am fully aware of all his deals with the City of New York, by which he pays kickbacks to get municipal trucking contracts. I am aware of his right-hand man, Mike Murphy, who uses threats of violence to force saloon owners to use O'Donnell's trucks to deliver beer. And I have a list of two dozen other stinkers that I am more than willing to release to the press. In fact, the corruption of my opponent, the *Dis*honorable William Ryan, and his boss, Casey O'Donnell and the Irish machine, is going to be my *other* platform in this campaign. The people of this district have been exploited by political *hacks,* whose only desire is to make money for themselves and entrench themselves in power. I say it's time to clean out these bums! I say to you that *I*, Marco Santorelli, who came from the same poverty and background you did . . . I swear that if you elect me to the Congress of the United States, I will do everything in my power to clean up this district and give you *honest* representation in Congress."

He had spoken with passion, and his speech worked. The Italians went crazy for him, cheering and clapping. The hecklers were forgotten. Marco's past peccadilloes weren't important. Here was someone young, strong and Italian who was presenting himself in a leadership position. The immigrants, most of them desperately poor and weary from the incessant struggle of their daily lives, had found someone exciting who was offering to fight for them.

Nellie, who hadn't understood a word of the Italian but had caught the passion of Marco's speech, was as excited as the immigrants.

"He's really good," she said to Jake, who was applauding as wildly as she. "He's going to win!"

"You're right, he *is* good. Hurray for Marco!"

The crowd began chanting "Marco, Marco, Marco" over and over. Nellie joined in: "Marco, Marco, Marco . . ."

My God, I've got to have him, she was thinking. *He's the sexiest, most exciting man I've ever seen in my life.*

"Marco, Marco, Marco . . ."

PART IX
Love Affairs

Chapter 39

On a rainy late-September day, Violet Weiler returned to her parents' Fifth Avenue town house from Mme. Levitska's ballet studio. The butler told her, "Your parents wish to see you in the drawing room, Miss Violet." She went into the gold room. Her father came up and hugged her.

"Be brave, Violet," he said.

"What's wrong?"

Her mother, who was standing by one of the Fifth Avenue windows, turned. Her hands were clasped together in front of her in a tragic pose.

"My dear, I'm so sorry," she said.

"So sorry about *what*?" she almost screamed.

"It's Craig. His mother called a while ago. She received a telegram from the Italian ambassador. Apparently, his ambulance was hit by a German bomb."

Violet was stunned. Death seemed so remote in her young life. Death seemed almost impossible.

"Is he . . . ?"

Her father put his arm around her again.

"Yes."

She remembered a young boy swimming with her in an Adirondack lake ten years before, and she began to understand what the Great War was all about.

It was all about death.

* * *

Craig Wertheim's death threw her into a deep depression. For the first time in her young life, Violet began to realize emotionally the ugliness that lay beyond the gilded walls of her protected world. It was one thing to read about the war and to hear her parents talk about charities for the poor in the slums. But Craig had been killed in that distant war; Jake Rubin had been poor and had lived in those slums. More and more, her thoughts kept returning to the songwriter who had offered her love in the Chinese restaurant. But what exactly was this love he was offering? What was the great secret? Why were certain women spoken of in whispers? For that matter, what had Oscar Wilde done that was so horrible her mother wouldn't allow his name mentioned in the house?

She decided she had to find out. She walked downtown to the Public Library, that magnificent building that had recently been opened, went to the third floor and looked up Biology in the card catalogue. She had taken biology at Vassar; the hypocrisy of the curriculum was reflected by the fact that Violet knew more about the sex life of frogs than human beings. Checking out two books, she sat down in the huge Reading Room and began to study.

"So *that's* it," she whispered to herself a while later, trying to imagine her beloved, fat father making love to her mother. It was difficult to imagine, but it must have happened, because here she was.

She returned the books, left the building and started walking back uptown. Now she understood what Jake was proposing in the Chinese restaurant, and she realized that if she called him, she was committing herself to a course of action that would inevitably lead to what her mother called ruin. Did she want that? Her world might be stuffy and in its way unreal, but it was also undeniably comfortable. If she broke the rules by going to bed with Jake Rubin, she might never find a husband—at least one of her own kind, like Craig Wertheim.

By the time she reached Fifty-seventh Street, she had weighed the pros and cons to the point of exhaustion. To her, Jake was glamorous. Jake had suffered. Jake felt things more deeply. Jake had lived. She liked him enormously, perhaps was even in love with him. Most importantly, she *wanted* him.

Did she want him enough to make the phone call that might destroy her? Did she want him enough to take on the outraged opprobrium of her mother? She was in an agony. If there were only someone she could talk to!

She was just starting to cross Fifty-seventh Street when it struck her: Of course! *She'd* know what to do.

Hadn't she been the mistress of the Tsar (or so she said)?

Nadeshda Maximova Levitska lived in a three-room apartment directly above her Carnegie Hall ballet studio, and her living room was, in Violet's opinion, something straight out of Dostoevsky. Heavy burgundy velvet fringed draperies almost shut out the light entirely, casting the room into a perpetual gloom which Mme. Levitska's glass-globed table lamp barely pierced. There was enough furniture for six rooms—Victorian sofas, ottomans, étagères; the dark Oriental rug was spotted where her two supposedly house-trained dogs had repeatedly peed and pooped; Russian magazines, books and scores were scattered everywhere; the top of the black Bechstein grand was piled with more scores and silver-framed photographs of the Russian royal family, including one of her alleged lover, Alexander III. Over the mantel was an oil portrait of the young and beautiful Mme. Levitska poised *sur les pointes* as Odette. Below it, the fifty-year-old Mme. Levitska—still beautiful, but wrinkled—was seated in a dusty armchair, wrapped in a fringed shawl, pouring tea into a glass cup from a silver samovar.

"So you tink you're in love?" she said in her heavily accented English, which she peppered with Russian phrases, such as *Bozhe moi,* meaning "My God!" "To whom, please?"

"Jake Rubin, the songwriter," replied Violet, who was sitting on an ottoman beside the samovar. "Oh, madame, he's the most wonderful man! He's—"

"Yes yes, I know," she interrupted, handing her the tea glass. "He's handsome, nice, funny, loving—they *all* are. He's also married, dollink. And from what I hear, she's not a nice woman, this Nellie Byfield. You're asking for *beeg* trouble. And what about your momma? *Bozhe moi!* I hate to tink!"

"I know," groaned Violet. "That's why I've come to you. I don't know what to do."

"When I was mistress of His Majesty . . . " She closed her eyes and smiled. "Ah, what a lover! What a *bear* of a man! *Bozhe moi!*"

She opened her eyes again. "Anyway, when I was mistress, I learned most important rule of game: *negotiate*."

Violet looked puzzled. "Negotiate what?"

"Take a leetle step forward, see what he does. Then take *another* leetle step. See what he offers. *Negotiate*. Don't rush in, dollink, and say 'all or nozzink.' Never *never* rush. Go slow. Negotiate. You got what he wants. Make him *pay* for it."

"But I don't want money. . . . "

"*Bozhe moi,* you don't know from *nozzink*! You tink you're in love; he talk beeg about him loving you; okay, let's see how much he loves you. Does he love you enough to give up that beetch of a wife of his and make *you* his wife? Hm? Have we tought of that?"

Violet looked pensive. "That would certainly solve a lot of problems," she said.

"Of course. You're not good mistress material, dollink. You're too bourgeoise—no offense intended. But lead him on! Let him *tink* you want to be his mistress. But of course, mistress must have her own apartment, no? Okay, let's see if he'll get you an apartment. And you're rich girl, used to finest everytink, no? It's got to be *nice* apartment, okay? Let's see what he comes up with. Meanwhile, dollink, talk sweet, but hang on to what you got. Understand? Drive him a leetle crazy. Is always good for men. More tea, dollink?"

"No, thank you. But what if he comes up with a nice apartment? What do I do then? Not that my parents would *let* me move into an apartment someone else was paying for . . ."

"Is not necessary to move. You keep negotiatink. You'll need the apartment repainted before you can move in. You don't like the curtains. The kitchen steenks. There's always sometink. Meanwhile, he's investink more and more; time is passing; he's going crazy with love, dollink; and that's when you suggest maybe he's married to the wrong woman. Understand? *But hang on to what you got!* Is money in the bank."

"Is that how you handled the Tsar?"

"Ah, is different with tsars. Besides, by time I met him, I didn't have nozzink to hang on to."

She refilled her tea glass from the samovar, her five silver bracelets jingling merrily.

Negotiate, mused Violet. *Well, it's not very romantic, but maybe she has a point. And it would be sort of fun to see what Jake comes up with....*

But as to moving out of her parents' house into an apartment of her own, Violet was having some new ideas about that.

Jake's workroom on the third floor of his town house had formerly been another maid's room and consequently was extremely small, the physical comfort of maids not having been foremost in the mind of the house's builder. But the room was perfect for Jake. He had moved in his black upright piano, a piano stool, a small desk and chair, and a sofa to lie on when inspiration seemed flagging. When he worked, he generally pulled a green blind down over the one window so as to block out any distraction. The room was almost monastic, but in it Jake was writing a phenomenal amount of music. He had become known on Tin Pan Alley as "The Song Factory," and it was meant as a compliment, albeit a jealous one.

Jake was sitting at his piano working on a new song called "I Remember You, But Why Have You Forgotten Me?" when his business phone on the desk rang. Expecting a call from Abe Shulman, he answered it.

"Hello?"

"Jake? It's Violet Weiler."

He sat down slowly. Violet. Delicate, delicious Violet. It had been two weeks since his lunch with her at the Chinese restaurant, and since he hadn't heard from her, he had assumed she wasn't interested in his proposition. But the sound of her voice brought back his memory of her, which was one of pure pleasure.

"I've missed you," he said. "How have you been?"

"Thinking about you," she replied, and he thought her voice seemed different, perhaps lower, perhaps . . . seductive? Violet? "I wanted to talk to you about your offer."

He was all attention.

"Yes . . . good! When can I see you?"

"Well, it's difficult with Mother, you know. But they're going to a gala at the opera tonight, and I could slip out."

"What time?"

"The curtain's at eight, so they'll leave here at seven-thirty. Mother always likes to get to the opera early so people can see her jewels. Why don't I meet you in front of our house at quarter till eight?"

"Fine. I'll take you to dinner in the Village. I know a wonderful French restaurant down there."

He heard the click of her phone as she hung up.

Because Nellie was at the theater every evening, Jake was at liberty at night, which had obvious advantages, and at quarter of eight he was sitting in the back of a taxi in front of the Weiler mansion, watching the front door. Ten minutes earlier Mr. and Mrs. Weiler had climbed into their limousine as their chauffeur held an umbrella against the drizzling rain.

Now, Jake saw the front door open, and Violet hurried out. She wore a raincoat over her yellow dress and carried an umbrella. Jake got out to hold the taxi door for her; when they were both in the back seat, he gave the cabbie a Village address, then took Violet's hand and smiled at her.

"I'm glad you called," he said. "*Very* glad."

He leaned over and kissed her on the mouth. She enjoyed it, but Mme. Levitska's voice rang in her mind: *Hang on to what you got.*

The restaurant was called Le Bec Fin—French slang for gourmet—and it was on West Fourth Street, very near the Hudson River, in a charming block of brick Federal houses. The restaurant was in the basement of one of these houses, which had a thick, gnarled wisteria vine climbing its front to the roof. Jake led Violet down three steps from the sidewalk, then held the door for her. After they had checked their raincoats, the captain, who knew Jake, led them to the best table by the window, which gave a nice view of the shoes of the pedestrians passing on the wet sidewalk above.

"Monsieur has ordered a bottle of champagne." The captain smiled as he seated Violet.

"Oh, Jake, how wonderful!"

The captain opened the bottle and poured the champagne.

"To us," said Jake, raising his glass.

"To love," sighed Violet.

After she had taken a sip, she put her glass down.

"Now. Where do *you* think we should look for an apartment?"

"I beg your pardon?"

"The apartment. I mean, if we're going to have a love affair—and, oh, Jake, I'm *so* looking forward to it! The thrill of your passionate kisses!—anyway, we can't do it in my house, certainly, and obviously not in yours, and I'm certainly not going to live in some second-rate hotel. So we have to find an apartment I can move into, like a proper mistress. And it has to be on the Upper East Side. Mother would never let me live anywhere else."

Jake was a bit dazed.

"Do you think your mother will let you move into an apartment? I mean, even one on the Upper East Side?"

"It's going to be difficult, obviously, but my mind's made up. She can't dominate me forever. Now, you'll have to pay the rent, obviously."

"Of course."

"And I suppose you'll have to give me some sort of allowance to live on. I have a funny feeling my parents aren't going to want to support me if I become your mistress, so *you'll* have to do it. I come into a trust fund when I'm twenty-one, but right now I'm flat broke."

Jake was looking even more dazed.

"An allowance. Yes, of course ..."

"And then there's clothes and things ... but let's not talk about that now."

"No, let's talk about you and me. I can't tell you how happy this is making me. ..."

"Oh, I know, darling." She smiled. "I'm happy, too. My first love affair!" *Negotiate.* "But we have to be practical. I'll start looking at the real estate ads tomorrow, but I have to have an idea of what you'll be willing to pay. How much would you, darling?"

Jake was staring at her, thinking, *Jesus, what happened to the airy ballerina? What happened to Miss Innocent? This is like talking to a goddam real estate broker.*

"Uh ... well, I don't know. Whatever you want ..."

"Well, I'll look, and if I see something I fall in love with, I'll show it to you. All right? And we'll want a piano, won't we? So you can play your songs for me? May we have a piano, Jake? That would be so romantic."

"Uh ... sure. Why not? I'll rent one ..."

Jesus, this is going to cost me a fortune!

Violet saw the terror in his eyes, and his look tickled her funny bone so much, she couldn't help but burst out laughing.

"What's so funny?" he asked, surprised.

"Oh, you! Oh ..." She covered her mouth with her napkin, trying to stifle her giggles. "I think I've overnegotiated you."

"You've *what?*"

"Madame Levitska ... I went to her for a 'mistress' lesson, because I figured she'd know how to handle you. ..." More laughs. "And she told me to negotiate with you ... except I think ..." She bounced up and down in her chair with laughter. ". . . I think I've scared you into a panic!"

Jake started laughing also. "*You* went to Madame Levitska?"

She nodded, giggling.

"Well, you *have* scared me into a panic."

And he was laughing as hard as she.

The Diamond Horseshoe of the Metropolitan Opera was one of the most conservative bastions of New York society— Mrs. Astor's box, Number 7, was called "the social throne of America"—and it was also a stronghold of anti-Semitism. Jews were simply not allowed to buy a box, though they could rent one for various performances, and this despite the fact that two Jews, Otto Kahn and Simon Weiler, were the two greatest individual donors to the house at Thirty-ninth Street and Broadway. The gala performance of *Tosca* being given that evening was for the Belgian Relief Committee, and because Simon had contributed fifteen thousand dollars to the committee, he was graciously allowed to rent Box 32 for the occasion. The cream of New York society was there, and Mrs. Weiler pulled out her heavy ammunition for the evening. In Rebecca's case, this meant a diamond and ruby tiara, a three-strand diamond and ruby necklace, matching pendant earrings, three diamond bracelets, a forty-carat diamond solitaire ring, and a jewel-encrusted pair of opera glasses that had cost seventy-five thousand dollars. Even with that much jewelry, she felt neither over-diamonded nor vulgar; the woman in the box next to her wore *seven* diamond bracelets.

The custom at the opera was to leave after the first act, for no one in society was much interested in the singing or the music—

the opera was attended mainly because people needed someplace to dress up for—but on tonight's occasion, because it was a gala and because *Tosca* was a deservedly popular opera, most of the audience, including the Weilers, stayed till the end. After the curtain calls, Mrs. Weiler rose from her gilt chair, and Simon put her full-length ermine cape over her shoulders. Then they swept grandly out, chatting with their bejeweled and befurred friends as they made their way to the entrance, where a long line of limousines waited and a crowd of "rich-watchers" huddled in the autumnal chill to see the parade.

When they reached home, the butler took their coats and Rebecca said, "Is Violet in bed, Jarvis?"

"No, madame. She went out."

"Out? She said nothing to *me* about going out. Out with whom?"

"She didn't say, madame."

Rebecca's ample bosom swelled, and seven hundred thousand dollars' worth of diamonds and rubies swelled with it.

"But she *must* have said something."

Just then the front door opened and Violet hurried in. When she saw her parents, she tensed. She had meant to beat them home from the opera, but she had been having such a good time with Jake that she lost track of the hour. Now her mother turned on her.

"Where have you been?" she thundered.

"I got hungry and went to a delicatessen," she said, closing the door. Her mother looked at her yellow party dress.

"You went to a delicatessen in *that* dress? To go to a delicatessen at *all* strikes me as a foolish extravagance, considering the lavish way you are fed in this house, but to *dress* to go to a delicatessen seems absurd!"

"Nevertheless," Violet said haughtily, passing her parents on her way to the stairs, "I went to a delicatessen. Good night, everyone."

Her mother watched her as she climbed the marble stair.

"The child is lying," she whispered to her husband.

"Now, Rebecca, let her alone. I sometimes think you're too strict with Violet."

She turned on him. "One can *never* be too strict with one's

329

daughter," she intoned. Then she said to the butler, "When did she leave the house?"

"I believe it was shortly after you left for the opera, madame."

"You see?" she exclaimed to Simon. "She lied! *Four* hours at a delicatessen? She must have eaten all the chicken salad in New York. I'll have a talk with that girl. Delicatessen, indeed!"

And she swept up the stairs, her action stations manned.

Violet was brushing her hair when her mother came into the room. She sighed as she saw the bejeweled battleship in the red velvet evening gown bearing down on her.

"Jarvis informs me you left the house shortly after we did," she said. "Surely you don't expect me to believe you spent four hours at a delicatessen?"

Violet continued brushing her hair.

"You can believe what you want, Mother."

"Violet, I want the truth! Where were you tonight?"

She slammed down her brush and turned on her mother.

"Would you stop *bullying* me?" she exclaimed.

"I am not bullying you. I am merely performing the normal duties of any concerned parent. Where were you?"

"It's none of your business!"

Violet ran into the bathroom and slammed the door.

"Violet!"

Rebecca hurried across the room and pounded on the door.

"Violet, come out here! Come out here this instant!"

The door reopened and a sulky Violet appeared.

"Yes, Mother. What do you want?"

"You know very well what I want. Where were you this evening?"

Violet took a deep breath. "All right, if you want the truth, I went to dinner in Greenwich Village with a man I think I'm falling in love with. And you'd better get used to this, Mother, because I think I really *am* falling in love with him."

"I see." Her tone was lethal. "And who is this man you think you're falling in love with?"

Violet went to her bed, sat down and took off her shoes.

"Jake Rubin," she said.

An extremely long silence. Violet got up from the bed to carry her shoes to the closet. "I know what you're thinking, Mother, so don't waste your breath on a speech. I *know* he's a 'Russian,' I *know* he's not one of 'our kind,' and I *know* he's married. Nevertheless, I'm falling in love with him. He's the most wonderful man I've ever met."

She opened the closet door and put her shoes inside. Then she took off her dress and hung it up, wondering why her mother wasn't fulminating at her.

When she stepped out of the closet, to her surprise her mother was gone.

Nellie had brought her black maid, Fanny, with her from Sniffen Court when she moved uptown with Jake, and the next morning Fanny came into her bedroom. Nellie was sitting up in bed reading *Variety*.

"Miss Nellie, you got company downstairs," said Fanny.

Nellie put down *Variety*.

"Company? Fanny, who is it?"

"Someone *very* important, if you asks me. She done drove up in a Rolls-Royce a block long with a good-lookin' chauffeur. Mm-*mm!* Do I like that chauffeur!"

"Fanny, who *is* it?"

"Here's her card, Miss Nellie. Her name's Mrs. Weiler, or something."

Nellie examined the card.

"Mrs. *Simon* Weiler," she said, in awed tones.

"She looks mighty rich, Miss Nellie."

"She *is* mighty rich," said Nellie, throwing off her covers. "Did you ever hear of the Weiler department store chain? That's *her*."

"Really? I *like* Weiler's. I saw the prettiest dress there last week in the window, but I couldn't afford it. Do you suppose I could jew her down a couple-a bucks?"

Nellie groaned as she hurried into the bathroom.

"Don't use that word around her, you idiot. *She's* Jewish! Get out my ivory dress—the one with the lace—then go down and tell her I'll be down in ten minutes. Ask her if she wants coffee or tea. And be *polite*."

"Yes'm, Miss Nellie."

I wonder what she *wants,* thought Nellie as she began brushing her teeth.

* * *

Fifteen minutes later, Nellie came into the drawing room. Rebecca Weiler, wearing a tweed suit the hem of which brushed the top of her spats, and a toque hat with an enormous feather, was sitting ramrod-straight in a chair.

"Mrs. Weiler? I'm Nellie Rubin," she said, coming over to shake the gloved hand.

"How do you do, Mrs. Rubin," said Rebecca, shaking her hand but not getting up. "I do apologize for making this unannounced call and trust I haven't inconvenienced you?"

"Not at all. Did Fanny ask if you'd like coffee?"

"She did, and I declined. I have already had two cups of coffee this morning. A third cup would be an indulgence, which I do not approve of."

"I see." *Friendly type,* she thought, sitting down. *And so warm and informal.* "Well." She smiled. "What can I do for you, Mrs. Weiler?"

Rebecca turned her cool eyes on Nellie. *Attractive but cheap,* she thought.

"Mrs. Rubin, I fear this will not be pleasant for either of us. Is your husband here?"

"Yes, he's upstairs in his workroom."

"There is, I hope, no possibility of his overhearing our conversation?"

"Oh, no." *What is this?* she thought.

"Then I will proceed to speak with the utmost candor. I perhaps may be accused of having old-fashioned views on the subject of marriage, but I firmly believe that when the marriage vows are pledged, it is the duty and obligation of each partner to remain faithful to them. Do you share these views, Mrs. Rubin?"

"Well . . ." Nellie squirmed slightly. She had cheated on Jake twice without his knowing it. "Yes. I suppose."

"You seem somewhat ambivalent, Mrs. Rubin. Can one possibly 'suppose' the marriage vows are sacred?"

"Excuse me, Mrs. Weiler, but I would like to know what this is all about?"

"It's very simple. Your husband is philandering with my daughter."

Nellie looked amazed.

"Jake?" she gasped.

"I believe that is his unfortunate name."

"But when? How?"

"They have known each other for some time now. Violet is a child of extreme refinement and delicacy, but she is innocent, Mrs. Rubin. *Very* innocent. She has no defenses against your husband's guile, and I fear for her purity. Of course, my sympathy is extended to you, too, for being the victim of this man's duplicity. Which is why I have come here this morning to warn you of the danger to your own domestic tranquillity. You must stop your husband, Mrs. Rubin. Stop him before he *ruins* my daughter! And your marriage, too, of course."

"How old is your daughter?" Nellie asked.

"She will be twenty next month."

Jake's robbing the cradle! she thought. *Can you beat that? That sneaky little bastard . . .*

She assumed a tragic look.

"I can't tell you how grateful I am you've told me this, Mrs. Weiler. Of course, I'm shocked—shocked!—to hear that my husband is 'philandering,' as you put it. But you need have no fears. I'll stop him right away."

Rebecca relaxed a bit.

"And I, dear lady, am relieved to hear you say that. We live, unfortunately, in an age of loose morals. It is good to know that there are some wives, like yourself, who still believe in the eternal verities." She rose to her feet and extended her hand. "It has been a great pleasure meeting you, my dear. It is obvious to me your husband was extremely fortunate to have won you."

Nellie also rose.

"Why, thank you, Mrs. Weiler. And it's been a pleasure meeting you."

"I feel a tragedy has been averted."

As Nellie accompanied her to the front door, she thought, *Damn Jake! But I know how to get back at him. . . .*

Chapter 40

That night, as her chauffeur dropped her off at the New Amsterdam Theater, Nellie said, "I'm going to be running through a new number after the show tonight, Billy. I don't know how late I'll be, so I'll take a taxi home."

"Yes'm, Miss Nellie."

But after the show she took a taxi downtown to the Village instead. "That's the house," she said to the driver, and the cab pulled up in front of Marco's campaign headquarters. The house was dark except for the third-floor windows. The third floor was what Nellie was interested in.

She got out, paid the cabbie, then climbed the three steps and rang the bell. When the light in the stained-glass overdoor turned on, Marco opened the door. He was in his bathrobe and barefoot. He looked surprised to see her.

"Nellie! What are you doing down here . . . ?"

"Well, since you never invited me to that lunch I mentioned, I thought maybe you'd invite me in for a midnight drink."

He didn't look happy about this.

"I was just going to bed. . . ." He looked up and down the deserted street, realizing that if he were seen, it wouldn't be exactly a political asset. He stepped aside. "Come on in," he said.

She came into the narrow entrance hall and he quickly shut the door. Then he turned to look at her. She was wearing a sable-collared black velvet coat over a lavender dress; on her head was a drooping-brimmed black velvet hat with a large rhinestone buckle in front. She looked gorgeous and hell-bent for trouble.

"Does Jake know you're here?" he said.

"Of course not." She smiled. "Aren't you going to ask me upstairs?"

"No. And, Nellie, I think you'd better go home. *Now.*"

The short hall was so narrow they were inches apart. She put her arms around him.

"I know how you feel about Jake," she whispered, "but he'll never know. I want you, Marco. I want you more than any man I've ever known. . . . Don't make me beg . . . please. . . ."

"You don't think Jake's faithful to *me,* do you?" she went on, slipping one hand inside his bathrobe and running it slowly over his chest. "He's got a nineteen-year-old girl he's seeing on the sly. If he can have fun, why can't we?"

The feel of her hand on his skin was driving him crazy. Slowly, he put his arms around her. Half opening his mouth, he put it against hers. They kissed in the narrow entrance hall for almost a minute.

"Make love to me," Nellie whispered. "Make me happy, darling. . . . "

Suddenly he pushed her away.

"Get out of here," he said softly. "Go on, get *out!*"

She smiled slightly and returned to him, putting her hands inside his bathrobe again.

"Don't tell me you don't want to," she said.

He grabbed her wrists and pulled her hands away.

"Of *course* I want to. That's the problem! But I'm not going to do that to Jake. Christ, sometimes I wish I were a goddam eunuch! Now get out of here before I fuck you right here on the floor."

"*Do* it. . . ." She smiled. "I'd love it."

"Don't I know it!"

"I love you angry. It's exciting."

He closed his eyes.

"Oh Jesus, Nellie, don't make it worse. I'm not going to do it. Not Jake's wife . . . the *one* person in the world!" He opened his eyes again, and they were blazing. "Now get the hell out of here! And you're *stupid* to cheat on that man. He's the best thing that ever happened to you."

Now she was angry. She wrenched her wrists free from him.

"All right, I'll go," she said. "But you know what I'm going to tell Jake? That you made a pass at me. No, I'll make it better than that: I'll tell Jake you asked me down here, and then tried to rape me."

He slapped her so hard she stumbled back against the wall.

"You tell him that, and I'll kill you! You understand? You can cheat on him with anyone else, but you're not going to tell him you cheated with *me*. Because Jake's my friend. So don't try anything!"

He said it with such intensity she was actually rather afraid. But she wasn't going to show him. Holding her cheek, which hurt fiercely, she went to the door and opened it.

"I'll pay you back for this," she said quietly. "Somehow. You *and* Jake."

She left the house.

Marco closed the door, then leaned against it, his testicles aching with desire. *Oh Christ*, he thought as he put his hand on his genitals, squeezing them to ease the ache. *Jake, you helped me when I escaped from Ellis Island, and for that I'd never play around with your wife.*

But oh Christ, how close I came to doing it!

Straightening painfully, he walked slowly to the stairs and started up.

After his dinner with Violet Weiler at Le Bec Fin, Jake was more delighted with her than ever. But after he got home, he told himself that despite Violet's hilarious negotiating, she had a point: She had a right to understand exactly what the arrangements would be. After all, she was still a minor, legally. Her mother— laughably "correct" as she might be—still reflected the general moral outlook of Society with a capital S; and by making Violet his mistress, he knew that he would be ruining her in the eyes of her parents and most of their friends. Violet might now be hankering for freedom and free love, but five years from now, might she not change her mind and start wanting respectability when it was too late? And did Jake want to take on that responsibility? He began to realize that his feeling for her was more complex than he thought. Mixed with his sexual desire for her and his delight in her youthfulness was a sense of almost paternal care about her that was perhaps a result not only of their age difference but a reaction against the tough independence of Nellie as well.

The answer would be to divorce Nellie and marry Violet, but the problem there was Laura. Laura the innocent, Laura the hopelessly retarded. Jake knew that Nellie had mentally rejected her daughter when she found out she was not normal, but would Vio-

336

let be any better as a mother? All human compassion aside, Jake knew that Laura was not an easy child to live with. She needed constant watching and protection, and her health was much more fragile than a normal child's. Jake's money eased the situation; he could hire Mrs. Fleming. But would Violet want to be saddled with a problem child who wasn't even her own?

As if to underline the difficulty, two mornings after his dinner with Violet, Mrs. Fleming told him that Laura had caught a bad cold.

Mme. Levitska had planted the seed in Violet's mind, but it blossomed into a decision on Violet's part to find an apartment for herself and pay for it herself—and, most importantly, to live in it herself. Several of her contemporaries had managed to break away from their parents and go out on their own—though never without a fight, for the custom was still deeply ingrained that girls lived with their parents until they were married. The freedom of living away from the domineering personality of her mother had intoxicated Violet, for she knew that much of her trouble with Mrs. Weiler derived from the fact that they both lived under the same roof. So Violet began searching the real estate ads in the newspapers, circling the apartments that seemed interesting. And two days after her dinner with Jake at Le Bec Fin, she decided to call him and tell him that he would be relieved of the necessity of paying her rent. She was going out on her own.

She knew that Jake was usually in his workroom by ten, so she waited until five after, then called his private number. To her surprise, no one answered. She went back to the window seat in the circular bay window at the corner of the house which gave such a wonderful view of Fifth Avenue and the park. She would miss that view. She would miss her bedroom, which was white, with white lace curtains at the windows. Violet's bed was brass, with a high, round, white lace canopy that made her feel like a princess when she woke up. The bed was covered with her collection of stuffed animals—her favorite was a bear she had named Gordon, for no particular reason—and there were photographs everywhere of her favorite ballet stars, with a half-dozen of Nijinsky. (The great Russian dancer had occasioned a fight between Violet and her mother. The previous April, Nijinsky had arrived in New York to make his American debut at the Metropolitan

Opera, and of course Violet had wanted to see him. But her mother refused on the grounds that Nijinsky's dancing was indecent. Mrs. Weiler knew all about Nijinsky's infamous performance of *L'Après-midi d'un Faune,* during which he had mimed masturbation on stage with a silk scarf, and Mrs. Weiler wasn't about to have her daughter see *that*.)

Fifteen minutes later, Violet tried Jake's number again and this time he answered.

"It's Violet," she said.

"Oh."

"Is anything the matter?"

"My daughter's sick. She caught a cold, but the doctor's afraid it's developing into pneumonia."

"Oh, I'm sorry. . . ."

"She's running a pretty high temperature. I'm . . ."

She waited for him to finish the sentence, but he didn't.

"I hope she'll be all right," Violet said.

"Well, we're a little nervous."

"Then I won't take any more of your time."

"I'm sorry. . . ."

"No, no, I understand. Goodbye, Jake. I miss you like crazy."

She hung up and went back to the corner window seat to look down on Fifth Avenue. He had mentioned his daughter briefly, suggesting that she was not entirely normal, but Violet had sensed he didn't like talking about her.

For the first time, she began to realize that he led another life, that she had spent only a relatively few hours with him, and that she really knew very little about him. She knew what the world knew: that he had come from Russia nine years before a penniless immigrant, and that he had achieved a meteoric success on Broadway. She knew he was kind and gentle and fun to be with. She knew she was attracted to him. But she had never even met his wife; she had only seen her on the stage.

She began to see that she was, with Mme. Levitska's encouragement, planning to destroy someone else's marriage by stealing another woman's husband. When looked at in that light, it started to become rather ugly.

She decided she would continue apartment hunting for herself.

Chapter 41

"My dear, this is the *only* party of any importance being given in New York tonight," announced Una Marbury as she escorted Vanessa up the steps of the town house on Barrow Street in the West Village. "Carol has hired a black jazz band that was the *hit* of Paris, if you can believe it. The leader's name is Roscoe Haines. He and his wife have just come to New York from Rio, and Carol says his jazz is quite, quite pagan and utterly irresistible. Like you tonight, my pet. I could *devour* you with kisses! In fact, I very probably shall." She patted her cheek lovingly, and Vanessa tingled with pleasure and apprehension.

Being with Una was like being back in girls' school, where Vanessa had had many crushes on girls—crushes of such intensity that they had included love letters and impassioned kisses. But then, she had never felt ashamed of them or guilty, because the thought of going further into an openly sexual relationship had simply never occurred to her. At a time when Violet Weiler had to go to the public library to learn the facts of life, it was hardly remarkable that Vanessa had never heard of lesbianism, and at first her friendship with Una had seemed as innocent as those schoolgirl crushes Vanessa remembered with such fondness. Not only was Una funny and an out-and-out rebel against society, which appealed to Vanessa, but also Vanessa had always felt more comfortable with women than with men, and she had practically locked her husband, Marco, out of her life, so that she was looking for someone new to fill the vacuum.

But lately Una's caresses had become almost embarrassing, her kisses hungrier, to the point that Vanessa was beginning to feel a sexual response that frightened her. Una had told her enough about Carol de Witt and her friends that Vanessa realized if she went to the sculptress's Bohemian party, she was committing herself to something as fascinating and attractive as it was dangerous. But she was so curious that she couldn't say no.

The door to the house was opened by a tall woman in a man's tuxedo. Her brown hair was cropped mannishly, and she wore a monocle in her left eye. She was in her early thirties, rather attractive, and she held a champagne glass in her hand. Behind her blasted the sound of very hot jazz mixed with the babble of many voices.

"Carol, my dear," said Una, coming into the house and kissing the hostess's cheek. "This is Vanessa. I've told her she will be shocked and possibly revolted by your party. I *do* hope you won't let her down." She added, in a whispered prompt, "She bought 'Promise of Spring.'"

Carol's smile was the first frost of winter. Vanessa could understand why this sculptress daughter of a rich Chicago grain dealer thought herself a vampire. She looked like one of Count Dracula's sisters.

"I know who Vanessa is," said Carol, with all the warmth of a great white shark. "You're welcome, but I don't think your husband will get many votes here."

The jazz was almost too loud to think, but Vanessa cringed slightly at the mention of Marco. As much as she had come to dislike him, he was still her husband and the father of her son, he was running for political office in the Village, and his wife's presence at Carol de Witt's party could hardly be an asset to his campaign. As if reading her thoughts, Una took her hand and led her into Carol's packed, smoke-filled studio. The guests were of both sexes, but women were dancing with women and men with men, as well as a few examples of the more conventional arrangement. Some of the men wore dinner jackets, but the male attire tended toward the more flamboyant: arty velvet jackets, some strange outfits that were versions of toreador suits, and one very drunk young man sprawled on the floor totally naked. The women wore either men's outfits, like Carol, or else rather sloppy blouses and skirts. Una was one of the few women there who dressed with any feminine style at all; she wore a burgundy dress with a crepe de chine cape flung over one shoulder.

"There!" she exclaimed. "Isn't it deliciously decadent? So much more interesting, my dear, than men dancing with women, which is, when you think of it, terribly common. Shall we dance?"

Before Vanessa could say yes or no, Una took her in her arms and, leading, danced her into the crowd. Vanessa was initially tense, but as Una placed her soft cheek against hers, she found herself rather enjoying it.

"Did you know, my dear, that *jazz* derives from an African dialect and that it means 'sperm'? So that jazz music is *prima facie* sexual, which I find absolutely fascinating. Of course, a century ago the waltz was considered so daring as to be provocative. I'm sure someone could write a tedious doctoral thesis on the evolution of sexual looseness as demonstrated by dance forms. Why did you look so upset when Carol mentioned your husband?"

"Can't you imagine?"

"Ah, dear heart, you're feeling a teensy bit guilty about being here at Number Twelve, Sodom Street. Oh well, I suppose that's understandable. Do you love Marco, my dear? Since you hardly see him anymore, I can't imagine your bosom is heaving with desire for him."

"I'd rather not talk about it."

"Oh, but we must! Here we are, dancing cheek-to-cheek, *comme on dit*, and it must be painfully obvious by now that I am madly, passionately in love with you. Is Marco madly in love with you?"

"No . . ."

"Nor are you in love with him—am I right?"

"Please, Una, let's change the subject. . . ."

"No! It's time we were utterly frank with each other. Why did you marry him? You must have known he was after your money."

"I didn't know at the time. . . . He seduced me. He looks like a god, you know."

"You can have all the gods on Olympus, as far as I'm concerned. Filthy, hairy beasts. It's obvious God made Adam first and decided He'd made an inferior product. *Eve* was the triumph. But you *let* him seduce you, didn't you? Because you wanted a husband?"

"Yes . . . oh, I don't know. . . ."

"You wanted a husband because you were afraid to be different, to be your true self. And your true self is really not attracted to men—isn't that right? You don't have to answer. I know. Furthermore, you thought Marco was a poor nobody you could handle. He was *there,* and you grabbed him. Isn't that the truth?"

"Please!"

"Face the *truth,* Van: We love each other."

And she stopped dancing to plant a kiss on Vanessa's mouth, a kiss so nakedly lustful Vanessa couldn't resist it.

"God *damn!"* said Roscoe to Flora as he continued leading the combo. "There's more lesbos here than in Paris. What's happened to New York?"

"I don't know," replied his wife. "Looks to me like it's gone queer as a preacher in a whorehouse with his fly buttoned. I'm not sure this was a smart idea, Roscoe."

"Hell, she paid cash. And you know these pansies: If they like you, they can make you chic as all shit. Okay, get up and sing 'Where's My Man?' That'll get the boys peein' in their pants."

Flora got off her chair and followed Roscoe to the piano.

"Ladies and gentlemen," he announced with a grin, adding, "though it's *raw-ther* hard to tell which is which . . ."

A laugh from the half-drunk crowd.

"My wife is gonna sing the song she introduced in Paris, '*Je Cherche Mon Homme,*' or 'Where's My Man?' Let's hear it for Flora Mitchum!"

Flora was wearing a gorgeous, black-sequined, tight-fitting dress that had black feathers around the top. It showed off her fabulous figure to perfection, and Una was ogling it appreciatively.

"My dear," she said to Vanessa over the applause, "I hear they're fabulous in bed."

Vanessa looked shocked.

"You wouldn't!"

"Oh wouldn't I?"

And she laughed. Flora started singing the torchy song, first in French, then in English. Vanessa's thoughts drifted back to her husband and her son and her father . . . to Garden Court and the *North Star.* How staid and stuffy that world seemed compared to this, and how wonderfully this represented the ultimate rebellion against it.

And yet, she missed the old world and missed her father dreadfully. Would he ever accept *this*? No, sophisticated as he was, he would hate this. . . .

She felt Una's arm slip around her waist. Then Una's mouth was at her ear, licking it delicately. Vanessa felt herself grow weak.

"Let's go upstairs," whispered Una. "Carol has a guest room."

"No ..."

"I *love* you, my darling. I adore you. I must have you now ... tonight...."

She took Vanessa's hand and led her back through the crowd to the front hall. Vanessa followed, at first resisting slightly, but then giving in completely to Una's forcefulness. Una led her up the narrow stairs to the top. The smoke and the music wafted up the stairway as Una put her arms around her and began kissing her, hungrily, her mouth half open, her tongue dancing inside Vanessa's mouth. Vanessa had never known such desire.

Una broke the kiss and whispered, almost angrily, "Say you love me!"

Vanessa, eyes half-closed, nodded.

"I love you."

"Say you *want* me!"

"I want you...."

"Good. Come on."

Una grabbed her hand and led her into one of the small bedrooms. She had just closed the door when they heard the police whistle downstairs. Then screams and shouts.

"What is it?" asked Vanessa, terrified.

Una was headed for the window.

"It's a police raid. Damn!"

"*Police—?*" Vanessa looked in shock.

"Come *on*! There's a balcony out here. Hurry!"

Una had thrown open the window and was climbing out. Vanessa, numb with fear, hurried after her.

Four blocks away, Marco was sitting at his desk in the small back office of his first-floor campaign headquarters, working on a speech when he heard the doorbell ring. It was eight-thirty. The office help had gone home; he was alone and not expecting anyone. He opened the desk drawer and pulled out the gun he had bought, at Phipps's urging. So far in the campaign, Sandro Albertini had given him no trouble, but Marco was prepared.

Going into the front room, which was littered with full ash-

trays, newspaper clippings and overflowing wastepaper baskets—
Gene Fairchild was a good campaign manager but not much on
housekeeping—he went to the front door. Holding the gun in the
right pocket of his suit jacket, he unlocked the door with his left
hand and opened it.

Standing outside was his wife.

"Van! What—?"

She pushed by him and slammed the door. She was looking so
desperate, he thought at first she was drunk. She leaned against
the door, trembling.

"Marco," she whispered, "will you love me? Will you take me
back? Oh God ..." Bursting into tears, she threw herself into his
arms.

"What in God's name has happened?"

"I was at a party ... there was a police raid. ..."

"Jesus, what kind of party was it?"

She didn't answer.

"Van, *tell* me. What kind of party was it?"

She pulled away from him and took a deep breath.

"A party where ..." she hesitated. "... Men were dancing
with men, women with women. ..." She put her fists to her cheeks
in a gesture of total despair. "Oh, I don't know *why* I went. ..."

"Who invited you? Who were you with?"

"This friend I met at Silver Lake ... Una Marbury. She runs
a sculpture gallery in the Village. She. .. " She stopped, lowering
her still-clenched fists. "Oh, you wouldn't understand. Why in
God's name did I come to *you*?"

He was looking at her intently, for the first time beginning to
understand her.

"Van," he said softly, "what kind of friend is this Una?"

She looked at him with bloodshot, guilty eyes.

"You wouldn't understand," was all she said. Then she
opened the door. "I'm sorry I bothered you."

And she left as abruptly as she had arrived.

Marco locked the door, then returned to his office. He walked
slowly, as if in a trance. He sat down at his desk and returned the
gun to the drawer.

Jesus Christ, he thought. *Now I understand why she never
wants to make love. ...*

344

* * *

Jake sat on the empty bed in his daughter's nursery and stared at the fairy-tale figures Maxfield Parrish had painted on the walls. Dorothy going down the Yellow Brick Road to meet the Wizard. Alice falling down the rabbit hole.

Dully, he wondered what to do with the room now.

"Jake," said Nellie, coming into the room. "You mustn't stay up here. It'll just make you morbid, and it's not going to do any good."

He didn't answer, and he didn't move. She came across the room and smoothed his hair.

"We knew she'd be lucky if she lived to be twenty," she went on. "So perhaps it's just as good this way. Perhaps she's better off."

"Better off *dead?*" he said.

"Yes, better off dead. What kind of life did she have? I used to look at her, and it would break my heart thinking how little she was getting out of life."

"Nellie, it's me, Jake. Don't put on an act."

"It's no act. It's true!"

He got up from the bed.

"In the first place, you don't have a heart to break. And in the second place, you never looked at her. The only person who's better off now is *you,* because you won't have to be bothered with her anymore."

"That's a helluva thing to say!"

"But it's true. Look, Nellie, I don't care anymore. That's *you.* I was amazed you stayed home from the theater last night to be with her at the end. I was sure you'd send an understudy."

"Well, I'm not staying home from the theater *tonight,*" she said icily. "And if that's your attitude, you can make the goddam funeral arrangements yourself."

"I intend to. And I have an appointment with Rabbi Sobol at Temple Emmanuel in an hour."

"With a *rabbi*? Laura wasn't Jewish! *I'm* not Jewish, and the mother has to be, doesn't she?"

"I'm not seeing the rabbi about the funeral. I'm seeing him about myself. I haven't been to temple since I came to America, and I think it's time I went."

345

"A little late to get religion, wouldn't you say?"

He ignored the barb. "Late for Laura. Maybe not for me."

"Well, you can do what you want to about your religion, but just don't bring a lot of prayer shawls around *here*. I'm not going to have our friends thinking we've become fanatics."

He looked at her sadly. "God," he said, "how could I have ever fallen in love with you?"

"And just what does *that* mean?"

"I think it means it's time we got a divorce. I'm not in love with you anymore, Nellie. It's all dead inside me, as dead as Laura. Let's get a divorce before I begin to hate you."

She didn't say anything for a moment.

"Maybe I don't want a divorce."

"I'll give you plenty of money. You'll be a rich woman. Why would you want to stay married to a man who hates you?"

She sank onto Laura's bed, put her hand to her mouth and started crying.

"Oh Christ, Nellie, stop *acting*!"

"I'm not acting, you son of a bitch," she sobbed. "After all these years, how could you be so cruel to me? Particularly *now*, with my daughter dead . . ."

Jake had grown cynical, but in fact she wasn't acting. Suddenly, one of the emotional seismic shocks that quakes lives had occurred, and she was realizing she wasn't as young as she once was, she had lost the terrific hold she had had over her husband, and the only thing that had ever come out of her body was dead.

She looked at him. "Well? *Say* something, Jake."

"What's there to say?"

"Say you still love me."

"But I don't."

And the second seismic shock occurred. She realized he didn't believe her anymore even when she was being genuine.

"It's that Weiler girl, isn't it?" she sniffed, drying her eyes.

"What Weiler girl?"

"Oh, come on. I know all about it. That old steamroller of a mother of hers was here last week, trying to get me to stop you from 'philandering' with her daughter, as she put it. She said the girl's not even twenty. Are you going to tell Rabbi Sobol you're letching after a baby? *That* should make a fascinating conversation at Temple Emmanuel."

"I haven't *touched* her!"

"And pigs have wings. I know how horny you are."

He stared at her.

"What do you want?" he said, softly.

"I'm perfectly happy the way things are. I like being Mrs. Jake Rubin. You're the best songwriter in New York, and I'm the best singer. We're the perfect pair."

She smiled.

"And what if I stop writing songs for you?"

"Why would you do that?"

"Because you can't write love songs for someone you hate."

"Then write them for Miss Weiler. Besides, you don't hate me, Jake. You're just overreacting because of Laura. How could you hate the mother of your son?"

He looked confused.

"My son? What do you mean?"

She came to him and took his hand.

"I've been unfair to you," she said. "I'm willing to have another go at it. I know how much you want another child. Maybe we'll have better luck this time."

"Nellie," he whispered. "Do you mean it?"

"Try me." She smiled. "Tonight. After I get back from the theater." She kissed him, then went to the door. "And to show you how broad-minded I am," she added as she left the room, "I don't even care if you keep seeing that child. Now, how can you hate a wife like that?"

She blew him a kiss and was gone.

In his bewilderment, he kept telling himself there had to be a catch in it. But he couldn't figure out what the catch was, unless she had spoken the truth and really *didn't* want to lose him as a husband. The question was, could he still stand her as a wife, even if she bore him another child?

And what about Violet?

Chapter 42

"Georgie," he said softly, "it's Marco."

She looked up from the reception desk. The sound of his voice after so many years aroused a half-dozen conflicting emotions inside her, and she couldn't tell which was dominant.

"So it *was* you," she whispered. The library was less full than usual. "I thought so."

"Georgie, I know what you must think of me, but ... I'm in trouble. I need to talk to you."

She didn't answer for a moment. Then she said, "Marco, you really are a loathsome man. After all you've done to me, now I suppose you want to get me to spy for you against my uncle...."

"This has nothing to do with politics!"

"Keep your voice down. This is a library."

He looked around at the two blind women at the reading table whose faces were turned toward them. Then he turned back to Georgie.

"It's about my marriage," he whispered. "I have no one to talk to—*no one*. Please, Georgie. I understand how you feel, but ..."

"You want *me* to help you with your bloody marriage? You can go to hell! Tell me about *my* marriage—the one that never happened."

He winced.

"I guess it's no use," he sighed. "I'm sorry I bothered you. It won't happen again. Goodbye, Georgie."

He started away from the reception desk. He was almost at the front door when she called out: "Marco!"

"Ssh!" hissed the two blind women.

"Ssh yourself!" snapped Georgie. "Marco, come back!"

He was already halfway back to the desk. When he reached it he whispered, "Yes?"

She was nervously twisting a pencil.

"If you're *really* in trouble . . ." she whispered.

"I am."

"Then I'll talk to you if you want."

"Have dinner with me tonight. I'll pick you up at your sister's house at eight."

"All right. But, Marco . . ."

"Yes?"

"Don't hurt me again." The words stabbed him. "Be *very* careful with me."

There were tears in his eyes.

"Oh God, Georgie," he whispered, "I swear I will."

By now, Marco knew personally most of the Italian restaurant owners in the Village, so when he led Georgie into Tony's Villa d'Este Restaurant on nearby Thompson Street, the eponymous Tony treated him like a conquering hero. "*Il candidato!*" crowed the little man with the huge black moustache, pumping Marco's hand. "Hey, everybody: our next congressman!" he yelled, and the Italian customers in the small basement restaurant applauded and cheered. Marco nodded to them as Tony led him and Georgie to a booth in the back. Quickly brushing the oilcloth with his napkin, Tony seated Georgie and said, "Tonight, everything on-a me! Dinner, *vino, tutti! Va Bene?*"

"No, no, Tony . . ."

"I eenseest! Ees-a my campaign *contribuzione*. I got-a great Sicilian wine—Il Corvo. I bring you a bottle, eh?"

And off he went before Marco could make any further protest.

"You said you're in trouble," said Georgie flatly. She was staring straight ahead, her face emotionless. "I'm listening."

"I have a son named Frank. He's a good kid—a wonderful kid, in fact."

"I'm glad to hear it."

"But my marriage is falling apart at the seams."

"I'm glad to hear that, too."

"You see, my wife is a lesbian."

For the first time her face registered emotion, and the emotion was shock.

"You mean," she whispered, "one of those strange women who like *women?*"

"Yes. That's why I need advice. I don't know what to do about Frank. Vanessa's never been much of a mother to him, but now . . . I mean, if he finds out about her at his age . . ."

"Oh, he mustn't!" she interrupted. "And there's no reason why he should, is there?"

"Well, yes, there is. You see, Vanessa has a friend named Una Marbury. . . ."

"When you say friend," she whispered, "do you mean they go to bed together?"

"Yes. She's spending more and more of her time at Una's house on Patchin Place. Now she tells me she wants to bring Una out to the senator's house so Una can meet Frank and her father. I think she's crazy to do it. If my father-in-law guesses what's going on . . . well, I don't know what he'll do, but I think there'll be a lot of trouble. And Frank's bound to find out about it sooner or later."

"Have you met this Una?"

"No, and I don't want to. I mean, if my wife ran off with another man, I could deal with it. But she's run off with a goddam woman! It's driving me crazy."

"Do you love her that much?"

"I don't love her at all. I married her for her money. She knows that—I suppose everyone does, by now. I was in love with you. . . ."

"Marco, be careful!"

"But it's the truth. I *was* in love with you—I was *crazy* about you. But I saw all that money just sitting there, waiting to be grabbed. . . . Well, it's ancient history now. The point is, you were hurt. But if it's any satisfaction to you, my private life is miserable."

"Hey, signor, here's the vino!"

Tony brought up an ice bucket containing a bottle of white wine, which he deftly uncorked.

"I pour a glass for the lovely signora, eh?" He smiled. Then his smile froze as he saw the tears running down her cheeks. Shutting up, he quickly filled the glasses, stuck the bottle back in the bucket, whispered nervously to Marco, "You let-a me know when you want-a the menus, okay?" and hurried away.

Marco reached across the table and took Georgie's hands.

"Why are you crying?" he asked softly.

"Because you caused so much unhappiness," she said. "You

have no idea how miserable you made me, but it's no consolation to know *you're* miserable, too. Misery doesn't love company. Misery just wants to have a few laughs."

He squeezed her hands.

"Is it too late for *us* to have a few laughs?" he asked.

"I don't know. Where's my napkin?"

He released her and handed her the red napkin. She dried her eyes and rubbed her nose.

"Have you seen any of the Little Tramp comedies?" he asked.

"I don't go to the movies. I haven't since . . ."

She stopped. He took her hands again.

"I tell an awfully good movie." He smiled.

Vanessa was doubly nervous.

She had finally invited Una out to Garden Court for lunch with Phipps and Maud, and she was nervous about her father's reaction to her new friend—and "friend" was how she had described Una to her father. Would Phipps perceive her as a friend, or as what she really was? Una was certainly not as obvious as Carol de Witt or some of the other lesbians at Carol's party. On the other hand, Una was hardly an everyday young woman. She was conservatively dressed today—at least by Una's standards—but she still wore her African ivory bracelets that were a bit bizarre, and her "my dears" and other affectations were a bit *de trop* for the horsey North Shore. What if her father guessed?

Vanessa was also nervous about Una's reaction to her sculpture. She had taken her first to her studio in the playhouse, and Una was circling Vanessa's latest work, her first attempt at something modern: a large clay abstraction that was a horizontal S with two "arms" sticking out of the upper curve.

"It's evocative, my dear," Una finally said. "Very evocative. It reminds me of a corpse."

"A corpse? Why?"

"The curve . . . It could be a body sprawled on the floor, with its arms outstretched . . . perhaps a murdered body. Do you have a name for it?"

"No."

"Call it 'Mayerling.' Yes, Mayerling! The ultimate mystery! I like it, my dear. Cast it in steel and I could sell it for you. This could be the beginning of an important career."

Vanessa was pleased, but confused.

"But why 'Mayerling'?" she asked.

"This is either the body of Crown Prince Rudolf or his lover, Marie Vetsera. He has just killed her, then blown his own brains out. No one knows exactly why. . . . It's mystery and romance. The ultimate act of love: death! People love Mayerling. It will help sell it, believe me."

Vanessa still didn't quite understand, but she decided to bow to Una's superior knowledge of how to sell modern art. Una came around the pedestal the sculpture was on and took Vanessa's hand.

"And now, my dear, it's time I met your family. Don't be nervous. I'll behave. I'll break the ice by quoting a few paragraphs from Marx and Engels, then amuse your father by discussing Freud's interpretation of masturbatory fantasies in adolescent dreams."

"Oh, my God . . ."

"You've lost your sense of humor."

"I don't have one when it concerns Father. Please be careful, Una."

"And what if he knew?" She smiled. "So what? You must learn to be brave, my dear, as I learned. You must learn to accept yourself. We are not evil."

She whispered the last. Then she kissed Vanessa on the mouth. The kiss made Vanessa tingle, but it was the tingle of apprehension.

"Now, come on, my dear," said Una, heading for the door. "Into the fight! And why aren't I meeting Marco, the mighty immigrant?"

"He's only out here on weekends during the campaign."

"A pity. I'd like to meet him. He may turn out to be my congressman, you know." She opened the door and went out into the mammoth tiled pool room. "And who's this darling young man?"

Vanessa saw Frank dive into the opposite end of the pool. With him was his new tutor, a thirty-one-year-old Harvard graduate named Barclay Simmons.

"That's Frank."

For the first time, Vanessa saw Una's cool public facade melt a little.

"I envy you," she said softly. "You have a son. That's something I'll never have." She watched him swim a moment. Then her usual artifice returned. "Come, my dear, introduce me. And don't pity me. I'd make a rotten mother. My children would probably bite me as I breast-fed them—or they'd get drunk. My mother's milk is probably pure gin."

She started down the side of the pool, Vanessa behind her. When they reached the opposite end Vanessa said, "Barclay, this is my friend Una Marbury. Una, this is Frank's new tutor, Barclay Simmons."

"How do you do?"

"And this is Frank. Frank, stop splashing. I want you to meet my friend Una Marbury."

Frank grabbed the edge of the pool and looked up.

"Hello," he said.

"Hello," said Una. "You're a very handsome young man. And you swim well, too."

"Barclay's teaching me the backstroke. He was captain of the Harvard swimming team."

"Good for Barclay. And good for you."

"I'm going to grow up to be Tarzan!" he yelled, diving back into the water and starting to backstroke down the pool.

"He's adorable," said Una then, rather tersely. "Well . . . shall we have lunch?"

"What do you think?" said Phipps two hours later as he and Maud were having coffee in the library of Garden Court. Vanessa had taken Una on a tour of the gardens.

"Of Miss Marbury? She seems all right. Rather arty-tarty, but if she can sell Vanessa's sculptures as she says she can, then more power to her. She certainly couldn't sell one to *me*."

"I don't like her."

His sharp tone surprised Maud.

"Why?"

"She's a bad influence on Van."

"Really, darling, you must realize Vanessa takes her art seriously, and she's bound to meet bohemian types. I know that's not your cup of tea, but . . . "

Phipps was shaking his head.

"You don't understand. There's no reason you should, either, because even Van doesn't know this. But there's a skeleton in the Ogden family closet, and this Una—who's suddenly appeared out of the blue—is rattling that skeleton."

"How delicious! I adore family skeletons. Who is it?"

"*Was.* My Aunt Alicia. She was my mother's younger sister, and she painted. She was rather good, actually.... I suppose that's where Van gets her talent. At any rate, when she was in her twenties, Aunt Alicia took off for Paris to study art. And three months later she disappeared."

"To where?"

"My grandfather got a letter from her the following Christmas. She was living in Siena with a friend, as she put it. She lived with the friend for ten years, then she died of diphtheria. This happened thirty years ago when I was still a young man, but I've never forgotten how the family shut up about Aunt Alicia; it was as if all of a sudden she didn't exist anymore. I found out years later from my father that Aunt Alicia had been very quietly written out of the will."

Maud was looking past him out one of the windows where, in the distance, Vanessa and Una were walking together toward the Sound. Suddenly, she was seeing her stepdaughter in a new light.

"I take it," she said, "Aunt Alicia's friend was a woman?"

"Exactly. Now, I don't know if Van has inherited Aunt Alicia's tendencies along with her talent, and I don't want to find out. But I'm going to get Miss Marbury out of Van's life. I don't want another Aunt Alicia in my family."

"But, darling, how will you do it?"

"There are ways," he said, quietly.

It was the height of the Chaplin craze.

The English-born comedian, who was currently earning ten thousand dollars a week, had conquered the world with his Little Tramp character, whose wiggling walk Chaplin based on his recollection from childhood of the shuffle of an old drunk who used to hold horses outside a London tavern. The European war was sending nervous audiences to comedies to seek release from their anxieties in laughter; the monumental success of Griffith's *Birth of a Nation* the year before had finally made movies respectable to

354

the huge middle-class audience; and the resultant enormous popularity of moviegoing had caused theater owners to begin building the mammoth picture palaces that would reach their peak a decade later.

"This place is gorgeous!" said Marco, as he led Georgie down the aisle of the newly renovated Rialto movie house on Times Square. "They've made it look like Venice: All around the walls is the skyline of Venice, with gondola poles . . . and the ceiling is like the night sky, filled with stars. . . ."

"It's big, isn't it?" said Georgie, once again breathless with excitement as the smell of popcorn, like Proust's madeleine, conjured up remembrance of things past.

"Huge. It seats twenty-two hundred people, and it's packed. Oh, good, here comes the organist. . . ."

They found two seats on the aisle just as the organist began playing the rousing song hit, "America, I Love You!" As ten thousand organ pipes tweeted, boomed and blared, Georgie settled back in her red velvet seat, started munching her popcorn, and began experiencing her first real happiness in over five years.

"The name of the movie is *The Bank*," whispered Marco after the organ's peal died away and the titles appeared on the big screen. "It's with Charlie Chaplin and Edna Purviance. Charlie looks like a little tramp. He wears baggy pants, big dirty shoes, a bowler hat, and he has a funny little black moustache and carries a sort of rickety cane. Okay, the movie's starting. We're outside a bank. Charlie is walking down the sidewalk. Coming the other way is a mother with her little boy who's eating an ice-cream cone. Oh oh . . . the kid spills his ice cream on the sidewalk right in front of Charlie . . . Charlie slips on it and falls on his bottom . . . the kid is bawling, blaming losing his ice cream on Charlie . . . the kid's mother is furious, and now she's beating Charlie over the head with her umbrella. . . ."

At which point, he was drowned out by the laughter of the audience.

Georgie began laughing too.

The Italians gave the world, among other things, the Roman Empire, the Roman Church, the Renaissance, Michelangelo, Leonardo, Titian, opera, pasta, forks, Venice and the Mafia. They almost gave the world Sandro Albertini, but he was born, in 1880, a month after his parents arrived in New York from Brindisi, so that he was a native-born American. His father was a street peddler, and Sandro grew up in appalling poverty. At the age of ten he began stealing. When he was eighteen he was convicted of burglary and served four years in Sing Sing, where he got smart. Realizing loan sharking was safer than burglary, upon his release he set himself up in the loan business, operating initially out of a café on Houston Street which later, after his business flourished, he bought. Sandro was a cunning, cold and utterly ruthless man. By the time he was thirty he had branched out into whorehouses, gambling, the protection racket, quasi-legitimate real estate operations, and pornography. He bought a warehouse in Queens and converted the second floor into a movie studio of sorts where he would film crude "smokers," using the girls from his bordellos. Since his own sexuality had a strong sadistic streak, these films usually contained at least one whipping scene, and one whore was so badly mauled in a film that only a death threat stopped her from going to the police.

Sandro had a wife and two daughters, whom he kept in New Jersey; all they knew was that Daddy was in "the loan business." Sandro spent the weekends in New Jersey, but during the week he operated out of a small apartment on King Street, and it was in the King Street apartment that he met with his ex-prizefighter goon, Paolo.

"Santorelli's attacking me," said Sandro as he sipped a glass of milk. Despite his kinky sex life, Sandro was something of a puritan and neither smoked nor drank. "And he's whipping the shit out of Bill Ryan in his speeches. He's going to win this goddam election."

"So what do we do?" asked Paolo, passing a silver dollar over his fat fingers. Paolo's hobby was magic.

"Kill him," said Sandro, finishing his milk.

Marco was pushing the crude wooden plow while the bony horse pulled it. The blazing Calabrian sun beat down on him and his two younger brothers, Nino and Claudio, who were following him, planting sugar beets in the furrow Marco's plow dug up. It was April, and the snows in the distant Sila Piccola mountains

356

were melting, bringing down moisture and silt to the arid, treeless coast. The tiny, three-hectare plot of land Marco's father rented was being planted with the region's biggest cash crop. It was hard work, hot work, endless work, work Marco's family had done for generations.

Too many generations, Marco was thinking, when suddenly the sun became even hotter, so hot he stopped plowing, wondering if the sun were exploding. It became so hot that the field began to fill with smoke. "Run!" he yelled to his brothers, and he started to run. But his legs were strangely heavy, so heavy he could barely move. As he strained to escape in slow motion, his lungs filled with the acrid smoke. Run . . . escape . . . run . . .

He woke up to find his bedroom on the third floor filling with smoke. It took him a moment to shake out of his dream into reality, but then he threw off his sheet, got out of bed and ran to the bedroom door, beneath which fingers of smoke were curling. He opened the door and saw that the stairway was clogged with thick black smoke. He realized the house on Jones Street was turning into an inferno, and he panicked.

He slammed the door and ran to the window, throwing it open. The third-floor bedroom was at the back of the house. As he leaned out to look down, he could see the light of the flames on the first floor throwing their eerie illumination through the closed windows into the tiny, paved backyard. Opposite, on the other side of a concrete wall, was the rear of a similar town house facing Cornelia Street. The house was dark. On either side of his house were two other houses of the same vintage which were also dark. Greenwich Village was asleep, and most likely no one had yet turned in a fire alarm.

He was trapped on the third floor of a burning house with no fire escape.

In his panic, he realized this fire was too well timed not to be arson, but that knowledge wouldn't help him escape. He started yelling "Fire!" out the window. He looked at the ancient ailanthus tree growing in the back yard, its roots defying the cement paving. One of its branches came within four feet of the window and looked strong enough to hold him, if he didn't miss it when he jumped. As a last resort, he'd try it.

"Fire! Goddammit, somebody WAKE UP!"

Finally, he saw a light go on in the Cornelia Street house. He kept yelling but by now the bedroom was choking with smoke. He turned. The paint on the door was bubbling with heat; the flames must be shooting up the stairwell.

He heard a voice yell, "We turned in the alarm," and he looked out the window to see a man in a nightshirt standing in the backyard of the Cornelia Street house. Other lights were coming on as the neighborhood woke up. In the distance he heard a fire-bell clanging.

He grabbed a wooden chair and smashed out the entire window. He climbed on the windowsill, eyes fixed on the bough of the ailanthus tree, tensing his body.

"Don't jump!" yelled the neighbor. "The firemen are coming!"

Just then a resounding crash shook the entire house. The second floor had caved in. Now the bedroom door was in flames. Marco, standing barefoot in his nightshirt on the windowsill, looked behind him at a furnace.

Where are the goddam firemen? his mind screamed.

He looked again at the tree branch. Most of its leaves had fallen, creating a yellow rug at the base of the tree. But the leaves wouldn't save him if he missed. *Three stories! Jesus . . .*

Now he could hear the shouts of the firemen from the front of the house.

"Tell them I'm back here!" he yelled at the neighbor.

The flaming door had set the room on fire, and sparks were flying at him. He felt something hot burn the back of his left thigh and looked down to see his nightshirt on fire. He beat out the flame, nearly losing his balance.

"We're bringing a life net!" yelled a fireman below him.

"A *what?*"

"Something you can jump into!"

"Well, hurry up, for Chrissake!"

The heat was blasting him now, and there was so much smoke that even at the window he began choking. Something hot nipped the back of his neck; then another spark bit his leg. Coughing, gasping for fresh air, he decided he couldn't wait for the life net.

He jumped.

Chapter 43

The fire and Marco's escape down the ailanthus tree made big headlines, and Marco, whose campaign had already turned him into something of a folk hero in the Italian community, was now a celebrity all over the city. As the reporters mobbed him, he announced that the fire had been arson and a deliberate attempt to get him out of the way before the election. Though he was too careful to name names, the reporters hinted broadly in their coverage of the fire that the villain was the Irish machine backing Ryan; and the New York reading public, always avid for news of political skullduggery, licked its collective chops over this latest, blatant example of the crude way the city's politicos operated. "Mr. Santorelli has had the courage to attack corruption in Greenwich Village," pontificated the *Times.* "If political candidates risk their very lives by speaking out, then the democratic process in our city is in mortal danger." Father Domenici of Saint Anthony's Church was so outraged he sat down to write a blistering sermon attacking the Irish machine and praising Marco.

Casey O'Donnell read the papers with dismay, because he knew that the fire and the resultant publicity were ruinous to Ryan's prospects. But when his niece Georgie heard the news at the breakfast table in Carl and Bridget's Grove Street house, she exclaimed, "Thank God he wasn't hurt!"

It was so heartfelt that her sister and brother-in-law exchanged looks.

"Georgie," said Carl, "are you falling in love with that man *again?*"

Georgie turned red.

"Well, I . . ."

"Are you suicidal?" continued Carl. "He hurt you once. Are you going to let him do it again?"

359

"Carl, don't pick on her," said Bridget.

"Well, *someone* has to make her face facts. Here she is, running off to the movies with him again . . . Georgie, there's no future for you with him. He's married—"

"And he's miserable," interjected Georgie.

"What difference does that make? If he wants to be in politics, he certainly can't get a divorce. And even if he did, you couldn't marry a divorced man in the Catholic Church. There's absolutely nothing for you with Santorelli unless you want to become his mistress, which I *assume* you're not thinking about. You're just setting yourself up for another big fall, and I think you're *crazy* to do it! Dammit, I wish the man had never sneaked back into your life."

There was an embarrassed silence. Bridget got up and came around the table to hug her sister.

"He's right, darlin'," she said, tenderly. "You have to be careful for your *own* sake."

Georgie said nothing. Taking her sister's hand, she stood up.

"I'll clear the table," she said.

She started feeling for the breakfast plates. When she had stacked two of them, she suddenly burst out, "But he makes me *happy*! I can't help it if there's no future for me with him—there's not much of a future for me *without* him. I'll take a little happiness right *now*."

She carried the dishes into the kitchen. Bridget looked at her husband, who shook his head helplessly.

"She's asking for it," he whispered.

By the fall of 1916, that mysteriously powerful force called fashion had made the Nepenthe Club at Fifty-second Street and Broadway the hottest cabaret in town. Its owner, the fast-talking Phil Brinkman, was always looking for the newest sensation, and when he heard about Roscoe Haines's jazz band with its sultry singing star, Flora Mitchum, he auditioned them and hired them for a six-week engagement at the whopping sum of three thousand dollars a week. Word quickly spread, and on their opening night Jake had to use his pull with Roscoe to get in the packed restaurant. He sent flowers to Flora and a case of Scotch to Roscoe, put on his tails, dropped Nellie at the New Amsterdam, then went on to the Nepenthe Club, where he went as wild as the rest of the celebrity crowd when Flora, wearing the same black-sequined, black-feather dress she had worn at Carol de Witt's bohemian bash, leaned against Roscoe's piano and sang "Where's My Man?"

Afterward he went back to their dressing room, where he hugged and kissed Flora, pumped Roscoe's hand and said, "Fabulous! It was fabulous, and Ziggy's got to see you! He'll put you in the next *Follies,* and I've got an idea for a song for you, Flora. . . ."

"Wait! Hold on," said Roscoe. "Forget the Follies."

Jake gaped. "Forget the *Follies?* Are you crazy?"

"Tell him, honey," Roscoe said to Flora. "I got to go change. Then afterward, the three of us is goin' out to get gassed." He looked at Flora. "Is it okay if I get gassed tonight, Massa?"

"Listen to that man," she exclaimed, a look of mock disgust on her face. "He *pretends* that I run this act."

"Well, you do."

"Says *you.* Yes, you can get gassed tonight, but *only* tonight!"

Roscoe rolled his eyes as he went to the bathroom door.

"Somebody tol' me dey freed dee slaves," he said in an Uncle Tom accent, "but Ah tinks it ain't dee troof."

Winking, he went into the bathroom and closed the door.

"Now, what's the big surprise?" asked Jake.

"Well, the first big surprise is that Roscoe's stopped running. I had a helluva time with him in Paris, Jake. You know that man had a big grudge against this country."

"Oh, I know. When I first met him in Hamburg, he was saying America wasn't his home."

"Well, it's our home now. For better or for worse, and I think it's going to be for the better. We want to open our own nightclub, Jake. Up in Harlem. We've picked out a house on One-hundred-and-sixth Street, and we're gonna try and buy it. When Roscoe told me you were coming tonight, we had a fight because he didn't want to ask you to invest in the club. But I told him you owe us something, because I put over your first song hit, and I ain't shy, Jake. I'm asking you to invest. But I want to show you the place first—I think you'll *want* to invest when you see what we're talking about."

"Flora, I'd write you a check if you wanted to star in a musical about the Ku Klux Klan."

And they both laughed.

The next morning at eleven, Jake and Flora got out of a taxi on a crowded block in Harlem. Roscoe, having indeed gotten royally gassed the night before, was incapacitated by a hangover.

"You know what's going on up here," Flora said. "Harlem's going colored, block by block. As soon as one house goes colored in a white block, those For Sale signs go up so fast it makes your head spin. The whites are howling, but they're packing at the same time. Well, as you can see, this block's already colored. But this one house was owned by an old white lady named Mrs. Van Deventer, and she was too sick to move. She died last month, and the house is up for sale, cheap."

"How cheap?" asked Jake, eying the four-story brownstone.

"Ten thousand. I figure I could put the kitchen in the base-ment, use the first and second floor for the club, Roscoe and me could live on the third floor and maybe we'd rent out the fourth. Maybe not. Anyway, I think I could convert the whole place for another twenty thousand. Roscoe and I have saved a little under ten thousand and we can get a ten-thousand-dollar mortgage, so what we'd want from you would be the third ten thousand."

They were joined by the estate agent, who let them in and gave them a tour. The house, which had been built in 1890 and wired for electricity seven years later, was dusty and needed painting badly, but Jake could see it was solidly built.

The agent left them alone on the first floor to check some-thing in the basement.

"I'll loan you fifteen thousand," said Jake. "That'll give you an extra five thousand as a cushion. You can pay it back at three percent interest in ten years."

"I ain't got no collateral," she said.

"You already gave me that when you sang 'Raggedy Ragtime Man.' "

"How much of the club do you want?"

"None. It's yours and Roscoe's. Just guarantee me a table opening night. By the way ..." he hesitated. "I do have a ques-tion."

"Oh oh. What's that?"

"Is the club going to be colored or white?"

"I *knew* you'd ask that. I'd like to do something for my people, but this is business and right now my people is Roscoe and me. It's gonna be a white club. No colored customers allowed. The whites got the money, and they won't come if we let in coloreds. That's the way it's got to be."

"But how's Roscoe taking this? After all he's gone through trying to learn to live with his own color . . ."

"I know. We had another big fight about it. But I told him we can't change this country overnight. It's got to be *baby* steps, and if we can open a successful white club in Harlem, at least we'll be gettin' the white folks uptown and at least white folks and colored are gonna be *seein'* each other and maybe that'll do some good. And Roscoe said, 'Honey, I guess you're right. Baby steps is about the best we can do now, but that's better than sittin' on our asses.' "

Jake smiled. "In that case, I'll be proud to invest in a baby step."

Flora bit her lip. "I think I'm gonna cry," she said. She quickly pulled a handkerchief from her purse and in fact started crying. "I'm crying because I'm *happy,* you know," she sniffed.

"I am too," he sniffed, and she looked and saw that there were tears running down his cheeks, too. "I'm happy for you and Roscoe, and I'm happy I can write a check for fifteen thousand dollars. It wasn't so long ago I thought that was all the money in the goddam world."

"Is it nice being rich?" she asked, blowing her nose.

"It's wonderful. Try it—you'll see."

"God damn, maybe I will!"

He started laughing. Then he took her hands and they danced a little jig around the empty room, hooting and hollering and cackling with glee.

Chapter 44

Violet Weiler was rehearsing the *"Danse des petits cygnes"* from *Swan Lake* with four of her co-cygnets at Mme. Levitska's studio when she saw Jake come into the room. It was a cool October morning, and he was wearing an astrakhan-collared overcoat and held his bowler in his hand. Mme. Levitska, at the piano, kept on playing, but she was burning with curiosity about why he had appeared so unexpectedly. She saw the way he couldn't take his eyes off Violet and muttered to herself, *"Bozhe moi,* love!"

When she finished the number, she stood up from the piano, saying, "All right, girls, ten minutes." Then she lit a cigarette, watching Violet as she hurried across the room to Jake, her tutu fluttering daintily as she moved.

"Jake!" she said as he took her hand. "I didn't know whether to call . . ."

"I know. I'm all right now. But I've been doing a lot of thinking since Laura's funeral. I've decided I don't want to have another child with Nellie. I want to have one with you."

She stared at him, beginning to panic.

"I haven't had a chance to tell you," she said, "but I'm going to ask Father to give me enough money to rent an apartment. But I was going to rent it for *myself,* and I really couldn't lie to Father. . . . I mean, it wouldn't be fair. . . ."

"What are you talking about?" he interrupted, a look of total confusion on his face.

"Well, I want to be on my own, and . . ." She gulped and took the plunge. "Jake, I'm not sure I want to be your mistress after all. And I *certainly* don't want to be an unwed mother."

He started laughing.

"What's so funny?"

"I'm asking you to be my *wife.*"

She gaped. "Oh."

"Well? Do you accept, or do I have to get down on my knees? Mme. Levitska would love to see *that*."

"But what about Nellie?"

"It's all over with Nellie. It has been for a long time, but I guess I couldn't bring myself to admit that my marriage was a failure. I love you, Violet. I love you with all my heart—you're the most beautiful love song I've ever heard. I swear to you, *our* marriage will be a success. Will you marry me?"

Her beautiful face became radiant.

"Oh . . . *yes*."

She practically leaped into his arms. As they kissed, the four other cygnets began giggling.

"Sshh," hissed Mme. Levitska. "This is what ballet is all about: romance!"

The girls, abashed, quieted down, entranced by the long embrace at the end of the room.

"But what about Mother?" Violet suddenly asked.

"Don't worry about her. *I'll* take care of her. I'll *buy* my way into her affections.

Violet looked pensive.

"Yes, that probably will work," she said.

"Meanwhile, this is our secret," he continued. "I haven't told Nellie yet, but it's only a matter of days. By the way—do you love me?"

"Are you kidding? I'm *crazy* about you!"

She kissed him again.

"Violet, dollink!" rasped Mme. Levitska. "Back to *Swan Lake, pliss!* This is a ballet class, not a tea dance."

"Coming," Violet called. And she went back to the center of the room, beaming.

The Diamond Horseshoe of the Metropolitan Opera sparkled with jewels as it did every Monday night—Monday being "the" night at the Met—but no woman was more bejeweled than Mrs. Weiler as she opened her program for *Don Giovanni* and savored the supreme social triumph of her life: Tonight was the first night she sat in her own box, Number 12. Finally, in recognition of the millions Simon Weiler had given to the Opera, a Jew had been allowed to buy a box. It had cost Simon another fifty thousand, but for his wife it was worth every penny. She positively radiated triumph as she looked around the crowded house through her jeweled opera glasses. And she dripped diamonds, from her huge tiara down to the enormous stomacher attached to her black velvet dress. Every time she breathed, she twinkled like one of the big, new advertising signs on Times Square.

Eight minutes before the first act, a man in white tie and tails stepped into the box.

"Good evening, Mrs. Weiler," said Jake Rubin.

Mrs. Weiler turned, and her face became red with hostility. Was her triumph to be ruined by this Russian?

Simon Weiler stood up. "How are you, Mr. Rubin?" he said, shaking Jake's hand.

"I'm fine, sir. Mrs. Weiler, some time ago, I sent a check to the charity you head, the Amalgamated Hebrew Fund. It was a rather large check. I was a bit surprised when I received a form letter thanking me for the donation."

"I instructed the staff to send the form letter," said Mrs. Weiler glacially. "We receive many donations, Mr. Rubin. We cannot be expected to answer each one with a personal note."

"Still and all, I think a donation of twenty-five thousand dollars might have gotten some kind of personal recognition, particularly since you know me?"

Simon looked surprised.

"Twenty-five thousand? And you didn't thank him, Rebecca?"

She glared at her husband.

"I sent the *form letter*," she reiterated thunderously. Then she turned back to Jake. "Mr. Rubin, your generosity—if generosity was indeed what prompted your donation—is appreciated. However, I will remind you that organized charity is often used as a path toward social acceptance by those who have gained newly acquired wealth, or a certain amount of prominence. This charity social-climbing, to put it crudely, I thoroughly disapprove of. If your motives were—as I believe—to try and buy my approbation, then you wasted your money. Now, sir, I will ask you to leave this box. It is neither my desire nor my custom to be seen in public with Broadway 'personalities,' as I believe people like yourself are called."

Simon was burning.

"Rebecca," he growled, "shut up."

She looked apoplectic.

"Simon!"

"If you disapprove of charity social-climbing, why have you forced me to spend millions so you could get in the Diamond Horseshoe? And *this* isn't even a charity! It's a sideshow for the rich."

"Simon, I insist you retract that."

"And *I* insist you apologize to Mr. Rubin."

"I will not!"

Jake pulled an envelope from his jacket.

"At any rate," he said, "I've talked to a number of other Broadway 'personalities,' and I managed to raise another ten thousand from them for your charity. Here's the check. And don't bother to send the form letter. Good night. And enjoy the opera. Oh—and, by the way, Mozart was something of a social climber, but he never got anywhere because people in his day thought of composers as dirt. I'm not trying to compare myself with Mozart, but I'd like to think that in a hundred and fifty years, things had improved a *little* for us poor tunesmiths."

He handed the envelope to Mrs. Weiler, giving her a meaningful look, then left the box.

"Oh!" she snorted, sticking the envelope in her purse. Her husband sat down.

"Rebecca," he said quietly "for the first time in my life, I'm ashamed of you."

She sniffed angrily.

"You're going to write him a note the first thing tomorrow morning, and you're going to *apologize*. Understand? *And* you're going to invite him to our reception tomorrow night."

"Never!"

"Rebecca, need I remind you who *your* grandfather was?"

Just then the houselights lowered for the overture, and Mrs. Weiler thanked her lucky stars for the timing, because her face was turning red from embarrassment.

"Your grandfather would be *ashamed* of you," whispered her husband.

Rebecca Weiler squirmed a little. *Grandfather*, she thought. *Simon's right, I suppose. And at least Jake Rubin has a good tailor. He looked rather dashing this evening....*

"I'll write him," she whispered as Mozart's first ominous minor chord thundered from the orchestra pit.

The next morning Mrs. Weiler's Rolls-Royce pulled up in front of Jake's town house, and the chauffeur got out to deliver two letters to Fanny, who in turn delivered one to Jake in his workroom and the other to Nellie, who was still in bed. Jake tore open the envelope and pulled out the letter. Written in Mrs. Weiler's stiff, up-and-down hand, so curiously reminiscent of her personality, it said:

My dear Mr. Rubin:
I must apologize for my behavior last evening. Your kind generosity to the Amalgamated Hebrew Fund is certainly appreciated, and the remarks I addressed to you in our opera box were—as my husband so rightly pointed out to me—uncalled for on my part. It is not my role to question the motives of our donors; indeed, I suppose there is a certain amount of the "social climber" in all of us. But perhaps that is what makes life interesting.
I hope it will be possible for you and Mrs. Rubin to join Mr. Weiler and myself this evening for a *soirée musicale* we are giving for the benefit of the Belgian Relief Committee. Mme. Schumann-Heink will sing several Schubert *lieder* (we cannot blame poor Schubert for what his horrid countrymen are doing today!) and Maestro Rachmaninoff will play the Liszt "Dante" sonata and one of his own bravura compositions. It promises to be a culturally stimulating evening, and any contribution you may feel moved to make will of course be going to a *most* worthy cause. I apologize for the short notice, but you were, to be frank, not on my list. Evening attire, of course, and a buffet will be served at ten. The programme will begin at eight.
Again, dear Mr. Rubin, my thanks for your strong support of our Fund, and my apologies for my rudeness. We live, alas, in an age of surfaces. It has perhaps been my misfortune not to have perceived earlier your warm and generous personality.

Sincerely,
Rebecca Weiler

368

P.S. I have written an invitation to your charming wife. Hope to see you tonight! R.W.

Smiling slightly, Jake folded the note, then went upstairs to his wife's bedroom.

"Can you believe it?" said Nellie, who was sitting up in bed holding Mrs. Weiler's note. "We're invited to the Weilers tonight! Has the old cow gone crazy?"

"Maybe," said Jake. "Do you want to go?"

"I wouldn't miss it for the world! I'll call Ziggy and tell him I have a cold. . . . He'll be furious, but it'll give that bitch, my understudy, some experience. . . . I wonder what made Mrs. Weiler change? When she was here a couple of weeks ago, you were the Frankenstein monster. Doesn't she know you're laying her daughter?"

Not laying her yet, Nellie. But soon . . . soon . . .

"You know something, Nellie?" he said, going to the door. "You're a bitch."

He walked out, leaving her with a look of surprise on her face.

The war that in 1914 most people had thought would be "over by Christmas" had turned into a savage stalemate of appalling carnage. The casualty lists for the Germans and French in one battle alone—Verdun—amounted to 700,000, and that was a conservative estimate. Despite the length and carnage of the American Civil War, most people prior to 1914 had thought of war as a sort of romantic jousting between professional armies commanded by an aristocratic officer corps, which would leave the civilian population more or less unaffected. And weren't most of the ruling houses of Europe related? Despite the boorish bellicosity of the Kaiser, he was the King of England's cousin, and cousins simply didn't go to war, did they?

But two years of slaughter had shattered those naïve illusions, and the shock waves from Europe were affecting America as well. Thus, Mrs. Weiler, who thought of herself as a German and who earlier had found preposterous the idea of Germany being the enemy, had been forced to swallow her cultural pride and admit that the behavior of the Hun was barbaric. And though the great opera singer, Mme. Ernestine Schumann-Heink, had been born in Austria (which was, of course, Germany's ally), she too had been appalled by what was happening in Europe and was only too happy to accept Mrs. Weiler's invitation to sing for the Belgian Relief Committee.

Mrs. Weiler's hallowed list (the one Jake and Nellie had not been on) included all the great "our crowd" families. But an indication of how the Great War was subtly changing social mores in New York was the fact that for the Belgian Relief Committee, Mrs. Weiler had included many of the Goyim Grandees as well, borrowing the list of Mrs. Oliver Belmont, the mother of the Duchess of Marlborough and the former Mrs. William Kissem Vanderbilt. So on that evening, the crowd of over one hundred of the city's moneyed elite that squeezed into the Weilers' ballroom to sit on gilt chairs and listen to the heavyset Mme. Schumann-Heink included Astors and Vanderbilts as well as Loebs and Lehmans, two worlds that only a few years before had kept at respectful arm's length.

Nellie had put on one of her most beautiful evening gowns, as well as her flashiest jewelry, and she looked so stunning in her taupe satin that Violet, who was sitting not far away from her, could hardly take her eyes off her. *She's so beautiful*, she thought morosely; *what does Jake see in me?*

But Nellie knew what Jake saw. As she looked at Violet, she thought: *Just what I expected. Little Miss Innocent. Jake's a sucker for innocence. But I'll admit she's pretty. Not a knockout like me, but pretty.*

Mme. Schumann-Heink's rendering of the Schubert *lieder* was meltingly beautiful, and she received an ovation. Then Rachmaninoff sat down at the Steinway and thundered his way through the magnificent "Dante" sonata, followed by his own brilliant transcription of the scherzo from Mendelssohn's "Midsummer Night's Dream." He played so dazzlingly that even Nellie, who was usually bored by "classical" music, was impressed. After he whizzed through the Black Key Etude as an encore, the crowd rose to move to the dining room for the buffet. War might have been raging three thousand miles to the east, but it had never even occurred to Mrs. Weiler to stint on the food, and the buffet was a staggering display of the art of her French chef, Emile. The Weilers were faithful members of the congregation of Temple Emmanuel, but it was typical of their somewhat casual Jewishness that they ignored the dietary laws, and one of the prominent items on the buffet was a huge sliced ham.

"*Trayf,*" Jake whispered to Nellie as they stood in line, plates in hand.

"What?"

"The ham. Jews aren't supposed to eat it."

"Well, *you* eat it. And you love pork chops."

"Not anymore."

She looked surprised. She knew that Jake had started attending temple, but she hadn't been aware he had started observing the dietary laws. But in fact, he passed up the ham.

"I hope you don't expect *me* to start eating kosher?" she said, defiantly piling her plate with ham.

"Did I say I did?"

"No, but I won't do it. I hate Jewish cooking. All that chicken fat . . . ugh."

Keep on digging your own grave, Nellie, he thought.

"Speaking of ham," he said aloud, "you're making a pig of yourself."

"Oh, shut up."

Mrs. Weiler greeted them as they took their plates back to the ballroom, and even Jake was surprised at how cordial she suddenly seemed.

"Dear Mrs. Rubin." She smiled, her four-strand necklace of luscious pink Burmese pearls riveting Nellie's eyes. "I'm so delighted you could come. And your charming husband! Did you enjoy the music?"

"Oh, yes," said Nellie. "Rachmaninoff is a fantastic pianist."

"But so is your husband. Mr. Rubin, when I told Maestro Rachmaninoff that you were here, he expressed a great desire to meet you and hear you play some of your own compositions. Might I impose on you?"

Jake—remembering that only the night before, she had kicked him out of her opera box, saying she didn't want to be seen publicly with Broadway "personalities"—savored his revenge cocktail.

"I'd be honored to meet the maestro." He smiled.

What a nice smile, thought Mrs. Weiler.

"Then I'll tear you away from your lovely wife. You will excuse us, dear Mrs. Rubin?"

She took Jake's arm and led him through the crowd.

"It looks as if the old battle-axe is taking your husband up," said the tall young man behind Nellie.

She turned around to see a blond Apollo in tails drinking a glass of Simon Weiler's best Burgundy.

"I beg your pardon?"

"Mrs. Weiler. She's taking your husband up. That means she wants to promote him socially. She'll turn him into a salon star. My name's Peter van Rhynn, and I'm a big fan of yours. I saw the *Follies* four times this year."

"Then you must have enjoyed it."

"I enjoyed watching *you*—especially when you came down the stairs in your Cleopatra costume. You've got the best legs in New York."

His cold blue eyes undressed her.

"Van Rhynn—I suppose that's *the* Van Rhynns?"

"That's us. Stuffy, rich..." He smiled. "...And very wicked."

"I hear you're inbred and boring."

"Want to find out?" he said.

Just then Mrs. Weiler, standing by the Steinway, called for attention.

"Ladies and gentlemen ... may I have your attention, please? We have with us tonight a very talented young man, whom I'm sure you've all heard of ... the composer of so many of our popular songs ... Mr. Jake Rubin. Maestro Rachmaninoff has asked Mr. Rubin to play us a medley of his compositions, and Mr. Rubin has graciously accepted."

Jake got a big hand as he sat down at the keyboard. Rachmaninoff ... Fifth Avenue ... It was a long way from Russia.

As Jake played "Raggedy Ragtime Man," Peter van Rhynn whispered in Nellie's ear, "How about lunch one day?"

She looked at him coolly.

"Please. My husband's playing."

She turned back to watch Jake.

"Keen's Chop House. Tomorrow at one."

She pretended to ignore him, but she was not unaware of his cocksure maleness.

"*I'll* be there," he went on. "Tomorrow at one."

She looked at him again.

"I suppose," she said, "that just because you're a Van Rhynn and reasonably good-looking, you think that every woman in New York will throw herself at your feet?"

"Oh, and they *do*. My bedroom is carpeted with beautiful women. You really ought to see it."

She turned back to Jake, who was playing "The Night That We Fell In Love."

"One o'clock tomorrow," he whispered. "I'll be there, waiting for you."

And he walked away.

Mrs. Weiler's dramatic change of attitude toward Jake convinced him that his strategy was working and that it was only a matter of time until he could pay his way through the last barrier left to him in America, and the formidable woman would accept him as her son-in-law. Thus, as he drove home with Nellie, he decided the moment had come to make the final break with his wife.

He waited until they had changed for bed. Then, when Nellie came out of her bathroom in her negligee, he looked at her, remembering how he had gawked at her so many years before at the Cavendish Club, and said, "Nellie, I want a divorce."

He was standing at the foot of their bed. Nellie gave him a look, then sat down to brush her hair.

"Oh?" she said. "I thought we were going to try for another child?"

"I've changed my mind. I don't want another child by you. It wouldn't be fair to the kid, raising it in a home where there isn't any love. And there isn't any love here, Nellie. You know that as well as I."

She said nothing.

"I'll be generous with you," he went on.

"How generous?"

"Why don't we let our lawyers figure that out for us?"

She put down her brush and turned to look at him.

"I suppose you're going to marry the Weiler girl?" she said.

"Frankly, that's none of your business."

She stood up. "All right, Jake. I could make it messy for you. I could drag Little Miss Innocent Weiler's name into it and stir up a lot of dirt and make life hell for you.... But I won't."

"There's no dirt to stir up."

"Maybe. But anyway, you're right. Let's get a divorce. It's time."

She was thinking that perhaps she would be at Keen's Chop House the next day at one after all.

"That's decent of you, Nellie."

"Oh, I'm not as bad as you like to think. But there *is* one thing."

"What?"

"Your old friend Marco." She smiled. "I thought you'd be interested to know that he and I ... well, use your imagination."

Jake slowly shook his head.

"No, Nellie. I don't believe it."

"It's *true!* It happened at his house down in the Village. He made mad, passionate love to me—and you know something? It's true what they say about Latin lovers. They're great in bed. They're sure as hell a lot better than certain Jews I know." And she gave him a contemptuous look.

"Nellie, you're consistent to the very end. You've got no class."

He walked to the door.

"It's *true!*" she screamed, picking up her hairbrush and throwing it at him. "I was his mistress!"

Jake calmly ducked the brush, which banged against the door.

"Why don't you believe me?" she yelled furiously.

"Because Marco and I are friends, which is something you couldn't understand."

He walked out of the room, closing the door behind him.

Alone, Nellie stared at the door.

"Good riddance!" she yelled. "I never loved you anyway! I could make you *crawl* back to me if I wanted, but I don't want you. You hear? I don't *want* you! I'll get somebody better. I could have any man in New York I want. *Any man!*"

Silence.

"Jake?"

Silence.

She sat down on the edge of the bed, her anger cooling.

"*Any* man," she repeated to herself. "That rich guy at the party tonight—I'll get *him*. I'll just *snap* my fingers."

She lay back on the bed and stared at the ceiling.

Suddenly she felt very much alone. She told herself that Jake *hadn't* meant anything to her. But now that he was gone, she was beginning to wonder....

Chapter 45

A few months earlier, in England's Pentonville Prison, a thin, bearded Irishman of fifty-one, whom friends had described as having "a face by Van Dyke," was awakened by the prison chaplain, Father Carey. Carey gave the condemned man communion and spent an hour with him in prayer. "He feared not death," Carey wrote later, describing the last moments of Sir Roger Casement. "He marched to the scaffold with the dignity of a prince." To Ellis, the hangman—presumably something of an authority on the subject—Casement was "the bravest man it fell to my unhappy lot to execute."

To Irish people all over the world, the execution by the British of Sir Roger Casement caused consternation, and Bridget O'Donnell Travers was no exception. Casement was no ordinary martyr. He had twice achieved worldwide acclaim—and a knighthood—before the war: the first time for his heroic exposé of the atrocities committed by the Belgians against the black rubber-workers in the Belgian Congo, and the second time for his exposé of similar atrocities committed against Indian rubber gatherers in the Putumayo section of the upper Amazon by Peruvian and Brazilian plantation owners. But Casement was a fervent Irish nationalist, who liked to compare England to the Sipo Matador, a lethal South American fig vine which attached itself to the roots of a healthy tree—Ireland—then slowly sapped its vital juices until the tree died. At the outbreak of the war, Casement had gone to Germany. The English later accused him of trying to win German support for the Easter Rising in Dublin, when the truth was that Casement returned to Ireland in a German U-boat to try to prevent the uprising as premature. However, the rebellion occurred; its leaders were captured and summarily executed; Casement himself was caught and brought to trial at the Old Bailey on charges of treason; his reputation was smeared by the prosecution's leakage to the press of portions of Casement's so-called "black" diaries, which contained hair-raising accounts of his rapacious homosexual sex life (the diaries were later said to be forgeries, but they were probably real); and despite petitions to the Crown for leniency signed by some of the most eminent writers and scholars in England, Casement was hanged.

To Bridget, whose once-refulgent beauty had now been dimmed somewhat by motherhood and the passage of time, the Easter Rising and the execution of Sir Roger Casement reopened the Pandora's box of her own private terrors. Her involvement with the kidnapping of Jamie Barrymore, the Earl of Wexford, was still vivid in her memory, and she knew from occasional articles in the press that the British authorities had never closed the case and were still looking for Maryanne Flaherty, the beautiful chambermaid who had vanished with the kidnappers. Her life in America—her marriage to Carl Travers, her work on Ellis Island, her three children in the house on Grove Street—all had seemed so secure and serene.

But as the Irish Troubles aroused ever more bitter passions in the English, Bridget wondered how secure and serene her life really was.

Una Marbury had also been incensed by the trial of Sir Roger, but not because he was Irish. Una, a committed lesbian, had been furious because of the English leaking of Sir Roger's diaries to the press; she considered it an unscrupulous attempt to swing public opinion against him because of his sexual proclivities—an issue that had nothing to do with the charge of treason brought against him. Furthermore, Una's attitude toward the war was that it was a conspiracy of the capitalists and imperialists to crush worldwide socialism, a view shared by many of the Greenwich Village intellectuals and bohemians. The whole bloody mess in Europe was a plot to exterminate the things she held dearest: free love, free expression and art. Thus, when one October morning she answered the bell of her Patchin Place gallery and saw that pluperfect capitalist with whom she had the closest contact through Vanessa—namely, Senator Phipps Ogden—Una stiffened, on instant guard.

She had to admit he looked dapper and elegant in his dark-blue suit, custom-made shirt, kid gloves and bowler hat. How frumpy Vanessa had sprung from the loins of this capitalist dandy was something of a mystery to her.

"My dear Senator Ogden," she exclaimed with a false smile. "Don't tell me you're interested in *l'art moderne*?"

He removed his bowler as he came into the house.

"Possibly," he replied. "I may even buy something. Any nibbles on my daughter's work?"

Una closed the door.

"It has created a *rapturous* response among my artist friends," she replied. "But so far, the Philistines have not placed pen to check. It will sell, though. These things take time. Of course, a clever collector would gobble it up."

"Is this it?" said Phipps, walking over to the horizontal S, which had been cast in steel.

"Yes—'Mayerling.' The mystery of romance and death captured in the cold embrace of steel. Seven hundred and fifty dollars. For you, her father, ten percent off."

Phipps gave her a frosty smile.

"You're an efficient saleslady," he remarked.

"I try."

He removed a small black notebook from his jacket and flipped through it.

"Una Marbury," he said, checking his notes. "Your father is the distinguished Professor Ian Marbury, who holds the chair of Central European Historical Studies at Yale." He looked up. "Is that why you're so interested in Mayerling?"

"Perhaps," she said, rather tersely. "Have you been checking up on me?"

"Van told me you suggested calling her sculpture 'Mayerling.' A world-famous murder-suicide pact is a curious thing to name a sculpture after." He looked back at his notebook. "You have a small trust fund, but you have an outstanding note at the Chase Bank for seven thousand dollars, and you owe two thousand, four hundred and twelve dollars in back taxes to the federal government."

She turned to ice.

"You *have* been checking up on me."

Phipps returned the notebook to his pocket.

"I'll buy every piece of so-called 'art' in this gallery for fifteen thousand dollars," he said, "provided you agree never to see my daughter again."

Now he turned his eyes on her, and Una saw what she had read in the Socialist press: that when aroused, the elegant Senator Ogden had the instincts of a killer tiger.

"My dear Senator," replied Una, "how deliciously trite! Couldn't you think of something more original than to try and buy me off? However, one must learn to deal with the *mammoth* unoriginality of the political brain. You represent everything I *loathe* about this country. If you think you can play the bully with me, you are *sadly* mistaken. Vanessa and I share a love that transcends your Philistine imagination. So it is with exquisite pleasure that I tell you to take your fifteen-thousand-dollar check and shove it, my dear, up your rotten, capitalist ass!"

Phipps, unfazed, came up to her.

"If you're after Van's money," he said quietly, "I think you should realize *I* control everything, and I'm perfectly willing to cut her off without a cent if she continues seeing you. Think about it. Furthermore, if you don't agree within three days to stop seeing Van, I'll instruct the head of that Philistine organization the Internal Revenue Service to close this gallery down for nonpayment of taxes and confiscate all the junk art in it. And I might add, *you* represent everything *I* loathe about this country!"

Slapping on his bowler hat, he walked out of the gallery.

Vanessa was horrified by the news.

When Una called and told her about Phipps's ultimatum, immediately after Phipps left the gallery, Vanessa burst into tears on the phone.

"He guessed!" she sobbed. "I *knew* he would. . . . Oh God, *now* what do we do?"

"We go up to my place in Provincetown and think things over," said Una firmly.

"But what's to think over? I *love* him! I don't want to have him hating me—!"

"Don't you love me?"

"Yes, but that's different."

"Different?" howled Una, losing her habitual self-control. "Are you going to let that man dictate your life to you? What's more important: his money or your self-respect?"

"Don't bully me, Una...."

"Your father's bullying *me*, and I have the guts to stand up to him! With all your *talk* about socialism, when it really gets down to brass tacks, you don't want to risk losing your inheritance— isn't that it? Why should *I* risk losing my gallery for someone like you, who doesn't have the courage to face what she is? Good*bye*."

And she slammed down the phone. She lit a cigarette and waited. As she expected, four minutes later the phone rang. She picked it up.

"Yes?"

It was Vanessa, and she was in a wretched state.

"Una, I'm sorry," she sobbed. "Oh God, I don't know *what* to do...."

"It's very simple, my dear. Either you stay what you are, married to a husband you can't stand, and be Miss Rich Proper Heiress the rest of your life, kowtowing to your father and all the repressive things he stands for. Or you come with me to Province-town, devote yourself to your art and your talent, lead the kind of life you love and be an adult human being. Your father's just bluffing anyway."

"You think so?" she sniffed.

"Of course."

"I'm not so sure ..."

"Oh, Vanessa, grow *up*. If you want to be with me, meet me at Pennsylvania Station at three o'clock this afternoon and we'll catch the train to Boston. If you don't want to be with me, then don't bother. I *thought* we had something beautiful between us, but now I'm not so sure."

"Una, it *is* beautiful! I love you, you know that. But it's a horrible decision you're forcing me to make."

"Anything worthwhile in life is a horrible decision, my dear. Three o'clock at Penn Station. I have to pack. And, Van ..."

"Yes?"

"If you don't come, I'll always treasure our friendship. *Always*."

She hung up and stubbed out her cigarette. She was about sixty percent sure Van would be there.

"What's this doing here?" asked Vanessa, pulling the .22 caliber pistol out of one of the kitchen drawers.

Una, who was putting on a teakettle, looked at the gun.

"It belongs to Mr. Evans, the man I rent this cottage from. He's a bit of a fanatic and is convinced the Germans are going to invade the United States by U-boats. He told me he's going to go down shooting."

"How bizarre." Vanessa replaced the gun in the drawer, then continued exploring the tiny house, a block away from the Provincetown beach. The red cottage had been built in the seventeenth century by a fisherman. Set on a postage-stamp lot and surrounded by a white picket fence, it had a kitchen and low-ceilinged living room on the ground floor and two small bedrooms and a twentieth-century bath on the second floor, reached by an almost perpendicular flight of creaky stairs. The house was furnished with genuine colonial pieces and a few modern sculptures Una had brought up from New York. But cozy and charming as the place was, already, after less than an hour in Provincetown, Vanessa was beginning to regret her decision to join Una. She had acted on impulse, telling no one where she was going but her son's tutor, too afraid to confront her father or her husband. Now she kept asking herself, was *this* what she wanted? Was *this* worth losing the love of her father, giving up her son, giving up her old life?

After they had tea, Una stood up and said, "Come on, my dear, I'll give you a guided tour of Provincetown." The small town at the end of Cape Cod was already an artists' colony, the summer home of some of the country's most creative people, but it was also still a fishing village. Una, who had rented her cottage for two years, had typically taken no trouble to hide her sexual preference—in fact, it amused her to flaunt it for its shock value—so that when the two women left the cottage and started walking down the main street, there could be no question as to Vanessa's status, and the looks they got from the townspeople were hostile, if not contemptuous. Vanessa, who was used to being treated as a princess, was cringing.

"What do they think we *are*?" she whispered to Una.

"Lovers," said Una matter-of-factly. "Don't let them bother you, my dear. They're stupid, narrow-minded people."

Yes, thought Vanessa, *but practically everyone else in the country is narrow-minded....*

They had walked a few blocks when two neighborhood boys skipped by them singing, "Dutch girl, Dutch girl, stick your finger in the dike!," which so upset Vanessa she had to return to the house.

"You *have* to ignore them!" said Una, angrily slamming the door.

"But I can't!" said Vanessa, bursting into tears. "I feel like a freak."

"We *are* freaks in their eyes. So what? Be proud to be a freak. *I* am!"

"But you're used to it—I'm not. It's horrible!"

Una took her in her arms to soothe her.

"It will be all right," she said. "You'll see. Maybe it'll be better if you stay inside for a few days."

"Like a prisoner?" said Vanessa, wiping her eyes. "And what will we be in forty years? Those two weird old women who never go out of their house? Doesn't it bother you a *little*?"

Una closed her eyes. "Well ... yes, a little, I suppose. Do you want to go home?"

"No," Vanessa sniffed, hesitating.

"Then be brave. I'll make some more tea. No—to hell with tea. You need a drink."

Vanessa, who hadn't touched alcohol since Silver Lake, suddenly decided that alcohol was the only thing that could get her through this ordeal.

"Yes," she said, sinking into the worn armchair in front of the fireplace. "I *need* a drink."

Una, who previously had seemed so fascinating in small doses, now as a steady diet began to become something of a morbid bore. The news in the papers the next morning that the Emperor Franz Josef was dying in his palace in Vienna launched her on the subject she was almost obsessed with: the suicide of Franz Josef's son, the Crown Prince Rudolf, at his hunting lodge, Mayerling, in January 1889. Una knew all the gory details and chattered on cheerfully about the discovery of Rudolf's and his mistress's bodies by the valet, Loschek, as she dried the breakfast dishes in the kitchen. Vanessa, who had never washed a dish in her life, was not exactly overjoyed at suddenly being pressed into kitchen duty, and the morbidity of Una's recital, along with her hangover from the previous evening's drinking, finally outraged her.

"Oh, for God's sake, talk about something *else*," she almost screamed. "Suicide, murder, suicide—it's *depressing*!"

"But it's fascinating, my dear."

"No it *isn't!* The rest of the world thinks Rudolf was an insane murderer; *you* think he was brave."

"But he was! He and his mistress gambled their lives on the greatest mystery of all: to find out what's on the other side."

"Maybe there wasn't anything on the other side. Or maybe they went to hell, where they *should* have. But I don't *care*, don't you understand? I want to talk about something cheerful. And I'm sick to death of being cooped up here!"

She threw down the dishtowel and ran out of the kitchen. Una hurried after her into the living room, where Vanessa was standing in front of the fireplace.

"Van," she said, coming up behind her, "you've chosen this way of life. Now you have to accept it and make peace with it. The only reason you're 'cooped up' here is because you're afraid to go outside the door. If our love isn't more important to you than the sneers of a few snotty-nosed schoolboys, then you really should go home."

"Do you think I *can* go home?" Vanessa said quietly. "Can *you* go home?"

Una looked troubled. "My father talks to me. On the phone."

"On the phone," repeated Vanessa. "What a warm family relationship *that* must be. Be honest. Didn't you go through the same thing I am?"

"Yes, but I got over it."

"*Did* you?"

Una said nothing.

Our love, thought Vanessa gloomily. *Oh God, am I worse off than I was before?*

On their third morning in Provincetown, a nor'easter blew in from the ocean, drenching the town with gusty squalls. Vanessa, standing at one of the living room windows watching the tears run down the ancient bottle-glass panes, finally said, "Let's get drunk."

Una, who was reading an art magazine in front of the fire, looked up and said, "It's a *teensy* bit early, my dear. It's not even noon."

"I don't care."

Vanessa went into the kitchen and pulled a bottle of wine from the icebox. She quickly uncorked the bottle and filled a glass with cool Chablis. Una, coming into the kitchen, said, "You can have the wine. Mother's milk for me," and she pulled out a bottle of gin.

By one o'clock, when they heard the knock on the front door, they were both well on the way.

"Who's that?" slurred Vanessa, sitting up in her chair before the fire.

"How the hell would I know?" said Una, getting up and going across the wide-planked floor to the front door. She opened it. Outside, holding an umbrella, was Phipps Ogden. He gave her a look and came into the house, not waiting for an invitation. Una closed the door, trying to clear her brain for action.

"You *might* have asked to come in," she said.

Phipps, closing his dripping umbrella, said nothing. Leaving on his wet raincoat, he jammed the umbrella in a porcelain stand, then came over to his daughter. Vanessa put her glass on the floor, got up and came to him.

"Daddy," she said, "I've missed you *so*. . . ." He took her in his arms and hugged her.

"Will you come home?" he said gently.

"Now *wait* a minute," exclaimed Una, crossing to them. "*I* have something to say . . ."

"You have *nothing* to say!" exclaimed Phipps. "You've caused enough trouble already."

"What have *I* done? Given your daughter the first real love of her life!"

Phipps turned back to Vanessa. "Get your things, Van," he said. "I'll take you home. Don't listen to her. Everything's going to be all right."

Vanessa wiped her eyes and backed away from her father.

"Under . . ." she started to say when she bumped into her

chair and abruptly, almost comically, sat down again. "Under what conditions do I come home?"

"This is a disease," said her father. "I've discussed it with several doctors. They say it can be treated. There's a new technique called psychoanalysis. . . ."

"*That* quackery!" snorted Una. "And do you think even *dear* Dr. Freud could change Vanessa from what she is?"

"A properly qualified analyst can *try*," snapped Phipps. He turned back to his daughter. "Will you come with me?"

Vanessa looked at him drunkenly. Una came to her chair, grabbed her hand and pulled her to her feet. Then she put her arms around her, pulled Vanessa against her and kissed her on the mouth, hard. Vanessa struggled a moment, then relaxed. Phipps watched icily. Una released her and smoothed her cheek, a smile on her beautiful face. Then she turned to confront Phipps.

"You're overlooking one thing, my dear," she said triumphantly. "Your daughter loves me." She turned back, adding, "He'd never let you see me again, Van. He'd never let you do with me or any other woman what you love to do. Is that what you want? A life with no love or passion?"

Vanessa had tears in her eyes.

"I don't know. . . ." she said. Then she looked at her father. "Couldn't I have *both*?"

"No," he replied coolly. "You've broken the fundamental laws of nature. If you come home, you'll never break them again."

She hesitated. Una took her hand and squeezed it, her gorgeous eyes burning into Vanessa's.

"I might add," said Phipps, "this is your last chance. Either you come with me today, or you'll never see me again. I'll make a financial settlement that will leave you comfortable the rest of your life. But I'll disinherit you, Van. Everything will go to Frank, with Marco as executor. The sum involved is around one hundred million dollars."

Una squeezed her hand harder.

"I don't know what to *do*!" cried Vanessa. "Somebody *help* me. . . . " She sank back into the chair, sobbing hysterically. "Why can't I be what I am? Why can't you accept me as I am? What have I done that's so evil . . . ?"

She broke down completely. Her father looked at her a moment, then said, "Goodbye, Van."

He walked back to the door and took his umbrella out of the stand. He looked at Vanessa again.

"Don't go!" she cried. "I haven't made up my mind yet!"

"Yes, you have," he said. "And so have I."

He opened the door and stepped out into the rain, raising his umbrella.

"Father!" she screamed, pushing Una away and running to the door. "Don't go! Don't GO!"

He was walking down the narrow path to the gate. She ran out into the rain and hurried up behind him. "Don't GO!" she screamed again, grabbing his hand. He turned on her, his face furious.

"You disgust me," he said, jerking his hand away from hers.

Then he continued to the sidewalk. Vanessa put both her hands to her mouth, watching him go, horror in her eyes, as the rain poured down her face. Then, still sobbing, she ran back in the house and slammed the door. Una was still standing in front of the fire.

"Darling," she said, with a smile, "I'm proud of you. You stood up to him. Let's have a drink to celebrate."

"*Damn* you," cried Vanessa, running around the sofa into the kitchen. "DAMN you!"

"Of course you're upset, but it's for the best, Van. Really."

She heard her opening kitchen drawers.

"What are you doing?" Una called. "Come out here and finish your wine. Then we'll go upstairs and make love. We'll forget all this . . ."

She stopped. Vanessa had reappeared in the kitchen door. She held Mr. Evans's .22 pistol in both hands, and it was aimed at Una.

Una tensed.

"My dear," she said coolly, "I think you're overreacting a *teensy* bit. Now put that nasty toy away."

"Mayerling," whispered Vanessa, and she fired, hitting Una in the stomach. Una doubled over, stumbling against one of the chairs. "The triumph of love!" said Vanessa. She fired again, hitting Una behind her right ear. She fell to the floor, dead. Vanessa stumbled across the room and fired two more bullets into the body. Then she sank to her knees, the smoking gun still in her right hand.

"What's there, Una?" she laughed. "Is there *anything* there? It's *got* to be better than what's here!"

She was placing the gun to her right temple when her father reopened the door.

"Van, *don't* . . ."

She turned to look at him.

"*Don't* . . ."

She could hardly see him for the tears.

"You don't want me as I am," was all she said. Then she pulled the trigger.

The fifth bullet splattered part of her brain across the stone fireplace.

Chapter 46

Marco was just leaving his new campaign headquarters on Thompson Street to make a speech before the Italo-American Society when he was called back to the phone. It was Maud.

"Something terrible has happened," she said. "You'll have to come out here as soon as possible."

"What is it?"

"Phipps just phoned from Provincetown. Vanessa apparently went mad. She killed Una, then committed suicide."

"Jesus . . ."

"Phipps is a wreck, and I don't know how to break the news to Frank. I think you'd better do it."

Marco looked at his watch.

"I'll catch the next train," he said.

He hung up, thinking of Vanessa. Crazy Vanessa, drunk Vanessa, tortured Vanessa, pathetic Vanessa.

Dead Vanessa.

* * *

Frank was in the second-floor schoolroom at Garden Court with his tutor when Marco came into the room.

"Daddy!" exclaimed Frank, relieved to be rescued from the subjunctive of the French verb *rompre,* which he had forgotten. "What are you doing here?"

He ran to kiss his father.

"Mr. Simmons," said Marco, hugging his son, "I'd like to talk to Frank for a moment. Do you mind?"

"Not at all."

The tutor left the room. Frank was looking at his father, sensing something was wrong.

"What's happened?" he asked.

"Frank, I know you're a brave boy, aren't you?"

Frank was smart.

"It's Mommy, isn't it?" he said. "Something's happened to her."

Marco took a deep breath.

"She's dead," he said.

Frank winced, and Marco's heart went out to him. He kneeled down to be at Frank's level and opened his arms. The boy came into them, and Marco hugged him.

"How did she die?" Frank whispered.

"It was an accident," Marco lied. *He can learn the truth later,* he was thinking. *Much later.* "A gun accident."

Frank started crying softly as his father hugged him. *I'll get him a new mother,* Marco was thinking. *A better mother. I'm sorry about Van, but she's given me my freedom.*

Oh God, Georgie . . . at last!

As Casey O'Donnell's fortunes had waxed, he decided he wanted to move out of the city, so in 1914 he bought a sprawling Victorian house overlooking the Hudson in Irvington. The new white house, set on four acres, bristled with gingerbread and was girdled by a wide covered porch on which Casey envisioned himself sitting to watch the sunsets, sipping a whiskey. Kathleen, whose taste had not improved with time and success, insisted on keeping her old furniture; but since the new house was four times as big as the old, she was forced to buy new furniture which, with lethal consistency, turned out to be as ugly as the old. The house was surrounded by a big, tree-shaded lawn, and it was in Irvington that Georgie spent her weekends.

On the Saturday following Vanessa's funeral, she was walking around the lawn when she heard a car pull up. The car door opened, then slammed. She heard Marco's voice say, "Wait for me."

She turned toward the voice.

"Georgie!"

She heard him running across the sidewalk, then silence as he ran across the grass toward her. Then he took her in his arms and was kissing her.

"I love you," he said. "I've loved you through all this nightmare—it's always been you, Georgie. Will you marry me?"

She ran her fingers over his face, seeing him again, tears of joy in her eyes.

"Oh, Marco, you darlin' man—YES!"

He let out a triumphal whoop, then began dancing her around the windswept lawn as once they had danced on the fantail of the *Kronprinz Friedrich*. Casey O'Donnell, hearing them laughing, came out on the porch and stared. A moment later he was joined by Kathleen.

"What in the world—?" she said.

"Something tells me Santorelli's back in our lives *permanent*," said Casey, rather sourly.

His wife looked at him.

"You think—?" Then she clasped her hands together and beamed. "Mary, mother of God—is the poor girl gettin' a husband at *last?*"

"Looks that way. He'll lose the election, though."

"Why?"

"The scandal. All those headlines—his wife killin' that woman, then committin' suicide ... Bill Ryan tells me even the wops in the Village won't stomach that."

"*Italians*, Casey. If we're gettin' one in the family, we'll be callin' them Italians from now on."

"All right, Italians," grumped her husband.

Kathleen had an idea. "But couldn't you help Marco? I mean, now that he's marryin' Georgie ..."

"I've already thought of that," interrupted Casey, leaning

388

against one of the porch columns, his hands in his pockets. "It'll be our weddin' present to them."

"Thought of what?"

"Givin' the district to Marco. Bill Ryan's been hintin' that he's tired of Washington anyway. The city needs a new sanitation commissioner, so we'll give it to Ryan and send Marco and Georgie to Washington."

Kathleen kissed him. "You *are* a good man, Casey O'Donnell." She smiled.

"Good, hell. This way, we'll keep the graft in the family."

He winked at Kathleen.

Marco and Georgie kept on dancing.

Chapter 47

Bridget O'Donnell Travers was bored.

The excitement of the hordes of immigrants going through Ellis Island had died with the outbreak of the war in Europe. The young men who previously had immigrated to America were now being conscripted into the huge armies of the kaisers and kings and marched off to the battlefields. The result was that the flood of immigration had slowed to a trickle, and Ellis Island was almost out of business.

As she stood on the balcony above the Great Hall, leaning on the rail and looking down at the few immigrants going through the inspection procedures, Bridget became aware of one of them looking up at her.

"Maryanne!" he yelled, pointing to her. "Maryanne Flaherty!"

When she recognized him, Bridget recoiled as if from a rattlesnake. Then she backed away from the rail.

"Maryanne, it's *me*, Denny Flynn. Don't you remember?"

Now she was running down the balcony to her husband's office.

"Maryanne!"

She ran into Carl's office and slammed the door. He looked up at her from his desk chair and saw the terror on her face.

"What's wrong?" he said, standing up and hurrying to her.

"It's him!" she said. "Downstairs, goin' through the line."

"Who?"

"Denny Flynn! Dear God—and he *recognized* me."

That night, Bridget and Carl took the train to Irvington, then taxied to Casey O'Donnell's Victorian house overlooking the Hudson. They had called Casey, and he was expecting them. He opened the door when they rang. Bridget kissed his cheek, Carl shook his hand, then Casey said, "Come back to the library."

"You didn't tell Aunt Kathleen?" whispered Bridget nervously.

"I told her you wanted to see me about some money matters."

"Good. I don't want her to know—*or* Georgie."

Casey, who had no idea why his niece wanted to see him, led Bridget and Carl into the library, then closed and locked the door.

"A drink?" he asked as Carl helped Bridget off with her fur-collared coat.

"No, thanks."

"Well, you've got me so curious, I'm goin' to have a whiskey. Now, what's this all about?"

He went to one of the shelves, where he pushed a button, and the spines of a set of twelve of *The Collected Novels of Lord Lytton* jumped up to reveal a bar. As he poured some Irish whiskey, Bridget looked at Carl, then said, "You weren't ever supposed to know this, Uncle Casey, but Georgie and I didn't just *happen* to leave Ireland. You see, I was involved in a Fenian plot."

Casey almost dropped the whiskey bottle.

"You were *what*—?"

"There was a very important English landlord named Jamie Barrymore. Well, *I* called him Jamie. His title was the Earl of Wexford."

Casey's eyes widened even farther.

"The one they *murdered*?" he said, lowering his voice.

Bridget shot her husband a look of desperation.

"The same." She looked back at her uncle. "Except I swear I

didn't know they were goin' to kill him. I would never have gotten mixed up in it if I thought Jamie would be hurt. All I did was agree to help them kidnap him."

"Then you didn't use your head," exclaimed Casey. "The Fenians play rough!"

"I *know*," groaned Bridget, sinking into a chair. "It was stupid of me, and I've gone through a million hells since, thinkin' of Jamie."

Casey gulped down half his whiskey.

"My God," he said, "*my* niece a bloody Fenian! I don't know whether to kick you or congratulate you."

"There's *nothing* to congratulate, believe me," said Bridget. "Anyway, we came to America—the way it was planned—and I learned they'd killed Jamie and realized the Limeys would put out a reward for me, but I figured I was safe *here*. Then, this morning, who shows up at Ellis Island as an Irish immigrant but Denny Flynn."

"Who's Denny Flynn?" asked Casey.

"He was one of the servants at Wexford Hall who had a crush on me. And he *recognized* me!"

"Bridget's afraid," said her husband, "that this Flynn will turn her in to the British to claim the reward, which is two thousand pounds. I've told her she can't be deported because she's an American citizen now...."

"But it's *different* now, Carl," interrupted Bridget. "It's wartime, and the Limeys are hangin' Irishmen like laundry for spyin' on the Germans. Look what they did to Sir Roger Casement! The English aren't playin' games over there, and Jamie Barrymore was a very important man to them. What's to stop them from puttin' pressure on Washington to deport me?"

"But we're neutral," said Carl.

"Yes, but for how long?" said Casey. "Bridget's right. If the English want her, sooner or later there's a good chance they might get her."

"See?" she said to Carl, almost shrilly. "I *am* in danger! Oh, Uncle Casey, can you do something? I mean, with all your political connections..."

"But my connections are in New York. We need someone in the State Department, or with access to the White House.... My

God, Bridget, you sure as bloody hell picked a fine time to be spotted. I finally get Georgie settled, then *you* ..." He stopped. "Wait a minute ... Marco! Yes, *Marco*. That damned wop—er, Italian—has given me enough headaches. Now he can pay me back."

"How?" asked Bridget.

"His former father-in-law—Senator Ogden. He's a close friend of the Secretary of State *and* the English ambassador. And he's leading the pro-Allied faction in the Senate, so the English could hardly refuse *him* a favor.... That's it, Bridget. You can stop worryin'. We'll get Marco to fix it."

He finished his whiskey, thinking that things had turned out pretty well after all.

Rebecca Weiler enjoyed wines with her meals—as well she might, considering her husband's excellent cellar—but she did not approve of the modern habit of the cocktail hour, which in her opinion led to "excesses" and "intemperance." Tea was her preference, and the next afternoon she was, as usual, having tea with her husband in the drawing room of their Fifth Avenue town house when the butler appeared to announce: "There is a Mr. Rubin to see you, madame. I didn't know if ..."

"No, no, show him in, Jarvis," said Mrs. Weiler. "From now on, we are at home to Mr. Rubin."

"Yes, madame."

A moment later Jake came into the room, dressed in his best business suit.

"Dear Mr. Rubin." Mrs. Weiler smiled. "What a pleasant surprise. Will you have some tea?"

"No, thank you, Mrs. Weiler. Good evening, sir."

Simon Weiler stood up to shake his hand. "It's a pleasure to see you." He smiled, offering a chair.

Jake sat down. The two Weilers looked at him.

"My wife and I," said Jake in a firm tone, "are getting divorced."

"Divorced?" said Mrs. Weiler darkly. "That is a *serious* step."

"I realize that," said Jake. "I wanted you to know, because..." He took a deep breath. "... After the divorce, I want to marry your daughter."

Mrs. Weiler sipped her tea.

"I see," she said. "Well, not being entirely blind, I have not been unaware of your interest in Violet. But to a *divorced* man ..." She looked at her husband. "Of course, divorces *are* occurring more frequently. . . . There was a divorce in the Soloman family only last month. I suppose a divorce would not be an insurmountable objection."

"It wouldn't?" said Jake, who had been expecting at the very least a minor explosion.

"No. We must learn to live with the times."

He couldn't believe his luck.

"Then it's all right?" he almost shouted. "You *approve?*"

"Why shouldn't we approve?" said Simon.

"But ... I'm not very classy," he blurted out, having primed himself with a memorized speech about how the Weilers must overlook his humble origins.

"Dear Mr. Rubin," said Mrs. Weiler, putting down her teacup. "You are a very extraordinary young man who has given great pleasure to millions of people and whose success should be an inspiration to us all. I have discussed you with my husband, who has become a great admirer of yours. It was unfair of me to disapprove of your immigrant background. To be perfectly candid, *my* grandfather was an immigrant."

Jake looked amazed. "He *was?*"

"Yes, a pushcart peddler who came from Germany in 1847 and rose to considerable wealth. So, if you have won Violet's heart, neither of us will stand in your way. The marriage would, of course, be held in *our* temple."

"What is your temple, Mrs. Weiler?"

"Temple Emmanuel, of course."

Jake broke into a smile. "I just joined!" he exclaimed.

Mr. and Mrs. Weiler exchanged approving looks.

"Perhaps, Mr. Rubin," said Mrs. Weiler with a smile, "it's time we called you Jake."

The club was called Roscoe's, and its opening night—December 14, 1916—was a memorable event in the history of New York's night life. Thanks to Jake Rubin, who invited everyone he knew in show business, limousine after limousine filled with theatrical celebrities invaded Harlem for the first time, and dozens of photographers were on hand to flash their cameras as the celebrities stepped out in front of the converted brownstone. A small sign over the front door spelled out the club's name in white bulbs, but otherwise, Flora and Roscoe had saved their money for the interior.

The dining room was on the first floor, and they had tricked the place out with balloons and striped canvas walls to give the look of a circus tent, with the white-clothed tables facing the small curtained stage in the center of the back wall. The room quickly filled with the gala crowd, and promptly at ten the three-man combo (drums, clarinet and bass) struck a chord. A spotlight hit the curtain and Roscoe stepped out, dressed in a sharp tuxedo. He raised his hands for silence.

"Ladies and gentlemen," he said, "welcome to Roscoe's—and believe me, this is a *big* night for me!" He got a round of applause. "For tonight's opening celebration, an old friend of mine has done something special for us. But then, he's *always* doing something special, and he's a very special person. You all know him: Broadway's greatest songwriter—Jake Rubin!"

The spotlight switched to a table in the center of the room, and Jake stood up to take a bow. At the table with him were Violet, who looked radiant, and, incredibly, Mr. and Mrs. Weiler. Mrs. Weiler looked as if she couldn't *quite* believe where she was, but she was fascinated nevertheless.

"A long time ago," Roscoe went on from the stage, "Jake wrote a song called 'Raggedy Ragtime Man,' which I know you all remember and which my wife had the honor of introducing. Well, Jake's written a new song for Flora to sing tonight called 'Hungry For Love.' But first, for old times' sake, she's opening this club with 'Raggedy Ragtime Man.' Here she is: Flora Mitchum!"

He jumped off the stage to take the piano with the combo. The curtains parted, and Flora came out in the same slinky outfit she had worn that night so long ago in the second-rate vaudeville house. As the crowd applauded, the combo hit the intro and she sang:

> "Some women fall in love with millionaires;
> Others to society aspire.

> Well, my man's no patrician,
> He's just a poor musician,
> But when he plays me ragtime, he sets my heart on
> fire!"

As Flora swung into the chorus, Violet leaned over to kiss Jake's cheek.

"*My* musician's a patrician," she whispered. "And I'm crazy about him."

Jake kissed her back. He was about as happy as a man could be.

They were married in Temple Emmanuel, at Fifth Avenue and Forty-third Street, on March 3, 1917. Mrs. Weiler invited all of society, and Congressman Marco Santorelli—the first man to go through Ellis Island to be elected to the Congress—was best man. Marco married Georgie the next week at Saint Patrick's, and Jake was his best man for the second time.

Both marriages were lavishly written up in the society pages, with pictures in the rotogravure section.

In May 1917, Marco resigned from the House of Representatives and took a commission as lieutenant in the army. He was gassed at Belleau Wood and temporarily blinded, but unlike his wife's, his sight returned. After the war, he was reelected to Congress, where he served for twelve years. He had three children by Georgie and died in 1937.

His son, Frank, inherited his grandfather's colossal fortune in 1924. Haunted by his mother's tragic death, he became first a doctor and then a psychoanalyst. In 1940 he gave the Museum of Modern Art five million dollars to endow the Vanessa Ogden Santorelli Sculpture Gallery. He died in 1967, leaving two sons and four grandchildren, who were all remarkably good-looking. After the death of Phipps, Maud returned to England, where she married Lord Saxmundham, the "whisky viscount." Living in palatial style, she became active in charity work and occasionally acted in amateur theatricals. Lord and Lady Saxmundham were both killed in 1944 when a V-2 bomb struck their Belgravia house.

Nellie Byfield married two other husbands, lost her looks, took to drink and died in 1956 in an old-people's home in Greenwich Village, her theatrical career forgotten except by theater buffs, who thought of her primarily as Jake Rubin's first wife.

Jake Rubin had four children by Violet Weiler and lived to write the staggering total of forty-six Broadway shows. He died in 1970 of a heart attack. In his memory, all the Broadway houses dimmed their lights for one minute.

In 1926 a bronze plaque was unveiled by Della Banicek in the field next to Aunt Edna's farmhouse. The plaque commemorated the thirty-two men, women and children who had been killed in the field eight years before. When the Staunton Mining Company was finally unionized in 1938, the union named the local chapter after Tom Banicek. Della died in 1944, one year after her son Stan was killed in the Pacific. Her other son became a prosperous druggist in Pittsburgh.

Ellis Island is empty now, except for curious tourists. There is talk of turning it into some kind of national monument, or museum, or perhaps even a recreation center. But the walls still crumble, the roof still leaks, the dock where once the tenders landed with the immigrants is still rotting. The island that was once the dream of millions of poor foreigners is now the home of rats and seagulls.

But the ghosts are there, and the memories.

America's haunted house is a derelict, but a proud one.